THE PREGNANCY PROPOSITION

BY
ANDREA LAURENCE

MILLS & BOON

First Published in Great Britain 2016
By Mills & Boon, an imprint of HarperCollins*Publishers*
1 London Bridge Street, London, SE1 9GF

© 2016 Andrea Laurence

ISBN: 978-0-263-91880-9

51-1016

Printed and bound in Spain
by CPI, Barcelona

Andrea Laurence is an award-winning author of contemporary romances filled with seduction and sass. She has been a lover of reading and writing stories since she was young and is thrilled to share her special blend of sensuality and dry, sarcastic humor with readers. A dedicated West Coast girl transplanted into the Deep South, she's working on her own happily-ever-after with her boyfriend and their collection of animals.

To my boss Lawanda and my coworker LT—

You were right, Hawaii was worth the long flight.
Thanks for covering for me whenever my writing
takes me around the world and being so
supportive of my writing alter ego.

One

"Well, Papa, you finally made it back to Hawaii."

Paige Edwards gripped her grandfather's urn as she followed the driver to the town car waiting outside the Honolulu airport. He loaded her bags and opened the door for her to climb into the backseat.

As they drove through the busy, winding streets toward her hotel on Waikiki beach, she couldn't dismiss the surreal feeling that had hovered over her for the last few weeks. It started with the call from her mother to tell her that her grandfather had finally passed on. For the last year, he'd battled with congestive heart failure. As a nurse, Paige had felt the need to spend time with him and ensure he was receiving the best possible care.

It wasn't really necessary. Her grandfather was ridiculously wealthy and could afford the best doctors and treatments in Southern California. But she cared, and so she'd spent a lot of time there. Toward the end, it was easier than facing how big of a mess her life had become.

And once her grandfather died, she was able to distract herself with the plans for his memorial service and listening to her parents fret about how the estate would be divided.

Paige honestly didn't care about that. Papa's money was always there in the background, but it wasn't something she felt the need to clamor for. She'd actually encouraged her grandfather to donate his money to a cause that was important to him. That would cut down on the sharks circling around his estate.

What she hadn't been prepared for, however, was that her grandfather had bigger plans for her than she had ever expected. Those plans had forced her to pack her bags and get on a plane to Hawaii with his ashes.

Looking out the window, she could understand why her grandfather would want to have his ashes left in Hawaii. It was beautiful. As they got closer to the hotel, she could spy glimpses of golden sand and turquoise waters against the cloudless blue sky. Palm trees swayed in the breeze and people in various states of beach dress crowded the sidewalks and outdoor eateries.

The car finally slowed to turn into a resort named the Mau Loa. Paige hadn't really paid a lot of attention to the details of the itinerary her grandfather's executor had put together. This wasn't supposed to be about a vacation for her, so she didn't care where she stayed.

When they stopped outside and the bellhop opened

ANDREA LAURENCE 9

the car door, she realized that her grandfather had had very different ideas about this trip.

This wasn't a Holiday Inn five blocks from the beach. It was on the beach itself. The bellman was in a nice uniform with pristine white gloves. The entryway was open to the breezes, allowing a view through the lobby to the ocean beyond it.

The bellman escorted her to the VIP check-in station. She handed over the paperwork the executor gave her, and the woman at the counter's eyes widened for a moment before a large smile crossed her face.

"Aloha, Miss Edwards. Welcome to the Mau Loa." She came out from behind the desk to drape a lei of magenta orchids around her neck. They smelled like heaven.

The woman then turned to the bellhop with her bags. "Please take Miss Edwards's things to the Aolani Suite and then let Mr. Bishop know we have a new VIP guest checking in."

Paige's eyebrows rose. A suite? VIP? Papa really had gone all out, although it wasn't necessary. As a nurse at a veteran's hospital, she wasn't used to being pampered. She spent most of her time chasing away nighttime demons from traumatized ex-soldiers and trying to convince them that losing their leg wasn't the end of the world. The suicide rate was far too high amongst the servicemen and women who returned home. Pampering herself seemed a little ridiculous after coming home from that day after day.

She glanced around as the woman completed her check-in. Beyond the lobby, a trio of men were playing instruments by a lagoon-like pool with a waterfall. An employee was lighting torches around the area as the sun started to go down. The sound of the waves mingled with the melody of the traditional Hawaiian music, and Paige could almost feel her blood pressure lowering.

She had only made it ten feet into the hotel and she already knew she adored Hawaii.

"Here is your key card, Miss Edwards. Your suite is ready for you now. Just follow the pathway through the garden to the Sunset Tower. There will be live music until ten by the pool. Enjoy your stay."

"Thank you." Paige took the key and started down the stone path toward her hotel room.

The resort was large, with multiple towers surrounding a common courtyard. *Courtyard* didn't really do it justice, actually. There was the massive pool with a waterfall and a pair of slides, multiple restaurants and tropical plants at every turn. It was like a lush garden in the middle of the rainforest.

The Sunset Tower was the closest to the beach. She looked at her key as she entered the elevator. Her suite was room 2001. Paige tried not to frown as she pushed the button and the elevator spirited her up twenty stories to the top floor. As the doors opened, she expected a long hallway, but instead found herself in a small vestibule. To her left was a door marked Private. To the right was the door to room 2001 with a plaque that noted it was called the Aolani Suite. Where were the rest of the rooms on this floor?

She was about to slip her card into the lock when the door opened and the bellman came out. He held the door open for her. "Your bags are in the master bedroom suite. Enjoy your stay at the Mau Loa."

He got back on the elevator and disappeared, leaving her standing in the doorway at a complete loss. She crept into the room and let the door swing shut behind her.

This couldn't be right. This was...the penthouse suite.

It was bigger than her apartment and made almost entirely of windows. It had a living room with plush leather couches and a big-screen television, a dining room table that seated eight and a kitchen with state-of-the-art appliances. The neutral color palette, pale wood floors, white furniture and shiny modern metallic accents created a sleek, clean design that was very soothing. One side of the room overlooked downtown Honolulu, the other overlooked Waikiki.

Paige was immediately drawn to the balcony over the ocean. She shifted her grandfather's urn in her arms to slide the glass panel door open and step outside. The breeze immediately caught her long, straight brown hair, blowing it around her face. She brushed it aside and approached the railing to take in the view.

It was stunning. The colors all around her were jewel-like. Diamond Head crater stood like a sentinel guarding the beach on her far left. The crescent of pale sand edged the water, which was dotted with surfers. A pod of dolphins leapt through the waves, spiraling through the air and splashing back into the sea. It was unreal.

"Papa, what have you done?" she asked. But inside, she knew what this was about.

Yes, her grandfather wanted his ashes to be in Honolulu. He had been one of the few remaining sur-

vivors of the Pearl Harbor attack that sunk his ship,
the USS *Arizona*. As such, he had the option of returning to the ship to be interred. The ceremony was
a week away.

Until then, however, this trip was all about her.
There was no other reason that his service would require her to fly first class or stay in the penthouse
suite of a five-star hotel. He had done this for her.
And boy, was she grateful. Paige's life had taken an
unexpected turn recently, and a week in Hawaii was
exactly what she needed to figure out what the hell
she was going to do.

With a sigh, she stepped back into the suite and set
her grandfather's urn on a nearby table. Beside it was
a large wicker basket overflowing with fresh fruits,
cookies, macadamia nut candies and other local deli-
cacies. Tucked inside was an envelope that said "Miss
Edwards" on the outside. She opened it and read the
card on the fancy, embossed Mau Loa stationary.

*"Welcome to the Mau Loa. We hope your stay is
a magical one. Aloha."*

"Aloha," she replied to the empty room, putting
the card back on the table.

Looking at her watch, she realized it was a good
time for dinner. She was fresh off a few weeks on the
night shift at the hospital. Combining that with a long
flight and time change, she was exhausted. But she
had to eat. If she hurried, she might be able to watch
the sunset. Paige rushed to her bedroom and opened
her luggage. She traded her jeans and sneakers for a
sundress and a pair of bejeweled sandals. That was
all she needed.

She grabbed her purse and her room key and set

out to enjoy her first night on Oahu while she could keep her eyes open.

Pulling the door closed, she turned toward the elevator and slammed into a solid wall of muscle. As she stumbled back, a man's hand sought out her elbow to steady her. The man was several inches over six feet, making Paige seem petite at five-foot-ten. He wasn't just tall; he was large, with broad shoulders and biceps the size of her calves beneath his tailored suit. He had on a pair of classic black Ray-Ban sunglasses and a black earpiece that curved behind his ear and blended with the dark brown waves of his collar-length hair.

What she could see of the man's face was unbelievably handsome, and—she quickly noted—completely out of her league. But that didn't keep her body from clenching in response to such a potent specimen of man nearby. Her surprised intake of breath drew in his scent, a heady mix of musk and male that sent an unexpected shiver of need down her spine even as she recovered from their collision.

"I'm so sorry!" she exclaimed as she gathered herself. "I was in such a hurry I didn't see you there." The fact that she'd missed such a mountain of a man right in front of her was a testament to how scattered her thoughts were lately.

The man smiled, flashing bright white teeth against the warm tan of his Polynesian skin. The slight hint of a dimple in his cheek made her knees soften. "That's okay. I didn't see you, either."

Paige noticed the man didn't look directly at her as he spoke. Glancing down, she spotted the large chocolate brown Labrador retriever on his other side. In a service dog harness.

Good job, Paige. She'd just plowed into a handsome, incredibly sexy blind man.

"Ohmigosh," the woman said with increased angst in her voice. Apparently, she had gotten his joke but hadn't found it funny. Few people found blind jokes amusing, but he'd developed a dark sense of humor over the last ten years where his disability was concerned.

"Are you okay?" she continued.

Mano had to laugh. He might be blind, but he was hardly fragile. The woman could've plowed into him at a full run and he would've hardly felt it. "I'm fine. Are you all right?"

"Yes. Just embarrassed."

Mano could almost envision the blush that rose to the young woman's cheeks. He didn't imagine that many of the women he met on a day-to-day basis blushed much. This one seemed different from the usual guests of the Aolani Suite, though—nervous and easily flustered. The kind of money it took to afford that room usually came with a certain hardness that he didn't detect from her.

"Don't be embarrassed," he soothed. "Feel free to run into me whenever you like. I'm Mano Bishop, the owner of the hotel. I was just on my way to welcome the newest guest of the Aolani Suite. That means you must be Miss Edwards." He switched Hōkū's lead to his left hand and held out his right to her.

"Yes," she said, taking the hand he offered and shaking it. "Paige, please."

The touch of her small hand in his sent a bolt of awareness down his spine, forcing him to shift on his feet. The unexpected thrill made Mano take a more thorough notice of his new guest. She didn't just sound unlike his usual penthouse guest, she felt different, too. Her skin wasn't as soft as he expected a young woman's to be. There was a roughness to it as though she worked with her hands. It made him wonder if she was an artist of some kind. She certainly wasn't a pampered princess. "How did you find the suite, Paige? I hope it met your expectations."

"It's amazing. I mean, it's more beautiful than I ever expected it to be. And the view is incredible. Of course you know what...*er*...oh dear."

"Actually, I do," he interjected quickly, saving her from her awkward statement. "I didn't lose my sight until I was seventeen. I may not be able to see the view any longer, but I remember it well."

The elevator chimed and the doors opened. He heard Paige's sigh of relief and tried to hide his smile.

"Please—" he gestured "—go ahead." He listened for the shuffling of her movement as she got on the elevator, then Hōkū pulled at his harness and led Mano into the elevator behind her. He ran his hands over the control panel, finding the lobby button marked with the braille symbol. Then he turned to face the door and reached for the railing to steady himself.

"What is your service dog's name?" Paige asked as they descended.

"This is Hōkū," he said. The brown lab had been at his side for seven years, and he'd become almost a part of Mano. "You may pet him if you like."

"Are you sure? I know you're not supposed to do that when they're working."

Smart. Most people didn't know that. "Unfortunately, I am always working, so Hōkū is always working. Give him a pet, he'll love you forever."

"Hello, Hōkū," Paige said in the high voice people reserved for babies and animals. "Are you a good boy?"

She was rewarded with Hōkū's heavy, happy panting. She was probably scratching his ears. He was a sucker for a good ear scratching.

"What does *Hōkū* mean?"

Mano enjoyed the melodic quality of Paige's voice, especially as she used some of his native Hawaiian language. It wasn't too deep or too high, but he could hear the smile when she spoke. "It means 'star' in Hawaiian. Before navigation systems and maps, sailors used to guide their ships by the stars, and since I use him to guide me, I thought that was an appropriate choice."

"That's perfect."

A cloud of her scent rose up as she stood. Paige had a unique fragrance, and yet it was somehow very familiar to him. Many women, especially those from the Aolani suite, nearly bathed in expensive perfumes or scented lotions. Most people wouldn't even notice it, but Mano was overpowered by smells, good and bad. Paige's scent was subtle but appealing, like a hint of baby powder and a touch of…hand sanitizer. That was a different combination.

The elevator chimed and the system announced that they were on the lobby level. He'd had the elevators updated several years back to include that feature for

himself and any other visually impaired guests. The
doors opened and he held out his hand for Paige to exit
ahead of him. He expected her to rush out the door toward her destination. Most people were a little uncomfortable around him. She obviously was, but it didn't
repel her. Her scent lingered at his side as he exited.

"Are you eating dinner at the hotel tonight?" he
asked.

"That's where I was headed. I'm not sure where
I'm going yet."

"If you want your first meal to be an authentic one,
I would recommend Lani. That is our traditional Polynesian restaurant, so you'll get a great taste of what
Honolulu has to offer in its culinary basket. There's
also a beautiful outdoor seating area. If you hurry,
I believe you can still catch the sunset. It's not to be
missed. Just tell the hostess that I sent you and she'll
make sure you get the best seat available."

"Thank you. I'll do that. I hope we'll see each
other...er...run into each other again soon."

Mano smiled as she stumbled over her words
again. "Enjoy your evening, Paige. *A hui hou kakou.*"

"What does that mean?"

"Until we meet again," he said.

"Oh. Thank you for your help. Good night."

Mano waved casually and then listened as the slap
of her sandals faded in the direction of the beach and
hotel restaurants. Once she was gone, he turned toward the registration desks and let Hōkū lead him
through the guests. Hōkū stopped just short of the
counter where they went through the swinging door
to enter the area behind the registration desk. The
concierge station was just to his right.

"*Aloha ahiahi*, Mr. Bishop."

"Good evening, Neil. How are things going tonight?"

"Fine. You've just missed the check-in rush from all the stateside flights arriving."

Good. He did well to move about the hotel, but he tried to avoid the busiest times when he was most likely to run into an issue with people dragging roller bags or children running around.

Since it wasn't busy at the moment, he also wondered if he could take advantage of his concierge's eyes. He was curious about his new guest, Paige. "Did you happen to see the young woman that got off the elevator with me?"

"Briefly, sir. I didn't get a good look at her."

It amazed Mano sometimes how those with sight spent most of their time not taking full advantage of it. "What of her did you see?"

"Just a basic impression because I noticed her speaking with you. She was tall for a woman; with long, straight brown hair. Pale. Very thin. I didn't really see her face since she was turned toward you."

Mano nodded. That could've described a thousand women at the hotel, easily. It was a start, though. "Okay, thank you. Let me know if you have any issues. I'll be in my office."

"Yes, sir."

Mano and Hōkū continued down a hallway and through the area where hotel management worked to keep things flowing smoothly. They went down another hallway and turned to enter his office. He flipped on the light and made his way to his desk. Neither he nor Hōkū needed the light, but he'd discovered that his employees found it strange that he would sit in a dark office and would think he didn't want to be disturbed.

Mano settled into his chair and Hōkū curled up to sleep at his feet. His dog always laid his head on his shoe, so Mano knew he was there. He leaned down to pat the dog on the head, hit a few keys on the keyboard to wake up his computer and slipped the headset he used to control it over his free ear. It allowed his system to read emails and files to him, and he could control it with voice commands. He wished he could tell his high school keyboarding teacher that no, he wouldn't need that skill in the future.

As he checked his email, his attention was drawn to his other earpiece that was connected to the hotel security system. Mano knew everything that happened at his hotel even if he couldn't see it occur. It had been a quiet day with a lot of idle chatter. That would change as the sun went down. The weekends got a little wilder at the resort with nightly luaus, fireworks shows and plenty of mai tais to go around.

At the moment, two members of his team were trying to determine if a gentleman at the outdoor bar needed to be cut off. He was getting loud. Mano didn't worry about those kinds of issues. His staff could handle them easily.

A soft tap sounded at his door. Mano looked up expectantly toward the sound. "Yes?"

"Good evening, Mr. Bishop."

Mano recognized the voice as his head of operations, Chuck. They had grown up together and had been friends in school since second grade. "Evening,

Chuck. Anything of note happen while I went upstairs?"

"No, sir."

"Good. Listen, did you happen to be around when our Aolani VIP checked in this afternoon?"

"I was not, but Wendy was at the desk around that time. I can check with her if you need something."

Mano shook his head. He felt a little silly even asking, but it wasn't as though he could find out otherwise. "Don't trouble her, no. But if you happen to see Miss Edwards, let me know what you think. She seemed…different. She piqued my curiosity."

"Hmm…" Chuck said in a tone that Mano didn't like. "If she's caught your interest, I want to get an eyeful for myself. It's been a long time since you allowed yourself a little companionship. Could she be your latest lucky selection?"

Mano sighed. Chuck would likely torture him mercilessly now. He was a lot like his older brother, Kal, in that way. It was his own fault for telling his friend about his unusual dating habits, but it was the only thing that kept people from trying to fix him up all the time. "I don't know about that. I just wanted your opinion before I ask her to dinner tomorrow evening."

"So you *are* asking her out to dinner?" Chuck asked.

"Not on a date," Mano corrected. "I was going to ask her to join me at the owner's table." It was a tradition his grandfather started at the hotel, and he had carried it on when he took over. It was just the first time it involved a young woman traveling on her own. "I was curious about her being here by herself."

Chuck was right to a point, although Mano

wouldn't tell him so. He was interested in Paige. He didn't like dating guests at the hotel, but considering he almost never left the property, it was that or celibacy. From time to time, if he found a woman who interested him, he'd propose that she spend a week with him. No strings, no emotions, just a few days of fantasy before she returned home to her regular life. That's all he was willing to offer a woman. At least since Jenna.

His personal experiences had taught him that a short-term fantasy was the best thing he had to offer. His disability always seemed like the third wheel of every relationship. He may have adjusted to being blind, but he hated to ask someone else to deal with it long-term. He did his best not to be a burden on his family, but it would be harder to shield a woman in his life from it. He didn't want to be a burden on the woman he loved.

"I'll look into it, sir."

Chuck disappeared, leaving Mano to return to his work. He started to give a voice command, but he stopped. He wasn't really interested in reading any more emails tonight. Mano was far more intrigued by the idea of going down to Lani and finding out more about this mysterious Paige. He wanted to sit and listen to her speak a while longer. He wanted to draw in more of her scent and find out exactly what bizarre combination she was wearing. He wanted to know why her hands were so rough and why she was staying all alone in such a huge suite in such a romantic location.

He considered it for a moment, then dismissed the idea as foolish. It was her first night in Hawaii. Certainly she had better things to do with her evening than to tell her life story to the blind, lonely owner of the hotel. Yes, she'd intrigued him, and yes, her mere touch had lit all the nerve endings in his body, but she didn't necessarily have the same reaction to him. He was handsome enough, or at least he was the last time he'd seen his own reflection. But there was no overlooking his disability.

Pushing the thought and sensation of her touch aside, he barked out another command to his computer and continued to work.

But perhaps he'd get his answers tomorrow night.

Two

Holy jet lag, Batman.

Paige found herself wide awake the next morning before the sunrise. It was only a three-hour time difference from San Diego, but she hadn't been able to sleep that night. A long stint on nights before her vacation had her clock all turned around. But with a return to sleep eluding her, she decided to stop fighting it. She got dressed and headed downstairs with her camera in the hopes that she could catch some nice pictures of the sunrise.

The hotel was quiet and mostly dark. The occasional employee walked by as they readied the hotel for morning, but she was the only guest in sight. Even the coffee shop was still closed. It was just as well, she supposed. Coffee was on the no-no list her doctor had given her. She was limited in how much caffeine she could have, and she'd rather get it from chocolate. At least when she wasn't awake at 5:00 a.m. Later today, she might feel differently.

Recently, Paige wished she could drink something a little stronger than coffee. Her grandfather's death was just the latest news to upend her world. Before that, she'd gotten wrapped up in an unexpectedly passionate relationship with a man named Wyatt. He was a landscaper working for her grandfather, and they'd met while she'd been there taking care of Papa. She'd never expected such a handsome man to pay any attention to a woman like her. He had shaggy blond hair, a deep tan and strong hands. His dark blue eyes focusing on her was a welcome change after years of being looked over in favor of her pretty and popular older sister, Piper.

Paige knew she wasn't what most men wanted. It wasn't so much a matter of self-esteem as it was fact. She was thin without any hips or breasts to speak of. Her face was oddly angular, and her skin was ghostly pale despite living in sunny San Diego. After spending all of her hours working at the VA hospital and taking no time for herself, Wyatt's attentions were like a breath of fresh air. At least until the dream turned into a nightmare. Two months into their relationship, Wyatt dumped Paige for Piper. And a month after that, Paige found out she was pregnant with his child.

She was a nurse. She knew better than to skip protection in the rush of desire. And yet it had happened, anyway. Paige felt like such a fool. Wyatt had seemed so sincere in his attraction to her. All her guards went down and the next thing she knew, she was heartbroken with a bad case of morning sickness. She hadn't spoken to her sister since Wyatt left her.

Before she could figure out what to do about the mess she was in, her grandfather had died and shifted her focus. She had about six months to deal with the impending arrival of the baby. Her grandfather's death and final wishes were a more immediate issue.

Paige couldn't ignore it forever, though. Like it or not, she needed to start telling people about her pregnancy, including Wyatt and her sister. She needed to get a bigger apartment so she could decorate a nursery. She needed to tell her boss about her upcoming maternity leave. So far, she'd kept it all a secret to herself. Only her doctor knew.

It was a lot to think about, but it was easy to forget all that as she kicked off her sandals and stepped onto the sand. Paige hadn't told her grandfather about what happened with Wyatt, and yet he seemed to know she was unhappy. His final gift to her couldn't have had better timing.

With her shoes in one hand and her camera in the other, she ventured out to the shoreline. The sky was starting to lighten, making everything a dull gray before the brilliance of sunrise. A few dedicated joggers ran past her on the footpath that followed the Waikiki shore. A couple surfers were tugging on their wetsuits and preparing to paddle out. Day was arriving.

Approaching the ocean, she stopped as the cool water washed up over her bare feet. It was then that the magic happened. The rising sun started illuminating the sky in beautiful pastel shades of blue, pink and purple. The palm trees and boats in the harbor were black silhouettes against the horizon.

Paige took a few photos, then watched as the shape of Diamond Head crater grew more pronounced and the sun rose above it. Daylight had finally arrived in earnest. The whole island seemed to wake up then.

As Paige turned back to the hotel, she noticed employees setting up chairs and putting out towels around the pool. A larger crowd was walking up and down the jogging path now, and some were sitting on benches along the beach with their cups of coffee.

She suddenly had a burning need for a skinny mocha latte. She'd have to soothe the urge with a vanilla steamer to get that calcium in.

Back on the sidewalk, Paige rinsed the sand off her feet at the provided foot wash and slipped back into her sandals. She followed the winding path through the dense, dark foliage that would lead back to her room. At some point, she took the wrong fork in the sidewalk and ended up in an unfamiliar area of the resort. There was a large stretch of green lawn, and beyond it was the sandy lagoon where guests could paddleboard or practice snorkeling.

She also found the owner of the hotel and his dog out there. Paige almost didn't recognize Mano in his jeans and a fitted T-shirt. He seemed like the kind of man who wore a suit to sleep in. Then again...why would he go to all that trouble just to take his dog downstairs for an early morning potty break?

She certainly didn't mind seeing him again. She'd relived their encounter all evening. Just the sight of him again made her cheeks burn with embarrassment and her body tingle with the memory of his innocent touch. She'd reacted to him instantly in a way that was extremely inappropriate for someone she'd just met.

Paige didn't know if it was the pregnancy hormones getting the best of her or the superromantic environment, but she'd lain in bed all night, aching and unfulfilled with thoughts of the hotel owner on her mind.

His muscles were even more defined than in the suit he'd worn yesterday. He might be blind, but he clearly knew how to find his way to the hotel gym. His brown, nearly black hair was mussed but swept back from his face as though he'd combed through it quickly with his fingers. From a distance, she could make out some kind of tribal tattoo on his left forearm. Just the thought of tracing her fingers over the design made her stomach clench with a renewed need.

Paige immediately tried to suppress the feeling as she had the night before. The last time she'd let herself fall prey to her desires she ended up pregnant and alone. She couldn't get pregnant this time, but that didn't mean she couldn't do something else stupid.

Before she could turn and try to find her way back to her room, she noticed that Hōkū saw her standing there. His cheesy Labrador grin was wide and his tail wagged so frantically his whole bottom wiggled from the force of it. Paige realized that Mano recognized the change in the dog and knew she needed to make her presence known.

"Good morning, Paige," he said before she could greet him.

She walked the last few feet across the lawn to where Mano and Hōkū were standing. "Good morning," she said, patting the dog on the head. "How did you know I was out here?"

"You're wearing the same sandals you had on yes-

terday. They make a very distinctive clip-clop sound
when you walk. I could also smell you coming."

Paige frowned and tried to sniff discreetly at her
armpits. She hadn't taken a shower yet that morning,
but it couldn't be that bad. Could it? Here she was
fantasizing about the sexy hotelier while he was not-
ing how bad she smelled. She was marching straight
upstairs and scrubbing every inch of her body with
the provided coconut soaps.

"Relax," Mano added when she didn't respond.
"It's not a bad scent, just a distinctive one."

She wasn't sure how he knew she was silently pan-
icking, but she was glad she wasn't recognizable by
her trademark funk. "Thank goodness," she said with
a sigh.

Mano smiled, revealing his blinding white teeth
against his rich, tanned skin. He truly was an amazingly handsome man. Last night, she'd wondered
if perhaps she'd embellished him in her mind. No
man could really be that attractive. But now that
she looked up at him again, she realized it was true.
Paige had thought Wyatt was good looking, but he
couldn't hold a candle to Mano. Not even the T-shirt
and slightly askew morning hair could dampen his
masculine appeal.

He was a strange juxtaposition of traits that seemed
incompatible in her mind. He had heavy, sharp eyebrows over his sunglasses, one with a scar that sliced
through it. It made him look more like he should be
an ancient warrior or in some badass motorcycle gang
instead of the suit-clad owner of an exclusive hotel.
Upon closer inspection, she could see that his forearm tattoo was of some kind of black triangle design.

That sealed his bad-boy appeal in her mind. It also made her wonder what else his professional suit and polite demeanor were hiding.

Paige had always had a thing for the bad boys. It wasn't practical, or really even smart, but most of the time they didn't give her a second glance, so she couldn't get herself in too much trouble. Wyatt had been the first bad boy to look back at her. Giving in to that attraction had landed her on the path to single parenthood. Even knowing that didn't make her take the step back from Mano that she knew she should.

He never looked at her directly, but she could feel his attention completely fixated in her direction as though he knew she was admiring him. "Do you have plans this evening, Paige?"

Paige frowned. She really didn't have plans for the week. The only thing on the books was the memorial service on Friday. "I don't have plans at all. I figured I would talk to the concierge about booking a few things this week, but right now, I'm winging the whole vacation."

"Are you the kind that normally wings a vacation?"

"God, no," she admitted. "I'm a super planner, but this was a bit of a last minute adventure for me. I read some of a travel guide on the flight over, but that's about it."

"A last minute trip to Hawaii to stay in the penthouse suite, eh? There are worse things, I suppose."

Well, she supposed that some people lived a life with random tropical vacations, but Paige wasn't one of them. "I'm not complaining, that's for sure. I do feel a little like I'm flapping in the trade winds, however. I'll feel better once I have a plan."

"Well, start your plans with having dinner with me tonight," he said.

Paige narrowed her gaze at him, wondering if perhaps she'd heard him wrong. It was one thing for her to fantasize about him, but why would a Polynesian god like him want to have dinner with her? Was he just being polite because he knew she was here alone? "*You* want to have dinner with *me*?"

Mano chuckled and shoved his free hand into the pocket of his jeans. "Why is that such a ridiculous proposition? You eat, don't you?"

"Well, yes, of course I eat. It's just—"

"And you don't have plans, do you?" he interrupted.

"No plans," she confirmed reluctantly. She wasn't sure why the idea of having dinner with him unnerved her so much. She should be relieved. This was one meal she could have with a man where she wouldn't have to worry about him watching her critically across the table the whole time.

She could just imagine her family's response if she told them she was having dinner with a blind man— "He'd be perfect for you!"

Perhaps that was the key to his interest. He didn't know what she looked like. Her sister, Piper, had once suggested she try dating one of her blind patients. The helpful idea in Piper's mind had only sounded cruel in her own head. Maybe her sister was on to something, though.

"Excellent. I'd love for you to join me tonight at the owner's table of The Pearl. It's our seafood restaurant and was rated as one of the best on the island the last five years running. You'll love it."

The owner's table? That made more sense to Paige than the idea of a date or something, although she had to admit she felt a pang of disappointment that went straight to her core. This was some kind of "schmooze with the rich hotel guests" kind of thing. With her luck, he'd probably try to talk her into buying a time-share or something. Mano would certainly be disappointed to find out she wasn't the usual wealthy penthouse guest. Of course, a nice dinner with him was certainly better than anything else she had planned, which was a big nothing all by herself.

"I can give you some suggestions on how to spend your time here," he added almost as if to sweeten the deal, as though a free meal and looking at his hand-some face all night wasn't enough.

"Okay," she said at last. "You've talked me into it."

"I usually don't have to try this hard to get a woman to have dinner with me," Mano said with a wry smile. "I was about to be offended."

Paige felt a blush of embarrassment rise to her cheeks. "I didn't mean anything by it. I just can't fathom why you'd want to spend your evening with me."

For the first time, Mano looked at her, as though he were looking into her eyes. Even with his gaze hidden behind his dark glasses, she felt an unexpected connection snap between them and her body reacted. Her tongue felt thick in her mouth as her lips dried out like a desert. Her heart started racing in her rib cage and she suddenly wished this dinner was more than just politeness and tourist tips.

"Why wouldn't I want to spend time with you?" he asked.

Paige didn't want to list out all her flaws. Normally, she didn't have to tell a man what was wrong with her. They knew all too well just by looking at her. "You're busy. And you don't even know me," she replied.

"Hōkū likes you. He's the best judge of character I know. Anyway, by the end of dinner tonight, we won't be strangers any longer. I'll meet you at six."

Paige stood dumbstruck on the lawn as Mano and Hōkū continued on their morning walk. She wasn't quite sure how any of this had happened, but now she was having dinner with him. A bolt of panic shot through her, sending her on a fast path back to her hotel suite.

What was she going to wear?

"She's traveling alone, sir. Her reservations were made and paid through a travel agency. I tried to Google her and I didn't come up with anything but an obituary for her grandfather, who died a few weeks ago in Southern California. She doesn't even have a Facebook account."

Mano listened to Chuck report back on his penthouse guest as he dressed for dinner. "Is my tie straight?" he asked, turning to him.

"Yes, sir. Don't you think it's odd that there's nothing about her anywhere?"

These days it was a rarity, but that didn't mean there was something wrong with it. "Maybe she's mastered the fine art of living under the radar. It's a highly underrated skill these days. Not everyone feels the need to broadcast their every thought and feeling into cyberspace. I don't."

"I was able to get a little information on her deceased grandfather," Chuck added. "Apparently, he was a former military man that went into real estate development after World War II. He's credited with starting the tract house boom of the 1950s, creating affordable housing for returning soldiers to start families. That, along with the population growth in California at the time, made him a fortune."

That was interesting. His shy flower was an heiress to quite a large chunk of money. She certainly didn't act like one. "So her grandfather invented cookie-cutter suburbia? That's quite an accomplishment." Mano straightened his suit coat. "Anything else?"

"I did ask Wendy about her. She handled her check-in."

That caught Mano's attention. "And?"

"She said Miss Edwards was very willowy, tall and thin. She was pale with an unremarkable face."

That was an odd way to describe her. "Unremarkable? Is that good or bad?"

"I don't know, sir."

Mano sighed. People with eyes simply didn't use them the way they should. If he had his sight back, he would study every detail the way he did now with his hands. He'd talked to multiple staff members, and none of them could tell him what Paige looked like. It was as though she was a ghost that only he could sense. "What time is it?"

"Almost six."

"I'd better get going then." Mano made his way through the suite. He counted his steps, knowing his path through the rooms to the front door like the back of his hand. At the door, he whistled for Hōkū and waited for the sound of clicking toenails across the marble floor to come closer. He put on the dog's service harness and gave him a good scratch behind the ears. "Thanks for the information, Chuck."

"Sure thing. Have a nice dinner," he added with a teasing tone that Mano ignored.

Chuck disappeared into the elevator as Mano rang the doorbell and waited for Paige to answer. It took her a moment, probably because she was wearing heels. He heard the slow, unsteady steps approaching the door. She must not be used to wearing dressy shoes.

The door swung open and he was greeted with the scent of the hotel's coconut soap, a touch of Chanel No. 5 and the underlying hint of hand sanitizer he'd come to associate with Paige. His muscles tightened as he drew her into his lungs, making him more eager than he should've been to spend the evening with one of his hotel guests.

"I'm ready," she said, almost breathless.

He took a step back, then offered his arm to escort her over to the elevator. Mano noticed she leaned a bit more on him than he expected. Definitely the heels. It couldn't possibly be that she wanted to huddle close to a blind man, could it? The tightened muscles throughout his whole body hoped so.

"Does Hōkū get to join us for dinner?" she asked as they made their way to the restaurant.

"Yes. Hōkū goes everywhere. Even before I lost my eyesight, it was the policy of the hotel to welcome all service animals throughout the site. This close to the military base, we've hosted a lot of former military over the years with PTSD and injuries that require assistance. Everyone here knows Hōkū, anyway. The chef is known to make him his own treat to enjoy under the table while we dine."

"I guess that's not a bad job to have. He's like the hotel mascot."

Mano chuckled. "I suppose he kind of is." The doors to the elevator opened and he led her down the path to The Pearl. The restaurant wasn't original to the hotel, but Mano had added it not long after he took over the resort from his grandparents. The hotel was famous in its own right for being the oldest and most authentic resort on Waikiki, but he'd wanted to add something to put it over the top. It had taken him weeks to interview executive chefs and discuss menu plans to complete his vision, but within a few years, they'd earned a Michelin star. Even people who couldn't stay at the hotel went out of their way for reservations at The Pearl for dinner, especially on Saturday nights.

Hōkū slowed ahead of him and Mano knew they were getting close to the restaurant.

"Good evening, Mr. Bishop," the hostess said as the outer doors swung open and the cool blast of air-conditioning hit them. They stepped inside, waiting to be escorted to their table. "Right this way."

"This restaurant is beautiful," Paige said as they wandered back toward his reserved table. "That fish tank is amazing. I don't think I've ever seen a salt water tank that large outside of an aquarium."

Mano had always enjoyed snorkeling as a teenager. When they opened this restaurant, he wanted the centerpiece of the dining area to be a saltwater tank that showcased the beauty under the surface of the ocean just beyond the hotel. "It's a custom designed tank," he said. "It had to be built inside the restaurant otherwise there was no way to get it through the doors. It has over twenty different species of tropical fish, anemones and sea urchins. There's even a small nurse shark. None of which are on the menu," he said with a smile. "That would be a little creepy."

"Here's your table. Your server will be right with you both. Enjoy."

Mano gestured for Paige to take a seat to the left of the curved booth and he sat to the right. Hōkū found a spot beneath the table and curled up, resting his head on the top of Mano's shoe.

"Do you like seafood?" he asked. "I guess I should've asked that this morning when we made plans."

"I do. I'm trying to avoid the fish that's higher in mercury and anything raw, but I've been known to eat my weight in shrimp when the opportunity arises."

"That means the ahi tuna is out, sadly, but if you like coconut, we have an amazing coconut shrimp here. It's served with a spicy pineapple marmalade."

"That sounds wonderful."

Mano ran his fingers over the custom braille menu to see what tonight's fresh catch was. The specials changed depending on what was available each morning at the Honolulu fish auction. He was pleased to find smoked Hawaiian swordfish poached in duck fat with roasted purple sweet potatoes. That was one of his favorites.

"Everything here sounds delicious," Paige said.

"It is. But save room for dessert or you'll regret it."

The server came a moment later, taking their orders. Paige had taken his recommendation of the coconut shrimp with passion fruit rice pilaf. She turned down his suggestion of a mai tai, though, opting instead for a sparkling water. With that done, they handed away their menus and he was finally able to focus on figuring out his newest guest.

"So, Paige, tell me what it is that brought you to Oahu so unexpectedly, and alone?"

"I suppose that isn't normal, especially considering I'm staying in a suite that could sleep a dozen people. I'm actually here for my grandfather. Next Friday, his ashes are being interred at the USS *Arizona*. He arranged this trip for me to bring him here."

That was not the answer he was expecting at all. He hadn't connected her grandfather's recent passing to the trip. "I'm sorry to hear about your grandfather. Were you close?"

"Yes. I took care of him the last few weeks of his life. It was hard to watch the illness eat away at him, but I could tell he was ready to be done with it all. That's when he let go."

He noticed a sadness in her voice that he didn't like. He wished their conversation hadn't taken such a somber turn, but there was nothing he could do about it now. Few came to Hawaii for a funeral, but Paige was the exception to the rule.

"I knew he always wanted to return here when he died, but I never expected to be the one to do it. I thought for certain my parents would come out here for the service, but his instructions were very clear—I was the one to bring him. All the arrangements were made in advance and no one told me what to expect, so when I arrived it was quite a shock. I certainly didn't need the penthouse or the first class airfare. I guess it was his way of taking care of me since I take care of everyone else all the time."

Over the years, Mano had entertained scores of ridiculously wealthy couples vacationing from around the world, corporate bigwigs doing business and the rich and famous of Hollywood looking for a tropical escape. Chuck had mentioned that Paige's family had money, so he'd assumed that she was just another guest like the rest.

But the more Paige spoke, the more he began to doubt his assumptions. She seemed to be very ill at ease in the luxury of his hotel. Rich heiresses were normally quite comfortable traveling well and rarely noted that they spent their time caring for others. It seemed there was another confusing layer to Paige. Was it possible that she'd been raised without the benefit of the family fortune?

"What do you do for a living?"

"I'm a registered nurse."

He couldn't suppress his groan at her response. That wasn't what he'd thought she would say. Everything about her surprised him.

"What's wrong with being a nurse?" she asked.

"Nothing is wrong with it. It's a noble calling. I've just spent more time than I ever wanted to around nurses. I was hospitalized for quite a long time with my injury. They were all great and cared for me very well, but I avoid hospitals at all costs now. I couldn't imagine working there every day."

"It's different when you're not the patient. I was a born caretaker. My mother told me I was such a little mama as a child. I was always carrying around my baby doll, and when I got older, I wanted to babysit at every opportunity. I thought maybe I would work in pediatrics one day. But when I spent time with my grandfather, he would tell me stories about World War II. At least ones that were okay for a little girl to hear. It made me want to work with soldiers when I grew up, so that's what I did instead. I got a master's degree in nursing and I work at the veteran's hospital in San Diego on the orthopedic floor. I work mainly with soldiers that have lost limbs or had their joints replaced or rebuilt."

"That sounds like a hard job to have."

"It's difficult work, but it can be so rewarding. I love what I do. Almost all of my time goes to my job, which leaves little for me. I think that's why my grandfather wanted me to come here, to get a break."

Mano tried not to stiffen at Paige's words as she spoke about her work. It wasn't that there was anything wrong with her answer, but it did give him pause. Chuck had been right when he asked if Mano was considering Paige for more than just dinner. He'd only used it as an excuse to learn more about her. She'd caught his attention without even realizing it.

But knowing she was a nurse...that changed things.

She herself had said she was a caretaker. One of his aunts was a nurse. Since the day of his accident, she'd fawned over him, treating him as nearly helpless. People who went into nursing had a strong desire to care for others. Mano didn't want to be taken care of. He didn't want to be fixed or babied, and he certainly didn't want to be pitied.

Then again, there was something about Paige that

his body reacted to instantly. He didn't know what she looked like or anything other than the feel of her hand in his, but he wanted to know more. As the pieces of her history started to click together in his mind, he found himself more interested instead of less. Of course she was a nurse. That explained the rough hands after washing them dozens of times a day and the scent of hand sanitizer.

"My grandfather knew this is something I never would've done on my own," she continued, oblivious to his thoughts. "He wanted me to take a break and enjoy life, if for just a week. So I'm trying. I find it's easier to do in Hawaii than it is at home."

"Everything is easier in Hawaii. It's a state of mind." Mano considered his options for this evening and decided that he didn't mind if she was a nurse. So far, she'd let him take the lead, not once going out of her way to help him when he didn't need it. Being a nurse might not be all bad. If things worked out, maybe she could give him a sponge bath...

He suppressed a wicked grin and tried to focus on what to do next. He didn't want their evening together to end so soon. It was Saturday night, which meant that the resort fireworks show was starting soon. He could take Paige somewhere to watch it, but he knew that the best view on the property was from his own balcony. Typically, he didn't allow anyone into his sanctuary, but for some reason he was almost eager to invite Paige upstairs. He could offer her dessert and an amazing show. But would she accept?

"Do you like fireworks?" he asked.

Three

Paige only thought her penthouse was the pinnacle of luxury. That was before she stepped into Mano's suite.

The whole space was very clean and modern. Every detail, from the industrial light fixtures overhead to the abstract paintings on the walls, exuded elegance and masculinity with a hard edge. The floors were seamless white marble, the couch was covered in buttery soft gray leather and the tables looked like sheets of glass floating in the air with only the slightest bit of metal supporting them. It was the kind of almost austere look that at first glance might seem plain, but in fact was extremely expensive.

There were no fussy elements, no flower arrangements or lace or knickknacks. Everything seemed perfectly placed, as though an interior designer had handled each detail down to where the dog's leash hung on the wall. She supposed that things being out of place could cause a problem when you couldn't see to track down errant items.

There wasn't much for Paige to break, but what was there, she could tell, was fragile. She was anxious about being in Mano's suite for dozens of reasons, but now that she was here, she added the new worry of being someplace where she could stumble and put her fist through a priceless Jackson Pollock painting.

It had been hard enough for her to shake the surreal feeling as she followed him upstairs without those other worries. She wasn't really sure why she was here, anyway. She understood the polite dinner invitation, but why ask her to join him in his suite for dessert just to be nice to a lonely hotel guest? Maybe her initial reaction to their dinner date was closer to the truth and this was about more than just treating the VIPs.

Mano removed Hōkū's harness and the dog trotted over to his corner pillow where a rawhide bone was waiting for him. "We do fireworks at the hotel every Saturday night," Mano explained as he slipped out of his suit coat and laid it over the back of a chair that he seemed to know would be positioned just there. "It's a long-standing tradition at the Mau Loa that my grandparents started decades ago. My suite has one of the best views, ironically enough."

Paige bit at her lip as he noted the obvious issue. She followed him out onto the balcony and he was right—his view was even better than hers. The fireworks over the lagoon would be center stage for the spectators waiting along Waikiki beach, but their view had it all beat. "It's a shame you can't enjoy them."

"Actually, I can," Mano said as he gripped the railing and looked out over the water as though he could see it.

The moonlight highlighted the sharp angles of his face, reminding Paige just how handsome and unobtainable a man he was. She wished he would take off his glasses so she could see his eyes. She understood why he wore the glasses, but she felt like a part of him was hiding behind them.

"I remember what they looked like when I was younger. As I mentioned earlier, I didn't lose my eyesight until I was seventeen, so I have the memories. I can sit on my patio and listen to the pop of the fireworks and the cheers of the crowd. The smell of the smoke in the air brings back the experience for me. I don't need to see them anymore."

The doorbell of the suite rang just then, robbing Paige of any questions she might want to ask. With her medical background, she was curious about what had happened to him, but she needed the right opportunity to bring it up. She didn't want to pry, but she knew from her experience with soldiers that they often wanted to tell their story, but only when they were ready.

"Dessert has arrived," Mano said.

"I'll go get the door," Paige replied, beating him to the sliding door. He was able-bodied but so was she, so there was no reason why she couldn't let room service in for them.

At the door, a man was waiting with a cart. On top of it was a large silver-domed dish like the kind you'd see in old movies. "Good evening, ma'am. Where would you like your dessert?"

"Bring it out to the balcony, please," Mano called. He'd followed her into the living room even though he didn't need to.

They both trailed the cart back to the patio, where the waiter placed it on the glass table. "The famous Mau Loa Black Pearl," he announced, raising the lid with dramatic flair.

Paige couldn't help the gasp that escaped her lips when she saw the beautiful chocolate delight hidden beneath the silver dome. Mano had told her it was the showpiece of The Pearl, and the dessert looked exactly like a giant black pearl in an oyster. A thin hinged cookie shell was the bed and backdrop for a dome of layered chocolate mousse. It was enrobed in a dark chocolate fudge ganache and dusted with toasted coconut and macadamia nuts on the edges. It was the most beautiful and delicious-looking thing she'd ever seen in her life.

"I don't think I can eat it," she said.

Mano chuckled as he gave the waiter his tip and he disappeared from the suite. "You'll change your mind about that pretty quickly. It's the most incredible thing you'll ever put in your mouth."

They sat down in the patio chairs and armed themselves with spoons. Mano broke through the dark chocolate outside first so Paige didn't have to do it. One bite and she knew he was right. The different layers and flavors of chocolate mousse and cream melted together on her tongue. The decorative starburst of passion fruit puree on the plate gave a sharp sour bite to break up the richness. The cookie was crunchy, almost like a fortune cookie, but much more flavorful. It was amazing. And gone before they knew it.

"That was incredible," Paige said as she laid her spoon down on the empty plate. "I think I might burst, though."

"It will be worth any suffering." Mano paused for a moment, putting his hand to the tiny headset that always seemed to be in his ear. "Ah, perfect timing. The fireworks show is about to start. Are you ready?" He held out his hand to her.

Paige took it and they walked together to the railing. Heavy drums and traditional Hawaiian music sounded from the lagoon in the distance. A moment later, the sky lit up as a firework exploded and bathed the darkness in streaks of white fire. One after the next, bursts of color danced across the sky. For about ten minutes it continued, illuminating the dark water. Down below, she could hear the crowds gathered on the beach as they cheered and gasped in awe.

"That was wonderful," Paige said as the last of the smoke started to clear. "You were right, you do have the best view for the show."

"I'm glad you enjoyed it."

Paige turned away from the beach to look at him. "I want to thank you for all this."

He shrugged it away. "It's nothing."

"No, it's not nothing. You've taken me to a lovely dinner, brought me up here for an amazing dessert and fireworks. You've saved me from a lonely night in a beautiful place. That's more than other people would've done for a stranger. More than other people typically do for me."

Mano's brow furrowed as he listened to her. "What do you mean? Do the people in your life back at home take advantage of your kindness?"

Paige sighed and leaned onto the railing. "It isn't that simple." She wasn't bullied or abused at all. She just didn't quite fit in. It was mostly a case of being invisible. "More often than not, I'm just ignored. No one really seems to see me. I just blend into the background noise no matter how loud I yell. Sometimes I wonder if, when I die, anyone will even remember I existed."

"Your patients will remember you. I know I'll never forget the kind nurses that cared for me after my accident."

"I hope you're right," Paige said. She tried to make a difference in their lives, even when it didn't seem like she was getting anywhere.

Mano's hand slid along the railing until he found hers. He covered her with his reassuring warmth. "And I'll remember you, Paige Edwards."

Her breath caught in her throat at his words and his caress. Her skin seemed to sing beneath his touch. A thrill ran up her arm and jolted her heart to beat double time in her chest. She knew she shouldn't get excited. Mano wasn't putting the moves on her; he was being kind. And yet, her body didn't seem to know the difference. "I'll remember you, too. You are the first person in a long time that truly seems to see me."

"Sometimes people depend too much on their eyes," Mano explained. "They make all their judgments based on what they see, ignoring everything else. I may not know what you look like, Paige, but I know a lot of other things about you that make you a person I want to know more about."

She really couldn't understand why he felt that way. She was a nobody—certainly not the kind of woman who captured the attention of a rich, handsome man like Mano. "I don't know what you see that others don't. Frankly, I don't even see it. I've never thought I was very special."

"That's odd," Mano said. "I find myself wanting to know everything about you. It seems I uncover a surprise with every layer I peel away. May I ask you something?"

Paige shifted nervously, pulling back from his touch. Usually when someone prefaced a question like that, it was going to be bad. Like when her sister asked if Paige's relationship with Wyatt was really serious. She was just testing the waters before she jumped in. "Why not?" she said at last. After what she'd been through lately, there wasn't much he could ask that would make things worse.

"May I touch your face?"

Except for maybe that.

"I know that sounds odd," Mano continued, "but it's how I see people. I'd like to see you better."

A part of Paige was happy that Mano couldn't see her. He seemed so interested in her. Would finding out how she looked ruin their perfect night together? She supposed that telling him no would end it just as awkwardly. "Okay," she agreed.

Mano turned to face her, but his expression was as concerned as hers likely appeared. "You sound nervous. You don't have to do it if you don't want to."

"No, it's okay," she argued, placing a hand on his forearm. "If you had your sight, you would've known what I looked like from the first moment, so you've waited long enough to know. I just hope you're not disappointed with what you find."

* * *

Disappointed? Most of the women who had drifted in and out of Mano's life had a healthy sense of self-esteem, but not Paige. Whether or not she was right, she seemed to think she was invisible or even unattractive. He didn't think that was actually possible, but now he'd find out for himself.

Taking her wrists in his hands, he let his palms glide up her arms to her neck. There, he cradled her face in his hands. Paige was tense and still beneath his fingertips as they traced the lines and angles of her face. She had a delicate brow, large, wide eyes and a sharp nose. Her face was thin, as was the rest of her, judging by her narrow wrists and protruding collar bones.

He realized then that she was too still and too silent beneath his touch. "Breathe, Paige."

She moved slightly with a sudden exhale and intake of breath. Once she relaxed, his fingers ran over her hair. It was long, straight and silky. Paige hadn't twisted it up or tortured it with curling irons and hair spray. It just flowed naturally down her back.

"What color are your eyes?" he asked, trying to envision them in his mind.

"They're a hazel color. Not quite green and not quite brown."

Mano nodded, the picture coming together. "Now, tell me about what you're wearing tonight so I can see it."

"I overdressed a little," she confessed. "It's a blue satin cocktail dress that I found on sale at the mall. I don't even know why I bought it—I have nowhere to wear it normally—but I threw it into the suitcase when I was packing. I figured if I didn't wear it tonight, I might as well donate it to charity."

He didn't know why she had to cut herself down with every description of herself. "What shade of blue?"

"A dark royal blue, kind of like the deeper waters off Waikiki."

Mano could see that color vividly in his memory. He wished he could continue his exploration, run his hands over her body to find out more about her. Feeling bold, he traced the neckline of the gown with his finger, finding the V plunged deep. His fingertip lingered at the apex for a moment as Paige let out a ragged breath. He expected her to pull away or tell him to stop, but she didn't. She leaned closer to him. The scent of her mingled with the Plumeria and orchids that perfumed the breezes. He was intoxicated by it and drawn to her in a way he simply didn't understand.

Gently cupping her face in his hands, he lowered his lips to hers. Her response to him was cautious, but curious. After a moment, the caution gave way to enthusiasm. She wrapped her arms around his neck and arched her body against him. Mano felt his every muscle tighten as her lithe body pressed into his own.

He let his tongue explore her mouth as his hands explored her body. She had the taste of decadent chocolate lingering on her lips. Her body was lean and angular to the touch, with few curves to cup in his hands. Considering how tiny she'd felt when he'd touched her earlier, he wasn't surprised. It was just another way that his Paige was different.

As his hand strayed near her belly, she went stiff as stone in his arms. "Paige?"

He felt her pull away and the next thing he knew, her loud and unsteady clomp of heels against the marble floors grew softer and softer until the front door of his suite slammed shut. She'd just run away.

He'd had a lot of reactions to his kisses in his life, but he'd never had a woman turn tail and run. For a moment, Mano wasn't exactly sure what to do, but in the end, he decided to give chase. He wasn't going to let Paige run away from this. If nothing else, he would apologize for crossing a line and making her uncomfortable, but he felt like it was more than that.

Mano made his way cautiously through the suite to the entrance, then across the vestibule to Paige's door. He pressed the doorbell of her suite and waited as patiently as he could. His heart was still pounding in his chest and his muscles were still tight with tension from their kiss. It was possible that Paige just wouldn't answer the door, but he didn't think she was the kind to just ignore him. That would be impolite.

Mano heard her soft shoeless footsteps approach the door and it unlatched with a metallic pop. The door swung open.

"Yes?"

He could tell by the harsh tone of her voice that she was upset. Mano just wasn't sure if she was upset with him or herself. "Did I do something wrong?" he asked.

"No. You were wonderful. Everything I could've asked for and more on a night out in the most romantic place in the world. It's just me. I'm sorry," she said.

And here he thought he'd been the one apologizing. "Sorry for what?"

"For everything," she said with a sadness in her voice that told of more than just tonight's worries on her mind. "For kissing you, then for running. In the moment, I wasn't really sure what to do. I don't trust myself when it comes to these things. I make poor decisions, and I'm not saying that kissing you is a mistake, but I'm really not at a place in my life where I need this kind of…complication."

Complication? Paige seemed to have tied herself up in knots for no reason. He could feel the anxiety and tension damn near radiating from her body in waves. "It was just a kiss, Paige. There's no need to make more of it than that. How complicated can things get with you leaving in less than a week?"

He reached out for her and placed a hand on her waist. He waited until she relaxed and the throbbing pulse beneath his fingertips slowed. "Listen, Paige, I want you to know this isn't something I do very often. I've never even invited a guest up to my suite before."

"Really?"

"Really." It was true. Only Chuck, housekeeping and room service were allowed inside from the hotel staff. When he did indulge in a short romance, he always went to the woman's room or sought out an empty suite. And yet, he'd wanted to share his retreat with Paige. He wanted to experience those fireworks with her, knowing it would be as though he could see them again. "Like you, I don't really trust myself in relationships, either. My condition puts me at a disadvantage. Every time I'm with a woman, I wonder what her angle is, or if I'll be a burden on her. To be honest, your work as a nurse is a huge red flag for me. I should walk away from you right now."

"Why?"

"Because I don't want to be someone's project. I can't be fixed and I don't want to be coddled. Some women see me as someone they can care for and, as a nurse, it's in your nature to do it."

Paige chuckled softly. "You'll find that I'm more drill sergeant than babysitter. Sometimes it takes a firm hand to get a patient out of bed and make him stop feeling sorry for himself."

"Maybe that's the difference. There's just something about you that makes me want to throw all my rules out the window. I want to know more about you, Paige. I want to touch you again."

Paige gasped. He took a step closer to her and drew her hand to his chest. "I don't want to make you uncomfortable. If you tell me to, I'll walk away right now and leave you alone for the rest of your time here in Hawaii. But I don't want to. Whatever we share doesn't have to be serious or complicated, Paige. I'm proposing we spend the week together. I'll let you set the boundaries so there's no unwanted complications. I simply enjoy your company."

"You do?"

Her voice was soft and small, so insecure it made his chest ache. What had Paige been through that she thought so little of herself? She questioned his every interest in her. "I absolutely do. I don't know why every man you meet doesn't feel the same way. You're charming, thoughtful and kind."

Paige laughed softly, but he could tell it wasn't with amusement but with disbelief. "You're the first person to ever say that. The people that don't ignore me entirely find me to be awkward and quiet. I don't know exactly what it is that a man like you sees in a woman like me."

Mano frowned. "What kind of man am I?"

He felt her shrug. "I don't know…handsome, wealthy, successful… The kind that could have a dozen supermodels in his contact list if he wanted to. That kind of man doesn't really belong with a woman like me."

"Supermodels aren't much for interesting conversation. I have different priorities. I might be blind, Paige, but I see more than most because I rely on more than just my eyes. What I see of you, I like. So, will I see you tomorrow?" he asked.

After a moment's hesitation she said, "I'll think about it."

Mano smiled and took a step back from her doorway. "You do that. When you decide to accept my proposal, and you will, just ask any hotel employee for me and I'll find you. Good night, Paige."

As he reached the doorway of his room, he heard Paige's door click shut behind him. Inside his suite, he went to the kitchen and sought out a bottle of locally brewed beer. Sinking into his leather couch, he took a sip and hoped that the muscles in his body could uncurl with the help of the alcohol.

Hōkū trotted over to the sofa and jumped up beside him. He laid his heavy head onto Mano's lap and sighed. That was pretty much how he felt, too.

He wasn't sure if Paige would take him up on his offer to spend time together or not. He hoped so, but nothing was certain.

Since his accident, Mano had become very distrusting of women. Before, when he was the vibrant younger Bishop brother with everything ahead of him, he liked it when the girls swarmed him. Even then, he only had eyes for Jenna. He had been dating her since their sophomore year, and they had everything going for them. Like his older brother, Kal, he was about to graduate and go on to the University of Hawaii. He and Jenna had plans to take over the family business with his brother and branch out to new locations, turning the Mau Loa into the most luxurious hotel chain in the islands. First Maui, then Kauai. He was young, rich, handsome and soon to be very powerful. He felt invincible with her at his side.

Then, in the blink of an eye, everything changed. On the way to his brother's football game an oncoming SUV strayed from its lane and plowed head-on into his parents' car at fifty miles an hour. Their parents were killed on impact. Mano hit his head with enough force to blind him permanently, break his arm and earn about twenty stitches across his brow.

Suddenly, he wasn't the golden child he always thought he'd be. Recovering from his accident had been a challenge. Kal and their grandparents tried to convince him that he'd only lost his vision, not his life, but Mano knew better. Even the girls around him knew better. Jenna disappeared, carrying on with her plans and leaving him behind. She said she was too young to dedicate her whole life to loving a man with a lifetime of challenges ahead of him. Suddenly, he went from being a catch to a charity case.

Over the last ten years, Mano had managed by only allowing himself the physical comforts of a relationship—nothing emotional. A week with a woman every few months or so was enough to soothe the beast. He didn't want or expect anything more than that.

He certainly looked forward to a week with Paige. *If* she agreed to it.

A buzz of conversation in Mano's ear distracted him from his thoughts. There was an issue downstairs that he needed to tend to. Giving Hōkū a pat on the head, he took one last sip of his beer and left the rest to go flat on the coffee table. He sought out his suit coat and Hōkū's harness, preparing to head back downstairs.

Thankfully, work was always there to distract him from everything, including his own life.

Four

Mano didn't sleep well. Being completely blind, he usually had some level of difficulty because he didn't have the light cues to regulate his circadian rhythm. Medication usually helped, but not last night. Though last night had less to do with being blind and more to do with Paige.

He'd tossed and turned thinking about that kiss. Her eagerness countered by her quick retreat was a beautiful collision of contradictions. She'd called what happened between them last night "a complication." He hoped he was able to convince her otherwise. She would only be on Oahu for a few days, but he wanted to take advantage of every moment he could with her. He wanted to taste her lips again and feel her body press against his. He wanted to ask her more questions because she surprised him with every answer.

His brain had circled around those thoughts until the wee hours when he finally fell asleep. The morning alarm came early. Hōkū didn't really care that he hadn't slept. He was ready to go outside, so down they went. Mano grabbed a latte with a double shot from the coffee shop on their way back upstairs so he could wake up and get ready for work.

Mano was stepping out of the shower when he heard the doorbell. Hōkū barked and stood anxious at the door as he slipped into his robe and made his way to answer it. He couldn't fathom who would be at the door at this hour. It was too early for him to even have his earpiece in yet.

Tightening the belt around his waist, he asked through the door, "Who is it?"

"It's Paige," a soft voice answered back.

Without really considering that he was wearing nothing more than a robe, Mano whipped open the door. He didn't know why Paige was on his doorstep at dawn, but he wanted to find out immediately.

A muffled gasp was her response. Mano adjusted the wrap of the robe around him to make sure he wasn't exposing anything and ran his hand self-consciously through the wet strands of his hair. "Is everything okay?" he asked.

"Y-yes," she stammered. "I'm sorry to come by at such a miserable hour. You're obviously still getting ready. I haven't adjusted to the time change and I just uh… I wanted to catch you before you went to work. I wanted to see if you'd be interested in playing hooky with me today."

"Hooky, *pulelehua*?"

"Yes, that's why I came by when I did. Last night

you said you wanted to spend some more time with me. You proposed a week together in the most romantic place on earth. I said I would think about it and I did. All night, actually. And I've decided that if you want to spend these few days with me, I'm not going to be the one to turn you away."

A wide smile spread across Mano's face. When he'd left her last night, he hadn't been certain of Paige's answer. In his mind, she seemed like a skittish doe that would flee at any sudden movements. But now his doe was getting bolder. "I'm glad to hear that."

"I thought that we could spend the day out. I mean, it's a Sunday, after all, and you own the place. You could take the day off without asking permission, right?"

Mano's brow furrowed in thought. "I don't know. I don't usually leave the property. This is a little short notice for my staff."

She didn't bother to disagree with him. Her silence spoke volumes. He supposed she was right. He could leave, he simply never did it. His world completely revolved around the Mau Loa, and mostly by his own design. Nothing required him to be there, on call, twenty-four hours a day. He could have a home he returned to each night instead of converting one of the penthouse suites into his private apartment. He could take vacations and sick days the same as every other employee on site did. He simply didn't do it. Mano couldn't think of the last time he'd taken a day off.

"It'll be fun," she encouraged with a musical lilt to her voice. "Come on, Mano. Show me everything your beautiful island has to offer. I may never come back. I've got to make the most of every minute."

"You absolutely should. I can make some great recommendations—"

"No, I want *you* to show me Oahu. You can't spend all your time in this hotel, Mano. There's a whole island outside your property lines, and I want us to see it together."

"I don't spend all my time in the hotel," he argued, knowing it was a lie. He only made the occasional trip to Maui to see Kal. What was he going to do? Go sightseeing? Snorkel? That was kind of pointless.

"Sure you don't." Paige sounded anything but convinced. "What was the last thing you did outside the resort?"

Mano couldn't answer that question. He had no clue. His groceries were delivered. Most of his other needs were handled at the hotel. He had his assistant order whatever he needed online. His last trip out might have been to the tailor to get some suits fitted the year before last, but he certainly wasn't going to admit that. Instead, he pushed up his sleeves and raised his hands in defeat. "Okay, you win. You really are a bit of a drill sergeant. Hooky it is." He took a step back from the door. "Please, come in. I'll go put some clothes on."

"You don't have to—I mean, put clothes on. That didn't come out right. I'm not asking you to *not* put clothes on. I just meant that I can wait until you're dressed. You don't have to invite me in. Take whatever time you need."

Mano did his best not to laugh. Paige had the ability to get twisted in her own words in the most endearing way. It was charming. Of course, he wasn't helping the matter by opening the door fresh from the shower. In this robe, it was likely that she could see his native tattoos and his scars, two things he usually kept hidden beneath his Armani armor. Hell, he hadn't even remembered to put on his sunglasses before he answered the door. She just seemed to have thrown him off balance last night and he had yet to recover, making one mistake after the next.

Paige sighed heavily. "I'll wait outside," she said.

"Okay. Just give me a few minutes."

Mano closed the door and headed back to his bedroom. He wasn't entirely sure what to wear for a day of fun on his island home. It had been a long time since he'd even tried. He started by picking up his earpiece from the charging station beside the bed.

"This is Mr. Bishop. Who's listening?"

"Good morning, Mr. Bishop," a man's voice responded. "This is Duke. What can I do for you?"

Duke was the night shift operations manager, second in command to Chuck. "Morning, Duke. Would you let Chuck know when he gets here that I won't be in today?"

There was a long hesitation. "Are you unwell? Should I have the resort doctor sent up to your suite, sir?"

He did need to get out more. "No, Duke, I'm fine. I'm just taking the day off."

"Very well. I'll let him know, sir."

Mano took off the headset and put it back on the dresser. It felt weird not to leave it on, as he did every day, but it wouldn't work once he left the resort. And today, that was apparently what he was doing.

Reaching into the bottom drawer of his dresser, he pulled out cargo shorts and a polo shirt. He added his only pair of flip-flops. He wasn't sure which color polo he was wearing, but he knew his flip-flops were brown and would go with anything. With that handled, he returned to the bathroom to finish grooming and drying his hair. Feeling carefree, he skipped shaving. He always shaved, but if he was going to play hooky today, he was going all out.

The last thing he did before reopening the door was slip the harness onto Hōkū and his glasses over his eyes. When he reopened the door, he called out to see if Paige was still waiting for him. "Paige?"

"I'm right here." He heard the opposite door shut and listened to her steps as she approached him. "I wanted to grab a few last things before we left. I'm not sure what we'll do today, but I figured my sunglasses and my camera were a must. Are you ready to go?"

Mano nodded. "Yep." He held his arm out to her and once she slipped hers through it and snuggled beside him, they went to the elevator.

After he pressed the button she asked, "So, what *are* we going to do today?"

That was a good question. He'd just come to terms with the idea of "hooky" so he hadn't fully developed today's itinerary. Normally, he handed guests a couple brochures from the display by the concierge desk and sent them on their way. But what would he do if he was going along? That might be a little different. For one thing, he was hungry. "I was thinking we'd start with pancakes."

"Pancakes?"

Mano nodded. "Every decent day of hooky needs to start with an indulgent breakfast. I recommend we go to Eggs 'n Things for macadamia nut pancakes with coconut syrup and whipped butter. There's a lot of pancake houses around the island, but this one was my favorite as a kid. I haven't been there in ages."

"Those pancakes sound wonderful," she said with a smile in her voice.

The doors of the elevator opened and they stepped in together to start their day's journey.

Paige was exhausted and she was pretty sure she had the start of a sunburn, even though she'd put on sunblock, but she didn't care. She was having too much fun with Mano and they hadn't even strayed from the Waikiki Beach area yet.

They started out with pancakes, then they continued to stroll down the main path that snaked around the beach. Mano took her hand as they walked. It was probably just so he didn't lose her in the crowds, but the feel of her hand in his made a shiver run down her spine. Although she was a tall, lanky woman, she felt petite and feminine beside Mano. She rarely felt like either of those things.

They went through the narrow aisles of an open air market, where she was nearly overwhelmed by vendor after vendor selling every type of souvenir she could think of. Mano and Hōkū were remarkably patient as she looked at things they'd been surrounded by their whole lives. He explained different items they had for sale and helped her negotiate a better deal on a few things. She picked up something for her parents and something for her best friend, Brandy. Brandy was a nurse on her shift at the veteran's hospital and one of the few she could call a friend.

Somehow her work environment had evolved into

a sorority house, with veterans hanging around instead of football players. The other nurses weren't necessarily mean, but she wouldn't call any of them friends, either. Paige had never been very good at fitting in, no matter what she was trying to do. Even now, she was getting odd glances from people as they passed, trying to figure out the two of them together.

Fortunately, she didn't have to try to fit in with Mano, so she could ignore everyone else. He seemed to find her differences charming, although she really didn't understand why. He laughed at her jokes, held her hand and looked as proud to be with her as if he was with a famous Hollywood actress. She almost didn't know how to act around him. The last guy she met who was this charming was just using her, but Mano seemed totally sincere. He'd given up a whole day at work to spend time with her, after all, with no promise of anything in return.

It was late in the afternoon when she spied a Hawaiian shaved ice place and begged to go inside. He bought them each a huge snowball of sugar and ice and they found a table under a shady palm tree where they could eat and Paige could watch the ocean.

"It's been a long time since I've had one of these," he admitted as he took his first few bites. "My mother used to take me and my brother down to the beach and buy us one from time to time. It's as good as I remember. I wonder if I should put in a Hawaiian ice place at the hotel."

"You absolutely should." She took a bite of her Tiger's Blood flavored ice and let it melt on her tongue. "Maybe near the big pool so people can get a cool treat while they're enjoying the sun. Honestly, I can't believe you don't have one already."

Mano shrugged. "Well, when my grandparents opened the hotel, Waikiki was a different place. It wasn't long before it exploded into an endless strip of hotels and gift shops. There were more US soldiers than tourists back then. Hell, Hawaii wasn't even a state yet. Their goal was first and foremost to have the most authentic, yet luxurious, experience for guests. The resort grew and expanded over time under my family's watchful eyes, just as Honolulu grew and changed. When it was handed over to me, I was mindful to make sure that my grandfather would approve of anything I did. My grandparents are still alive, so my whole life I've gotten an earful about the tacky and cheap things other resorts are doing every time I go to visit them."

Paige understood those family expectations. She supposed she failed in most areas, while her sister, Piper, excelled. That was okay with her, though. Her patients loved her and that was more important to her. "I am certain you can open up the classiest shaved ice shop on the whole island."

They chuckled as they sat together and finished their frozen treats. As Paige set her cup aside, she noticed the tattoo on Mano's left forearm again. This time she had a much better view of the design. It was simple and geometrical, with rings of black triangles encircling his forearm. She'd never seen a tattoo like it before.

"What does your tattoo mean?"

She watched as Mano self-consciously ran his palm over the black ink etched into his forearm. "This is a traditional Hawaiian tattoo. These triangles symbolize a shark's teeth. My parents named me after the Hawaiian word for shark because my grandmother had a dream of me swimming with sharks while my mother was pregnant. It's considered to be my spirit animal. My people also believe that if I were to run across a shark in the ocean, it would see the tattoo and recognize me as kindred."

Paige reached out and traced along the rows of triangles that went from just below his elbow to his wrist. She could see the line of a scar hidden beneath the ink. It was probably the companion scar to the one on his brow and the smaller spatter of scars she'd seen on his chest that morning. She noticed that Mano stiffened under her touch and a ragged breath escaped his lips. Instantly, she forgot all about the tattoo and was focused entirely on the beautiful man it belonged to.

It was nice to sit so still and close to him. His skin was warm to the touch from the sun and when the breeze blew just right, she got a whiff of his scent. It was something earthy and masculine like sandalwood and leather. It made her want to lean closer and press her nose against the line of his throat to draw it fully into her lungs. As much as she was tempted, Paige resisted. Instead, she studied the interesting lines and angles of his face without worrying that he would notice her staring.

He had such an interesting face. The scar across his brow and the flat distortion of his nose could be considered flaws to some, but it gave him so much character. He had his glasses on now, but that morning, she'd gotten her first glimpse of his eyes. They had been more striking than even the sight of his bare chest. They were a dark brown that seemed to see right through her despite their lack of focus. She could just imagine those eyes looking at her through the dark lenses. She could watch him like this for hours.

Well, at least until he mentioned the awkward silence between them. "What?" he asked, turning to look in her direction.

"Nothing," she said as she cleared her throat and turned her attention back to his muscular and inked forearm. "It's just such a beautiful piece."

That made Mano smile. "I'm glad you think so. It's almost a rite of passage for the men in my family to receive their tattoo. I went through almost nine hours of traditional Hawaiian tapping to have it done. I'd like to think it was worth it, although I've never seen the results, myself."

Paige was surprised, although she supposed she shouldn't be. He'd mentioned losing his vision as a teenager, so if he'd gotten the tattoo as an adult, he wouldn't have seen it. "That's a lot of pain to protect yourself from sharks when you never get into the ocean."

Mano nodded softly and pulled his arm away from her touch. He ran his hand hard over the skin, almost scrubbing away her touch, before moving it out of her sight. "There are plenty of sharks to be wary of on land, as well."

She certainly knew that to be true. She wished the music from *Jaws* had played when Wyatt started circling her. Maybe then she wouldn't be in the predicament she was in—a predicament she still hadn't confided in Mano about. She wondered if it would really matter to him. They had a week together, not

a lifetime. He'd likely never even know if she didn't
bring it up. Yet at the same time, the grave seriousness with which he'd just spoken was the voice of
experience. She didn't know everything he'd struggled through in his life, but she would do her best
not to add to it. She should definitely tell him about
the baby. At least before things got any more serious.

Paige turned to the ocean, searching for a way
to mention it before they got too close. Instead, she
caught a glimpse of a pod of dolphins buzzing past
a few surfers. "Oh!" she cried out, gripping Mano's
arm.

"What?" he asked with an edge of panic in his
voice. Mano came across much more confident at
the resort than he was out with her today. Being unable to see the world around him seemed to make him
a little edgy. He must know every inch of the Mau
Loa like the back of his hand, yet out here he was at
a disadvantage.

"Nothing bad," she said soothingly. "Dolphins.
There's about twelve or fifteen of them."

The tension disappeared from Mano's body. "Oh
yeah. They're all over out here. It's too early in the
season for the humpback whales, but spinner dolphins are here year-round. If you go out on the water
while you're visiting, you'll get a chance to see them
up close for sure. They like the wake of the boats."

That was an interesting idea. She hadn't given
much thought to that yet. Including Mano in her plans
had both enhanced and limited her options. He was a
very capable man, but there were just some things that
were either difficult or pointless when you couldn't
see. But there were still options… "You know, I saw

a brochure at the hotel for a dinner cruise that departs from the pier near the Mau Loa."

"It's a nice operation. I recommend it to a lot of hotel guests. Half of Hawaii is underwater. You've got to get out there or get in it to have the full island experience."

Snorkeling or kayaking with Mano might not be feasible, but Paige thought a dinner cruise was very doable. "What about tonight?"

"What about tonight, what?"

Paige frowned with a touch of irritation. "What about you and I take that dinner cruise tonight?"

"Hmm." It was a thoughtful yet noncommittal sound that nonetheless drew her attention to his full lips and made her more interested in kissing him again than going out on a boat. Of course, there was no reason why she couldn't do both. The dinner cruise might be romantic.

"Please?" she asked with a hint of begging in her voice.

Mano twisted his lips in thought then finally sighed in defeat. "Okay. I'll call the concierge and see if I can book for tonight. They fill up early sometimes, though, so don't get your heart set on it yet. We might have to go another day."

He pulled out his cell phone and Paige sat with baited breath while she listened to him complete the call. He asked several questions, all positive from her side of the conversation. In a few minutes he hung up and slipped the phone back into his pocket.

"You're one lucky lady, *pulelehua*. They just had a cancellation for tonight, and I confirmed that they're okay with service dogs on board."

"Yay!" Paige cheered and wrapped her arms around his neck. She startled him, but he quickly recovered by returning the embrace. His arms were warm and strong around her, the hard muscles of his chest pressing against her small breasts. She felt her body start to respond to the simple hug and began to pull back, but he wouldn't let go.

Instead, his lips met hers. It was an easy kiss, sweet but firm. His lips tasted like watermelon shaved ice and his tongue was still slightly cold against her own.

"Okay," he muttered against her lips as they came apart. Mano pressed a button on his watch, announcing the time aloud as just after four. "I think we'd better head back to the hotel. I don't think cargo shorts will meet the dinner dress code. And besides that, I think you need to put on more sunblock."

Paige sat back and looked down at her pinkening skin. "How do you know that?"

"Your skin is hot to the touch. Either you're sunburned or feverish."

Paige smiled. She was always amazed by how much he noticed when it seemed like he would miss most things. "How do you know I'm not just all warmed up from that kiss?"

Mano laughed and pushed back from the table. "It's possible, but if you get that hot from a simple kiss, you're going to be in trouble later."

Five

Mano couldn't remember how long it had been since he'd gotten on a boat. He might have been on one catamaran since the accident. Kal had made him do it, but that had been enough for him. The charter to Lanai from Maui was on choppy seas and he'd clung to the railing for dear life. It had seemed like a stupid thing for a blind man to do.

Kal was never really interested in acknowledging Mano's limitations. He tried to stay positive about the whole thing, insisting that Mano could do anything he wanted to do. His brother didn't like the idea of him being trapped inside the Mau Loa. Paige favored his brother a lot in that way. He supposed it was her work with veterans. They overcame disabilities every day. Why should Mano be any different?

Because he *was* different. He'd learned to function

as well as possible in the world he knew now. Part of that was knowing his limitations.

As Hōkū led them up the ramp to the dinner yacht, Mano hoped he wasn't making a mistake. It was hard to say no to Paige, though. It was just a dinner cruise around the south side of the island. The boat likely had stabilizers to keep them from rocking everywhere or guests might end up wearing their dinner instead of eating it.

"Thank you for doing this. I know it isn't your first choice for a way to spend the evening."

Mano pushed aside his doubts and tried to give her his most confident smile. "I don't have to steer the boat, so we should be fine. To be honest, I've always wanted to try the cruise, but I figured the view would be lackluster."

"Very funny."

"Well, it's true. The company makes up for it, however."

"Mr. Bishop," a man's voice greeted them as they neared the deck. "Thank you for joining us tonight. Just take one big step up, sir, and you'll be secure on the ship."

Mano sensed Hōkū move ahead of him and felt out his step before climbing onto the boat with Paige at his side.

"If you'll come right this way, I'll show you to our rear deck where we're serving wine and canapés."

They followed the host around the ship, where they were greeted with their choice of beverages and some small bites to tide them over until dinner. Paige opted for sparkling water once again and this time, he opted for the same. Alcohol seemed a poor choice given the situation.

Mano held Paige tight at his side as they mingled with other guests on the cruise. Everyone seemed enamored with Hōkū, who basked in the praise. Mano was far more interested in the bare skin he ran across when his palm came to rest on Paige's lower back. His fingers felt around, casually searching for fabric, and found the silky edge just shy of indecency. Moving up, he realized she hadn't worn a bra tonight, either. Her back was one bare expanse of skin. The realization made his blood hum in his veins, and he wished dinner would go ahead and start so it would end. He was far more interested in getting her back to his hotel suite.

When they were finally shown to their table, he was happy to find they were at a private table for two. He would rather talk to Paige alone than continue the small talk. She read the menu choices to him since a braille menu wasn't available and they gave their selections to the waiter.

"Is the table nice?" he asked once the server was gone.

"Oh yes," Paige said. "Our table is right at the window so we have the best view of the water. The sun is just starting to set."

Mano nodded. "Sounds nice. What about you? How do you look tonight?"

"Well," Paige began thoughtfully, "I think I pale in comparison to an Oahu sunset, but I tried."

"I don't know," Mano said thoughtfully. "I felt a whole lot of skin earlier. I'm envisioning you in something pretty slinky."

"I'm wearing a halter gown. It ties around my neck and it's open in the back. It hangs fairly loosely to the ground."

"What color is it?"

"Red."

"I like it. What shade of red?"

"A dark red. Not quite burgundy. I'm just now noticing how it's highlighting the sun I got today. I probably look like a lobster."

"Stop it, Paige," he said softly but firmly. He didn't understand why she always cut herself down. A lot of women were prone to dismissing compliments, but she took it a step further. She didn't seem to think very highly of herself at all, and that was a damn shame. Here he was envisioning her in a sexy red dress and she thought she looked like a boiled crustacean.

"Stop what?" she asked.

She cut herself down so easily, she didn't even know she was doing it. Reaching across the table, he sought out her face with his hand. "Don't pull away," he insisted and finally felt her cheek against his palm. "I've spent enough time with you, Paige, to know you are a beautiful woman, inside and out."

"You don't know anything," she said flatly.

"Don't I? I've touched your face, kissed your lips, held your body... I've drawn the scent of you into my lungs and tasted you on my tongue. I've heard your soft sighs and melodic laughter. I don't need eyes to see you, Paige. Every word out of your mouth convinces me more and more how lovely you are. It pains me to hear you insist otherwise."

The silence answered him back. He withdrew his hand and waited for her response.

When it finally came it was quiet, nearly a whisper. "You're right. Thank you."

It wasn't very convincing, but it was a start. They might only be spending a week together, but he wanted Paige to return to the mainland feeling like a million bucks. It wasn't normally his style to double as lover and therapist, but he'd never met a woman so…broken before. She had no reason to be. He was the broken one, and he had more confidence in his little finger than she had in her whole body. It simply wasn't right, and he was determined to fix it.

At the same time, he started to regret chastising her on their evening out. Whether or not what he said was true, it seemed to quiet her. Their dinner went by with him trying to make conversation and her giving as many one word responses as she could muster. It was nearly painful. When the crew announced that there would be dancing and live music on the upper deck, he jumped at the chance.

"Would you like to dance, *pulelehua*?"

More silence. "I'm not a very good dancer," she said at last.

"That's okay. I can't see how bad you are."

That earned a chuckle out of her. "All right. What about Hōkū?"

"He has four left feet. We'll leave him to the side for a little while."

He took her hand and he let her lead them around the ship to the stairs and up to the main deck. There, the warm breeze ruffled his hair even as he could feel the night start to cool with the setting of the sun.

One of the servers offered to attend to Hōkū, so Mano passed off his lead and followed Paige onto the dance floor. The band was playing something a little jazzy and slow. He slipped one arm behind her back and took her hand in his. They rocked in a slow, easy motion to the music. He could feel the hesitation in Paige's every step, but after a few minutes, she finally relaxed against him.

"This isn't so bad, is it?" he asked.

"No," Paige admitted. "It's nice. I've never really slow danced with a man before."

"Really?" Mano didn't know why he was surprised after all she'd told him, but he was. "Not even in high school?"

"Definitely not in high school. I wasn't very popular. What about you?"

"I was very popular," Mano said. "All the girls loved me. And I loved them. Things were going great for me in that department until the accident."

"Did the girls really walk away from you when you lost your vision?" She sounded aghast at the mere idea.

"Some," Mano said. One in particular, but he wasn't in the mood to tell her about Jenna. He'd rather Paige think he was a playboy than a broken-hearted teenage boy who lost almost everything he loved in a single moment. "I think I pushed most of them away. I was so angry for so long that I hardly wanted to be around myself. I don't blame them for taking a step back."

"I see that a lot in my patients," Paige said. "So many of them intended to be soldiers for life. It was what they felt they were made to do. Then some IED blows their arms off and they're shipped home to live a life they never envisioned. It's hard on them. A lot of them don't adjust well. I spend a lot of my time not only helping them heal physically, but emotionally. Too many walk out the door and put a bullet through their head. But if you can get through to them, they can really live a full life. They have to make adjustments, but they can still do anything they put their mind to."

"Do you really believe that?" Mano asked.

"I do. I've seen it happen. Determination can take you far. I mean, look at you. You run that hotel like a well-oiled machine. It's amazing. I have no doubt that if you wanted to take on some new challenge, you'd succeed."

"You remind me of my brother."

"Is that a bad thing?"

"Not entirely. Only when he's pestering the snot out of me. He was always very positive about how I could still lead the life I wanted to lead after the accident. I've never been as certain. I think for him, it was mostly guilt. He wanted me to do everything I'd wanted to so he wouldn't feel like he cost me my dreams."

"Cost you your dreams? How would he be responsible for that?"

Mano stiffened. They'd already put a bit of a damper on the night. He didn't want to drive another nail in the coffin by talking about something that dark. "Let's not discuss it anymore tonight. I promise I'll tell you all about it another time."

"Okay."

The tempo of the music slowed and Paige surprised him by wrapping her arms around his neck. He pulled her close and they swayed together on the dance floor. Through the thin fabric of her dress, he could feel every inch of Paige pressing against him.

Suddenly, he wasn't interested in talking anymore. Or even dancing. He couldn't wait for the ship to return to the marina so he could slip off this dress and make love to Paige.

As they exited the elevator at their floor, Mano reached out and captured Paige around her waist. She allowed herself to press against him, relishing in the feeling of being in the arms of a man so strong and masculine. Walking with him this afternoon was nothing compared to how he made her feel now. He insisted that she was beautiful, and she almost believed it when he held her like this. Being as commanding of presence as he was, it was hard not to agree with anything he said. She couldn't understand how anyone could see him as handicapped. He simply couldn't see.

Everything else about him was amazing. He made *her* feel amazing and desirable. Just the touch of his hand against the bare small of her back tonight had sent a sizzle of need through her whole body. She could still feel the heat of his touch lingering there, as though his handprint had seared into her skin, branding her as his property.

She'd never imagined that she could capture the attention of a man like Mano, and yet here she was outside her hotel room, on the verge of asking him in. This wasn't like Paige at all. She'd never been one to indulge in casual sex, mostly because it was rarely offered. But something about the beauty of Mano and Hawaii mixed with pregnancy hormones made her feel braver than usual.

"Thank you for playing hooky with me today," she said instead of asking him in.

Mano tipped his head toward her face, although his gaze settled near her lips. "You're very welcome. I'll play hooky with you anytime you like, Paige."

"What about tomorrow?" she asked.

"Tomorrow?" Mano's voice was low and gruff. "Tomorrow is hours away. Right now I'm more concerned about tonight."

"Tonight?" Paige shifted just enough in his arms that she could feel the firm heat of Mano's erection pressing into her stomach. He wasn't just paying her lip service. He truly did want her, and he left no question of it. She wanted him, too, but in the heat of the moment, she felt a flutter of panic. This was really going to happen. She just had to say the word. Was she ready to take the leap?

Mano's hand reached up to caress her cheek. He stroked her skin and let the pad of his thumb brush across her bottom lip. His mouth followed, pressing his lips insistently to hers. She realized quickly that the answer was a definitive yes. She couldn't deny him. Not when he kissed her like this and held her as though he couldn't get enough of her.

Paige wasn't used to that kind of adoration. Wyatt's kisses had been nice enough, but they lacked a certain spark. Mano clearly enjoyed every second, and so did she. When her lips parted and his tongue glided across hers, he groaned. The low, primal sound made her insides pulse with a need she'd rarely felt before.

At last, reluctantly, she pulled away and tried to steady herself in his arms. The warmth of his skin and his masculine scent made her head swim with desire. Thoughts of tomorrow had faded away and all that mattered was here and now. She'd known they were spiraling toward this moment since they'd kissed on the balcony last night and he'd chased after her. She wanted him. She just had to be brave enough to ask for what she needed. "I would invite you into my room, but I don't know if you'd prefer us to go to your own suite. For Hōkū's sake."

Mano smiled at her. "That's an excellent idea. And very thoughtful." He pulled away, but not before taking her hand in his. "My suite, then?"

Before she could start to panic, they moved across the hall to his doorway and the reality of it all began to sink in. Inside, he cut Hōkū loose and went into the kitchen. "Can I get you something to drink? I have a couple kinds of beer, a bottle of Moscato, some pineapple juice and sparkling water."

"The water would be great," she said. His offer of alcohol was one she'd had to turn down repeatedly. It was a reminder that she wasn't being as forthright with Mano as she should be. She couldn't put this off any longer. She'd told herself that if things got serious, she would tell him about the baby. Well, things were on the verge of seriousness. If it put a damper on their evening together, or ended this vacation romance altogether, so be it.

"Shall we drink on the patio?" he asked.

"Sure." She waited for him to open the bottle for her and a beer for himself. He handed hers over and they walked together to the sliding doors of the patio.

They were both seated in the plush lounge chairs and gazing out at the dark sea before she worked up the nerve to say what she needed to say.

"Mano, before this goes any further, I need to tell you something."

He picked up his beer and took a sip. "Tell me anything, *pulelehua*."

Paige hesitated for a moment. Did she really need to tell him about the baby? Their short vacation fling would long be a distant memory when her child was born, but somehow it didn't feel right to keep it from him.

"I'm leaving in less than a week, so it really doesn't matter, but I feel like I should tell you. I don't like keeping secrets, especially one that could be a potential turnoff for you."

Mano turned to her, a frown furrowing his brow. He sought out her hand and held it in his. "What is it? You're not married are you?" he asked with a joking grin.

"No," she said with a chuckle and a shake of her head. "But I am pregnant."

"Pregnant?" Mano's jaw fell slack with shock. She could tell it was the last thing he was expecting to hear.

"I know," Paige said, avoiding his gaze in favor of watching the waves below. "When I told you that my life was a little complicated right now, that's what I meant."

Mano put his hand over his heart. "You'll have to forgive me. It's the first time a woman has ever said those words to me. I had a moment of panic even though I know it couldn't be mine."

"I understand. It's not the kind of thing you'd expect me to say."

"When we touched, you didn't feel pregnant."

Paige remembered the surge of panic she'd felt the night before when he'd touched her stomach. "I'm only thirteen weeks along. I should start showing soon."

At last, Mano exhaled and took another big sip of his beer. "This explains a lot, actually. I couldn't fathom how someone could come all the way to Hawaii and not at least try a mai tai. I was wondering if you were a recovering alcoholic. This, however, is a very good reason."

"It is. I'd love to have a mai tai, honestly. With the way my life is going, I could use a stiff drink." Or a dozen.

"That doesn't sound good. Are there problems with the baby's father?" he asked. "There must be if you're here with me."

"You could say that. Long story short, you don't need to worry about him. What happens between us won't be some kind of torrid affair. He's out of the picture. Permanently." Paige struggled to keep the sound of tears out of her voice as she told the truth about Wyatt, but the look of concern on Mano's face was enough for her to know she'd failed.

"Does he know about the baby?"

Paige wished he hadn't asked that question. She'd wrestled with that since she found out. She didn't know how to tell him, or if Wyatt would even care. He was with Piper now. The kind of man who would dump one sister for the other was not likely to be candidate for father of the year. She would tell him.

Maybe when she got back from Hawaii. But she didn't expect the conversation to go well.

"Not yet," she admitted. "Like I said, it's complicated. I'm not going to bore you with my sob story, but no matter what, I'm not going back to him. That's the important part. I just wanted to tell you the truth so you knew I wasn't trying to pull a fast one on you and play it off as yours or something else foolish. But at the same time, I hope it really doesn't change things for us." She held her breath, waiting for his response.

"I beg to differ," Mano argued. "It does change things. For example, I'm certainly not going to send you parasailing or windsurfing now that I know you're pregnant."

Paige laughed at his protective response, relieved that he was joking about the whole thing instead of escorting her out of his suite. "I'm not fragile, I'm just pregnant."

"You're housing a life inside you, *pulelehua*. Enjoy yourself, but there's no need to be reckless."

Paige let out the breath she'd been holding, although her muscles were still tense. He seemed to take the news well, but she couldn't be sure. Would he handle her with kid gloves now? Send her back to her suite for a good night's rest without the sound bedding she'd hoped for? She didn't want to know, so she changed the subject by asking the question that had been bothering her for days.

"You keep calling me that Hawaiian word—*pule*-something. What does it mean?"

"Pulelehua," he repeated the complicated sounding word as though it simply rolled off his tongue. "It means 'butterfly.'"

Butterfly? Paige gasped aloud. Was this guy for real? He was like something out of a novel—the dashing romantic hero who says the right things and knows just how to touch a woman to make her melt with desire. She could feel the heat inside of her building and he hadn't even touched her yet. He was the kind of guy a girl like her would never have outside the pages of a book. And yet here he was with her, moments from the bedroom.

"That's sweet of you," she said, "but I feel more like a caterpillar most days."

Mano stood and reached for her hand. When she offered it, he pulled up her up and wrapped his arms around her waist. Paige relished the way her body fit so snugly against his. The press of her small and sensitive breasts against his chest created a sensation that made it almost hard to breathe, yet she wouldn't pull away. She couldn't. Her knees were so soft with desire that she'd melt to the floor if he let her go.

"You are no caterpillar, Paige, although sometimes I think you're still hiding in your cocoon, afraid to come out and spread your wings. You have challenges ahead of you, but I don't want you to think about them while you're here. This is your vacation getaway, and our fling is just the thing you need to get your mind off things. I don't want you to be afraid with me. I don't want you holding back. Especially not tonight."

She was holding back, but she had good reason not to leap into his arms and kiss him senseless. What if he wasn't there to catch her? "How can I not be afraid? You're like a dream I'm going to wake up from any moment now. I don't know why you chose me, but I'm on eggshells waiting for you to change your mind."

"I'm a very decisive man. I'm not the kind to change my mind. Especially not when I want you as badly as I do. So it's a very simple thing. Do you want me, *pulelehua*?"

Paige couldn't help the rush of air that purged from her lungs at the question. She didn't answer right away, instead reaching up to pull off his glasses. He didn't stop her, letting Paige gaze into his beautiful brown eyes, thankful she could see all of him. "I absolutely do. I'm scared to death, but I've never wanted a man more in my whole life."

Mano smiled and brushed the back of his hand across her cheek. His knuckles grazed her skin, leaving a trail of fire in their wake. "Good. Let's go back inside."

Six

Mano led Paige down the length of his balcony to the second set of doors that opened into his master suite. He circled behind her and drew her back until her bare shoulder blades pressed into his chest. He let his palms run up her arms from her wrists to her shoulders, stopping at her neck when he found the tie of her dress. Her hair was up tonight, out of his way, so he had full access to the bare skin he'd hungered over on the yacht.

His fingers pulled gently at the fabric as he leaned in to leave a trail of kisses on the side of her neck and along her shoulders. When the knot finally came undone, he let go to see how far the fabric pooled. He felt down her sides, finding her bare waist, then hips, then thighs. The dress had simply slipped all the way to the floor.

"Thank you," he murmured into the sensitive hollow under her ear.

"Thank you for what?" she asked, her voice near breathless.

"Thank you for wearing a dress that was easy for me to take off. I don't have the patience to fuss with a lot of buttons and fasteners tonight. I was afraid I might have to tear the dress and buy you a new one."

Paige gasped, but he wasn't certain if it was the words or his hands reaching around her to cup her breasts. They were small, but firm, with nipples that hardened instantly to his touch. He massaged them gently, squeezing the tips until he could feel Paige shiver against him. She arched her back and pressed her hips into his raging desire, making him groan aloud against her neck.

"Oh, Paige," he whispered as he held one breast and let his other hand travel down her stomach. He detected the faintest roundness to her belly that ended just as he reached the lacy trim of her panties. His fingers dipped below the fabric and gently stroked between her thighs.

Paige writhed in his arms, her body wracked with the sensations of his touch. Encouraged, he stroked harder, teasing her in slow circles until she was panting and desperately clinging to the fabric of his suit coat. He hadn't intended to take this so far before they'd even reached the bed—he was still fully clothed, after all—but he couldn't bear to tease her. He wasn't about to let go of her until she was screaming his name.

Mano stroked at her moist flesh. Paige's knees buckled beneath her and she leaned back against him for support, which he gladly provided. It gave him an even better angle to her body. He took immediate advantage of it, letting a finger slip inside of her. She was so tight, he could feel her muscles clamp down around him as she whimpered with need.

"Mano..." she said in a pleading voice. He could feel the rest of her body tense and her heart race beneath his other hand as she came closer to her release.

"Yes, *pulelehua*," he encouraged in a low growl. "Fly for me, butterfly."

With one hard stroke, Paige came apart in his arms. She shuddered and cried out, her hips bucking against his hand as he held her tight to keep her from falling to the ground.

Mano waited until her breathing slowed and her body stilled. "Let's get you to bed."

"I won't argue with you on that," she murmured.

When Paige was stable on her feet, she took Mano's hand and let him lead her to the bed. She collapsed just at the edge, then moved quickly to remove his shirt. She wanted to see and touch him—every inch of him. He didn't stop her. Instead, he helped her by slipping out of his suit coat and tossing it into his corner chair.

Paige opened his shirt, tugging it out of his pants so it could slip it off over his shoulders. That was when she paused and took a moment to appreciate the beauty of his body. His chest was solid muscle and just as tan as the rest of him. The few scars she'd glimpsed early that morning turned out to be more numerous than she'd expected. They were old and faded, standing out only because they were lighter than his unblemished skin. It looked almost like the chest of one of her soldiers that had taken shrapnel from an explosion.

She let her fingertips trace every ridge of muscle, tickling her way across his smooth chest and down his stomach to stroke over his six-pack abs. His skin was as soft and smooth as she wished her own could be. "I have to admit I'm a little jealous," she said.

Mano chuckled. "Of what?" he asked.

"You have the smoothest, softest skin. Almost no body hair at all. It's not fair, really."

"That's funny. I've always wanted some manly chest hair. Genetically, it's just not common for my people. My father was a white man stationed here in the military, but even then, no luck. My Polynesian genes, along with my heritage, won out in the e-end."

It seemed harder for Mano to get the words out as Paige continued to touch him. Her palms ran over his arms and shoulders, down his chest and finally to his belt. She was ready for the rest of him. Her belly burned for what would come next. The clink of the metal buckle gave way to the sound of his zipper drifting down. Impatiently, she slipped her hand inside, palming his massive erection and making a shudder run through his whole body.

"Paige," he groaned, but she didn't stop. It was her turn to play.

One hand stroked him while the other slipped off his pants and briefs. He stepped out of them, tossing them to the chair, as well. She figured that leaving clothing on the floor was like littering his space with land mines he would trip on later. She would be conscious to keep her own things out of his path.

Now Mano was naked, standing before her like an ancient Polynesian god. Not even the scars could detract from the carved beauty and masculinity of his body. Everything about him was large and strong. As her eyes took in his desire for her, she swallowed hard. She went to reach for him and then she remembered an important step. "Before we go any further," Paige said. "Do you have condoms somewhere?"

Mano nodded and pointed to the bed stand. "There should be a new box in there."

Paige opened up the drawer and pulled out the largest box of condoms she'd ever seen outside a bulk warehouse. She couldn't contain her nervous laughter. "A twenty-count box?"

He grinned and shrugged. "I was feeling hopeful yesterday after our kiss," he said. "I bought them at the gift shop last night. It might seem like a lot, but we are spending the week together, you know. I think a solid goal would be to use every single one before you leave."

Paige had a hard time believing they were having sex at all, much less twenty times, but she would be happy to aim high. "Ambitious. I like that."

Mano held still as Paige opened a condom and slowly rolled it down his length. He bit at his bottom lip as she took her time and stroked every last air pocket out.

"You're pretty good at putting those on for a pregnant lady."

At that, Paige laughed aloud. "Touché." She reached out and stroked his undercarriage to punish him in the best way possible.

Mano hissed through gritted teeth and pulled away

from her touch. He moved past her to the bed and threw back the comforter. Taking Paige by the wrist, he pulled her onto the bed beside him. The lengths of their whole bodies were touching, skin to skin at last, with his need for her insistently pressing against her belly.

His hands went back to her body, seeking out her sensitive center. He stroked and teased at her again until she was more than ready for him. He rolled her onto her back and she parted her thighs so he could settle there. Without hesitation, he surged forward and filled her.

Paige gasped as the pleasure-pain of it shot through her. Once the feeling faded, she lifted her hips to take all of him in, wrapping her legs around his hips to pull him in deeper. It was a delicious sensation, one unlike any feeling she'd experienced before. Judging by his tightly clenched jaw and tensed muscles, Mano was enjoying the position, too. She wanted to immediately give in to it and relieve the tension he built inside of her. They had nineteen condoms left, after all, but she knew he wasn't about to let this end so soon.

He started by stroking long, slow and deep inside of her. Propping himself up on one arm, he cupped her breast with his free hand. Since her pregnancy, they had become extremely sensitive. The nipple pebbled at his touch, growing hard against his caress and making her moan with pleasure.

"What color are your nipples, Paige?" he asked.

Paige was startled from the sensation by his bold question. "Um…" She didn't know what to say.

"If I could see them, I wouldn't have to ask. Tell me, please."

That was true. She needed to open up so she could share every aspect of this moment with him. "Dark pink. Almost a dusky rose, I guess."

Mano nodded slowly, biting his lower lip with his eyes closed as though he were picturing them in his mind. Bending down, he took one into his mouth. His tongue flickered over it, making Paige squirm beneath him. The moist heat of his mouth on her skin coaxed pleasure that made her core tighten and pulse around him.

He hesitated only for a moment and then he redoubled his efforts to pleasure her. His hips moved in a more circular motion, making his pelvis grind against her sensitive nub. He timed the strokes with the hard suction of her breast until Paige was a gasping, writhing, moaning mess beneath him. She'd never allowed herself to unravel like this before, but she could do it with him and not feel self-conscious about it.

"Are you close, *pulelehua*?"

"Oh yes," she whimpered. "So close."

"What do you want me to do?" he asked.

"Love me harder," she demanded softly. "Fill me and don't be gentle."

Mano made a growling sound deep in his throat before dropping onto his elbows on each side of her. He buried one hand in her hair and the other gripped her shoulder tight. He thrust hard once, making Paige cry out loud. He followed it with two more hard strokes, then he seemed to let go of whatever restraint he had left. He pumped hard and fast into her body, holding tight as his hips pounded into hers.

Paige's cries escalated from soft gasps and whimpers to loud screams as he unleashed his passion on her. "Yes! Yes!" she shouted, loving every minute of it. She loved the feel of his skin, slick with sweat against her own. Her cries echoed in her own ears, their scent growing stronger the harder he loved her. Her every sense was overloaded, pushing her closer to the edge as he climbed there himself.

Then it hit her. Her release was punctuated with a sharp cry of pleasure she couldn't hold in. He continued to thrust into her as her internal muscles tightened and fluttered around him. Before her last gasps faded, he finally gave in to it and poured into her with a loud groan of satisfaction.

Paige welcomed him into her arms as he collapsed, spent, against her. Finally rolling to her side, Mano sank into the pillows. With one hand curled over her left breast, they fell asleep together with her heartbeat serving as the soothing rhythm that lured them to sleep.

Paige woke up in the night practically starving. She never woke up to eat in the middle of the night, and she'd had plenty to eat at dinner. The pregnancy books she'd read said that once she reached her second trimester, the cravings would begin in earnest, and that must be what was behind it. Why did this have to happen when she was naked and in the bed of a sexy hotelier? He probably didn't have much food in that kitchen. Of course, she didn't have any in her suite, either.

As quietly as she could, Paige peeled back the covers and slipped from bed. With her only option being her red gown, she considered just going hunting for food in the nude. No one would see her but Hōkū, anyway. But propriety got the best of her and she found Mano's robe hanging in the bathroom like the one in her own suite. She wrapped herself up in it and padded barefoot through the bedroom into the living room area.

Hōkū was asleep on his pillow, but his head popped up when he saw her. He got up and followed her lazily into the kitchen. He sat by her side as she opened the refrigerator door and frowned. Beer, water, juice and fancy dog food.

"That's no help," she said to the dog, then turned to check cabinets for pantry goods. She found dog biscuits, some saltines and a box of Pop Tarts. Paige never thought of Mano as a Pop Tart guy, but she supposed everyone had their weaknesses. Unfortunately, that was not what she wanted. She got a dog biscuit out anyway and gave it to Hōkū. He happily wagged his tail and lay down on the floor to eat his treat.

"We found something for you, but nothing for me. My dorm room in college had more food than this and I was broke," she muttered.

"That's because your dorm room didn't have room service."

Startled, Paige spun on her heels to see Mano standing in the doorway to the kitchen. He had tugged on a pair of boxer briefs, but otherwise, he was still gloriously bare. Her heart was beating too quickly to appreciate it, though. "Lord," she swore. "You scared the hell out of me."

"Sorry. Usually people are sneaking up on me, not the other way around."

She supposed that was true. "I was trying not to wake you up. Sorry."

"No worries," he said, leaning against the wall. "I don't sleep well. To me, it's dark all the time, so my body never knows when it's time to rest and when it's time to wake up. What did you need?"

Paige sighed and opened the refrigerator door again as though things would change. "I'm hungry. I shouldn't be, it's two in the morning, but the baby has other ideas."

"Tell me what you want and I'll have it brought up."

"It's two in the morning," Paige repeated. "Doesn't the kitchen close?"

"Not entirely. There's twenty-four-hour service for special guests, including the two penthouse suites. So, lucky you, you can have whatever you'd like."

That was tempting. Or it would be if she could pin down what she was after. The baby wasn't quite specific enough. "Would you eat some of it?"

"Sure." He shrugged. Mano picked up his phone and dialed it. "This is Mr. Bishop," he said after a moment. "Yes, I'd like to place an order to be brought up. One second." He stopped and handed the phone to her. "Order anything and everything you'd like."

Paige felt like she was living out the *Pretty Woman* breakfast scene. Her brain wanted everything on the menu, but she held it in. "Hello?" she said.

"Yes, ma'am? What can we get for you?"

"I don't know. I don't have a room service menu."

"That's fine. We can make whatever you'd like."

Paige could get used to this. "Well, how about a cheese and fruit plate with some crackers?"

"Yes, ma'am. Anything else?"

"A Sprite. And..." Her hungry brain started to spin. "A chocolate milkshake. That's all."

"Very well, ma'am. It will be up shortly."

When she hung up the phone, Mano was smiling at her. "What?" she asked.

"Nothing." He took a few steps toward her and Paige closed the gap to walk into his arms. "You're just adorable."

"Adorable?" she repeated. "I'll take it, but it's not really what I was going for."

Mano laughed. "Well, earlier, you were a wild sex kitten, if that makes you feel better. Right now, you and your food cravings are cute."

Paige leaned in to rest her head against his chest. "They're cute now. They won't be cute when I'm huge and home alone and there's no room service to bring me what I want. Then it will just be sad."

Mano's expression fell and his lips twisted in thought. "Are you sure the father won't be there for you?"

Paige's mind drifted to the disturbing image of her sister in Wyatt's arms. It was almost as awkward as talking about the baby's father with her new lover. "Yes, I'm pretty sure. I'm also sure I don't *want* him to be there for me. He was a bad choice. My biological and emotional urges overrode my common sense. At the very least, I hope the baby will take after him physically. The father is very handsome, if nothing else. I can raise the baby to be more kind and thoughtful than he was. That will be easier without his influence."

Mano's furrowed brow didn't disappear no matter

how she tried to dismiss the father. "I don't like the idea of you doing this alone."

Paige nearly snorted. Join the club! "Yes, well, things are what they are. The baby and I will be fine on our own."

"What...what if you moved here?"

Paige froze. What the hell did he mean by that? The expression on his face was perfectly serious, but that couldn't be the case. "Moved here? I can barely afford a place in San Diego. I certainly can't afford anything on Oahu."

"You wouldn't have to," he insisted. "I could get you a place. Make sure that you had everything you needed for you and the baby. You could work or not, whatever you wanted. Wouldn't that make things easier for you?"

"Sure, but what do you get in return? Am I your on-call piece on the side whenever you're feeling lonely?"

"What?" Mano looked horrified. "No! I'm just being nice. I'm not buying your affections like a common prostitute. There are no strings to this, even if we never slept together again. I asked for a week with you and that's all I'd require."

No matter how many words came out of his mouth, Paige didn't understand what he was talking about. Why would a man offer to support a woman and another man's baby with nothing in return? "Why would you do that? You hardly know me."

"I know enough about you. I've got more money than I could ever spend, and it sounds like you are in a rough spot. Let me help you out."

Paige's eyes grew wide. "Oh no," she said dismissively. "I'm not going to be a charity case. Thanks, though."

"I can't win with you. Either I get something out of this and you feel cheap or I don't and you feel like I'm pitying you. I wish you wouldn't look at it that way." Mano approached her and put his hands on her arms. "Let me do this for you. I want to. And you could use the help if you'd just admit it. At least think about it."

The doorbell to the suite rang and Paige was grateful for the interruption. "I'll get it," she said, pulling away from his touch.

Paige opened the door and room service came in with a cart. "Where would you like it?" the man asked.

She motioned over to the dining room table. "That's fine."

She was handed the room service receipt, but the total was blank. The perks of owning the hotel, she supposed. She filled out the tip generously and handed it back. The man quickly disappeared, leaving her alone with a delectable chocolate milkshake and an uncomfortable conversation.

Paige opted to ignore their previous discussion and focused on her food instead. Under the lid was a beautifully arranged platter with at least five or six types of cheeses, an assortment of crackers, strawberries, grapes, pineapple and apple slices. It was just what she'd been wanting.

"Would you like to eat on the balcony?" Mano asked.

"Actually, if it's okay, I'd be happy just to take it to bed. I eat in bed a lot at home."

"Not a problem."

Paige gathered up her tray and carried it into the bedroom. She placed it on the foot of the bed, moving her drink and her milkshake to the nightstand. She stacked the pillows high behind her and curled up in the blankets. Mano joined her, snuggling to her side and thankfully not bringing up their earlier discussion.

They chatted about harmless things and nibbled on the food. Paige fed Mano grapes and even shared her milkshake with him. It was an easy, fun moment together in the middle of the night. She hadn't had many experiences where sex was followed by conversation and cuddling. It was nice. Being with Mano was nice.

But when the food was gone and they'd opted to go back to sleep, Paige couldn't turn her brain off. Thoughts swirled through her mind faster than she could process them. She lay there amongst the pillows with Mano snoring softly next to her. It felt amazing to be here beside him. Wonderful. She enjoyed spending time with him more than she ever expected to.

And maybe that was the problem she had with his offer. He didn't ask her to stay because he loved her. They'd only been together a few days, so she'd wonder if he was insane if he did. He didn't ask her to move here because he wanted to be with her for more than just a week. That might even be different enough for her to consider it. Instead, he was just trying to solve her problems and help her take care of her baby, which was noble, but it wasn't what she wanted from him.

Raising her baby alone would be hard. There would be long hours with day care or a sitter when she worked nights. There would be miserable sleepless days where they would both be cranky and exhausted. But there would also be the two of them together like peanut butter and jelly.

Paige had wondered often if she would spend most of her life alone. She'd never been in a serious enough relationship to imagine herself getting married or having children. She feared she might become one of those lonely spinsters who talked to cats. She liked cats. But she didn't like the idea of going through her whole life on her own.

Wyatt was a first-rate jerk, but he had given her something she never expected to have. No matter what, she would have this baby and she wouldn't be alone. It wasn't the same as having a partner in life, but it was something. There would always be a little part of her out in the world that loved her unconditionally, gave her sweet kisses and remembered her birthday. She looked forward to handmade construction paper and crayon cards, and jewelry made of macaroni and glitter.

And maybe one day in the future, instead of cats, she would have grandchildren to love and dote on. She couldn't ask for anything better than that.

No, as generous as Mano's offer was, she couldn't accept it. Paige would do this on her own.

Seven

"You work too much, Mano. I called you last night at nine thirty and it rolled over to voice mail."

"Aloha to you, too, *Kalani*," Mano responded to his brother's phone call. As much as he'd hated to leave Paige asleep in bed, he needed to get *some* work done today. He'd slipped downstairs early in the hopes he could perhaps take a half day. He liked playing hooky when Paige was involved, but he did still have a hotel to oversee. "What makes you think I didn't answer because I was working?"

"Is there another option for you?" Kal asked with a chuckle. "I mean, it's not like you were with a woman."

Mano grinned silently and waited for Kal to piece it together.

"You *were* with a woman? That's a welcome change."

"Shut up," Mano chastised. He didn't feel much like getting ragged on by his brother today, but he should've thought of that before he answered the phone. "It's not as though it's my first go out the gate. I've been with plenty of women."

"Oh sure. There was that belly dancer from Qatar, what, six months ago?"

"Five." It was just like his brother to keep track of his sex life just so he could rub it in his face.

"And the Australian opera singer? That was before Thanksgiving, I think."

He had him there. "Probably. You know how I am. Once or twice a year, if I'm lucky, I find a lady with whom I'm interested in spending a little time. It just so happens, I've found one to be with this week."

"What's this one? A Brazilian bikini model? You seem to be trying to cover every continent."

"You're one to talk, Kal. I can't help it I live in Hawaii and run a hotel. I'm surrounded by tourists. This time is no different. But no, she's not a bikini model. She's actually a nurse from San Diego."

"Interesting choice. So, what drew you to this one? It couldn't be the accent this time."

"Actually, no. It was her scent. And her total and complete awkwardness. It was charming."

"I have to say, I've never chosen a woman for being clumsy, but more power to you, man, if it gets you away from your desk for a while."

Mano smiled. Paige had certainly done that. "I took yesterday off to spend the day with her."

"Really?" He could hear the disbelief in Kal's voice. "I don't recall you doing that for Miss Qatar."

"That was because she was with a couple of friends that went out during the day. Paige is here alone."

"What kind of person comes to Hawaii alone?"

Mano sighed. He didn't really want to get into Paige's story with Kal. "The kind of person that could use a vacation and a knowledgeable tour guide."

"What good are you as a tour guide if you won't leave the property?"

"We left the property!" Mano snapped at his older brother. Kal always thought he knew everything. He was older and wiser, while Mano was just the baby. It had only gotten worse after their parents died. At that point, Kal decided he was the head of the family and needed to not only run the show but care for Mano as though he were still a child. Never mind he was nearly eighteen at the time he lost his eyesight.

"Okay, okay," Kal said. "How long is the nurse from San Diego in town?"

"Until Friday afternoon."

"That's a shame. I'm going to just miss her."

"How's that?"

"I'm flying over on Sunday for Tūtū Ani's birthday. You didn't forget about her party, did you?"

Yes. "No," Mano insisted. "I wouldn't forget our grandmother's birthday. I just thought you'd be too busy to come."

"You're the workaholic, little brother, not me. Of course I'm coming. After a week with your friend, I expect you to be in a good mood when I arrive."

"Don't get your hopes up on that. You know those big family gatherings always make me tense."

"Your family should be where you feel the most at ease," Kal argued.

"Yes, well, I only feel at ease at the Mau Loa. So unless they're having the party here and neglected to tell me so I could book the ballroom, I won't be having much fun. But I'll go for Tūtū Ani's sake."

Honestly, it wasn't just the location that stressed Mano out. The large crowd of family, the well-meaning but pushy aunts treating him like an invalid, the kids running in front of him and unnerving Hōkū…it all added up to an afternoon he'd sooner do without. He hadn't really even enjoyed the gatherings when his parents were alive and he could see.

"You know they're having it at Aunt Kini's place. It's the only place we can bury the pig."

Thank goodness Paige was here. That's all Mano had to say about it. She would be a welcome distraction from the upcoming chaos. Hell, he'd completely forgotten about his grandmother's birthday celebration until Kal mentioned it. He'd be happy to lose his memory once again in Paige's arms.

"Did we get her a gift?" Mano asked. He couldn't remember.

Kal just sighed into the phone. "Yes. We went in together to get her the golden South Sea pearl necklace with the diamond clasp. You don't remember sending me a check for that? People usually remember paying that much for something."

Mano just shrugged. "We both have more money than we'll ever spend. I really don't pay attention to things like that."

"Well, at least pay attention to your phone. I'm going to text you when my plane leaves Maui. I need you to send the car to pick me up."

"Okay." Mano made a note of his brother's arrival and his grandmother's party in his calendar so he wouldn't forget again. "I'll see you Sunday. Don't take it personally if I don't answer the phone between now and then."

Kal barked an evil laugh into the phone. "I won't. I know you're getting busy. I mean, you're busy."

"Goodbye, dork."

Mano heard his brother laugh again into the phone as he ended the call. He loved Kal, but he certainly didn't mind that they lived on separate islands now. He was happy to have his space, from his brother and from the rest of the family. At the Mau Loa, he was in charge and confident of his every move. Although they knew he ran the family business without a hitch, his family was still prone to treating him as though he were newly blind and incapable of doing anything for himself.

They certainly wouldn't believe what he'd done over the last few days. His little adventures with Paige had been out of the norm for him. While it made him uneasy, it also was a shot of excitement into a life he'd crafted to be very predictable and dull.

Paige was anything but, and he liked that about her. It made him wish, for the first time, that she wasn't a tourist. Going into these short-term flings, Mano could always guarantee that he knew when the relationship would end. There was no reason to worry about an ugly breakup or a woman walking out on him, like Jenna had. Paige was the first woman who made him want more. He didn't know what more he wanted, but he wasn't looking forward to the end of the week.

It would come, though, so he needed to mentally

prepare for that. She'd turned down his offer to stay on Oahu, flat. The offer had been part charity, part selfishness. He could help her, and he wanted to, especially if she might be in his life for a while longer. Her negative reaction stopped him cold. That meant that no matter how charming, sexy or wonderful Paige was, he couldn't let himself get wrapped up in this. It was just a fling. That's all he wanted. He just needed to keep reminding himself of that when he was around her.

Mano's phone chirped again, but this time it was a text. He pressed the button to have the phone read it aloud.

It was Paige. *"You snuck out on me! I thought we were spending today together."*

He laughed as the phone's voice read Paige's text aloud. He hit the button to dictate a response. "It's still early, *pulelehua*. We have plenty of time to be together yet, today." The phone repeated his words back to confirm the text before it sent his response.

It chimed again. *"Okay, but if we're going all the way to the North Shore and back today, we shouldn't get too late a start."*

Mano's brow raised curiously at her response. The North Shore? They hadn't even discussed that possibility. "Is that what we're doing today?"

"Yes. We're getting garlic scampi shrimp and sticky rice from a food truck and eating it on the beach."

Ah. She'd been reading some of the brochures he'd given her for sights around the island. "I hope you're driving," he replied and got a smiley face in return. "I'll reserve a car from the hotel fleet."

Mano got up to talk to the head of hotel transportation with a smile on his face. He knew exactly which car they needed to take out—the cherry red convertible roadster. The little BMW was one of the special touches he'd added to the hotel for exclusive guests to use to see the island. His teenage heart wished he could be the one to drive it—it was the car he'd dreamt of when he had turned sixteen—but he'd settle for riding shotgun. Being beside Paige was enough to make his heart race and his adrenaline rush through his veins.

They'd take this trip so she could experience more of his home, but he was far more interested in coming back to the hotel so he could have her again. Unless, of course, they could find a secluded enough spot on the North Shore…

This was potentially the messiest and best thing she'd ever eaten. An old white food truck in a patch of dirt off the highway had just served her a plate of shrimp so divinely garlicky and buttery, she had streams of butter and olive oil dripping down her forearms as she tried to eat. Mano had opted for the spicy shrimp, and she could already see beads of sweat forming on his forehead from the hot chilies. They'd taken their order to go and found a piece of rocky secluded shoreline a few miles away, where Paige spread a blanket out on a dry stretch of sand for them to have a picnic.

The sea was wilder here on the North Shore, less manicured and tourist friendly than Waikiki. The sand was decorated with chunks of black volcanic rock and large pieces of driftwood from trees that had fallen. The deeper water was a stormy blue, but the shallow tide pools just beyond them were perfectly clear. She was certain she would put her feet in them before they left. They called to her.

"This is a beautiful spot," she said, immediately feeling guilty that he couldn't see it. "It's such a nice day."

"I always liked it up here," Mano said as he sipped his drink. "When I was a teenager, some of the guys and I would come down here to pretend like we could really surf. I'm surprised none of us got killed. The waves out here are for professionals, but we wanted to show off for the girls."

"I can't believe you'd risk that just to impress a girl." That seemed crazy, but she'd seen boys do plenty of daredevil stunts to get a girl's attention.

"One girl in particular," Mano admitted. "We dated for two years. Jenna." He winced as he said her name, as though it pained him. "I was a fool for her. I would've done any stupid thing she asked to see her smile and beam at me with pride."

"What happened with Jenna?" She felt like she shouldn't pry, but at the same time, she wanted to know since he had brought it up.

"Like most things in my life, the accident happened."

Paige was afraid of that. "Will you tell me about it now, since you wouldn't last night?"

Mano sighed and set down his carton of food. "Do you really want to ruin a beautiful day on the beach in Hawaii with my sob story?"

"Yes."

He shrugged and leaned forward to pick at his food

with a fork. "My brother, Kal, was playing football at the University of Hawaii. My parents and I were driving to the stadium to see the game. On the way there, we came upon one of the little pop-up rainstorms we have around here. It wasn't a big deal, they disappear in minutes, but an oncoming SUV was going too fast through a curve. I was in the backseat, so I'm not entirely sure what happened, but the police seemed to think the SUV hit a pool of water and hydroplaned into us at full speed."

Paige held her breath as he told the story. She knew it wasn't going to end well, and yet she kept hoping she was wrong.

"They had to use heavy machinery to extract us from the car, but I don't remember anything about it. I woke up in the hospital a couple days later and started screaming because I couldn't see. They had to drug me and restrain my arms because I just went completely berserk. I didn't even care that my arm was broken. I accidentally hit a nurse with my cast and blackened her eye. I didn't know she was there, but in the moment, I just didn't care about anything but my sight and when it was coming back. It wasn't, of course."

Mano shook his head and frowned. "I was such a mess that they didn't tell me my parents were dead for almost a week. I missed their funeral while I was in the hospital. Kal and my grandparents had to face all of that on their own."

"I'm sorry about your parents. I didn't know about that." Paige never dreamed the story would be worse than she imagined. He hadn't mentioned his parents very often, though, so she should've anticipated it.

"Yeah. The hardest part for me, I think, was that I never really got to mourn them. I just snapped my fingers and they were gone. Once I got out of the hospital, I was in and out of rehabilitation and training for my new disability. I had to learn braille and adapt every aspect of my life to being blind. Technology is better now, but even just a decade ago, there was a steep learning curve. There wasn't really time to think about losing them and what it meant for my life."

"What about the rest of your family?"

"My grandparents took over hotel operations again. They'd retired when they handed it over to my parents, but they knew Kal and I weren't ready for the responsibility. Kal dropped out of school for the rest of the semester and came home to take care of me. I think he felt guilty. He wouldn't leave my side for a minute."

"Why? Survivor's guilt?"

"Not quite. I think he decided none of it would've happened if he hadn't wanted us to come to his game that night. It's ridiculous, really, but even though he won't say it, I think he believes it. His life has turned into a penance. He completely changed course and seemed to pick up my life where I left it off, so my dreams could still be fulfilled in some twisted way. The Maui hotel was my plan. He opened it for me, which isn't the same, but I appreciate it. When I was old enough, I took over the Oahu hotel since I was familiar and more comfortable with it. I converted one of the penthouses into my apartment so I didn't have to commute or worry about the world outside the Mau Loa. And here we are."

"And what about Jenna?"

For the first time since he started telling his story, Mano turned to face the sea. His jaw hardened. Hōkū seemed to sense the change in his mood and rested his head on Mano's thigh in support. Mano placed his hand on the dog and stroked absentmindedly. "We had big dreams, too. We were going to go to college together, get married and run the new resort as a team like my parents and grandparents had. At first, she was right there by my side, but I think she had a naïveté about the accident. Like if she hung on long enough, I'd get my vision back and we could continue on with our plans. When that didn't happen, she left."

"Really?" Paige's heart ached at the thought.

"Yes. She said that she was too young to throw away her whole life taking care of me. And she was right. I don't blame her for going. I was enough of a burden on my family. I've no interest in being a rock that drags her—or any other woman—down."

Paige sat back on her heels and considered this confession. She'd seen the same thing with her soldiers. While they would die for their brothers, they refused to hold each other—or anyone else—back. She worried that some of them would've rather died on the battlefield than come home and be a strain on their family and friends. A lot of them pushed people away, not letting anyone close.

"So, is that why a handsome, rich hotel magnate is single and sitting on a beach with me instead of charming his beautiful wife and playing with their children?"

He shrugged. Mano didn't seem to want to get too introspective about the whole thing. "There's no sense wasting my time in real relationships. Spending this week with you, or another week with another woman every now and then, is all I need. I get the excitement, the passion, and it all ends before things can turn sour."

Mano had been right. As much as she wanted to know about his past, the story had certainly taken their afternoon on a darker turn. The oily shrimp started to churn in her stomach. She knew their time together would be short and without strings, but somehow knowing that he deliberately kept women, including her, at arm's length made her sad. She wasn't entertaining any romantic delusions about the two of them, but she still found herself caring more for Mano than she intended to. He did care about her and the baby, too, in his own way. He wouldn't have offered to help her if he didn't. He wouldn't be trying so hard to make her feel better about herself if he didn't worry at least a little about her. But it was different. She wanted him to be happy and she just didn't see that in him, despite his protestations.

Instead of dwelling on it, she tried to make light of his confession. "So you just want me because I'll be gone in a few days," she teased, thankful that he couldn't see the glimmer of hurt in her eyes. "Tell the truth."

He instantly brightened, happy to put all that aside. "You bet. I want you more the shorter our time together gets." Mano leaned toward her and beckoned her to kiss him. She complied, pressing her lips against his. She let herself give in to the kiss. That was what this week was about anyway. Enjoyment. Pleasure. Not dwelling in the past or worrying about the future. She just found it hard to turn those parts of her brain off.

When Mano's hand found her breast and cupped it through her tank top, she finally succeeded in focusing on the here and now. She moaned softly against his lips as his thumb stroked her nipples though the thin cotton. She hadn't worn a bra today—one of the perks of being a thin, nearly flat-chested woman. That meant there was very little separating the two of them.

She lay back on the blanket and let Mano roll onto his side next to her. He tugged gently at the neckline of her top, exposing her breast so he could capture it with his mouth. Paige buried her fingers in the long, dark waves of his hair and pulled him closer to her.

Paige loved getting lost in the feel of being with Mano. His mouth and hands and body on her were like nothing else in her life before now. There was no hesitation in his touch. Mano seemed convinced that she was beautiful and, for now, she'd let him believe that. Maybe they'd make it through the week before he learned the truth.

Eventually, someone would tell him. Staff at the hotel, maybe? Perhaps he'd overhear someone ask aloud why a man like him was with a woman like her. That would have to make him wonder. But until then, she would try to enjoy it.

There was a freedom in being with a man who couldn't see her. It took a while for her to adjust to the idea of not feeling self-conscious all the time, but once she got used to it, she really loved it. Some might find it a cruel irony that an unattractive woman would end up with a blind man, but to her, it was such a relief. At least until he realized that he was the one getting the short end of the stick.

She tried not to let those thoughts ruin the moment and focused instead on his touch. Mano's hand slipped beneath her shorts and sought out her center. He started stroking her, gently at first, then harder. Her breath caught in her throat as the sensations starting exploding inside of her. Within a minute she was close to coming undone. She couldn't believe how quickly he could manipulate her body into doing whatever she wanted it to do.

Paige looked around in a panic as she got closer... Anyone could see them together like this. Mano didn't seem to care, of course, but he wouldn't know if someone was watching.

"Someone is going to see us," she panted.

Mano raised his head from her breast. "I doubt it."

"What if they hear us?"

Mano chuckled and nuzzled her neck, never slowing his sensual exploration of her body. "Are you planning to be loud?"

"I may not have a choice in the matter."

"Good."

Mano rubbed harder, dipping his finger inside of her and stroking her from the inside, as well. The combination was explosive, sending her over the edge without a care if someone were watching them or not. He kissed her just as she reached the pinnacle, smothering her cries with his mouth until she finally stilled beside him.

Just as she returned to reality, a sound caught Paige's attention. She pulled Mano's hand away and quickly adjusted her shirt as she sat up on the blanket.

Behind them, another car had pulled up beside theirs. A whole family climbed out, talking and laughing all at once. She watched the father haul out chairs and a cooler and knew that their private oasis was gone. They'd just barely made it.

"I think we'll have to finish what we started back at the hotel," she said.

"It's probably for the best," Mano agreed as he sat up and dusted the sand off his legs. "A little make-out session is one thing, but any more serious action and sand gets *everywhere*. It's very unpleasant."

Paige smiled and leaned in to give him a kiss. "So you're promising me some serious action when we get back to the hotel?"

Mano pulled her close and deepened the kiss. "You better believe it."

Eight

Paige pried one eye open in the early morning light. She could see Mano slipping into his suit coat and frowned. "Where are you going?" she asked with a pout.

"Work. Just for a little while," he said sitting down on the edge of the bed. He leaned in and she met him halfway for a goodbye kiss. "A couple of hours. I'll meet you for lunch. What are you going to do this morning while I'm gone?"

Paige considered her options. It was already Thursday and there was so much of the resort she hadn't seen. She really should take the opportunity to explore something other than Mano's bed. "I thought I might walk through the shops and browse at some point. I also thought about going to the pool. I haven't done that yet."

"That would be nice. Go swimming first. Most of

the shops don't open until ten. By the time you finish and shower, they'll be open."

Paige twisted her lips in thought. "That's a good idea. I doubt I'll buy anything, though. The shops I've seen are all very high end. I'm not coming back upstairs with a Louis Vuitton bag."

Mano reached out and stroked her cheek with the back of his hand. Paige leaned in to his touch, wishing more and more than he didn't insist on going to work so soon. "If you want one, you should get one. Have them charge it to me. Anything you want, just tell them."

Paige laughed aloud, eliciting a frown from Mano. "What's funny?" he asked.

"You. Since I arrived in Hawaii, it's like I live in an alternate dimension. Penthouse suites, room service, you offering to buy me anything I want…it's all kind of ridiculous. Really. You should see my apartment. You'd be horrified."

Mano sighed and shook his head. "Then consider your time here a little pampering. I mean it—buy something today. I'll check my charges, and if there isn't anything on there, I'll be very disappointed."

"Okay," she finally agreed. Paige fully intended to buy a pack of gum at the sundries store just to say she bought something.

He leaned in and kissed her again before whistling for Hōkū. "I'll meet you for lunch at about noon, okay? I'll text you to see where you are."

Paige nodded and watched him walk away. Rolling onto her back, she stretched leisurely across the king-size mattress and stared up at the ceiling. A few hours by the pool might be just what she needed. It was early enough that she might not have to fight for a lounge chair.

She pulled her hair up into a knot on the top of her head and slipped into the bikini she bought for the trip. It was a bright blue and purple design with a halter top and boy shorts for the bottoms. The cut gave her the illusion of curves where she had none.

Before she pulled on her cover-up, she decided to slather on some sunblock so it could soak in. As her hands slid across her belly, she realized she was finally starting to show. The change was subtle, just the slightest curve, but it was enough for her to notice on her slight frame. She turned sideways to look at herself in the mirror and admire her burgeoning baby bump.

At the moment it just looked like a big lunch, but she would be growing at a faster pace from here on out. The baby would be doubling in size every few weeks. It was easy to ignore her situation while her belly was flat, but soon her pregnancy would be common knowledge to anyone who saw her.

With a sigh, Paige slipped the royal blue cover-up over her suit and gathered things to take to the pool with her. She tossed the sunblock, her phone, earbuds and a book in the wicker shoulder bag she bought on the beach and headed downstairs.

It was hard to believe she hadn't made it to the pool yet. Paige had admired it every time she walked past but hadn't dipped her toe in even once. It was beautiful, beckoning to her. The pool looked like a natural, sprawling lagoon surrounded by large stone boulders and green, leafy plants, as though it were nestled in a tropical rain forest. Hidden among the boulders was a pair of slides and a couple waterfalls.

Paige found a lounge chair in a corner with a little bit of shade. The touch of sunburn she'd gotten on their first day out had started to fade, and she didn't want to make it worse. She laid out one of the fluffy pool towels and self-consciously glanced around to see if anyone was looking before she slipped out of her cover-up. The coast was clear, so she whipped it up over her head and settled down into the chair.

One of the poolside servers approached her after a few minutes. "May I bring you anything?" he asked.

She wanted coffee, but that wasn't on her menu. "Pineapple juice and seltzer water would be great. Thank you." The fresh juice and bubbles would be a nice change. Decadent, but not too much for the early morning.

The waiter disappeared and Paige relaxed back into her chair. As the sun warmed her skin, she closed her eyes and tried to enjoy it all. Her time in Hawaii had been filled with activity, both in and out of Mano's bed, so she hadn't gotten much R&R time. This was her chance. All that was missing was music. She pulled her phone and her earbuds out of her bag and cued up her favorite playlist.

Just before she hit Play, she noticed two women sit down in the lounge chairs nearby. She didn't pay much attention to them, though; she wasn't in the mood to chat. But as the first song ended with a short period of silence before the next song, she caught a bit of the conversation beside her.

"That's the woman I was telling you about," the blonde said in a harsh whisper that was anything but quiet.

"Her? *Really?*" Her friend, a brunette, sounded aghast.

Paige knew she could turn up the music and drown out their voices, but instead she hit Pause so she could listen without their knowledge. She was a masochist that way.

"It's unbelievable, right? I saw the two of them together the other night. Even when they were all dressed up, she wasn't anything to look at. I don't know what he sees in her. Oh wait." The blonde laughed. "He doesn't see anything."

The two women laughed, making Paige clench her teeth. She was used to people having opinions about her, but she didn't like hearing them mock Mano. That was uncalled for.

"She's got her headphones on, right?" the brunette asked.

"Yes, she can't hear us. But even if she could…she knows as well as we do that they're an aesthetic mismatch. There's no way a rich hunk like that would be with a woman like her if he wasn't blind."

Paige struggled not to react and hoped her sunglasses hid away the emotions that slipped out anyway. She never should've listened to their conversation. She had known what she was in for and now she'd let it ruin a perfectly good morning by the pool. The most painful part of the whole discussion was the fact that the woman was right. Paige did know they were an odd match, and she agreed with them. She'd had the same thoughts a dozen times since Mano kissed her. Would he feel the same if he could see her? She worried the answer was no, but he was the only one who disagreed.

"Someone sounds jealous," the brunette taunted her friend.

"I'm not jealous!" the other woman snapped. "I just think that if the guy could stand the two of us side by side and see us to compare, it would be me in the fancy suite with him, not her."

"Do you really want a blind guy? He wouldn't appreciate your new boobs."

The blonde chuckled. "He's got hands, doesn't he? And really, who cares? He owns the hotel. He's filthy rich. I'd happily live my life off his dime while he stumbled around with his dog. I mean, who would be dumb enough to say no to that, even if he's blind?"

The waiter returned with Paige's drink and a fruit and cheese plate she didn't order. "What's this?" she asked.

"I got orders from Mr. Bishop to bring you a snack. He insisted that the baby needs to eat." He left the plate on a table beside her and put the pineapple seltzer beside it. He didn't notice the gasp of the women nearby, but Paige did. If they thought she was pregnant with his child, their heads would probably explode. Let them think it.

"Thank you," she told the waiter.

"You've got to be kidding me," the blonde hissed. "God, I hope the baby looks like him."

That was all Paige could take. She cranked up her music and tried to focus on the snack Mano had sent for her. Even though she couldn't hear any more of their venomous words, she didn't need to. The damage was already done. What little ego Mano had built up in her over the last few days gave way, and she felt as ugly and unlovable as she had the day she found out Wyatt was with Piper.

She picked at the fruit and cheese because she knew she should, and eventually she tried to read. It was impossible to do with the music so loud in her ears, but she couldn't risk hearing any more of the women's conversation.

When she was done eating, Paige decided her time by the pool was over. She might as well go back upstairs to change and go shopping for a while. Maybe a little retail therapy would improve her mood.

Paige started gathering her things into her bag, finally removing her earbuds and noticing with relief that the women were now discussing their extensive grooming habits instead. As she stood up and slung her bag over her shoulder, she heard the brunette speak again.

"Aren't you going to get in the pool?"

"No," the blonde said. "I just had my hair colored before we came. My stylist said if I get chlorine on it, it will turn green. I don't like getting in pools, anyway. How do I know some kid hasn't peed in it?"

Paige tried not to roll her eyes as she left. Their chairs were nearer to the pool's edge than hers, so she had to get close to the water to move past them. Then she paused as she realized that she was leaving and she still hadn't gotten into the pool. Putting her bag down on another chair, she eyed the distance and slipped out of her shoes. She took a running leap, cannonballing into the pool right in front of the two women.

As she broke the surface, she could hear the women screaming about getting wet. A quick glance confirmed that the blonde was now completely soaked, including her hair. She really hoped that it did turn green.

Paige calmly climbed out of the pool and wrapped herself in a towel. As she left, she turned and gave a little wave to the women.

Damn, she thought as she disappeared down the path. That felt *good*.

"Let's go for a walk on the beach," Mano suggested. "The sun is about to go down."

Paige snuggled closer to Mano as they sat on the couch. "I'm happy right here."

"Perhaps, but in a few days, you can sit on the couch and do nothing whenever you want. You won't be able to walk along Waikiki beach and watch the sky change colors as the sun sets."

"Yes," she countered, "but I won't be able to do either of those things with you."

Mano hugged her tighter and placed a kiss on the crown of her head. "If your only requirement is being with me, I say you be with me while we walk on the beach."

Paige groaned but reluctantly sat up. Mano whistled for Hōkū, and they prepared to go downstairs. He hoped she didn't notice him slip the gift he bought her into the pocket of his cargo shorts. As he expected, she hadn't taken advantage of his offer to buy her something, so he'd taken the initiative to choose a gift for her himself. He was certain that he'd selected something far nicer and more expensive than she ever would've chosen on her own.

They headed downstairs and through the garden

courtyard to the beach, where they slipped off their shoes. Hand in hand, they walked together along the shore. Mano could feel the warmth of the sun move lower as it sank into the sea. The water washed over their feet as they walked, Hōkū's paws happily splashing ahead of them.

"You were right," Paige admitted after a few peaceful minutes of walking. "This is better than the couch."

"I told you it would be. I bet you it will get even better, too."

Paige didn't question him, and after they got a certain distance from the hotel, Mano decided it was time to give her the gift. She'd been a little quieter and more reserved than usual today. He hoped that the gift would bring out the excitement in Paige that he was missing. "I want you to close your eyes," he said.

Paige giggled. "Don't you think at least one of us should be able to see where we're going?"

"We're not going any farther. Just hold still and close your eyes. If you don't close them, I'll cover them with my hand."

"Okay, okay."

Mano brushed his fingertips across her cheeks and felt her thick lashes resting there. "All right." Hōkū came to a stop beside them and Mano held Paige's shoulders steady. "Okay, keep them closed."

"I am," she insisted.

Mano reached down into his pocket for the large velvet box he'd gotten from the high-end jewelry store in the hotel. As quietly as he could, he opened it and removed the necklace from inside. He felt the clasp, opening it the way the jeweler had taught him, and then draped it around her neck. "Keep them closed," he insisted as he fastened the necklace.

"This is killing me," Paige said.

"I know. Okay, open your eyes."

Mano held his breath waiting for her reaction. As far as he could tell, there was none. No squealing, no jumping up and down. He was certain the jeweler in his own hotel wouldn't sell him something subpar. Six figures should at least get him a thank-you, if not an enthusiastic kiss.

"Did you open them?" he asked.

"Yes." Her answer was barely a whisper.

"And? Do you like it?" He hoped she would. The jeweler had helped him pick out an exquisite three-strand multicolor black South Sea pearl necklace. She'd told him the pearls alternated in size and shade from near black to a silver gray and were separated with ten carats' worth of small micro pave diamond pearls. The jeweler said the luster on the pearls was remarkable. He knew it was the ideal gift for her—a tiny piece of sand transformed into a beautiful, rare gem. It was the perfect memento of her time here, where he hoped that she, too, saw herself as a precious gemstone instead of a tiny bit of sand.

"I do," she said after a moment of hesitation.

Mano frowned. "You don't sound like you do. I thought you'd like it. I told you to pick out something and you didn't, so I chose this for you. I wanted to get you something nice to help you remember this week."

Paige put her hands on each side of his face. "I don't need an expensive necklace to remember this week, Mano. I'm certain I'll never forget it."

He was glad to hear that, but it didn't change anything. "Well, then consider it a thank-you gift. You've gotten me out of the hotel, forced me out of my comfort zone and helped me realize that maybe I don't need to spend every moment of my day at the resort."

"A simple thank-you would've been enough. This necklace is…"

She was resistant, and he was certain she had no idea how much it cost. "No, a simple thank-you is not enough. I bought you this necklace because I wanted you to have it, Paige. I can make up a million excuses you can shoot down, but that's the long and short of it. What good is all my money if I can't spend it on the things I want to spend it on? Please humor me and just accept it."

He heard Paige sigh heavily. "Okay. Thank you. It's beautiful, Mano." She leaned in and gave him a soft thank-you kiss.

When they parted again, they turned toward the hotel and started their leisurely stroll back. "How would you like to spend tonight, Paige? The Moonlight Luau is going on at the hotel if you'd like to see that. We could go out to eat somewhere where we could dress up and you can show off your new jewelry."

"I don't think I have anything to wear that would do this necklace justice. At the moment, I feel silly wearing it because I'm in denim shorts and a tank top."

"A beautiful woman wearing beautiful jewelry doesn't need a fancy dress."

"There's an idea," Paige said leaning in close to him. "How about we stay in tonight, order room service and I'll wear the necklace. *Just* the necklace."

Mano felt his whole body stiffen at her suggestion. His blood started humming through his veins, making him eager to return to the hotel. No matter how many times he had Paige, he wanted more. "A tempting offer."

He tried not to wish for his vision very often. It was the kind of hopeless yearning that succeeded only in fairy tales. Rapunzel's tears wouldn't cure him because this was real life. And yet, Paige painted a picture in his mind that he wished he could see for real.

Paige made him wish for a lot of things that he hadn't ever expected. She was so many different things in one person, and he'd never imagined he'd find a woman like that. He'd indulged in a handful of affairs over the years, but he'd always been happy to let them come to an end when their time together was up. He'd never been tempted to search one of them out, invite them back for another visit to the island or really even give them much thought once they were gone. They had fun together, but that was all.

Mano had the feeling that it would not be the same with Paige. This week was not enough. Their time together was not enough. Her melodic laughter and tender caresses would haunt him for weeks.

But was it fair to ask more of her? Mano didn't think so. Would another week be enough to soothe his soul? What if it wasn't? What if he wanted more? Longer? What if he was thinking about forever?

Mano choked down that thought and wished it away. Those sorts of fantasies were even worse than hoping to see again. Why did he long so badly for Paige? Why did it have to be the one woman whose life was so complicated that their future together didn't really stand a chance? She had a life in California, one that wouldn't be so simple to just walk away from. She was certain the baby's father wouldn't want to be involved in her life, but what if she was wrong? Paige couldn't just take the baby out of state, much less half an ocean away.

Lost in his thoughts, Mano stumbled as he stepped into a hole in the sand. He landed face first in the water, soaking his clothes and covering the front of him in wet sand.

Hōkū whimpered beside him, licking at his ear to make sure he was okay.

"Oh, my goodness!" Paige exclaimed.

She crouched down beside him and offered him her arm to get up, but he wouldn't take it. He pushed himself up on his own and wiped away the sand from his face and chest. His jaw tightened with irritation. It had been a long time since he'd fallen. He wished that it hadn't happened in front of Paige.

"Are you okay?" she asked.

"I'm fine," he said stiffly. He grabbed Hōkū's collar and took her hand, continuing down the beach. Anger and irritation coursed through his veins as they walked together. This was part of the reason he didn't leave the resort. It was a carefully controlled environment that left few hazards for him. Out in the world, anything could happen. Hōkū couldn't see and avoid every obstacle in life.

It was hardly a major accident, but he knew the moment for what it was: a reminder. This entire line of thought about Paige moving to Hawaii to be with him was ridiculous. Even if Paige *would* stay, even if she loved him, even if the baby's father wanted no part in her life…he was still blind. He managed fairly well by himself, but would he be any help to her with the baby? More likely he would be an additional burden she didn't need.

"Are you sure you're okay?" Paige asked as they stepped off the beach and across the walking path to the Mau Loa.

"I'm fine," he insisted. They washed their feet off and slipped their shoes back on. "I've only bruised my pride."

Thankfully, Paige didn't press him about it again. They didn't even speak as they made their way through the grounds to the resort tower elevator.

"I've been thinking," Mano said at last. The words slipped out before he could really think it through.

"About what?"

Mano considered emptying his head into her lap. Maybe he was wrong and she could give him some insight or hope that they could have a chance together. Or perhaps not. She could shoot down the whole idea and the short time they had left together would be overshadowed by the dark clouds of her rejection. He needed to let the whole idea of a future go.

"About you wearing that necklace and not a stitch else." He covered with a sly smile.

"You're a naughty boy," she said with a laugh, clinging to his arm.

Better than a fool, he decided, as they headed back upstairs.

Nine

Paige didn't feel comfortable wearing this necklace in public. Not because it wasn't beautiful or because she wasn't proud to wear it, but because she was afraid of getting mugged. She'd seen this necklace in the window of the resort jewelry store when she was walking around after the pool incident. Smaller, far less impressive necklaces had dropped her jaw with the price, so she couldn't even begin to imagine what he'd paid for this.

When she got home, she'd have to look into things like insurance and a safety deposit box. This wasn't the kind of thing you tucked away in your underwear drawer with your class ring and the tiny diamond earrings your parents bought you for graduation.

Once they were safely back in his hotel suite, however, Mano went to take a shower and she could finally let herself enjoy it. She sought out her reflection in the sliding glass doors and admired the necklace. It was amazingly beautiful with different shades of gray and sparking stones that would be cubic zirconia on anything she bought herself, but she doubted that was the case here.

"Paige?" Mano asked after exiting the bathroom sand-free a few minutes later.

"I'm at the balcony doors admiring my new pretty," she said.

Mano made his way over to where she was standing. He pressed his bare chest against her back and wrapped his arms around her waist. The palms of his hands rested protectively across her newly rounding belly.

She watched their reflection in the glass as he planted a kiss on her bare shoulder. It was a little surreal to watch herself in the door with a man like Mano holding her. No matter how he flattered her or how many times he worshipped her body in bed, she couldn't believe how she'd ended up right here, right now. She was supposed to be spending a week reading a paperback on the beach.

Mano was an unexpected and very welcome surprise in her life. They'd only been together for a week, and yet, it felt like so much longer. It seemed like he'd always been a part of her life. She honestly didn't know what she was going to do when that was no longer the case. They'd agreed to a no-strings fling— a vacation romance to keep her mind off reality for a while. That didn't include a future. And yet she couldn't stop herself from wishing for it.

Unfortunately, what she wanted didn't exist. Mano

had offered to take care of her. As nice as that might sound on paper, there was no way she could accept it. She couldn't be around him, accept his money, raise her child, but not have him really in her life. If she moved to Hawaii, it was because Mano loved her and wanted her here with him. After their discussion in North Shore about Jenna and his emotional unavailability with women, she knew she was doomed. She'd made a joke out of it in the moment, but inside she'd realized that she was falling for a man who would never fall for her.

Mano's hands ran over her bare arms, his kisses sending a shiver through her body that made her skin break into goose bumps. Paige leaned back against him as he wrapped his arms around her and held her tight.

"I'm not ready to let you go yet," he said, echoing her own thoughts.

She only wished he truly meant it, in more than just the physical sense. All she could do was make the most of the time they had left together. "You don't have to," Paige said and turned in his arms to face him. "You can hold me all night if you want to."

She pulled her tank top up and over her head, revealing her bare breasts beneath it. She tossed her top aside so they could stand skin to skin. He was so hot to the touch. Paige was always cold despite the temperate climate of Southern California. Being wrapped in Mano's heat was like coming home to a warm blanket.

He kissed her then. It was the softest, most tender kiss they'd ever shared. There was no hesitation or resistance, no desire-fueled desperation, just a sweetness that made her eyes start to tear up. She was glad he couldn't see it. She didn't want to ruin this moment because her emotions were getting the best of her.

Maybe it was the pregnancy hormones. Yes, that must be it.

Paige took his hand and led him into the bedroom. She tugged away the towel from around his hips and then sat him down on the edge of the mattress. Her denim shorts followed the towel. Then, as they'd discussed, she was finally wearing nothing but the necklace.

The idea that he fantasized about her like this made her feel bolder. She stood between his thighs and took his hands in hers. She moved them all around her bare skin, then brushed his fingertips along the pearls at her throat. "As you requested," she said.

Mano's jaw clenched and he took a deep breath. Easing back farther on the bed, he took her hand and pulled her with him. Her body covered his as they lay on the bed together. Every inch of her molded against his hard muscles. He cupped her face and brought her lips to his again.

"What do you want me to do?" she whispered against his lips.

"Whatever you want to do."

Paige bit her lip, considering her freedom. She drew her legs up to sit astride him. It wasn't really a position she'd ever been comfortable in, but this was her chance to really, truly let go without feeling self-conscious.

Mano reached for one of their last condoms and slipped it on. She didn't need to wait for him. Paige had been ready the moment he touched her. His hands cupped her hips as she eased up and lowered herself onto him. The position pressed him deeper than ever before, filling her to where she was almost hesitant to continue. She slowed and let her body relax into it, finally seating herself fully against his hips.

Mano groaned and pressed his fingertips deep into her flesh. "Oh, Paige," he managed between clenched teeth. "You feel so good."

She did feel good. Her confidence increased with his reaction urging her on. She planted her palms on the hard wall of his chest and slowly rocked forward. Thrusting him deep inside her, she curled her lips into a sly smile. She liked this. A lot.

Paige watched every flicker of emotion on Mano's face as she moved, studying what got the best reaction out of him. When he was on the brink, she backed away, coaxing him closer and closer to the edge. She, too, grew nearer her climax with every move she made. Their bodies seemed perfectly fit for one another, with no move possible that didn't feel amazing.

She'd never been this in control, this confident in the bedroom. It was a rush of excitement that urged her on. She wanted to know exactly how to move to make Mano crazy, how to touch him to make his jaw tighten and body tense.

But most importantly, she didn't want this moment to end. There was a finality about their coupling this time. It wasn't likely to be their last sexual encounter before she returned to the mainland, but the sands of the hourglass were slipping away. Tomorrow would be about her grandfather and saying goodbye. Then her life would pick up where she'd left it off. A life without Mano.

The tears returned to her eyes. Paige couldn't help it. Even as she moved slowly and tortured him, she felt the emotions start to overwhelm her. How had he become such an integral part of her life in such a short time? How was she ever going to make it without the man she loved?

Paige hesitated for only a moment when she realized where her thoughts had turned. There was no point in denying it. She was in love with Mano. She'd broken the rules of their fling and fallen head over heels for a man she could never, ever keep. There was no joy in the realization; her heart didn't overflow with elation and adoration the way she'd imagined it would when she finally fell for someone.

It was just as she'd told Mano that night after their first kiss. She couldn't get involved because her life was complicated. Now she'd gone and made it ten times more complicated than ever before.

Mano reached for her, pulling her back into the moment. "Kiss me, *pulelehua*," he said.

She leaned down and gave herself over to his kiss. Paige surrendered everything she had because she didn't know what else to do. She didn't know what the next year would bring, but she had this moment with Mano, and she would treasure every second of it.

As their lips joined together, his fingers pressed into her hips and moved her harder against him. The friction created a delicious tension inside Paige that she knew she couldn't resist for long. Within seconds, they both found their release and their voices mingled and echoed in the open air of his bedroom suite.

She collapsed onto the bed beside him, and he

curled her body against his. "What am I going to do without you?" he whispered into her ear.

"Life goes on," she replied, knowing that for him it would. For Paige, living her life without him would be much harder.

"Why does the time go by so quickly in Hawaii?"

Mano turned to Paige with a frown. "What are you talking about?"

They'd been sitting on the balcony of his suite together while they drank juice and Paige watched the sunrise. It was hard to believe this was the last Hawaiian sunrise she would see. It seemed like only yesterday that she was standing alone on the beach at sunrise, wondering how she was going to spend all this time in Hawaii by herself.

"A week anywhere else would've taken far longer. It feels like I've only just arrived and yet I go home today."

He smiled and sought out her hand. "Have you considered that's because you've spent a good part of your trip in my bed? Time flies when you're having fun and all."

"Is that the problem?" she asked with a laugh. "It's all your fault, then."

Mano just shrugged off her accusations. "I told you I was a terrible tour guide." His expression grew more serious. "It is hard to believe that you leave tonight. What time is your grandfather's service at Pearl Harbor?"

"Two in the afternoon. Then it's time to pack up and head to the airport this evening."

"This is our last day together, then."

The words seemed to hang in the air between them. She didn't want to let go of this moment here with him. And yet she knew she had to. She'd cherished every moment of their last night together, especially when she'd fallen asleep cradled in his arms. Waking up had been bittersweet. Tomorrow would be back to reality. Back to home and plans for the baby. Back to her shift at the VA. Back to tell Wyatt he was going to be a father.

It had become too easy to lose herself here. She'd gotten used to room service and amazingly high thread count sheets. Her shower at home wasn't filled with coconut soaps and fluffy, freshly laundered towels. Her grandfather had given her this moment of paradise, but soon it would be time to face the life she'd ignored for the past week. She wished she could put off that eventuality for a little while longer, but she knew it would just hurt more if she did.

"I wish you could stay longer."

Paige sat up, startled, and pulled her hand away from his. He'd spoken the words that were on her mind, but she didn't dare say them aloud. He couldn't possibly mean what he'd just said. At least, not the way she wanted him to mean it. He probably wanted her to stay another week, not the lifetime she hoped for. "Don't say that," she chastised. "It will only make it harder for me to go home and deal with reality. Staying in Hawaii isn't an option, and you and I both know it."

"I don't know it. Who made that rule, anyway?"

"The universe did, Mano. And even if I *could* stay, what would it mean for us? Not much. You yourself said that you don't do relationships that last longer than a week."

Mano sat forward in his chair and rested his elbows on his knees. "You're the first woman I've met that makes me want to break that rule."

His words of longing for her made her chest ache, but she knew she couldn't let her feelings for him overtake her like they had last night. They'd urge her to make a hasty decision that she'd regret later, and in the end it would only complicate the matter further. "You say that now," she insisted. "I guarantee you'll be relieved when I'm gone."

Mano flinched as though she'd hit him. His brow furrowed deeply as he turned to her. "Why would you say something like that?"

Paige knew that she had to convince him of the truth. He would forget about her, and she'd rather he remember her fondly for a short while than grow tired of her and wish her away. "Because I know it's true. As much as I might like to be, I know I'm not the woman for you, Mano. We've come together for a short, beautiful moment in time, but it won't last. It can't. I'm sure there's someone here on Oahu that's perfect for you. Someone whose life isn't quite as complicated as mine."

"How do you know who's perfect for me?" There was an irritated edge to his voice.

"I know what I look like and you don't. I know you can do better. I want to thank you for everything you've said to me this week. It's really worked wonders for my self-esteem, but the truth is that you're out of my league."

"I am not," he snapped.

"Mano, if you really knew how I looked, you never would've laid a hand on me." That was the truth and she knew it. Those women by the pool had reminded her of the unavoidable reality of it.

Mano shook his head as he sat back in his chair and turned away from her. "That's not true. I know exactly what you look like."

Paige regarded Mano with suspicion. "Please tell me how such a thing is possible."

"Well, for one thing, I've touched you. Every inch of you. There's nothing boyish about you, Paige."

"It's not the same."

"Perhaps. But I also have a staff of a thousand here at the hotel. They are my eyes and ears. I asked around about you those first few days. They told me *exactly* what you looked like."

Paige's mouth dropped open. Could he really have known this whole time? It couldn't be true if he was sitting here, asking her to stay longer to be with him. And yet, she knew how often he wore that earpiece, how frequently he was in communication with his staff. It seemed perfectly natural, since they acted as his eyes around the hotel, that they would report on her to him if he'd asked.

"You think I've been operating under some kind of delusion this whole time, but I haven't. I know exactly what you look like, outside and in. Even a blind man can see the pure light that shines from inside you. You're a good person. I have spent this week with you, I've made love to you, because I like you just as you are, Paige."

She tried not to cry at his words. Never in her life had a man said that to her. All his assurances that she was attractive, all the compliments this week…she'd taken it all with a grain of salt because she didn't believe he knew the truth about her. Could he really have meant it all? He sounded so sincere.

"Do you want to know what a lot of my staff told me about you?" he asked.

Not really, but she supposed he would tell her, anyway. "What?"

"It really frustrated me at first because several of them didn't notice you at all. They would see me talking to you but couldn't tell me a thing about you. It seemed as though you were almost a ghost, invisible to everyone around you but me. I couldn't understand why so many of them didn't take notice of you. You certainly commanded my attention from the first moment we met."

"I ran into you. I'm sure those other people would remember me if I did that."

"That's the best way to get me to notice you, of course. But I couldn't help but wonder if you were deliberately wanting to be invisible and I was the only one you couldn't hide from."

"I don't deliberately try to hide," Paige began, but stopped herself. That was a lie and she knew it. "Okay, maybe I do. I've heard so many cruel and hateful comments over the years that maybe I've just wished myself out of existence and forgotten all about it. I've become accustomed to people not seeing me now. And really, I'd prefer that people didn't see me if all they have to offer are rude critiques. I'd rather be invisible than bullied."

Mano was quiet for a moment, turning back to the dark ocean as he seemed to be considering his words.

"Paige, do you think that telling me all this is going to change my mind about wanting you to stay? It sounds to me like you're trying to convince me to let you go."

She sighed. In a way the exact opposite was true. She wanted to stay, to give in to the feelings she was holding back and throw away her whole life to remain here with him. But Paige had already made one major relationship mistake this year. She couldn't afford another. What would she have if she gave in to this and he changed his mind? Mano's whole adult life had been spent avoiding real intimacy. Did she really believe she was the woman who could change him for good? No. She didn't.

"I'm just beating you to the punch, darling."

Mano shook his head, his lips turned down in a disapproving frown. "You're ridiculous."

"Maybe, but I know how the fairy tales end for girls like me." She sighed. "Do you want to know what happened with the baby's father?"

Mano stiffened in his seat, but then he nodded. "Please."

"Okay, I'll tell you. He left me for my prettier sister," Paige said, spitting out the most painful part up front so the rest would be easier to tell.

"Ever since junior high when boys started looking at girls with thoughts of things other than cooties, Piper was the one they wanted. Through high school, college and beyond, the men have always preferred Piper, and for good reason. We're only a year apart in age and people always had a hard time believing we were sisters because we looked so different. She's the opposite of me in every way, with all the best parts of our parents. I've always felt like I got the leftovers."

"Describe her to me," Mano demanded. "I want to know what it is about her that you think is so special compared to you."

"Well, for a start, her hair has natural golden highlights and a slight wave that makes it flow beautifully down her back. Mine is dull and stick straight, refusing to hold a curl for more than a few minutes. She's curvy in all the right places while I'm rail thin and built like a twelve-year-old boy. Her face is like an angel with big hazel eyes and full lips. My lips are thin and my nose and chin are too pointy. We just couldn't be more different."

"It sounds like it. But why would you compare yourself to your sister like that? If I compared myself to Kal, I'd make myself crazy."

"Because," Paige argued, "that's what everyone does. My whole life I've been looked over for Piper."

"I don't understand it. You haven't described any of the important things," Mano noted. "You'll have to forgive me, being blind and all, but my priorities are a little different. Is she smart or caring like you? Is she funny and kind? Would she spend her days caring for injured veterans or would she rather get her nails done?"

Paige was startled silent. She wasn't quite sure how to respond to that question, even though the answer was quite evident to her. Piper wasn't vapid and thoughtless, she just had different priorities. She was a hairstylist, so her focus in life was entirely visual. But she wasn't selfish. She'd tried to give Paige multiple makeovers, but they rarely took.

"You're in the minority, Mano. Most men can't help themselves around her, and as I mentioned earlier, Wyatt was no different. When Wyatt left me for Piper, it was just the latest incident in the story of my life. It was like I didn't exist to him any longer. He didn't even have the nerve to tell me we weren't dating anymore. He just ghosted me—stopped calling and texting—and then he showed up at a family event with my sister on his arm."

"Wyatt is obviously an ass, but what kind of sister would do that? Is she that cruel?"

Paige shrugged. "No, it's more a matter of ignorance. Piper is oblivious to everyone but herself. She always has been. I think to her it was natural for a man to prefer her over me, so I shouldn't be so hurt about it."

"Hurt about it?" Mano nearly shouted. "She steals the father of your child, but you're not allowed to be hurt about it?"

"Neither of them know I'm pregnant. I haven't told anyone but you."

"So that's why the baby's father won't be in its life? He'll be too busy being its uncle instead?"

That sounded terrible. A part of her hoped they would break up before that became a reality. "Something like that. Even if they stopped seeing one another, it's not like I'd take him back. I know better. I've had better, thanks to you. But I know what we have isn't something that can last. Tomorrow I'm getting on a plane to go home. I'll go back to reality and will finally have to deal with everything I've pushed aside while I was here.

"While I'm decorating a nursery and reorganizing my whole life, you'll be here, running your hotel. It may take a few weeks, or even a few months, but you'll forget about me. You'll spend another week with another woman, and life will go on. Maybe someday I'll cross your mind and you'll wonder how I am and if the baby turned out to be a boy or a girl. But that's all the future the two of us have together, Mano. It was just a fling. A wonderful one, but a fling."

Ten

"I'm going to get in the shower," Mano said.

After breakfast at sunrise and their depressing conversation, Mano had been at a loss of what to say to Paige. There was no convincing her to stay, no convincing her that she was good enough for him. She didn't want to drag him into the complicated life she was living, and the finality of her words convinced him that was the end of the conversation.

They'd returned to bed for a nap and a leisurely round of goodbye sex. Mano had taken his time making love to her, knowing it was the last time. Now that it was over, he knew he had to get up and walk away from it all before he did something stupid.

Crawling from the bed, he disappeared into the bathroom to get ready for the service. His thoughts were scattered as he shampooed his hair and considered his options.

Paige was distracted and distant today, which wasn't unusual considering they were about to sink her grandfather's ashes into the ocean. It felt like more than that, though. It was like she was anticipating the end and pulling away from him before it was over. That was probably the smart thing to do. How much longer did he have? Not much. Hours.

She'd insisted that she couldn't stay and that he wasn't serious about the two of them, but he knew that he was. This didn't feel like any other time before. Paige was different. He felt different. He just had to find a way to convince her of it. She wasn't like the other women in his life, and he wished she could understand that. He wanted her to stay. He wanted to help her raise that baby. Their baby. One day, he hoped that he could love her so well and so completely that she could even forget about Wyatt and what he'd done to her.

A plan formed in his mind as he stepped out of the shower. He would tell her how he felt. He would say the words he'd never said aloud before. That would convince her he was serious and then she would stay. Wouldn't she? He wrapped a towel around his waist and filled the sink with warm water to shave. Mano was rinsing the blade one last time when a strange sound in the bedroom caught his attention. It took Mano a moment to realize it might be Paige's cell phone. No one had called her the whole week, so he hadn't heard it ring yet.

"Hello?" he heard her answer.

He wasn't trying to listen in on her conversation, but he found it difficult not to with only a door between them.

"Wyatt? Why are you calling me?"

Wyatt? Just the mention of the man's name made Mano's blood start to boil in his veins. He turned off the water to hear them better.

"Piper will be furious if she knows you're calling me... No, I'm not at home," she responded to him. Her voice sounded stressed. "I'm in Hawaii... Yes, Hawaii."

Mano was nearly holding his breath as he listened to half of their discussion. Paige had sworn up and down that she wouldn't take Wyatt back. She said she didn't really want him involved in her life, or the baby's life, but she'd do what was right and tell him about the child. Her extended silence meant he had quite a bit to say for a man who had vanished from her life without an explanation not long ago.

"You're right, Wyatt, we do need to talk but not right now... No, I'll be home tomorrow morning. You know I've got to bury Papa today."

Mano could only think of one reason why Wyatt was calling Paige. He wanted her back. Unless he'd left his laptop at her apartment or something, it was the only thing he could come up with.

"I know," Paige said. "It was extremely difficult for me. I just can't talk about it right now. Call me tomorrow afternoon, okay? All right. Goodbye."

Mano waited a moment, drained the sink and then stepped out of his bathroom with his towel still slung around his hips. "Did I just hear you talking to someone?" he asked casually.

"Uh, work called," she said, the lie evident in her voice even if he hadn't overheard the conversation. "They thought I would be back in time to work the day shift tomorrow, but I told them I wouldn't be in until Sunday. I don't think I can go straight from a red-eye flight to work a twelve-hour shift the next morning."

He nodded and turned back to his bathroom to finish getting ready. His mind was racing with thoughts as he dried his hair with a towel. Why had she just lied to him about who called? There was only one real answer that made sense—that she hadn't been entirely truthful with him about her feelings for Wyatt. He'd called her out of the blue wanting to see her. Why? Had Piper dumped him? Was he going to make a play to get Paige back?

And more distressing...would Paige actually take him back after everything he'd done?

The thought made Mano sick to his stomach. Paige deserved so much better than a man like Wyatt. And yet, if he really did have a change of heart, who was Mano to interfere with that? He was the father of her child. Wouldn't it be best for everyone if they reconciled and raised their new family together?

The only odd man out of this scenario would be Mano, but he would survive. As Paige insisted, maybe he would forget about her in a few weeks or months and continue on as though she hadn't touched his heart. Or maybe he would throw himself into his work, heartbroken, and she'd never know it.

Either way, he knew it wouldn't really matter as long as she was happy. A future with her baby seemed to excite her; would having an active father in the baby's life be even better? It would certainly make things less complicated for her. She wouldn't have to uproot her whole life to be with him. Her child would

have a father. His real father. It would tie everything
up into a neat bow.

It would crush Mano. Make him that much more
emotionally unavailable. But that was what he needed
to do. If there was a chance in hell that Paige could
reconcile with the baby's father, it would be selfish
of him to go out there and declare his feelings for her
and beg her to stay.

He wasn't thinking clearly, Mano realized. He
was letting emotion cloud his decision-making skills.
Paige was right. It was better if she went home. He
would forget. He would move on. If he did manage
to convince her to stay and then one day regret raising another man's child and uprooting her from her
whole life, then what? It was better to let her life
take the path she'd chosen, and that was to go home.
If that meant going home to Wyatt, that was none of
his damn business in the end.

With a sigh, Mano combed his hair and splashed
his face with aftershave. He just needed to keep his
mouth shut.

Paige clutched her grandfather's urn as the boat
took them out to the USS *Arizona* Memorial on the far
side of the harbor. It was temporarily closed to tourists, allowing Paige private access for the ceremony.
She took in the markers that identified the locations
of the various boats in the harbor and the real ships
still in service to the far left.

The memorial was a gleaming white building that
seemed to float above the water. Beneath it, she knew,
were the sunken remains of the *Arizona* and the sailors who lost their lives that day so long ago. Only a

few small parts of the ship were visible above the waterline.

A man in full dress blues took the urn from her as they stepped off the boat and onto the dock. Mano took her arm, escorting her up the ramp to the memorial with Hōkū just ahead of them. They followed a large procession that included the firing squad, the officer carrying the urn and a bugler.

Inside, the memorial was filled with navy officers and personnel dressed for the most formal of occasions. As Paige was the only family there for the ceremony, there was only one row of chairs set up. They were led there and seated in front of the massive memorial wall. From floor to ceiling, the names of all the men who died the day the USS *Arizona* was bombed by the Japanese were etched into marble.

In front of the monument were two large rectangles made from the same marble. On it were the names of the sailors who had returned to the Arizona to be interred, like her grandfather would be. The stone memorials were draped with purple and white orchid leis. The names were fewer, but just as impactful to Paige. Twenty, forty, sixty years later…these men never forgot that day or the brothers they lost. They all chose to return to be with them in the end. Including her grandfather. His name was the latest to be etched into the stone. She was certain he was one of the last survivors remaining.

Seeing all those names at once brought a tear to Paige's eye. She tried to hold it in. Not because she was embarrassed to cry—it was her grandfather's funeral, after all—but because once she started, she was pretty certain she wouldn't be able to stop.

She'd already cried her tears for Papa. She cried most of those while he was still alive and clinging to existence no matter how miserably his heart was failing him. No, today she was mourning something different.

The loss of love.

Paige could already feel it slipping away. She was the only one to blame for her situation, but it didn't make it any less painful. Could Mano not understand how hard it was for her to say no to him? It was agonizing. It broke her heart to do it. Of course she wanted to stay. She could easily come up with some extended fantasy about what their life could be like together if she just threw caution to the wind and never returned home.

But that wasn't reality. If nothing else, Paige prided herself on being practical. Nothing about that scenario was practical. Especially the part where she expected Mano to raise her child as his own.

She couldn't ask that of him. Even as much as she loved him. Maybe because of how much she loved him. Paige wanted him to have a family of his own. It would happen for him, she just knew it, if he would open up to the possibilities. It was that, more than his disability, that was holding him back. He didn't believe his happiness was possible, so it wasn't.

Paige supposed she was just as guilty of sabotaging herself. Because she thought she was unattractive, she assumed that was what people saw. It was a cycle that fed on itself. Mano had helped to disrupt that, convincing her to feel better about herself and what she had to offer. Perhaps if she felt that way on the inside, she would attract more positivity in her life.

Not love. Just positivity. She didn't have room in her future or her heart to love anyone but the baby. Paige knew that as hard as it had been to cope with what had happened with Wyatt, it would be nothing compared to losing Mano. She didn't love Wyatt the way she loved Mano. It would take a long time for her to heal and let someone else in.

She didn't know what that call today from Wyatt was about. He hadn't spoken two words to her since he'd run off with Piper. She got the feeling he was sniffing around for something. Had her sister broken up with him and he was looking to come back? Fat chance. She might be naive, but she wasn't stupid. Whatever he wanted from her was irrelevant, really. She would meet with him, tell him about the baby and ask what kind of arrangements he wanted to make. That was it. Even if he declared his love for her, she wouldn't bite. She knew what real love felt like now, and it wasn't what he was offering.

The ceremony started with the chaplain reading scripture. Her grandfather's urn was placed on a table draped with the American flag. Mano took her hand for support, but she could feel the strained energy radiating off him like a wave. He hadn't been the same since their discussion this morning. She had rejected him before he could reject her, so she supposed he had a right to feel unhappy about it. One day he would understand why she had to do it.

The admiral in charge of the base stepped up to speak. It was an amazing honor to have such a high-ranking officer at her grandfather's service, but it was such a rare and important occasion that many officers in the navy wanted to attend. He spoke about the bombing and the soldiers like her grandfather who survived. He thanked Paige for his service to the country and for his dedication to his fallen brothers.

Two uniformed navy men picked up her grandfather's urn from the table and carried it to the window of the memorial where it was handed over to a dive team. Paige watched as the diver secured the urn, then slipped beneath the oil-slicked waters to the belly of the ship. All the navy officers silently saluted as he was interred.

"Unto Almighty God," the chaplain continued, "we commend the soul of our brother departed, and we commit his body to the deep; in sure and certain hope of the resurrection unto eternal life, through our Lord, Jesus Christ, Amen."

He continued with the benediction. When that was finished, the firing squad fired three volleys and the bugler played "Taps." The loud noise was a startling contrast to the rest of the ceremony. The vibration of the shots threatened to shatter what was left of her nerves.

By the time the flag was folded and presented to her, Paige feared a breakdown was coming. They were escorted out of the memorial and took the boat back to the shore. There, they got back into the hotel town car that had brought them to the service.

The farther she got from Papa and his final resting place, the more alone she began to feel. He was the one who understood her. He encouraged her, supported her, when the rest of her family didn't understand their awkward youngest daughter. Without Papa and without Mano, who would she have now? It would be just her and the baby, together against the world. Would that be enough? She supposed it would have to be.

As the car returned to the highway toward Waikiki, Paige was unnerved by how quiet it was. Mano hadn't spoken since they'd left for the service. He was a good enough man to stand by her through the memorial, but she could feel him pulling further away by the minute. Part of her had known this moment would come, but now that it was happening, it hurt more than she expected. It was almost as though she could feel him physically ripping away from her, leaving a gaping hole in his absence. She thought that trying to take a step back sooner would ease the pain, but it didn't. It only made her wish she'd clung more tightly while she had the chance.

"Thank you for going with me today," she said quietly. Paige clutched the flag in her arms and held it fiercely in lieu of the man she loved.

"You're welcome. It was my honor to join in on the ceremony to honor a sailor from such a historically important event." The words were stiff, almost practiced like a campaign speech.

"I can't imagine having to sit through that by myself. It was much easier having you there with me."

He didn't turn to look at her. With his dark glasses on, he simply stared ahead through the windshield. "No one should have to. I don't understand why the rest of your family didn't fly out here for this."

"My grandfather didn't want them to. He wanted a memorial ceremony in California for everyone to attend, but this service to be more private."

"Private is immediate family. This is beyond private. I have to say you have an odd family. At least compared to my own. If one of ours dies, you're not keeping the others away unless you rise up from the grave and drive them off."

"You're lucky."

Paige imagined that the upcoming months with her family would be difficult. Her parents wouldn't be thrilled about her unplanned pregnancy, especially when they realized their other daughter was dating the baby's father. While a landscaper might be as good as Paige could do, they'd certainly disapprove of Piper lowering her standards.

She didn't expect a big baby shower or a large showing of people to help her plan and prepare. Brandy would be there, of course. She had no doubt her friend would help her celebrate, but it wouldn't be like it would if she had a family like Mano's. The way he spoke about them, she imagined being smothered by their excitement over the baby. Would there be traditional Hawaiian music at their shower? Would they bury a whole pig wrapped in banana leaves in the backyard to roast over hot coals? Would his grandparents fawn over her rounded belly and bless the baby with a traditional Hawaiian name?

For the first time, she allowed herself to wish that Mano was the baby's father instead of Wyatt. That would make everything simpler. Then she wouldn't have to ask Mano to raise another man's child. She wouldn't feel guilty about staying on Oahu to be with him. There was also the fact that she loved Mano. Loving the baby's father was a critical element that she was missing from her reality. She didn't just not love Wyatt, she despised him. That wasn't the way it should be.

Although she'd vehemently rejected his suggestion that she stay, it was getting harder by the minute not to change her mind. She didn't like him turning a cold shoulder to her after how passionately he'd treated her all week. It was one thing to want to stay. It was another to know he felt the same way. If he would walk away like she meant nothing to him, it would still be hard, but she could leave knowing their affair was one-sided. She let her heart get involved, and that was her own fault.

And yet...

The car pulled up outside the hotel. Paige knew her chance to change her mind was slipping away. Would it change things if she told him how she felt? Would she just embarrass herself? Things were ending either way.

"Mano?" she said just before they got out of the car.

He paused and turned to her. "Yes?"

"I..." The words stuck in her throat. With his dark glasses covering the expression on his face, she couldn't read his emotions. She couldn't tell how he'd accept her words. He just seemed to radiate this protective wall that she wasn't sure she could penetrate.

"I've got a pretty busy schedule this afternoon," he said when she couldn't get the words out. "I've arranged for the car to take you to the airport whenever you're ready."

Paige felt her heart drop in her chest. "You're not seeing me off?"

He shook his head, his expression aggravatingly neutral. "I'm sorry, I can't. But I want to thank you for a lovely week. I enjoyed our time together very much. I hope you enjoyed your visit here at the Mau Loa, and I wish you the best for your future."

Without so much as a hug or a kiss goodbye, he opened the door and he and Hōkū got out of the car. He tipped the driver and disappeared into the hotel without the slightest hesitation.

Paige couldn't move. She couldn't breathe. Her heart started to crumble in her chest and she could feel every painful crack as it fell apart. The tears rushed down her face then. The seams holding her together unraveled completely, and she collapsed into broken, heaving sobs in the back of the car. It was an angry, ugly cry, making her face a blotchy red and her nose run. She simply couldn't hold it in anymore. Everything that had happened over the last month— her grandfather's death, the pregnancy, Wyatt's betrayal—had snowballed together with Mano's cold rejection.

She let herself give in to it. She didn't know if the driver was watching, but she really didn't care. Her life was unraveling before her eyes, and if she wanted to sit in the back of the car and cry, she damn well would.

When she was out of tears, she reached for a tissue she'd stuffed away in her purse for the funeral. Paige dabbed away the tears and blew her nose before throwing it away. This was what she thought she wanted, but she was wrong. So wrong. She pushed him away in self-defense and now she regretted it. She would rather confess her love to him and be rejected than to receive this cold, neutral goodbye. She'd hurt him. And now he'd hurt her. She had to fix this.

With a surge of bravery, she climbed from the town

car and ran into the hotel after him. She glanced every which way around the lobby, but he was nowhere to be found. Paige dashed over to the concierge desk.

"Did you see which way Mr. Bishop went?" she asked.

The man looked at her suspiciously, then shook his head. "I'm sorry, I didn't."

"Please," she insisted. "I have to tell him something very important."

"I'm very sorry, Miss Edwards, but Mr. Bishop has requested he not be disturbed while he works in his office this evening."

"But I—"

"He most specifically noted that he not be disturbed by you, miss," the concierge interrupted. "I'm sorry. I hope you enjoyed your time here at the Mau Loa. If there's anything we can do for you today before you check out, please don't hesitate to ask."

The polite, practiced speech mimicked Mano's parting words and felt like a slap in the face. He didn't want to see her. The man seemed pretty firm on his stance. There was no amount of begging or pleading that would get her behind the desk and into the business area of the hotel where Mano was hiding away.

That left her with no choice. "Thank you," she said softly and turned away. Paige sought out the elevator to return to her room.

It was time to pack and say goodbye to Hawaii and Mano for good.

Eleven

It was a long overnight flight home with a layover in LA. She should've slept or watched a movie to pass the time on the plane, but instead, she'd stewed in her thoughts.

Paige hated the way she and Mano left things. He'd seemed to completely shut down when she told him she couldn't stay. She wanted to. Her heart ached at the thought of telling him no, but how could she stay? He didn't really understand what he was taking on. He wasn't just getting her in the bargain, and it wasn't fair to burden Mano with another man's child.

Anyway, did he really think they had a future together? The man who didn't date anyone longer than a week? What if she said yes, quit her job, gave up her apartment and moved to Hawaii, only to have him change his mind? Then what would she do? It was bad enough that it would break her heart, but as much as she might love him, she couldn't do that to her child, either.

Exhausted, Paige finally arrived home early the next morning, slipped the key into her apartment door and stumbled inside. She dropped her bags on the floor, then shouted in surprise as she noticed a figure in her apartment, sitting on her couch.

Her heart was still racing double time when she realized it was her sister, Piper. "What the hell are you doing here?" she asked. She was too tired and emotionally spent to use her polite filter. Especially with the woman who had run off with the father of her child. Not that she wanted him any longer.

Piper stood up to greet her anxiously. Paige noticed her normally attractive face was blotchy and red and her eyes were puffy. She'd been crying. "I came by because I knew you were coming home today."

"What do you care?"

Piper flinched. "How was Papa's service?"

Paige folded her arms protectively over her midsection. "It was very nice. They took some professional pictures at the ceremony that they'll be sending to our parents. They should get them in a week or so."

Paige felt awkwardly trapped at her front door. She didn't want to get any closer to her sister. She wanted to collapse into her bed, but Piper was in the way. "You didn't bring him here with you, did you?" It was the kind of thoughtless thing her sister would do. She wasn't deliberately hurtful, she was just oblivious to other's feelings.

"No," she said with wide eyes. "Wyatt...is gone."

Piper broke down into tears again, but Paige had a hard time feeling sympathy for her.

At the same time, she got the feeling that her sister wasn't leaving anytime soon. "I'm going to make some coffee," she said. She'd have to use up her daily allotment of caffeine to get through this.

As the coffee started brewing, she noticed her sister standing in the entryway to the kitchen. "So what happened? Did he leave you for someone prettier?"

Piper winced at her sister's cutting accusation. "I don't know. Maybe. We didn't really talk about it. I just came home from work one day and he was gone."

"You don't know why?" Paige asked, pouring them each a mug full of steaming brew.

"I have my suspicions. He kept asking me what Papa left me in the will. I finally told him yesterday that he didn't leave me anything. That Papa left almost everything to a wounded veteran charity. I don't think he expected that. I think he was sniffing around me...around both of us...in the hopes that we'd inherit a fortune when our grandfather died. When I came out of it with nothing, he took off."

That made sense to Paige. She'd met Wyatt when he was working for her grandfather. He had firsthand knowledge of the sprawling estate and how much money the ailing man had to be worth. Paige must've been a convenient target for him. "That's probably why he called me yesterday. Maybe he thought I got something in the will even if you didn't. I feel stupid," she said. "It sounds as though he would've left me no matter what. He just jumped ship earlier because he thought he could get the money and a prettier woman in the meantime."

She held out a mug to Piper, who accepted it. "I'm so sorry, Paige. I don't know what the hell I was thinking. He was just so…"

"Mesmerizing." Paige remembered that much.

"Yes. And charming. And handsome. When he spoke to me, I felt like the most important person in the world. I got wrapped up in it. I never should've let myself get anywhere near him when I knew you two were dating. I never meant to hurt you. I mean, you're my sister."

Paige didn't know what to say. Would her sister be here apologizing if she hadn't been dumped? She wasn't sure. Instead, she just shook her head. "It's okay. I'm over Wyatt." And she was. She was madly in love with another man who lived an ocean away.

"Are you sure?"

"Absolutely."

Paige turned to face her sister and noticed that Piper's gaze zoomed in on her just-rounding belly. She knew better than anyone that Paige had always been rail thin, even underweight. A sudden belly was more than just too much food on her recent vacation. Her eyes grew round and wide, then she looked up at Paige with her mouth agape.

"You're pregnant?"

Paige looked down and stroked the tiny belly she'd earned as she started her second trimester. "I guess this shirt is tighter than when I wore it last. I should've tried it on before I packed it." She sighed and nodded. "Yes, I'm pregnant."

"With Wyatt's baby?" Piper didn't need her sister to answer that. The crestfallen expression on her face was proof enough of that. "Oh my god, Paige!"

Paige set her coffee down just in time to receive the sudden embrace of her sister. Piper clung to her with new tears dampening Paige's shirt. She thought she'd cried all she possibly could in the car yesterday, but she'd been wrong. In her sister's arms, she found she couldn't hold them in. The tears rolled down her cheeks almost faster than her body could produce them.

They stood like that for several minutes until their emotions were spent and their eyes had dried. At last, Piper pulled back and wiped her cheeks. "You come sit down right now," she said, launching into her older sister bossy self.

Paige was too tired to argue. She took a seat at her dining room table and Piper sat down beside her.

"How far along are you?" she asked.

"Almost fourteen weeks. I didn't find out about the baby until after…" Her voice trailed off, unable to finish with the words *after you stole him away*.

"Does he know?"

Paige shook her head. "I was going to tell him when I got back."

"Oh no," Piper said. "You're not likely to track him down. His phone is disconnected. His apartment is vacant. He's not even working for that landscaping company anymore. Wyatt seriously split town when he was done with us."

Paige felt a sense of relief when she heard the news. "To tell you the truth, I'm okay with that. I don't really want Wyatt in the baby's life. I just knew it was the right thing to do." She stared down at her coffee, thinking about all the decisions she'd made. "How could I let myself get in a position like this with a man like that?"

"He was a snake, Paige. He whispered whatever you wanted to hear into your ear and you melted like butter. I did the same thing. You're not to blame for this."

"It's not just Wyatt," Paige began before bursting into tears again. "It's Mano, too."

Piper perked up in her seat. "Mano? Who is Mano?"

"He's the man I'm in love with," Paige managed between sobs.

Piper put a hand on Paige's shoulder. "Tell me everything."

So she did. She'd never really been one to share with Piper, but she had to talk to someone. Paige started at the beginning and told her about everything that happened on her trip to Hawaii. How she'd been intrigued by Mano's attention, how he hadn't seemed to be able to get enough of her. How broken he seemed to be, but how much he'd improved even over the short time they were together. How she'd let herself fall in love with a man even though she knew it wouldn't work out because she was a fool.

"He asked you to stay? That's a pretty big deal."

Paige shrugged it away. "At best, he's infatuated with the idea of us. The reality would never work. How can I ask him to raise another man's child? I can't ask him to do that, especially knowing that this might not last."

"You're absolutely certain you won't change your mind?"

"Yes. He never wanted to be a burden on a woman,

and I refuse to be a burden on him. I don't think he thought it through enough to understand what he was asking."

Piper looked saddened by the way their enchanted vacation romance had ended. Paige understood.

"He only proposed a week. That's all it was ever meant to be."

At last Piper got a more cheerful expression on her face that reminded Paige of their mother when she was getting fired up. "You know what? Everything is going to be fine. You're going to get through this, and you're going to have the most amazing baby ever. You're going to be a great mom and you'll be so much better off without some loser in your life. Okay?"

Paige nodded and sniffled away the last of her tears. Her sister was right. She had a baby and a future to focus on now. She needed to make the most of that.

"Quit moping, Mano. I don't know what your problem is, but it's Tūtū Ani's day. Act happy for her."

"Of course I'm happy for her," Mano said to his brother, although it sounded more like a growl. Kal might have a point, but he couldn't help it. He'd been like this since Paige left on Friday. He'd tried to take a step back, protect himself from the sucker punch he knew was coming, but it still hurt. He'd much rather be at the hotel moping privately and not bringing down the family birthday festivities, but he didn't really have a choice.

He'd opted to find a corner where he could sit with Hōkū and be out of the way. These things were always too chaotic for him to walk around much.

Even his own family had the tendency to forget he was blind and trip him up, especially the children, who didn't really know better. From what he could hear, the women were fussing in the kitchen, the men were preparing to dig up the kalua pork from the pit in the backyard, and he was no good to any of them.

Mano heard the squeak of the metal chair beside him and knew Kal had sat down. "So what's with you?" he asked. "Even Hōkū looks depressed. The last time we talked, you seemed pretty psyched about your semiannual romance. Did it not end well? Did she get clingy or weird about it?"

"The opposite, actually. Things were going great. We were having an amazing time together. I was beginning to think I wanted more than just a week with Paige and I told her so. But she left, anyway."

"That's a lot to spring on a woman after a week together. I mean, how did you tell her? Did you ask if she could come back and visit? Confess your undying love and ask her to move here? Propose marriage after her grandfather's memorial service?"

Mano felt his jaw tighten at his brother's probing questions. He didn't really want to talk about this. It was too fresh. "I told her that I wasn't ready for it to end and asked if she'd consider Honolulu as a potential future residence."

"A potential future residence? Tell me you didn't say it like that."

"I don't remember what I said now. All I remember is that she said no."

"I can imagine she had a lot to think about. And you didn't exactly sweep her off her feet from the sounds of it. For a woman to pack up her whole life, give up her job and move here, she needs more than just the idea that you two might continue to date."

"I know." He'd run it through his mind a million times. But a part of him was too scared to push it any further. "I didn't know what else to say, so I just let her go."

"I thought that's how you liked it. Easy and string free."

Mano shifted Hōkū's harness back and forth in his hands. "It is how I liked it. Until I met her. Paige changed everything...but it's complicated."

"How complicated can it be?" Kal asked. "You either have feelings for her or you don't. Do you?"

Mano swallowed hard. "Yes."

"Are you in love with her?"

He hadn't been certain then, but since Paige left, he'd been miserable. Heartsick. It felt just like when Jenna left. Only worse because then he was a child losing a sweetheart and now he was a grown man losing the woman he loved. "Yes."

He could hear Kal sigh and shift in his seat. "Man. This woman really got to you. I didn't think I'd see the day. Tell me what's so complicated about it. It sounds pretty straightforward to me."

This was the part of the story, Mano knew, that would change everything. "Paige is three months pregnant with another man's child."

"What?" Kal nearly shouted, then leaned in closer and whispered it again. He'd likely drawn looks from the family.

"You heard me. It's not as simple as I love her and we can start a life and everything is hunky-dory. There's things she has to deal with back at home, like the baby's father. He called her the other day and wanted to talk. I can't get in the way of her reconciling with the baby's father. And even if they didn't, she can't just move to Hawaii if he wants any kind of visitation. She also would be moving over two thousand miles away from her family and any support system she might need to raise her baby."

"That's true. But what you don't know is if she loves you. If she does, none of those other things matter. You didn't tell her. For all she knew this was just a promise of another week-long fling, not a lifetime commitment. And a pregnant woman in her position isn't messing around. If she does love you, she doesn't just want another week of romance. She wants your love in return and she wants you to love her baby as your own."

That was the other issue he wasn't quite sure how to address. Paige had been so adamant about not staying, he hadn't really thought their future through. Was he ready for fatherhood? In one week, he'd gone from being a confirmed bachelor to a man in love. Could he make the leap to family man and raise Paige's baby as his own child?

"Could you do that? Raise another man's child?" Mano asked his brother.

Kal sat thoughtfully for a minute. "It is just the same as dating a single mother with older children. If I loved the mother, I'd love the child. I don't think it would be hard since you would be there through most of the pregnancy. You'd be there when she delivered, and you'd get to hold the child in your arms. That's powerful stuff. I think in that moment, it doesn't really matter who the biological father is anymore. And besides, you're blind."

Mano winced, following his brother's logic until the end. "What does that have to do with anything?"

"Well, I would think it would be easier for you to ignore that it isn't your biological child. If the kid is born with red hair and freckles, that's a physical reminder that you wouldn't have to deal with. If you and Paige had children together, there wouldn't be anything to physically distinguish the child that is yours from the child that isn't, at least not to you. This is one instance in which being blind is perfect."

"Being blind is never perfect," Mano grumbled.

"You know what I mean, Mano. If you love this woman and you want to be with her, you have to tell her."

Mano hadn't expected this kind of guidance from his brother. Kal was as stubborn a bachelor as he was, although his reasoning was different. To hear his brother encourage him to throw caution to the wind and chase after Paige and her baby was a revelation.

"Do you really think I could? What would she say? What if she says no?"

"You absolutely could. I don't know Paige, and I can't guess how she feels about you, but it sounds like something serious happened this week. She might be scared of taking the leap the same way you are. Making a big gesture could make all the difference."

"But if it doesn't?" Mano pressed.

"If it doesn't, then you did all you could. You come home content in knowing that you aren't the first man to fall in love with a woman that didn't love you back. Then you move forward with your life. Simple as that."

It didn't seem simple. None of it was simple. He hadn't left the islands since before his accident. Getting on a plane with Hōkū, traveling to San Diego, tracking down Paige and confessing his love was anything but simple.

"Why would she want to love me, Kal? Even if I love her and her baby, she's still inheriting a broken man. I'm never going to have my sight back. Does she want to raise a family with a man that can't contribute one hundred percent?"

"You know what?" Kal snapped. "You're full of it."

"Excuse me?"

"You heard me. You've been blind for over a decade. You run the Mau Loa like a corporate shark. You charm the ladies, you take care of yourself and Hōkū. Yeah, things would be easier if you could see, but you've learned how to live your life without your vision. You'll learn how to be a lover, a husband and a father without your vision, too. You just have to want to do it. You're only a burden on yourself because you allow it."

A roar of voices came from Mano's right. He turned his head to listen and was pretty certain the pig was up and ready. There was a commotion to follow as food was taken out to the long tables on the lawn.

"It's time to eat," Kal said.

"I know." His hand gripped Hōkū's lead. Part of him wanted to act on Kal's suggestions before he could change his mind. He could walk out the door right now and get a cab to the airport. He could be in San Diego tonight.

Then he heard his family start to sing to his grandmother. He took a deep breath and steeled his resolve. Kal was right. He would go to Paige, but he wouldn't rush things. He'd enjoy the day with his grandmother, make his plans and ensure that when he touched Paige again, he'd never ever have to let her go.

Mano stood and followed Hōkū to join the others in his grandmother's celebration. Before he could fall into line to make a plate, one of his aunts came up to him.

"Mano," Aunt Kini began, "Tūtū Ani would like you to sit with her to eat since she hardly gets to see you. Why don't you go ahead and I'll make you a plate?"

This was the aunt who treated him like he was helpless. "I can make my own plate, Aunt Kini," he tried to argue.

"I know that, Mano," she chided and put a hand on his cheek. "You run a whole empire. You can make a plate for yourself. But why? Today you don't have to conquer the world on your own. Your family is here. Let me do this for you and enjoy a few moments with your grandmother."

Mano couldn't argue with that. At least this way he wouldn't have to ask what each thing was in front of him and try to balance a plate in one hand while holding on to Hōkū with the other. He still needed to learn that accepting help wasn't the same as accepting defeat.

"Thank you, Aunt Kini."

"She's over to your left about ten paces," she said before disappearing into the crowd of his family.

Mano turned and started in the direction she provided, stopping when Hōkū sat down. "Tūtū Ani?" he asked.

"I'm here, child."

He felt his grandmother's hand grasp his. She guided him to a chair beside her at the table. *"Hau'oli Lā Hānau, Tūtū."*

"*Mahalo*, Mano. Are you enjoying the party?"

Mano shrugged. "This is your party to enjoy, not mine."

Ani made a thoughtful sound with her tongue, then laid her hand on his knee. "Who is she, *mo'opuna*?"

He perked up in his chair. How could she know there was a woman on his mind? He hadn't mentioned Paige to anyone but Kal. "What do you mean?"

"Mano, you think just because you are blind everyone else is, too. You look absolutely heartsick. What has happened? Why didn't you bring your lady today?"

"Because she went home Friday."

"But you love her. Why did you let her go?"

Mano stiffened in his chair. Even with his sunglasses on, his grandmother saw everything. He realized then that the problem was his feelings went far deeper than he'd imagined. "I don't know, Tūtū."

"You should go to her. Tell her how you feel. Then give her this."

Ani took his hand and placed something cold and metallic in his palm. "What is it?" he asked.

"It's my peridot engagement ring. The stone is native to the big island and has been in our family for generations. Your grandfather was given the ring by his mother. And now I'm giving it to you."

Mano didn't know what to say. He knew exactly

which ring she was talking about. She'd worn it every day he could remember. The stone was a brilliant green octagon set in platinum with tiny diamonds around the edge. It was art deco in style, and almost a hundred years old. He couldn't imagine his grandmother would ever part with such a precious piece of jewelry. "But Tūtū, this is your ring."

"No, this is a family heirloom, no more mine than anyone else's. Give it to your love. Bring her back to Hawaii and begin your life together here. I insist."

"I would love to, but it's not that simple."

"What about love is simple, Mano?"

She was right. Kal was right. He needed to take their advice and act before Paige disappeared from his life forever.

"Why are you still sitting here, mo'opuna?" Ani asked.

"It's your birthday party," he insisted.

"Hopefully it will not be my last. You can make it up to me by attending the next one with your new bride. Go!"

Mano raised his grandmother's hand to his lips and kissed it. "Thank you, Tūtū," he said before getting up and making his way out of the house. He slipped the ring into his coat pocket and called the hotel to send a car for him. He was a short drive and a long plane flight away from Paige, and he wasn't going to waste another second.

Twelve

Paige stood with her hands planted firmly on her hips. "Absolutely not," she said to her stubborn patient, Rick. "If you want a pudding cup, you need to walk with me down the corridor to get it."

"Are you a nurse or a sadist?" Rick snapped bitterly.

"A little bit of both. You've been fitted with that new prosthetic for a week now, and the doctor says you're to walk on it at every opportunity. The more you use it, the less it will hurt. You can even use the walker or the crutches," she offered.

"I'm not taking orders from a woman in scrubs with kittens on them."

Paige looked down at her purple scrubs and the cartoon cats wearing tutus on it. She had to wear scrubs every day, so she tried to keep it lively with fun designs. "They're not just kittens, they're ballerina kittens. They're tough cats, and they're not interested in your excuses, either. If you want the pudding, you're coming with me."

Rick glared at her from his hospital bed. She knew it hurt to use his prosthetic, but he had to get past that or he'd never regain an active lifestyle again. She hated being like this, but sometimes with soldiers you had to antagonize them like a drill sergeant to get results.

"It's twenty feet, Rick. Just past the nurses' station. You can totally do it."

Rick finally flung his sheets back and sat up, placing both feet on the ground. "Give me the damn walker," he said, and she scooted it over to him. He pushed himself up, and with a wince they started down the hallway together.

"You're doing great," she said in a bright voice as they neared the snack station. "Chocolate or vanilla?" she asked.

"For this, it better be chocolate. With a Percocet chaser."

Paige smiled. "You got it." She got the pudding and spoon and started walking with Rick back to his room.

"Have you seen him?" she heard one of the nurses ask Brandy.

"No. Who?"

"He's the most beautiful man I've ever seen in real life. It's a shame he's blind and can't see how handsome he is."

Paige usually tried to ignore most of the other nurses she worked with. Today, however, their words caught her attention. She tried to focus on Rick, getting him the last few steps back to his room.

"How do you know he's blind?" Brandy asked.

"The sunglasses and the service dog. They don't let just anyone into a hospital with a dog, you know."

Paige's heart stuttered in her chest and she froze in place.

It couldn't be. It just couldn't be. Paige refused to let herself believe that it was Mano. That was ridiculous. He didn't want to leave the resort; the idea of him flying to San Diego was out of the question. Besides…why would he come chasing after her? He was the one who had used his employee as a bouncer to keep her away from him.

"Is something wrong?" Rick asked.

Paige's eyes widened as she realized she'd stalled her patient on his walk. "I'm sorry. Just a few more steps." She tried to focus on helping him into bed and getting him settled. That was more important. The minute she rushed out of the room she'd be disappointed, anyway. It was a veteran's hospital; there were bound to be blind men with service dogs here who weren't the one she was desperate to see.

She tugged the sheets up and swung the bedside table over Rick's lap. She placed two pudding cups and a spoon on it for him.

"Two?"

"You earned it. I'll be back with that Percocet in a few."

Rick immediately dove into a pudding cup, freeing Paige to return to the nurses' station. She made a note in his file and tried to ignore her gossiping coworkers.

"It's a big hospital. I doubt he's coming up here," Brandy said. "Where was he?"

"In the gift shop. I ran down for a candy bar on my break a minute ago. He was getting flowers."

No. Paige shook her head and logged the dose of pain medication she was about to take to her patient.

"Excuse me," a man said from behind her. "Do you know where I can find Paige Edwards?"

She knew the voice in an instant, but she was certain her mind was playing tricks on her. She shot up and turned in his direction.

It was Mano. He was there in one of his tailored suits with his Wayfarers on. His hair was slicked back and his face clean-shaven. He was clutching a bouquet of crimson roses in his hands. She almost wanted to reach out and touch him to make certain this wasn't a hallucination. Mano wasn't just off the resort property—he was on the mainland. Thousands of miles from his comfort zone. Why?

"Paige?" one of the other nurses said. There was a noticeable incredulity in her voice.

"Brandy, would you please give this to Mr. Jones for me?" She handed the cup with two pills to her and walked around to the outside of the nurses' station.

When she got closer, she heard the telltale thump of Hōkū's tail on the wall. Mano immediately turned in her direction. "Paige?"

He was here. He was really here. "Yes?"

"I'm so relieved to find you," he said with a smile. "This has been quite the adventure for me so far."

"Congratulations on getting out and about," she said cautiously. "I'd tell you to check out the zoo, but all you'd get out of it is the smell of elephant dung."

Mano didn't laugh. He was far too focused on her. He took a few steps forward, closing the gap she'd deliberately left between them. "I didn't come here for the zoo." He reached out and handed her the bouquet of flowers. "These are for you. I hope they're as pretty as I imagined they are."

Her heart started pounding so loudly in her chest she was certain he would hear it. She accepted the bundle of bright red roses. "They're lovely, thank you. I'm confused, though. Why are you here, Mano?"

"I wanted to tell you that I'm a fool."

"A text would've sufficed," she said coolly.

"No, it wouldn't. I had to come here in person so you would understand how serious I am about this. I never should've let you walk away from me."

"It wasn't really your choice," she argued, and yet she knew that she would've turned and ran into his arms if he'd only asked her to. Hell, she'd tried and was cruelly shut down.

"Not entirely. You made your decision then and you can make your decision now, but I can't help but think the outcome would've been different if I hadn't been too scared to say what needed to be said to make you stay."

Mano didn't look like the kind of man who was scared of anything, much less of something as simple as words. Didn't he know he could tell her anything? "And now?" she asked. She bit anxiously at her lip as she awaited his response.

He reached forward and sought out her arm. His warm palm glided along her skin to her wrist and wrapped her hand in his own. "I'm still scared. Waking up with you gone was like waking up in the hospital all over again. I'd lost everything and it's terrifying. But I've got to say it, anyway. I came all this way because you need to know that I love you."

There was a loud gasp. Paige thought it might have

come from her, but when she turned to the nurses' station, she realized both her coworkers were watching them like a soap opera on television.

"Let's go down the hallway and finish this in private," she said. Paige didn't really want them in her business. If this ended poorly, the whole third floor would know about it before the shift was over. She loved Brandy, but she was a blabbermouth.

"I don't want to do this in private. I want everyone to know how I feel about you," Mano insisted. "I want to rent a billboard and shout it from the rooftops. I'm not going to push my feelings down anymore because I worry about getting hurt. I realized it hurt more to lose you knowing I didn't try my damnedest to keep you with me than to spill my guts and have you walk away, anyway. At least then, I would've tried."

"Mano…" She didn't know what to say. Her thoughts were racing as his words spun around in her brain. He loved her. Did he really, truly feel that way? She almost couldn't let herself believe it.

"Don't," he said, squeezing her hand. "I know that tone of voice. You're about to tell me all the reasons why we can't be together. The distance and the baby and anything else you can come up with. I don't care about all that. You may see them as obstacles, but to me they're just challenges that can be overcome. All I know is that I love you more than I've ever loved a woman in my entire life. A week was not long enough. A year isn't long enough. I want you in my life for always. You and the baby."

Paige's mouth fell open. She couldn't believe what he was telling her. The baby had been the one issue she was certain they wouldn't be able to get past.

"I know that Wyatt called you the other day. He probably wants you back and he's a fool not to. I told myself I should step back and let the two of you have another chance, but I just can't. I love you too much, Paige."

He thought she and Wyatt were reconciling? She never should've lied to him about the call. She hadn't wanted Mano to know she spoke to him, not because they were anywhere near a reunion, but because she was embarrassed that she answered the phone when she saw his name.

She stepped close to him and reached up to pull off his sunglasses. She wanted to see his face—his whole face—when he said this to her. Then, and only then, could she look in his eyes and see if he was telling the truth. "Say it again," she whispered.

Looking down at her, Mano clutched her hand against his chest. She could feel his heart pounding in his rib cage nearly as fast as her own.

"I love you, Paige Edwards. I love everything about you, and that means I love that baby, too. It's a part of you, half of you, and that means it's going to be an amazing child. And if I have anything to say about it, it's going to be my child."

His child? "I don't understand. How could it possibly be—"

"If we are married when the baby is born and my name goes on the birth certificate, he or she will legally be mine. I'll fight anyone who would say otherwise."

Paige stiffened. Any minute now she was going to wake up. This was like some extended fantasy playing out in her mind. She'd been awake too long and slept too little the night before. Any second now, she would snap out of it and realize that she'd fallen asleep in the break room over a lukewarm frozen meal.

Mano let go of her hand and reached into his lapel pocket. There, he pulled out a small wooden box. He opened the lid and presented the ring to her for her approval. It had a glittering green stone the size of her thumbnail in the same bright color as the foliage around the Mau Loa. It was surrounded by baguette diamonds and set in either white gold or platinum, she didn't know or care which.

Mano removed the ring from the box and held it up to her. "This ring has been in my family for generations. The peridot was mined on the big island over a hundred years ago. My grandmother gave it to me this weekend. For you. She insisted that no other ring would do if I wanted you to be my bride. And I do, more than anything. So Paige, will you do me the honor of being my wife?"

The silence seemed to go on for an eternity. All Mano could do was stand there, holding the ring like a dolt, and wait for her to answer. He couldn't see her reaction. All he knew was that she hadn't run away this time.

"Paige?" He palmed the ring and reached out to touch her face. Her cheeks were wet with tears. "You're crying. Why are you crying?" he asked. "I'm sorry. Do you not like the ring? I can get you a different one. Tūtū won't mind."

"Don't apologize. And you are absolutely not getting me a different ring. That's the most beautiful and special ring you ever could've chosen. It would be an insult to Tūtū and your whole family if I turned it down for some boring old diamond."

The panic started to subside in him. Despite her tears she sounded...happy. "So you *do* like it?"

"I do."

"Then will you please say yes and save me from all this suspense?"

"Mano, I want to say yes."

The anxiety returned. Why was it that Paige could never just go with her heart? She always had to rationalize and analyze everything. "Do you love me, *pulelehua*?"

"I do. You know that I do."

Okay, one obstacle down, he thought with a sigh of relief. "Did you like Oahu? Would you be happy living with me in Honolulu?"

"Oahu was amazing. I would be happy living with you there, but I don't know that I want to raise a family in the hotel. I want my child—"

"Our child," he insisted.

"*Our* child to have a normal life, and that means a house and dinners that are cooked, not delivered on a silver platter by room service."

That was a concern he could easily address. He would give her anything she wanted if she would just say yes. "Absolutely. That's how I grew up, and you're right, that's how it should be. We visited the hotel a lot, but we didn't live there. We had a home. And if that's what you want, we'll go house hunting the second we return. You can have whatever you want, Paige. You only have to ask it of me."

"Then what about my work? You know how important it is to me. I want to continue working with veterans, even if it's only on a part-time or volunteer basis while the baby is small."

Mano had anticipated this one. "There is an amazing VA hospital in Honolulu. I'm certain they would be lucky to have you there for an hour or forty hours a week."

He waited for Paige's next argument, but there was a long silence instead. Was it possible that he'd actually gotten through all of their excuses not to be happy?

"Mano," she said at last, this time in her smallest voice. "Are you sure this is what you want? You've gone your whole life dedicated to being a no-strings-attached bachelor. If I say yes, and I accept your ring and move to Oahu, I can't have you changing your mind."

"You keep trying to talk me out of what I've already decided. Why do you keep giving me an out from this, Paige?"

"Because usually the person takes it." The emotion in her voice made his heart ache in his chest. He wanted to go back in time through her life and punch all the people who had made her feel like she didn't deserve this.

"I love you, Mano. I do. But my heart can't take it if you offer me this fantasy and then snatch it away. You really, truly want me as I am, with this baby as your own? Wyatt has vanished, so I'm doing this by myself."

"No, you're not. You're not doing anything alone again. I'm going to be at your side until you're sick of me. And once the rest of my family finds out about you and this baby…you'll wish for peace and quiet.

I'm not going to change my mind, Paige. I wouldn't dream of doing that to you, to me, or to our child. We're going to be a family. Or we will be, if you would just say you're going to marry me."

"Okay." Paige moved closer to him, pressing her body against his. "I will marry you." Her hand caressed his cheek, and then her lips met his.

He felt a rush of happiness and relief wash over him as she kissed him, her acceptance of his proposal still ringing in his ears. She was going to marry him. He hadn't ruined this.

Then an odd sound captured his attention. Mano reluctantly pulled away from Paige, turning his ear toward what sounded like...applause. "What is that?" he asked.

Paige giggled softly in his arms. "Those are my patients and the rest of the nursing staff," she said. "Apparently, your dashing proposal has drawn a crowd of them from their rooms."

Mano laughed. He hadn't expected that. "Well, then let's put this ring on your finger and make it official."

He held out the ring and slid it up Paige's finger until it nestled tightly. This was met with another round of cheers and an enthusiastic bark from Hōkū.

He hugged her tight against him. "So, can we get out of here?" he asked. He didn't want to wait any longer than he had to to bed his new fiancée.

"I have two hours left on my shift."

Mano frowned. It was just like his Paige to be so responsible. She'd probably insist on giving two weeks' notice, as well. Any fantasies about sweeping her into his arms and flying her on a private jet back to Hawaii within the hour were likely just that.

"Did you really just say that?" a woman asked.

Paige shifted in his arms. "Brandy, I can't just walk out and leave you guys."

The woman snorted. "You're too nice a person, Paige. If a hunk proposed to me and wanted to kidnap me and take me to Hawaii, I wouldn't even say goodbye. I'll explain to the supervisor what happened, although she'll hardly believe me. Now go on, get out of here."

Brandy was joined by the shouts of what sounded like a dozen soldiers surrounding them and encouraging Paige to run off with him. Mano was glad to have backup on this.

"Come on, Paige," he said. "What do you say we play hooky today? You work too much and you need to get out more."

"My own words coming back to haunt me," Paige said.

"You and I are going to play hooky together for the next fifty years. We're going to teach our daughter to paddleboard and deep-sea fish. We're going to—"

"Wait," Paige interrupted. "What makes you think this is a girl?"

"I had a dream about her the night you left, like my grandparents did about me."

"And what did you see?"

"I saw you running down the beach chasing after a little girl with long brown hair. She was tan from the sun and leaping through the waves like she was born to be there."

"So we're having a girl?"

"Yes, *'Eleu*. It means energetic and agile."

Paige giggled, the melodic laughter reminding him of the first day they met. The day that changed his life forever. "It sounds like I'm going to have my hands full."

Mano smiled and gave her a kiss. "I can't wait."

* * * * *

*If you loved this story of pregnancy and passion
from Andrea Laurence,
don't miss the sequel
THE BABY PROPOSAL
available December 2016!*

*And be sure to pick up these other books from
Andrea Laurence!*

*WHAT LIES BENEATH
MORE THAN HE EXPECTED
BACK IN HER HUSBAND'S BED
HIS LOVER'S LITTLE SECRET*

Available now from Mills & Boon Desire!

"Don't kiss me. This isn't a good idea."

Did that protest sound weak?

He nipped at her jawline, traveled up to her ear and whispered, "Feels like a great idea." His hands curved over her backside, pulling her hips into his.

Graham's hands and mouth, his body for that matter, always seemed like the answer. He made her forget everything except for how her body seemed to zing to life. But she couldn't zing, not today.

Eve pressed her palms to his chest and eased back. "No. I won't be distracted by sex. I want your brother to back off with the media attacks and insults."

She turned, needing to put some space between them. Having him so close was difficult.

But just as she spun away, a wave of dizziness overcame her. The room literally tilted before her eyes. Her hand went to her stomach just as strong arms wrapped around her torso.

Secure against Graham's chest, Eve kept her eyes shut as she pulled in a shaky breath. The dizziness remained. This was her first symptom of pregnancy.

"Okay?" he whispered in her ear.

Not really.

* * *

His Secret Baby Bombshell
is part of the Dynasties: The Newports series—
Passion and chaos consume a Chicago real estate empire.

HIS SECRET
BABY BOMBSHELL

BY
JULES BENNETT

MILLS &
BOON

First Published in Great Britain 2016
By Mills & Boon, an imprint of HarperCollins*Publishers*
1 London Bridge Street, London, SE1 9GF

© 2016 Harlequin Books S.A.

Special thanks and acknowledgement are given to Jules Bennett for her contribution to the Dynasties: The Newports series.

ISBN: 978-0-263-91880-9

51-1016

Our policy is to use papers that are natural, renewable and recyclable products and made from wood grown in sustainable forests. The logging and manufacturing processes conform to the legal environmental regulations of the country of origin.

Printed and bound in Spain
by CPI, Barcelona

National bestselling author **Jules Bennett** has over thirty romance novels in print worldwide. She's written for Mills & Boon since 2008 and currently writes for two lines: Cherish and Desire. When Jules isn't working on her latest romance novel, she's spending time with her family or procrastinating on social media. Check out all of her upcoming titles, appearances and more on her site at www.julesbennett.com.

This book goes to my shelf buddies
and awesome friends Sarah M. Anderson,
Andrea Laurence and Cat Schield.
Love you all!

One

Déjà vu swept over Eve Winchester. *Not again. This* cannot *be happening again*.

The two pink lines mocked her denial.

Eve clutched the pregnancy test, gripping the side of her white pedestal sink with her other hand.

Sheets rustled in the bedroom. Through the crack in the bathroom door, Eve could see Graham Newport lying in her bed.

Now that she knew her predicament, she had no idea what step to take next. For someone who prided herself on plans, on spreadsheets and following through on details in a timely fashion, she was completely lost.

But her unknowns stemmed from the fear of what Graham would do. How would he react? How would their families, whose rivalry was legendary in Chicago, deal with this shocking news? The Newports and the Winchesters had enough drama on their hands lately.

The Newport brothers' paternity had been thrown into question earlier this year. Graham and his brother Brooks were still up in the air after their paternity tests came back negative, but their other brother, Carson, had discovered who his real father was—Sutton Winchester, who happened to be Eve's, too.

Yeah, they were all in a state of upheaval right now and this unexpected pregnancy would just toss a stick of dynamite into the fire.

With shaky hands, Eve quickly put the test back in the box and shoved it beneath some trash in the can under the sink. Finally, risking another glance over her shoulder, she peered through the slight opening in the door and noted that Graham was still asleep. He had one toned leg thrown over white sheets, one arm stretched out to the side. Eve closed her eyes and pulled in a deep breath. After the paternity test had proven Graham wasn't related to her in any way, they'd finally given in to the feelings they'd fought so hard against. They'd been so careful to keep this heated affair a secret. But when their instant attraction had become evident, they'd both gotten backlash from their siblings. Fine, they could sneak around and leave the siblings out of it, right?

Yeah, that had worked for the past six weeks. So much for keeping their families out of their private lives.

Now she was having a baby. A second pregnancy… this one much scarier than the last. This time she knew the ugly horrors that could happen. She'd lived through them, still bore the internal scars, and now she'd have to find a way to push through again. Could fate be that cruel?

Eve slid her hand over her silk chemise. Her flat stomach had once been round, once held another life taken all too soon. As much as she wanted to take her father's company global and focus on being in charge, she refused to let an innocent baby feel anything but loved and secure. And above all, this child would not be a victim in the war between the families.

That is, if she made it to full-term.

Fear coursed through her. The fear of telling Graham weighed heavily on her, but the fear of losing another child was absolutely crippling. Going through such grief again might very well destroy her. Added to that, her father was terminal. How much pain could one woman endure and still keep going?

The sheets rustled again and Eve knew she couldn't hide in the bathroom forever. Graham had come over late last night and they'd quickly tumbled into bed, as was their habit. No sweet-talking, no romantic walks for them. Eve had a passion for Graham and the family feud between the Winchesters and the Newports had no place in their affair.

Unfortunately, their worlds were about to collide in ways they never dreamed.

Stepping back into her bedroom, Eve pulled in a deep breath. Even though her entire world was completely turned upside down, she still had obligations, and Elite Industries needed their new president to be in top form at all times. The man in her bed would have to go because she had a meeting shortly and she needed to prepare. Plus, she needed some time alone to process her situation.

The second Eve crossed the room, Graham's intense aqua eyes were on her. That heavy-lidded gaze did amazing things to her body. Just one stare, one simple touch, and the man had her under his spell. The potency he projected was unlike anything she'd ever known.

With a cockeyed grin, he jerked back the sheet in

a silent invitation for her to join him. He never had to
say a word to get her right where he wanted her. There
had been an unspoken agreement that this was sex only.
Clearly they didn't want more because they were both
married to their jobs and the intensity of their passion
was off the charts. A committed relationship couldn't
be this hot this fast. But they were about to enter a committed relationship of a totally different nature.

Eve shook her head. "As much as I'd love to take you
up on your offer, I need to get some work done."

He raised one dark blond brow. "On Sunday morning? I can make you forget all about work."

Graham Newport could charm the crown from a
queen…which was why he was one of Chicago's finest
lawyers. Despite his young age of thirty-two, Graham
had made full law partner at Mayer, Mayer and Newport. And it wasn't just the charm that catapulted him
into his prestigious position. That reserved, quiet, yet
lethal strength had him soaring to the top.

"Maybe so," she agreed, trying to sound casual,
though the hidden pregnancy test mocked her. "But I
have an online meeting later with a group from Australia because it will be their Monday morning."

Graham sat up, the sheet pooling around his bare,
sculpted waist. Raking a hand through his disheveled
hair, he sighed. "I hate when you want to be responsible."

Eve nearly cringed. If he thought she was responsible now, wait until he discovered the pregnancy. But
that would have to wait. She needed to cope with this
shock first, needed to make sure everything was all
right. Granted, everything had appeared to be fine with
her last pregnancy…then suddenly it wasn't.

Even though she and Graham had a physical relationship only, he had every right to know. But until she saw a doctor, she was keeping this news to herself. The last thing she'd ever want anyone to feel was the empty void and crushing ache of losing a child.

"You okay?"

Eve blinked, pulling herself back to the moment. Graham's aqua eyes held hers. Pasting on a smile, she nodded. "How could I not be after last night?"

Get it together, Eve.

Graham jerked the sheet aside and stalked across the room to gather his clothes. The man was completely comfortable with his body and she was completely comfortable enjoying the view.

Eve smoothed her silk robe with shaky hands before adjusting the covers and pillows on the bed. She needed to focus on something other than the sexy man in her bedroom, who never failed to satisfy her every desire, and the unborn child they'd made.

Graham would demand to know how this happened. She'd told him she was on birth control, and she was. But she'd switched types right about the time of the children's hospital charity ball...their first night together.

Strong arms circled her waist as she fell back against Graham's hard chest. Her body instantly responded to his touch and when his lips caressed the side of her neck, Eve couldn't stop her head from tilting, her lashes from closing and a moan from seeping out. She had no willpower when it came to Graham and the bedroom. Obviously.

"Maybe I could help you with preparing for this meeting," he muttered against her ear. "I do my best thinking in the shower."

Eve had been prepared for this meeting for weeks. That was her thing. She was always professional, always prompt, and she always had a plan B. Her spreadsheets had spreadsheets, and her period was never a day late.

Which is how she'd known when she needed to buy a pregnancy test.

And, if Graham really knew her, he would've caught her in the lie about needing to get ready for a meeting. He would've known she had her notes and speech down pat in order to win over the prospective new company. Which just went to prove, they didn't know each other very well at all outside the bedroom.

With a quick, effective tug, Graham pulled the knot free on her robe. Eve gripped his hands. "You may think in the shower, but I guarantee I won't be able to."

Graham playfully nipped at her earlobe and released her. "You're always flattering me."

As if his ego needed any more stroking.

Eve finished making the bed as Graham sat in the corner accent chair and slipped his dress shoes on. The man was hot as hell naked, but designer suits did some amazing things for him. And each time he showed up after work, she had a hard time resisting that *GQ* look with a touch of unkempt hair going on. How could one look like one needed a haircut and still have the entire Chicago power-lawyer look going?

It was the side eye. He had the sexiest side eye she'd ever seen. He'd tip his head in that George Clooney kind of way and peer at you from beneath those thick lashes. Yeah, those aqua eyes were the main component of his charm to get you hooked. Once he had you under his spell, he pulled you in tighter, snaring you with the rest of all of his seductive ways.

"I actually have a case I'm working on." He came to his feet and rolled up the sleeves of his black dress shirt.

"Brooks and I are meeting later. Say the word, though, and I'll gladly cancel."

Laughing, Eve shook her head. "We both have meetings. And if our families keep noticing how you and I are both MIA at the same time, they're going to stage an intervention."

Without a word, he closed the space between them, wrapped her in his arms and kissed her. Could something so potent, toe-curling and heart-clenching be summed up in such a simple word as *kiss*? Being kissed by Graham was an event, something she should prepare for, but there was no way she could ever prepare her body for the onslaught of passion and desire that slammed into her each time he touched her.

He ran his hands up and down her back, the silky material gliding against her skin. Nipping at her lips, he murmured, "I'll be back tonight."

With that whispered promise, he released her and walked away. Eve remained still, clutching her robe, staring at the neatly made bed and trying to figure out exactly how this unplanned pregnancy would weave into her perfectly planned life…and how Graham would take the news that he was going to be a father.

"Sutton will not win in the end," Brooks threatened. "If it's the last thing I do, I'll expose that man for the cheating bastard he is."

Pinching the bridge of his nose between his finger and thumb, Graham blew out a breath. Sutton Lazarus Winchester had always been a thorn in their side—his real estate business was Newport Corporation's main competition—but ever since they'd discovered Sutton had had an affair with their mother, Cynthia Newport, things had been much worse.

It had all started when she had first come to Chicago. Her real name was Amy Jo Turner, which she'd used until she fled her abusive father when she'd been pregnant with twins. With a brand-new name and town, Cynthia had gone to work in a coffee shop, saving money to raise two boys. She'd ultimately been taken under the wing of Gerty, a retired waitress. It was at this coffee shop that Cynthia met Sutton and wound up going to work for him. Cue illicit affair and their half brother, Carson.

The entire string of events was a complete mess. But now that the DNA test was official, Graham and Brooks knew for a fact Sutton wasn't their father. Which had made Graham's seduction of Eve possible. The woman kept him tied in knots. He counted down the time to when he could get his hands on her again, have her panting his name and wrapping that curvy body around his.

"Are you even listening?"

Graham dropped his hand to the arm of the leather club chair in his brother's office and sighed. He was half listening, half fantasizing new ways to make Eve lose control.

"I hear you," he confirmed. "And I agree. Carson is entitled to an inheritance when Sutton passes. It's only fair seeing as how Carson is his child, as well. The estate shouldn't just be split among the girls."

Sutton's three daughters were fighting this battle, as well. Nora, Grace and Eve weren't quite ready to welcome another sibling, but too bad, because the tests proved Carson was indeed a Winchester no matter how many people disliked the fact.

And Graham despised that he and his brothers were technically teaming up against Eve and her sisters. But it was only fair that when Sutton finally passed, Carson got his fair share of what was rightfully his. It would be in the Winchesters' best interest not to fight this matter because Graham would fight back...and win.

This entire mess was just another reason Graham and Eve had to keep their affair a secret and 100 percent physical. Nothing too heavy, no commitments and nothing long-term.

And no way in hell could their siblings ever come to know the full truth of just how hot their attraction burned. They'd not been too secretive about their initial attraction, but quickly discovered discretion was the best way to go. Considering what he and Eve did was no one's business, they'd opted to take things to the bedroom and ignore the turmoil surrounding them.

Keeping things simple—no talk of families or wills and Sutton's health—was the only way this affair was working and Graham was in no hurry to end it. A physical relationship with a woman who matched his passion like no other wasn't something he was ready to toss aside.

"So I need you to subpoena Eve."

The cold, harsh words jerked him from his thoughts. Graham sat up in his seat. "Excuse me?"

"I didn't think you were listening," Brooks growled. "We need her and her sisters to testify at the hearing regarding Sutton's estate. I need you to hand deliver those subpoenas."

So much for attempting to keep his relationship with Eve impersonal. Damn it. He wholeheartedly agreed that Carson was due his percentage, but he didn't want to go to battle with Eve. Not that he wouldn't win. Winning had never been an issue because when Graham Newport went into a courtroom, he was there for battle and came out on top. Always. But to get into a war with Eve...

He blew out a breath. That would destroy this chemistry they'd discovered.

Not that he wanted anything long-term or serious with her, but he wasn't ready to put the brakes on this amazing secret affair they had going. And he had to admit, the whole sneaking-around thing did thrill him on a new level he never knew existed. Sex had always come easy for him, but to know Eve matched his passion, his fire, was something he'd never found before. So, for now, he'd really like to keep this subpoena out of his personal life.

"When's the court date?" Graham asked.

Brooks rested his forearms on his neat, mahogany desk. "Two weeks. I'd rather have it moved up because, with Sutton's health declining, I don't want to take any chances."

Sutton wasn't doing well at all. The man was on his last leg and Graham wasn't sorry the old bastard was fading. Sure, that sounded cold and harsh, but it was fitting for the man who was ruthless and conniving. The man had taken advantage of Graham's mother, whether she would've admitted it or not. He'd gotten her pregnant, unbeknownst to him, but he'd still tossed Cynthia aside when he was done with her. Clearly his high-society wife was all he needed at the end of the day, though she'd ultimately ended up leaving him.

Graham's own mother had recently died, too, which is how the paternity issues had come to light in the first place. But the loss was still too fresh, too heart wrenching, so he turned his focus back to Brooks. Letting the void in his heart consume him would be all too easy.

"What did Roman find out?"

The private investigator Brooks had hired to uncover Brooks and Graham's paternity had been working diligently on the case, yet hadn't come up with a name yet. They'd never known who their father was and, for a brief time, they feared Sutton was the one. Now that Roman Slater had found out that Sutton had fathered Carson and abandoned their mother, Brooks and Graham were out for blood. The only way to take Sutton down was to hit him where he'd feel it the most. Considering the man didn't have a heart, Brooks and Graham were going after his finances on Carson's behalf, and ultimately that would trickle down to his daughters. Graham ignored the guilt gnawing away at his chest. Business and sex were two areas where he never got emotionally attached.

"I'm waiting to find out, but he's almost positive he's uncovered more children Sutton fathered from his affairs. If that's the case, I won't hesitate to use it against him."

Graham muttered a curse and stared out the floor-to-ceiling window behind Brooks. The Chicago skyline was one he never took for granted. He loved his city, loved working here and taking charge. The ambiance of such a powerful city gave him ammunition each day to fight his battles.

"If he uncovers too many, they'll all want a share of Sutton's assets."

Graham crossed his ankle over his knee and raked a hand over the back of his neck. Maybe he should get a haircut. No. He liked Eve's fingers running through his hair. He liked the way she toyed with the strands on his neck when...

Damn it. He was here for Brooks. How could he concentrate when Eve kept creeping to the forefront of his mind?

"I thought of that, too," Brooks agreed. "Which is another reason I want this finalized before Sutton passes.

So those subpoenas need to be delivered as soon as you can draw them up."

Graham nodded. He might not want to do this, he might hate mixing this business with his personal life, but there was no other way. And Graham knew Brooks wasn't usually this ruthless. But his twin was angry, hurt. They both were. With Sutton so hush-hush about what he knew, and right on the tail of their mother's passing, there was just so much emotion and nowhere to put it all.

Sutton was a man who deserved to be destroyed, and if Eve and her sisters got in the Newports' way, well… they better just cooperate because Graham would win this fight for Carson. Taking prisoners along the way wasn't ideal, but he'd do so for the sake of his brothers. Family was everything, after all.

Two

Two days had passed since the test. Two hours had passed since her doctor had done an exam and confirmed the pregnancy, assuring her everything looked fine. She'd held it together until she made it back to her car. In the quiet of the parking garage, she'd wept for the innocent life growing inside her and prayed she'd have the strength to make it through.

Just because children weren't something she'd set her sights on for her future didn't mean she didn't want this baby. Years ago she'd been naive and unprepared for what life threw her way. Now Eve was ready to do anything and everything to keep her baby safe and secure. She'd started taking vitamins the day she took the home test. At this point all she could do was relax and attempt some sort of stress-free life...as much as was possible when she was planning global domination.

As president of Elite Industries, she was more than ready to broaden the scope of the company's dealings. Her father had created a good foundation, but she wanted more. She wanted to prove to herself, and to her ailing father, that she could make this company even better. Before he passed, she wanted him to be proud of what she'd done.

Back at the office, Eve closed her eyes and tipped her head back against her leather office chair. Her father's days were numbered, there was no denying the truth that faced them. Sliding a hand over her stomach, Eve wondered at what point she should tell him about this next generation. Would he be excited she was carrying on the name? But if she told him about the baby, she'd have to tell him about the baby's father. Eve wasn't ready to expose her child to this ugly war just yet.

Once she told Graham, then they could decide when to tell everyone else. He needed to know; she just had no idea how to go about telling him. Would he be angry? Would he blame her or would he embrace fatherhood? How on earth would they deal with shared parenting?

Questions whirled around inside her head as her office door burst open and slammed against the wall. Eve jerked upright, shocked to see Graham striding through, her assistant, Rebecca, right on his heels.

"I'm sorry, Ms. Winchester," Rebecca stated nervously. "I tried to stop him."

What was he doing here? Nobody knew about their affair and they'd purposely gone out of their way to avoid being seen together in public. His barging into her office could jeopardize everything.

"It's fine." Eve shot her assistant a smile and nodded in a silent dismissal. Once the door was closed, she glared at Graham. "What the hell are you thinking coming here? The last thing we need is gossip about your being in my office."

Graham crossed to her desk and slammed a piece of paper down, the force sending other paperwork fluttering to the floor. "We need you to testify."

Shocked, Eve came to her feet and braced her palms on the top of her desk, completely ignoring the paper. "What?"

"This is a subpoena regarding your father's assets and Carson's interest in them."

Rage bubbled within her. This is why he'd come? Was this also the same reason he looked so angry? What was he thinking doing this to her, to her family?

"How dare you order me to testify against my father?"

The muscle in Graham's jaw tightened, a tic she'd noticed when he was angry with himself. So, that was the real issue here. Why was he doing this if he didn't want to?

What was going on and why was he doing this to her?

"You have to see what your father is, Eve." Graham's bright eyes held hers. Those same eyes that had devoured her body just yesterday now held so much anger, resentment. "Carson is entitled to his share of the inheritance. Plus, our PI has uncovered some other nasty facts regarding Sutton."

As much as Eve wanted to close her eyes to battle the pain, she couldn't. Her father may not be a popular man, but he was still her father and she wouldn't let anyone stand in her office and throw ugly rumors around. Yes, he'd admitted to affairs while married to her mother, but that was in the past. Couldn't people change? Did he have to pay for his sins forever? He was dying. Couldn't everyone just let him live out his last days in peace?

Enough. She refused to allow this to happen, let alone

in her own office...her father's old office. Reaching for her phone, Eve started to dial her assistant. Instantly Graham's fingers encircled her wrist.

"What are you doing?"

She glared at him. "Having security escort you out."

The pressure around her wrist increased, but not to the point of hurting. "Hang up, Eve. Hear me out for two minutes and I'll go."

Still gripping the phone, Eve stared into his eyes, and her first thought was whether their child would have those mesmerizing baby blues. How could she resist him and tell him no when she couldn't get her own hormones in check?

And, how could she fault his loyalty for standing up for his brother? Wasn't she standing up for her father? They both held family bonds high and she had to admire that, but she still couldn't allow him to shove his weight around. Not here on her turf.

She hung the phone up and pulled away from his touch. Crossing her arms over her chest, Eve tipped her chin. "Two minutes."

A hint of a smile danced around those kissable lips. No. She couldn't think of him in those terms right now. The way he came barging into her office, forcing this subpoena on her had nothing to do with what they did in the bedroom. Right this minute, they were enemies... and soon to be parents. Talk about a conflict of interest.

"Carson is your half brother, too," Graham began in that steady, low tone of his that no doubt always had the judge and jury hanging on his every word. "He deserves part of your father's assets."

"Considering my father is very much alive, that's not my call," she argued. Eve hated discussing the fact that her father's health was failing, but the harsh truth was always at the forefront of her mind. "Is that all you barged in here for?"

"Eve, you have to see this is the right thing to do for Carson. Don't let Sutton's hatred and hardheaded notions trickle down to you. You're too good for that."

For a split second, Eve wanted to melt at his words, but then she recalled who she was dealing with. Chicago's youngest, fastest-rising attorney who marched through court and came out with a victory every time. He had Charm with a capital C. He oozed it and exploited it in order to get what he wanted.

"I have no hatred toward Carson," she stated firmly. Carson was just as much an innocent as she and her sisters were. "I simply don't feel it's my decision to say what happens to my father's things. He has a will, Graham."

"One that was implemented before he knew of Carson's existence." Graham pressed his palms on her desk and leaned forward. "Regardless of what you want to do, you've been served, Eve."

Part of her wanted to applaud him for holding his ground and having his brother's back. The other part of her wanted to slap him, tear this subpoena to shreds and toss it like confetti in his face. But she refused to let her emotions show.

"I believe your two minutes are up."

His eyes held hers for a moment longer, but he finally turned and walked out, his exit much less dramatic than his entrance. Once the doorway was clear, Eve's legs gave out and she sank back to her chair. With shaky hands, she unfolded the document and stared at the date she was due in court. Whatever was going on with the Newport brothers, she sincerely wished they'd leave her out of it. Her father was dying, she was pushing to acquire another real estate company in Australia and now she was expecting the baby of a man who should be her enemy.

What more could life throw at her?

"Ms. Winchester?"

Eve glanced up to see Rebecca standing in the doorway. "Do you want me to have security make sure Mr. Newport is out of the building?"

"No, Rebecca. That won't be necessary. Mr. Newport's business is done here. He won't return."

There. Hopefully that would help quash any rumors about Graham's unexpected visit. Rebecca wasn't one to gossip, though. Eve wouldn't have her as an assistant if she were, but she still wanted the utmost respect from her staff.

"We had a mutual client and he was dropping off some paperwork," Eve added. "Thank you."

With a slight nod, Rebecca stepped back out and closed the door.

So much for telling Graham about the baby soon. Now she had to figure out where they stood because he'd drawn a battle line the moment he'd opted to show up at her office. He could've had anyone on his staff deliver that subpoena.

Again, this proved how his family loyalties and his career were his top priorities. Which only made Eve wonder: Once he knew they'd created a baby, would she and the child be included in that inner circle?

The following morning, Eve's patience had run out. Graham hadn't contacted her since he'd burst into her office yesterday, and now the glaring headline mocked her from the front page of the paper: Chicago Kingpin Sutton Winchester's Infidelity Produces More Heirs.

She began reading the article and literally had to take a seat on a stool at her kitchen island when she hit the line about his "fathering numerous children out of secret affairs." Her stomach churned, and the nausea had nothing to do with the baby.

Tears pricked her eyes as anger rushed through her. There was only one family who wanted to stir the proverbial pot and that was the Newports. Brooks may be the ringleader in this agenda to bring down her father, but Carson and Graham were right there with him. And no doubt Graham had known all about this little media exposé when he was in her office yesterday.

Betrayal was a sickening feeling. But how could she feel betrayed? He'd never pretended to be on her side when it came to their families. They had sex, plenty of sex, but that didn't make them a couple. That didn't mean he had to be loyal to her or defend her to his family.

Eve knew very well who Graham was when she'd gotten together with him, so if blame was to be placed, she needed to point the finger at herself. She just wished she weren't getting so personally wrapped up in a man who was 100 percent wrong for her.

And what the hell was this about her father having "numerous" other children? Carson was the only child she knew of. Perhaps now that his secret son had come to light, others wanted a share of her father's holdings. The man was worth billions. Vultures would be swooping in wanting money, especially with his health failing.

An ache spread through her chest. People were picking away at her father. He was still alive, he was still in control of his will, and all of these people vying for a piece of something that didn't belong to them were seriously making her turn into someone she didn't want to be. If anyone, Graham included, wanted a fight, she'd give them one. She would protect her father, especially now, and she had no doubt her sisters would happily join her in the battle.

Eve finished her orange juice and dry toast so she could take her vitamin and keep it down. She'd learned on day one not to take that pill on an empty stomach and lately she was nauseous anyway. Whether from the pregnancy or from the constant roller coaster with the Newport men, she wasn't sure.

But if Graham expected her to show up in court and do dirty work on behalf of his brothers, she expected something in return.

She shot off a quick text to her assistant to reschedule any morning meetings. Eve already knew there were two, but both were with coworkers and could be adjusted. Nobody would second-guess the president's orders.

Once she finished with Rebecca, Eve sent Graham a text demanding an immediate meeting at her house. If he was going to play hardball, then so was she. Maybe he only knew her well in the bedroom, which was fine, but now the proverbial tables had turned. Hell, they hadn't just turned, they'd been flipped completely over.

Eve quickly showered and threw on her favorite crimson suit. The V of the jacket's lapels was just low enough to be sexy, yet high enough to be professional. She was gearing up for battle and she wanted to look her best.

She'd just applied her lip gloss when her doorbell rang. Eve's master suite was on the first floor of her Chicago mansion. Five bedrooms upstairs were available for any guests, but she rarely went up there. Maybe she'd reconsider once the baby came. She wasn't comfortable being on a separate floor from her child. Of course, at first she'd like the bassinet to be in her room so she could be close to her baby for nightly feedings.

Eve paused and pulled in a breath. That was the exact attitude she needed to keep in regards to this baby. A positive attitude, an outlook that planned for a future with her child. Because nothing would go wrong...fate wasn't so cruel as to take away a second child.

Eve gripped the door handle and gave herself a mental pep talk. The second she opened this door, she had to forget Graham was the father of her child and remember he was the man trying to ruin her father.

Opening the door, Eve stepped back and gestured for Graham to come in. They'd never been formal, and perhaps she should've had this chat on neutral territory, but she wanted to be here, on her turf. This was her day to win the battle.

The moment she closed them inside and turned to face him, her body heated. Damn it. Why did he have to slide that sultry gaze over her? When he started to step toward her, Eve held her hands up.

"This isn't a social call."

Her words didn't deter him as he closed the space between them and slid his hands over her waist, down her hips, and pulled her against him.

"I'm not in the mood to talk anyway," he replied with a slight grin.

When he went for her lips, Eve skirted out from his hold. One kiss and she'd be a goner. There was absolutely no room for hormones right now.

"What was that stunt in the paper all about?" she demanded. Certainly mentioning their family drama would douse any desire he had.

Graham shrugged. "The truth was uncovered."

"The truth," she repeated. "You expect me to believe

my father has Winchester heirs milling about Chicago? Sounds too convenient for this news to come out now."

"Our investigator turned up quite a bit on your father." Graham took one step toward her. "I don't want to argue with you about this. You have to see the truth and accept it."

With a very unladylike growl, Eve turned on her Christian Louboutin heels and made her way into the formal living room. This was one of the few rooms left in her home where they hadn't had sex. She had to focus on the fact that, even though she was expecting, this affair might be coming to an end. How could she continue when he was so adamant about destroying her family?

"I know you're trying to look out for the best interest of Carson," she started before he could say a word. "But you have to see it from my point of view, too. This is my father. I know you all hate him. I know he wasn't the nicest man to you guys."

"He's a bastard."

Crossing her arms over her chest, Eve forged on. "He's dying." Those words hurt to say, but she was fighting for him, so remaining strong was the only option. "This is not the time to drag his name through mud in the press."

"Eve—"

"No. If you want me to come to court, you better get your brother and that investigator to back the hell up." Eve hadn't realized she'd stepped forward until the tips of her shoes were touching Graham's. "I will not negotiate."

A corner of his mouth kicked up into a grin. Eve didn't want to give in to the ridiculous schoolgirl flutter in her belly; she couldn't let her emotions take over.

She was already personally involved with him, already carrying his child. She had to have some sort of hold on this…what? Relationship? Did they actually have a relationship? Was there a label that could be placed on whatever they were doing?

Not likely. They were both a mess. The only time things ever seemed to be going their way was in the bedroom. Sex had a way of making you think your world was perfectly fine. Then the cold slap of reality hit.

"If you start laughing—"

Graham snaked an around her waist and pulled her in tight. "Wouldn't dream of it."

"Don't kiss me." Did that protest sound weak? "This isn't a good idea."

He nipped at her jawline, traveled up to her ear and whispered, "Feels like a great idea." His hands curved over her backside, pulling her hips into his.

Graham's hands and mouth, his body for that matter, always seemed like the answer. He made her forget everything except for how her body seemed to zing to life. But she couldn't zing, not today.

Eve pressed her palms to his chest and eased back. "No. I won't be distracted by sex. I want your brother to back off the media attacks and insults."

The muscle in his jaw clenched. "Fine."

Narrowing her eyes, Eve shifted from his grasp. "It's that easy? You agree and know he'll just back down?"

Graham shrugged. "He's acting out of hurt, not rage. I can reason with him."

Eve wanted to believe Graham, but she didn't know Brooks very well. All she knew was how much of a mess they'd created with this secret affair. She was a fool to think their actions wouldn't trickle into their families' lives.

She turned, needing to put some space between them. Having him so close was difficult. They never just talked and she wasn't immune to his charm…much as she'd like to be.

But just as she spun away, a wave of dizziness overcame her. The room tilted before her eyes, and she reached out for any stationary surface. Everything seemed to be moving in slow motion, but Eve cringed, waiting for the hard hit to the floor.

At the last minute, her hand went to her stomach just as strong arms wrapped around her torso.

Secure against Graham's chest, Eve kept her eyes shut as she pulled in a shaky breath. The dizziness remained. It was the first time she'd experienced this pregnancy symptom.

"Okay?" he whispered in her ear.

Not really.

Eve patted the hand he had around her. "I'm okay." She hoped. "Just lost my balance."

Opening her eyes, she focused on the chair and eased from Graham's hold to have a seat. Crossing her legs, she wasn't a bit surprised when his gaze landed directly on her bare skin.

"I want to know what Brooks says and if he plans on getting your PI to ease up. You're attacking a dying man."

Graham unbuttoned his black jacket and crouched at her knees. "We're not attacking, Eve. We simply want your father to do what is right for our half brother. Surely you can see that he's entitled."

"My opinion is irrelevant."

Why was her stomach threatening to revolt? She'd been hoping to bypass this common symptom of pregnancy. She'd rather skip straight to that miracle glow so many raved about. Actually, she'd rather skip to the end when her baby was safe and healthy in her arms.

Heat washed over her. That clammy, instantly hot type of feeling that swept through you when you had the flu…or morning sickness apparently. Why now? Why did this have to happen with Graham here?

"I need to get to work," she told him, hoping he'd leave so she could be miserable all on her own. "Text me later after you talk to Brooks."

Graham's hand slid over her knee. "You're looking pale. Are you okay?"

Of course she looked pale. One minute she was fine, the next she felt like death. Why wasn't he leaving so she could battle this on her own? Why did Mr. Always-Polished-and-Sexy have to see her like this? She prided herself on being that sultry vixen he seemed to believe she was. If she tossed her toast on his Ferragamo shoes, she'd totally ruin her image.

"Eve?"

He wouldn't leave until she assured him she was fine. "Just tired," she told him, attempting to hold her head high and show as little weakness as possible, considering.

His brows dipped. "Are you coming down with something?"

Just a child.

If he didn't think she was fine, he'd never get out of here. With all the energy she had left, Eve pushed herself out of the chair, forcing Graham to come to his feet, as well. She ignored his worried look and started toward the open foyer. Time to show her guest the door before she made a complete fool of herself and he figured out she was pregnant. She couldn't tell him just yet.

"I'm running late," she lied. "You let me know how we're going to proceed after you talk to your brother."

As she reached for the door handle, his hand covered hers.

"Don't push me out."

"We both have work." Why was he so close? His familiar cologne enveloped her, but to her surprise, it didn't turn her stomach. His warm breath tickled her cheek, and any other time she'd relish the moment. Now was definitely not that time.

"I mean mentally," he corrected. Taking her by the shoulders he turned her around. "Whatever is going on with your dad, the courts and my brothers doesn't have to affect us."

Eve couldn't help the laughter that bubbled up. "You're a fool if you believe that. It has already affected us. Until today, we've never kept our clothes on when you came here."

His aqua eyes darkened. "I'm more than ready to rip that suit off you."

And he would. Graham didn't make veiled threats or empty promises. Right now, though, sex was not the answer.

Eve reached behind her and turned the doorknob. "You talk to your brother—we'll talk about the suit ripping later."

His eyes darted down to the V of her jacket, then back to her mouth.

"When I come back later, I want you to still have this on."

With a quick, promising kiss that was anything but innocent and sweet, Graham walked out. Eve shut the door at her back and rested against the wood. How could she feel so nauseous and yet still be reacting to this man?

One thing was sure: until she knew where he stood with this whole inheritance issue, and until the ultrasound came back okay, she wasn't telling him anything. They'd continue on as they had been…having sex and pretending the world around them didn't exist.

Three

"Tell me this is your idea and you're not being persuaded by a woman you should consider our enemy."

Graham eyed his brother, hating how much this paternity issue was eating away at them. They both just wanted answers…answers Sutton had, but refused to share. The man was dying. Why was he now choosing to be loyal to Cynthia? He hadn't chosen her years ago, so this sudden burst of emotion was completely out of character.

And Brooks's actions were also out of character. "This isn't you," Graham stated, eyeing his twin. "Being vindictive. I know you're reacting out of frustration and hurt, but attacking Sutton in the media isn't the way to deal with it."

Brooks grabbed a tumbler from behind the bar in his study and poured two fingers of bourbon. Gripping the glass, he stared down at the contents as if weighing his actions. Eve wasn't forcing Graham to do anything. What she said made sense, and Graham knew his brother wasn't a hateful man. Brooks was fair, honest and loyal...quite the opposite of Sutton Winchester.

"Are you sleeping with her?"

The quietly spoken question hovered in the air. Brooks didn't even look up, but Graham felt the punch to the gut just the same as if his brother had shouted the question.

"Are you going to ease off with the media?" Graham countered. "If you want Eve to cooperate, or any her sisters, we can't come at them like we're coming in for the kill."

Graham winced at his poor choice of words considering the state of the old man. But still, Nora, Grace and Eve weren't to blame. They didn't choose to be born to a man as evil and self-righteous as Sutton.

Brooks tipped back the contents and slammed his glass down onto the polished mahogany bar. "You can't be loyal to your lover and to your family. Your promiscuous ways are going to bite you in the ass."

Graham paced across the room to the floor-to-ceiling window overlooking the city below. This penthouse suite was perfect for a bachelor with a busy lifestyle. "I've gotten along just fine in my professional and personal life without your input."

"If you think getting into bed with a Winchester isn't going to do damage to our family, you're even more blindsided by lust than I first thought. Didn't we agree you'd stay away from her?"

Graham fisted his hands at his side. This was his brother, his twin. They were so similar, yet different. Brooks was the outgoing type, the go-getter, the grounded brother. Graham was definitely outgoing and a go-getter, but he also enjoyed a good time, a good woman. He'd been told often that his quiet charm won him cases and had women falling at his feet. He was just fine with that assessment.

But Graham wasn't ready to give up what he and Eve were doing. Why should he? He'd never experienced anything like Eve before and he sure as hell wasn't going to let Sutton Winchester's will come between them. He'd find a way to make everything work, play the peacemaker and get the job done. Isn't that what he excelled at?

"We didn't agree on anything," Graham stated. "Eve and I are adults. I know where my loyalties are and I won't let anything stand in the way of getting Carson what is rightfully his and getting Sutton to tell us the name of our father. But attacking him in the press isn't the way to go. We need to go in with a milder approach, for a stronger impact."

Brooks quirked a brow. "And how do you suggest doing that?"

Pulling in a breath, Graham turned from the window. "Stop the press war and put a hold on the legal proceedings."

Brooks opened his mouth, but Graham lifted his hand. "Leave this to me. We want Sutton to suffer, but not necessarily his daughters. They'll be hurt, but we can make it less of a blow to them. Sutton is still alive, so as long as he is, we go straight to him. Play hardball with him. Introduce the evidence Roman has discovered and let Sutton make a choice. Tell him we'll go to the media with all the facts, and the lineup of women claiming to have a child by him, or he can put Carson in his will as a beneficiary and give him his share. I'm demanding he give us the name of our father no matter what he chooses to do about the other issues. I refuse to back down on that."

Brooks raked his thumb back and forth on his glass of bourbon, considering all the options. Graham knew he could make this work. He knew Eve would see his side so long as they quit attacking her father. Damn, but he admired her loyalty. Graham just wished she didn't have to be so faithful to such a bastard.

"We'll try your way." Brooks came around the bar, leaned an elbow on top and shot Graham a look. "But you better remember what team you're fighting for."

Graham nodded. "I never forget who I'm fighting for. Carson and you are my top priorities."

Brooks nodded. "Good. I have another topic I want to discuss."

"Does it require more bourbon?"

With a shrug, Brooks crossed the room and took a seat on the leather sofa. "I want to talk to Sutton. In person."

Inwardly cringing, Graham glanced toward the ceiling and wondered why he was surprised. Brooks was a man on a mission. He was determined.

"You want to leave the girls out of this, fine. For now," Brooks added, aiming a hard look at his twin. "But the three of us—Carson, you, me—we're going to talk to Sutton. He's growing weaker every day and I know it may be cruel to go to him and put the pressure on, but we have to try."

Their mother had passed just months ago, taking the secret of who fathered them to her grave. Graham had no idea why she didn't tell them. At first, he'd thought for sure Sutton was their father and she'd been afraid, ashamed. But the DNA test had come back, proving Sutton had only fathered Carson, leaving Brooks and Graham confused and hurt.

While they yearned to know who their father was,

Graham was elated that old bastard wasn't his. Not to mention the fact that it had left the path wide open to seduce Eve the night of the charity ball for the children's hospital. He'd gotten the results right before the gala. Eve had shown up wearing a body-hugging gold gown. That honey-brown hair she'd piled perfectly on top of her head came tumbling down all around him when he'd finally gotten her to his penthouse. They'd barely survived the cab ride.

"I'll go with you," Graham stated, pulling himself back into the moment. He needed to be strong for his brothers, needed them to know they were a team. "Sutton isn't as strong as he used to be."

Brooks sent a malevolent grin. "That's what I'm counting on."

After a long day, exhaustion finally won. Eve nearly wept as she submerged herself in the soaker tub in her master suite. All the symptoms of her first pregnancy had come back full force: the need to rest at all times, the nausea that slammed into her with no warning, the emotions that were all over the place. Just trying to keep herself in check at work today had been trying. When someone from a newly acquired company in Barcelona offered condolences for Eve's father, she nearly lost it. Thankfully they had only been chatting on the phone and not via video conference because the tears welled up in her eyes and flowed, but Eve managed to clear her throat, offer thanks and keep her tone neutral.

Why were people acting like he was already gone? That was the part that completely gutted her. He was very much alive, though his health was failing.

Her hand slid down through the lavender-scented bubbles to rest on her flat stomach. Babies were a blessing. The innocence they injected into your life couldn't be matched. Eve wanted to tell her father, wanted to be excited about this new life, but first she had to talk to Graham.

Keeping their child from being a victim in this family war was going to be a struggle, but she refused to believe it was impossible. She knew Graham was loyal to his family—that much was obvious. But how would he react to this child? How would he treat her?

She didn't want him to hover, didn't want him to assume she wanted him as a permanent fixture in her life. She had a plan, goals, a career that was taking off better than she'd ever anticipated.

Tears pricked her eyes. She didn't want this career at the expense of her father's health, his life. She'd taken over as president when he could no longer run Elite Industries.

When her cell chimed, Eve jumped. She should've left the thing in her purse, but she'd been carrying it around like a pacifier lately…because one day she'd get the inevitable call about her father.

The cell lay on the edge of the tub surround. Eve glanced at the screen and saw Nora's name. Worried this might have something to do with her dad, Eve dried her hands off on her towel and quickly read the text.

Relief slid through her when she saw it was just a Halloween party invitation. Sounded fun. In terms of costumes, Eve could go as an overworked, worn down, emotional mess. Maybe she could go in her pajamas with bed hair to really play up the part.

Eve shot back a quick reply to tell her sister she'd be there. Asking if Graham could come as her date probably wasn't the smart thing to do.

Wait. Why was she thinking of taking him anywhere as her date? They weren't dating, they were...

Eve dropped her head against her bath pillow and groaned. She didn't know what they were exactly and that's what annoyed her. She had her life all mapped out with color-coded tabs to tell her when and where to do everything. She prided herself on being efficient, planning everything and knowing exactly what was coming her way.

What she hadn't planned on was the onslaught of desire associated with Graham Newport. One look led to another, then to flirting, which was put on hold when they both realized her father had been involved with his mother. The second they knew Sutton wasn't Graham's father, all bets had been off, all warnings from family ignored.

Eve hadn't been able to get Graham alone fast enough that first night after the children's hospital gala, and from the way he practically tore her dress off her, the feeling was mutual.

That had to have been when she got pregnant. She'd only switched her birth control a week before, thinking it was a safe time since she wasn't seeing anyone. They'd been all over each other before condoms were mentioned, but she'd assured him she was on the pill and they'd quickly had the "I'm clean" conversation.

Thinking back now, Eve realized he would blame her for this pregnancy. She'd assured him she was covered, that they were safe. Well, he could blame her all he wanted, so long as this child remained unaffected by any wrath from the Newports.

When her cell chimed again, Eve jerked from her relaxed position. Even though her body was calm and resting, her mind never shut off. She zeroed in on the screen and saw Graham's name this time. Once again, she dried her hands and checked his message, cursing herself for acting like a teenager.

Meet me at my penthouse. 30 min.

Eve gritted her teeth. While some may go for the demanding attitude, she did not. Besides, she was exhausted. If she could sleep in this warm bubble bath and not drown, she would.

Because she didn't want him to think she jumped when he texted, though she did, Eve set her phone back down without replying. There was no reason to pretend that the thought of Graham didn't have her body humming, but now she had to be realistic. She was expecting his child, and she was entering into a battle over her father... Sex couldn't be the main thread that held them together at this point.

Eve closed her eyes for just a moment, needing to push aside all the fears, all the questions, and just relax. Her doctor told her to try to take as much downtime as possible. Even if she could grab five minutes here and there, she would have to for the sake of the baby and her own health.

All too easily she could let her mind drift into the worry of whether she was carrying a healthy baby, but she wanted to focus on the positive. Would she have a boy or a girl? Would her baby have Graham's striking aqua eyes and her honey hair? One thing was for sure—this child would be strong-willed, determined and take charge, all qualities she and Graham possessed.

Eve's mind went to the nursery, and she instantly envisioned Nora and Grace helping her decorate. She could hire a decorator, but this wasn't a kitchen or bathroom job. No, Eve would take a hands-on approach to her baby's room.

The water had cooled, but Eve was still content to just lie there and relax. The quiet of her home was a welcome reprieve. She'd been in meetings all day, had made numerous decisions regarding offices in several different countries. She wasn't one to have idle time, but she had to admit this felt amazing.

She definitely had to listen to her body, and her body was tired and in need of some downtime.

"Eve."

Water sloshed as she jerked and opened her eyes to see Graham standing in the door separating her bedroom from the bath. Her heart beat out of control in her chest. He'd scared the hell out of her.

She blinked, realizing she'd fallen asleep. The water chilled her now and she shivered as she started to get up.

"What are you doing here?" she asked, stepping from the tub to reach for the towel from the heated bar. "How did you get in?"

His eyes raked over her, causing her chills to multiply for a totally different reason. "You were supposed to meet me an hour ago."

Eve wrapped herself in the towel and secured the edge between her breasts. She'd been asleep that long? Maybe she was more tired than she'd thought.

"First, I never agreed to meet you after you demanded it." She crossed her arms, rolling her eyes when his gaze dipped to her cleavage. "Second, you didn't tell me how you got into my house."

One slow step turned into two and suddenly he was in front of her. His fingertips trailed up her bare arms and shivers wracked her body. Without a word, he tipped his head to rake his lips lightly across her jawline. Eve fisted her hands at her sides. She wanted to clutch him and give in to what he was obviously offering, but she had to think with her head, too.

"You smell amazing," he muttered as his mouth continued to explore her skin. "I worried when you didn't show up."

Eve cursed herself when her head tipped back. With this man, she didn't have control over her body. The fact that he worried about her warmed her, but she couldn't think like that. They weren't in a relationship. In fact, last time she'd talked to him, they were more divided than ever.

"Graham." She pushed at his chest. "We can't do this."

Her slight shove did nothing to budge him. Wrapping his arms around her, he met her eyes.

"Brooks and I have an unspoken understanding."

Eve narrowed her gaze, waiting for him to elaborate. "And that's him keeping his investigator out of my family's business?" she asked when it was clear he wasn't going to go into detail.

"He's staying out of this for now. I don't want to talk about my brothers or your father." He nipped at her lips. "Trust me, Eve. I won't hurt you."

Trust him. Oh, how she wished she could. She had a secret she wasn't ready to reveal and *he* wanted *her* trust. And he may not intend to hurt her, but he was hell-bent on destroying her father, which in turn would most definitely hurt her.

With an expert flick, he had her towel open and gliding to the floor before she could stop him. Every intimate encounter before now had been frenzied, frantic, clothes flying and lips exploring. Something about this slow seduction in her bathroom seemed even more...intimate. Were they crossing a line or was she just reading into this?

"Stop thinking," he demanded in a whisper against her ear. "Feel, Eve. Only feel."

As if she had any other choice.

Four

He couldn't touch her, taste her enough. When she hadn't shown, he'd wondered if she was working, but then she hadn't even replied so he'd panicked like some lovestruck fool. Considering he was neither in love, nor a fool, Graham hated how he'd let his imagination run away from him.

But then he'd gotten into her place, using the security code he'd seen her type in one other time, and every worry fled. Seeing her wet in that tub full of disappearing bubbles, he'd had one mission and that was to get his body on hers as soon as possible.

But he wanted to go slow. She looked positively exhausted, not that he'd ever tell her. He wasn't an idiot when it came to women. Something about how vulnerable Eve looked resting in the bath stirred deeper feelings in him that he'd quickly tamped down, but he welcomed the rush of lust and desire.

He wanted her, he needed her and he planned on having her. Now.

Her bathroom was spacious, complete with a vanity island in the middle. Perfect. He scooped her up, sat her on the edge and stepped between her thighs.

Running his hands up her legs, over those rounded hips and over her waist, Graham wasn't surprised when she trembled beneath his touch. Trembling was a nice start, but he planned on having her writhing, panting his name.

Her fingers curled around his shoulders. "We shouldn't do this anymore," she argued, but her words came out on a whisper, betraying her true feelings.

Graham slid one fingertip between her breasts and down to her abdomen. "And why is that?"

Eve sucked in a breath as her lids lowered. Yes. That was the reaction he wanted to see. Complete surrender.

"B-because. We want…"

Graham leaned forward, his mouth trailing along the path his finger had just traveled. "Oh, yes. We want."

Her hands framed his face as she urged him back up to look at her. "We want different things," she stated, her eyes holding on to his.

"Right now I'd say we want the exact same thing."

"It's not in here that I'm worried about."

She had every reason to worry, but he meant it when he said he wouldn't hurt her. Eve was innocent, but she may feel some of the aftershock of her father's wrath. Everything that was coming down on them was a result of Sutton's actions. If anyone was hurting Eve, it was her father. Couldn't she see that?

"I told you to trust me," Graham reminded her. His hand settled between her thighs. "No more talking."

The second he touched her, she moaned. Leaning back on her hands, she offered herself up exactly the way he'd been fantasizing about all day. He'd wanted her in his penthouse with the city lights flooding into his living room, but this was fine, too. If anyone stopped by to visit, they wouldn't see his car because she'd given him a bay in the second garage in the back of the house for such eventualities. This sneaking around only amped up his desire. Graham never backed away from a challenge and he damn well wouldn't start now that Eve was having doubts.

The more his hand moved over her center, the more she let out those sexy little moans. Then she'd bite her lip as if she hadn't meant to show how much she enjoyed what they were doing.

He wanted to bite that lip.

Graham continued stroking her as he leaned forward and took her mouth with his. She instantly opened to him, matching his need with her own. And that's what made Eve so perfect in the bedroom. They had the exact same needs, they knew how to pleasure each other without a single word and neither of them expected anything beyond exactly this.

Eve tore her mouth away and shut her eyes as her entire body tightened. Watching her come undone was the sexiest experience of his entire life. She had no qualms about the noises she made, or the way her damp hair clung to the side of her cheek when she'd thrown her head to the side. This was Eve. His Eve.

No. Not his. She would never be his. This was temporary, no more.

The moment her body relaxed, Graham jerked her to the edge of the counter and unfastened his pants. He couldn't wait another minute. He needed to have her and didn't want her coming off the high she'd just had. She was everything he needed at this exact moment, and he refused to look beyond that. There was no future…not for them.

Her arms wrapped around his neck, her breasts pressed up against his dress shirt and he didn't even care that he was still technically fully clothed. That was the need he had for this woman.

Eve's ankles locked behind him and Graham bent his head to claim that precious mouth once more as he joined their bodies.

Would he ever get enough of her? He kept waiting for this new sensation to wear off, but it had been several weeks now and he was just as achy for her as ever. There was a desire inside him that he hadn't known before her. Part of him wondered if they'd still sneak around if their families weren't the Newports and the Winchesters.

When Eve arched her back, pulling her mouth from his, he took the opportunity to capture one perfect breast with his lips. His actions were rewarded with another soft moan as she gripped his shoulders. Her body quickened the pace, and he was all too eager to join her.

When she cried out his name, it was the green light he needed from her to follow her over the edge. He held her as they trembled together, held her after their bodies had cooled and then carried her into her bed.

And Graham refused to even think about why he was feeling so protective of her right now. This had nothing to do with Sutton, Brooks or Carson. His actions had nothing to do with how worn she'd looked when he'd arrived.

No, this was only sex. Nothing more. It couldn't be.

Eve finished the conference call with one of her father's established clients in Miami. Even though she was taking Elite Industries into global territory, there was still a need to keep the current clients satisfied. Now that Eve was president, she intended to not only continue building on current relationships, but also adding to their Elite family. This business was all she'd known; she was molded to fill this role and she took every bit of it seriously.

Eve popped in another peppermint and willed the flavor to calm her queasy stomach. She'd read from multiple sites—and her doctor had confirmed—that peppermint would alleviate the queasiness.

Two days had passed since Graham had shown up in her bathroom. Two days since she'd had the opportunity to tell him about the baby. But there was that whole family rivalry standing between them, driving the wedge deeper with each passing day. Graham had urged her to trust him, but that word was too easily thrown around. And what had he meant by that? He'd implored her at her weakest moment, and damn if she hadn't given in.

She wanted to trust him in more areas than just her body. She had to believe that he'd taken care of getting Brooks to stay away from the media. Dirty rumors could damage her family's reputation. Something that would start a domino effect and impact Elite Industries.

She refused to allow Graham, Brooks or Carson to destroy the only life she'd ever known. The life she needed to secure for her child.

A light tap on her door had Eve straightening in her seat. Shoving the peppermint into the side of her mouth, she called, "Come in."

The door swung open and Eve's younger sister, Nora, stepped in. Nora in all her beauty and radiance. She'd fallen in love with hotelier Reid Chamberlain and the two were deliriously happy. Reid had also taken to Nora's son and they were absolutely adorable together. Over the past several weeks, the trio had become inseparable. Eve was thrilled to see her sister find her soul mate. Being a single mother had to be so difficult, but Nora had always made life look like a breeze.

The tug on Eve's heart had her cursing herself. She wasn't jealous. Jealousy meant she wanted love, a man in her life. She didn't need, nor did she want those things. Staying focused on Elite, and now this precious baby she carried, was all she had time for. Being a single mom would be difficult, but women did it every single day and, damn it, Eve wouldn't fail. She refused to be intimidated by her fears.

"I hope you're not busy." Nora slid her plaid scarf from around her neck and dropped it, and her designer purse, onto the chair across from Eve's desk. "I was out and wanted to swing by. I haven't seen you in a few days."

Eve pasted a smile on her face. "I've been busy. I got your text about the party."

Nora beamed. "You have to be there, Eve. Grace won't tell me her costume but swears it's going to be awesome. Reid and I are thinking of either going as a Viking couple or as Superman and Lois Lane."

"Sounds fun."

Nora tipped her head to the side. "You're bringing a date, right?"

Everything inside Eve stilled. A date. Probably not, considering that she'd only been with Graham for the past six weeks. Plus, they weren't dating, not by any means. And with the way things were going in the press, there was no way in hell a Newport would be allowed inside a Winchester's home. Well, Eve's home didn't count, but her sisters would never stand for Eve and Graham being an item.

Eve cringed. An item? They'd never been on a date. They snuck around, they'd created a child and now she had to figure out a way to tell him, considering they were definitely *not* an item. So, no. No date for her at the party.

"I've been a little too busy to date." Too busy sneaking in time between the sheets with a Newport. "But I promise I'll be there in costume."

Nora rolled her eyes and dropped onto the other leather chair. "You work too hard, Eve. You need to date. There's not one man you can ask to be your date?"

Well, there was a man, but…

"I don't need a date," Eve stated, propping her elbows on her desk. "I'm happy for you and Reid, but not all of us want that happily-ever-after. I'm building Elite and taking it into the next generation. It's not easy work, so I haven't had much social life."

Okay, two days ago she'd done social life right on the vanity in her bathroom, but that wasn't necessary to point out here.

A solemn look instantly came over Nora's face. "Have you been to see Dad in the past couple days?"

Guilt ate away at Eve. She'd been busy building this company he'd left in her care. She wanted him to see how far she could take it before he…passed. But thinking about the inevitable had tears burning her eyes.

"I know," Nora whispered, swiping at her own eyes. "I'm on my way there, actually. Grace was there last night and said he was having a good day. I hope he's still the same when I get there."

Their father was in his home being nursed by the best caregivers they could find. He was a man of dignity; he didn't want his last days to be in a nursing home or hospital and Eve couldn't blame him. She and her sisters were just fine with granting him any wish he had right now.

"Have you seen Carson?" Nora asked.

Blinking away the tears, Eve shook her head. "I haven't."

Their new half brother. To find out after all this time they had a brother was definitely a blow. Sutton had been known to have affairs, or so the rumor mill had spun it over the past several years, but now there was proof. Eve wasn't quite sure how to handle Carson, but she did know he didn't deserve any of her father's holdings. He knew nothing of her father. They shared DNA only. There was no bond, there were no treasured moments. Not that any of that was Carson's fault, but Eve wasn't ready to embrace him just yet. And she certainly wasn't ready to argue over her father's assets while he was still alive.

"He's requested to see father."

Eve straightened. "What?"

"He wants to talk," Nora clarified. "We can't deny him, Eve. He has every right to see his father."

Before he dies. The unspoken words hovered between them, driving home the point that their father was human. He'd cheated on their mother, now he was dying. He shouldn't have to keep paying for his sins, and he shouldn't have his name tarnished when his days were numbered.

And that brought Eve's thoughts right back to Graham. Was Carson requesting to see their father because he was trying to gain ammunition for their media campaign? Every protective instinct welled up inside her.

"It's a bad idea," Eve told her sister. "He could be plotting with Brooks and Graham."

"I don't think that's what he's doing. Brooks hired a private investigator. If they want to dig up Dad's past, we can't stop them and I highly doubt Dad will give up any skeletons in his closet on his own at this point."

Nora's words sank in, and actually made sense. Still…

Graham had wanted her to trust him. Those words kept bouncing back and forth in her head and she truly wished she knew what the answer was.

"What does Grace think?" Eve asked.

Nora lifted a slender shoulder. "She's fine with letting Carson in. She's not as cynical as you are, though."

"I prefer the term *realistic*," Eve countered. With a heavy sigh, she nodded. "Fine. But one of us needs to be in the room."

Nora nodded. "I agree. I'll let Carson know and we can set up a time."

"Wait." Eve pressed her palms to her desk and eased back in her seat. "Have you asked Dad?"

"He wants to see his son."

Those simple words were what this all boiled down to. Carson was Sutton's son. The final say belonged to their father and he would never turn away family…especially a newly discovered son.

"Let me know when and I'll make sure I'm there," Eve told her sister.

Nora got to her feet and pulled her scarf back around her neck. After adjusting her navy cardigan, she grabbed her handbag and hooked the strap on her forearm.

"Try not to work so hard," Nora said, a soft, caring tone lacing her voice. "You're looking tired and you have assistants who can help."

Eve laughed. "Wow, thanks for the confidence booster."

Circling the desk, Nora embraced her. "I say this because I love you. Don't let work rule your life like Dad did. Take time for yourself. Who knows? You may change your mind about that happily-ever-after but find your Prince Charming has passed you by while you were stuck in your office."

Graham's face instantly came to mind, but he was far from Prince Charming. He was more the evil villain with charm and charisma that made him impossible to resist. Besides, she didn't need anyone to rescue her—prince or peasant.

"I promise to get more rest," Eve assured her as she eased back. "Now, go on and see Dad. Tell him I'll be by later."

Once Nora was gone, Eve fell back into her seat. She was exhausted, and it was showing. She was going to have to take better care of herself. Her life wasn't just about her anymore. She had an innocent child to care for, and she would do anything to keep her child safe.

Reliving the nightmare of losing a baby wasn't an option. But fear had a crippling hold over her. Between the worry of miscarriage and telling Graham, she had some legitimate concerns. Would this be a replay of the last time? Granted, before she'd thought herself in love. She wasn't as naive this time. But she still wanted Graham to be accepting of their child, wanted him to take part in the baby's life.

She had to tell him. Tonight. There was no easy way to drop this bomb and she wasn't a coward. No matter what happened after she told him, she'd be just fine.

Five

She'd avoided him for two days. Two. Damn. Days.

Graham had gone to bat for her, going against his brothers, and Eve had dodged his texts and calls. The fact that he'd thrown away all common sense when Eve had pleaded with him to not ruin her father spoke volumes. That's something someone in a relationship would do. They weren't in a relationship. They had sex. Private, sneaking-around, amazing sex.

Well, they had been. But when he'd been at her place and they'd been intimate, she'd turned down any further advances the morning after. Did she want to call this affair quits? Too bad. He wasn't ready and her body's response to his touch told him otherwise. Not that he would beg. Hell, no. And he didn't want a relationship, but he certainly wasn't ready to end this.

Even if he wanted something more, he was too swamped with being a partner in his law firm to feed any type of relationship. Sex was a stress reliever and Eve was definitely on the same page, though she may have been fighting herself on this matter. She was just as vigilant in her career and wanted nothing more. So, when she ignored his texts, it shouldn't have bothered him...but it did. Eve wasn't one to play games, and if she wanted to put on the brakes, he imagined that she'd just tell him so.

Then, as if she hadn't been silent for two days, she texted him to say she needed to talk.

He didn't like the sound of that. The whole we-need-to-talk thing was such a veiled subject and he didn't like how it eluded to the fact that she may want to call this quits.

Eve possessed every quality he'd ever wanted in a lover. She was career driven—so she wasn't monopolizing his time—she was passionate and damn if she didn't challenge him...in bed and out.

He'd never cared when another woman blew off his calls, though that rarely happened. The few times it had, he'd moved on. No worries. Yet with Eve, he wasn't going to have her call it quits without seducing her one last time. If she wanted to move on, he wouldn't stop her, but he sure as hell would give her a send-off she'd never forget.

Just the thought of getting his hands on her again had Graham hurrying to get to her office. He'd purposely waited until it was good and dark before setting out. With the skies darkening earlier this time of year, he was able to log in more hours with her.

Damn. He shouldn't keep track of the hours he'd spent with her. He should be going with the flow in this casual hookup arrangement. But he was human and

Eve turned him on like no one else ever had. So what if he wasn't ready to put the brakes on just yet?

Graham wasn't oblivious to the fact that he hadn't seen anyone else since that night at the ball when he'd seduced Eve. Had he ever gone this long with the same woman? Other women would think things were getting serious, but not Eve. She knew the boundaries. Besides, even if they wanted to make this something more permanent, no way in hell would their family feud allow that to happen. The last thing he wanted was his brothers or her sisters in their business.

No, it was all about sneaking and seducing. That was the name of the game. He'd been looking for a label and he'd found one. Simple as that.

So what if he had a designated bay in her second garage all to himself. He refused to believe this was serious. Hiding his car when he visited her at her house was merely precautionary, that was all. If one of her sisters or assistants stopped by, he could easily hide in one of the rooms of her sprawling mansion. A car would be a bit harder to explain if it was out in the open.

But now he was at her office, parking in a public garage, so there. Why the hell was he arguing with himself? He'd rather concentrate on Eve and how quickly he could have her on her desk panting his name. Ironically, she was the perfect distraction from the investigation and beating his head against the wall where Sutton was concerned.

Graham took the elevator up to her office. Nobody would be there this time of the evening, and Eve wouldn't have requested he come if her assistant or any other staff members were hanging around. Their offices had quickly become the go-to choice for late-night rendezvous.

As he made his way down the wide, tiled hall, the intense, familiar scent of Eve's jasmine perfume enveloped him. Would he ever tire of smelling it? When she'd wrapped herself around him after her bubble bath the night before last, he'd inhaled that sweet scent. Everything about Eve was a punch to his gut. The desire for her hadn't lessened one bit—if anything, he only craved her more. That was dangerous territory to venture into, but he was in complete control. He had to be.

Her office door was slightly cracked, a sliver of light slashing the dark floor tiles. Without bothering to knock or give a warning, he pushed open the door and found her at her computer. As Graham moved closer, he realized she was staring at her screen, scrolling with her mouse, but she didn't seem to be focusing in on any one thing.

She hadn't said a word, hadn't even turned to acknowledge his presence. As he came behind her chair, he glanced at the screen. Photo after photo of Eve with her sisters and their father in various places and times continued to scroll up the monitor. Sometimes she'd stop, scroll back down, then commence to go up again. Eve was a brilliant photographer. The images around the entire floor of her office proved that. She claimed her photography was a hobby, but he knew full well if she ever opted out of the real estate industry, she could turn pro without fail.

Graham swallowed. Whatever she'd called him here for had to do with that old bastard. Talk about a mood killer.

When she didn't say anything, Graham surveyed her spacious office overlooking the city. The floor-to-ceiling windows showed off a brilliant Chicago skyline dotted with lights. As he turned, he noted the built-in bookshelves on the far wall were full of books, mostly on photography and real estate. When Eve was passionate about something, she put her whole self into it. He could attest to that.

But the fact that he admired and cared about her hobbies was even more dangerous than having his physical desire escalate. Getting too personal meant setting down roots. He wasn't about to set down roots with any woman. Ever. Let alone a woman whose family bitterly rivaled his.

Graham walked back to the desk, setting his hip on the edge beside her chair. The picture she'd homed in on now was of a smiling Sutton surrounded by his daughters. This had to have been taken recently. Eve wore that killer red suit she'd had on a few days ago and Sutton wasn't looking well. But he actually smiled in these pictures. Graham didn't want to see his old rival as a human being capable of such emotions.

"I'm almost done," she told him, without turning. "I have a few more to upload."

Graham didn't want to see Sutton's face on the screen another second, especially not with Eve smiling back from the picture. Guilt twisted the knife in his chest. He had no right to hate the relationship between Eve and her father. He had no right to…what? Be jealous? No way was he jealous. That was absolutely…

Damn it. Maybe he was jealous. How did a man like Sutton deserve love and loyalty from someone so caring and trusting as Eve? Sutton was a bastard and that he'd managed to raise three amazing women was a miracle.

Sutton may have been a conniving jerk, but he'd made the right choice putting Eve in charge of his company. There was no one better to run Elite Industries. She had a vision, something fresh that would drive the company into the next several decades. She was brilliant, independent and charming. She had all the traits that would make Elite expand in the exact ways she wanted it to because she refused to take no for an answer, and she refused to fail.

"I saw my father today." Her soft words cut into the silence. "Grace and Nora happened to be there at the same time. Dad knows I always have my camera on hand, so he wanted family pictures in case…"

Graham didn't like that vulnerable, lost tone in her voice. Selfish as Graham was, and as much as he loathed Sutton, he wasn't going to let Eve grieve alone. The loss of a parent was still too fresh, too painful for him. Nobody should have to face such emptiness on their own.

Squatting down beside her chair, he gripped the arms and turned her to face him. Finally, her bright green gaze landed on his. "It's good you have these pictures. Many family members don't get to say goodbye, let alone capture the final memories."

Moisture gathered in her eyes as she nodded. When one lone tear slipped down her cheek, Graham reached to swipe it away. But his hand lingered on her cheek, his thumb sliding across the darkness beneath her eye.

"You're tired," he said before he could catch himself. "Maybe you should go home and rest."

"I'm fine. It's only seven. I wouldn't sleep now, anyway."

Stubborn. Hardheaded. So much like himself, he felt as if he were looking in a mirror. Still, he wouldn't let her work herself to death and that had nothing to do with their intimacy. He wouldn't want to see anyone this exhausted and worn down.

"What time did you come in today?"

She pursed her lips and looked away. "I think five. Or maybe it was five yesterday and six today. I can't remember right now."

He clenched his teeth and counted backward from ten. She was pushing herself too hard and someone needed to intervene.

"You have spreadsheets scheduling your bathroom breaks at work and you can't recall when you came in or how long you worked today?"

Eve's sharp gaze collided with his. "So?"

"You're working too hard. You're going to break if you don't slow down."

Narrowing her eyes, Eve stood up, but Graham didn't get out of her way. "That's the second time today someone has said that to me. My apologies if I look tired. I'm in negotiations with a company we want to take over, my sister is pressuring me to bring a date to some silly costume party and my father is dying. I'll try to look less exhausted tomorrow and double up on concealer."

Her words sank in and Graham got to his feet and reached up to cup her shoulders. Closing the miniscule gap between them, he brought her body flush against his.

"I'll be your date." Because no way in hell was another man going on her arm.

Eve blinked away her unshed tears. "You can't be my date. Nora and Reid are hosting the party at my dad's. You think they're just going to let a Newport onto the Winchester estate?"

Graham shrugged. "I'll wear a mask and a great costume. Introduce me as whoever you want. But I'm your date."

"No," she said with a shake of her head. "I'll go alone."

So long as no schmuck was escorting her, Graham

was fine. Still, part of him wanted to go with her, but she was right: that was ridiculous thinking. They weren't a couple, so why pretend to be one? He hated how his instant go-to idea was to be with her as her date. They didn't date. Sneaking around after dark, parking their cars where they couldn't be seen and sending texts in code was not dating.

Circling back around to the original topic, Graham asked, "What are you doing to yourself?" Sliding his thumbs beneath her eyes, he let out a sigh.

Eve blinked but remained silent. Something was going on with her. He wasn't sure what, but he wasn't leaving until he knew. Maybe it was the stress from her father's illness and from buying another company, just as she'd said. But could it be something else?

"If you want to end things, just say so."

Her eyes widened as she shifted back slightly. "What?"

Graham dropped his hands. He couldn't touch her and not want her, but he'd be damned if he begged. "If you want to bring this arrangement to a close, that's fine."

The color drained from her face. She started to step back, but hit her chair and lost her balance. Graham reached around to grab her, but she pushed away. Struggling out of his hold, she ended up moving around him and putting a good bit of distance between them.

"That's fine?" she repeated. "If you're that detached from this…whatever this is, then leave."

Careful of his next words, Graham slid his hands into his pockets. Eve was clearly on edge and his blasé words hadn't helped. He hadn't expected her to be so upset. Still, this was useful information to have. Clearly she wasn't calling him here to break things off.

He closed the gap between them, following her when she took two more steps back. Those expressive green eyes remained locked onto his, but her never-ending steely determination had her jaw clenched, her nostrils flaring.

"I'm not leaving," he finally replied. She may try to be fierce, but she looked as if she'd break at any moment. "Tell me why you called me here."

She blinked once, then shook her head. "It can wait."

When she attempted to skirt him once more, Graham reached out to grip her biceps. "Stop running. Tell me, Eve. I haven't heard from you in two days and I haven't felt you beneath me in just as long. What's going on if you're not ending things?"

She continued to stare at him as she bit the inside of her cheek. Whatever she was gearing up to tell him must be something major. Obviously she wasn't going to tell him to take a hike, but what else was there? Did she have news on Sutton she was afraid to share?

Eve pulled in a shaky breath, her body trembling beneath his hands. She was scared. Whatever was going on had her terrified because he'd never seen Eve this run-down, this unsure of her words.

"Just tell me," he stated, sounding harsher than he intended. "My mind is spinning and I have no clue what you want to tell me."

"I've rehearsed this in my head, but now that you're here, I can't find the words."

Worry coursed through him. They may not be a serious item, but Graham wanted to reassure her he wasn't some unfeeling ass. He framed her face and nipped at her lips.

"Whatever you need to tell me, we'll deal with it.

Are you sick? Is it something with your dad you think I won't care about? What, Eve?"

Her dark lashes rested against her cheeks as she let out a sigh. Finally, she lifted her lids, and her eyes locked onto his.

"I'm pregnant."

Six

Graham didn't release her. He couldn't even think, so getting his brain in gear to let go wasn't happening.

Pregnant. How could one word cause such panic and uncertainty? And why did this room seem to be closing in on him?

His hands fell from her arms. Graham raked his fingers through his hair and attempted to pull his scattered thoughts together. Over the past six weeks they'd been intimate so many times. He had no idea when this had happened. All he recalled was that first time when they'd been in such a rush and she'd assured him she was on birth control.

"Say something," she whispered.

"Did you plan this?"

Eve jerked as if she'd been slapped by his words. "I would never do that."

Graham shrugged. "How do I know? Despite the past month and a half, I don't know you that well."

Eve's cheeks pinkened with rage the instant before her hand came up in a flash and struck his face. The crack seemed to echo in the open office. Graham's head jerked, but he didn't reach up to touch the sting.

"You can't blame me for asking," he countered, refusing to feel sympathy despite the hurt in her eyes. "I assume this baby is mine."

Her eyes narrowed. "I haven't been with anyone else since we started seeing each other."

He firmly believed that. Eve was too busy at work for fun and he occupied her evenings, save for the past couple. Still, a paternity test would be required considering he had quite a padded bank account. Someone like Eve wouldn't be after a man's money, though. But he would be smart about this. And being smart, he wouldn't bring up the test right now or his other cheek may feel the same sting.

"I don't expect anything from you," she went on, crossing her arms over her chest. "In fact, maybe we should bring what's between us to a close and focus on what's best for the baby."

Graham didn't know what he wanted right now. His entire world had been flipped and control had never been so out of his reach. But he didn't want to just end things with Eve, especially now.

"That won't change the situation." Graham struggled to keep his distance, but he needed to play his cards right. "I will be here every step of the way, Eve. Whether you want me around or not. This child is a Newport and I never turn my back on my responsibilities."

"Is that what I am now?" she asked. "A responsibility?"

So maybe he hadn't chosen his words as wisely as he'd intended. "You're the mother of my child."

He watched her shoulders relax as relief slid over her. But then Eve blinked and her gaze darted away. Was she worried he'd reject her and the child? Didn't she know him at all?

Of course she didn't. He'd even thrown that fact in her face moments ago. They truly didn't know each other. And now they were going to be parents.

Brooks and Carson were going to…hell, he didn't know what their reaction would be. But for now, he was keeping this information to himself.

What would Sutton say? Once the man found out his responsible daughter was pregnant by his enemy, would he change his mind and give up the secrets he was keeping about Graham and Brooks's paternity? A plan started forming in Graham's mind.

"Have you told your sisters?"

Eve shook her head. "I haven't told anyone. I… I'm not sure they'll take this very well."

Most likely not. And he knew Sutton wouldn't take it well, either. The man probably had higher hopes for his daughter and new president of Elite Industries than having a child by a Newport. But Graham was serious when he said he'd be there through everything. He may not have planned on having a child with anyone, let alone Eve, but he would never turn his back on an innocent child…especially his own.

A possessive streak shot through him as he stared back at Eve. This was why she looked so tired, why she was likely running herself ragged. She was scared of the pregnancy, worried about the backlash when the rest of their world discovered the truth. Again, he would be there. Nobody would hurt his child or the child's mother, no matter what their relationship status was.

"Let's keep this between us until we know how to deliver the news."

Eve nodded. Her arms went around her waist, as if to somehow protect their child. "I don't want our baby to receive backlash from either of our families. No matter what's going on or not going on between you and me, please promise me you'll protect our child."

The urgency in her tone had Graham stepping toward her. "I promise."

The vow came easily because he'd walk through hell to keep his child safe. Odd how he'd only known about this baby for mere minutes and already his priorities had changed. And one thing was certain: his child would have his last name, even if he had to marry Eve.

The idea made him cringe. Not that being married to Eve would be terrible, but he didn't want to be married to anybody. Still, some marriages were made of lesser things. At least he and Eve understood the importance of each other's work and they would both love this child.

"When is your doctor's appointment? I want to go."

Eve shook her head. "That isn't necessary."

"I'm going."

Chewing on her bottom lip, she nodded. "Fine. It's next week. I went the other day for initial blood work. He said everything looked fine and gave me vitamins and my due date."

As Graham listened to her, he was already thinking about the time when the baby would arrive. All work would have to be put on hold. No way in hell was he missing the birth of his child.

His child.

Unable to stop himself, Graham reached out and

eased her arms aside before placing his flat palm against her stomach. To even think there was a life growing inside of her, a life he'd helped create, absolutely humbled him.

Eve stilled beneath him. When he glanced up to her face and caught sight of her wide eyes, he swallowed and stepped back.

"I have no idea how to act," he admitted, shoving his hands in his pockets. "I don't want to upset you, but I want you to be aware how serious I'm going to take this."

"Honestly, I just want to figure out how to make sure our families won't turn against us or this child. That's all I care about. Anything between us doesn't matter anymore."

A point he wholeheartedly disagreed with, but his actions would speak for him over time. He wasn't going anywhere, and keeping Eve close would be simple. No way was another man moving in. Eve and this child were his. Period.

Graham made sure that if there was something he wanted, nothing stood in his way. He may not want a family in the traditional sense, but letting Eve just put up a barrier between them was out of the question. His desire for her hadn't diminished one bit. In fact, knowing she carried his child was the biggest turn-on he'd ever experienced.

"How are you feeling?" He hadn't even asked her. He'd jumped straight into wondering if she'd trapped him, to asking about paternity, to wanting to feel her still-flat stomach.

"Fine."

The clenched half smile betrayed her. Graham tipped

his head. "You can't lie to me, Eve. You're exhausted—you admitted that earlier. But how else are you feeling? Does the doctor think you can keep working all these crazy hours or should you be resting?"

She stared at him, not answering, not even attempting to answer. Her eyes welled up once again and Graham waited. What had he said wrong? He had a million questions, but right now he wanted to know how she was feeling.

"I know this is your child, but..." Eve's words died away as she turned her back to him. Graham reached for her shoulders, but pulled back at the last minute.

The only sound in the room was Eve's shaky breathing. The lights of the Chicago skyline spilled in from the window. They'd shared some intense experiences in this office, but nothing compared to the intensity of this moment.

"Why do you care?" she whispered.

"Because you're carrying a Newport." Damn, that sounded heartless. Why was that his first response? Why did he have to sound so cold?

Because he couldn't let himself feel anything else for Eve. He had to remain detached. Their families made the Montagues and the Capulets look like besties and he couldn't cross the emotional boundary with her. Granted, having a child together was crossing the point of no return, but that didn't mean they had to set up and play house together. Plenty of children had parents who didn't live together. Whatever the arrangement, Graham wouldn't let his child ever want for love, stability or a solid foundation.

Squaring her shoulders, Eve turned and swiped her damp cheeks. "Well, I have some emails to send. I'll text you all the specifics about my doctor's appointment, but if anyone sees us coming and going—"

"You're dismissing me?" Unbelievable.

Her eyes didn't hold the heat or the light he was used to seeing. Now she stared at him as if he were merely a business associate. "I have work. Surely you understand."

"I understand you're trying to keep some ridiculous wall between us." Anger bubbled within him. He didn't know what he wanted her to do or say, but he sure as hell didn't want this unfeeling Eve. "I'll be at the damn appointment if I have to sneak in the back way."

Eve nodded and moved around him to settle back in at her desk. She wiggled her mouse until her screen came back to life. And right there was Sutton's face smiling back, with his hand holding Eve's. Graham had not only been dismissed, he was being mocked by a man who wasn't even in the room.

"We'll talk later," he promised, heading toward the door. "Don't believe for one second this changes what we had going, Eve. I still want you, and if you're honest, you want me, too. That passion isn't something that can be turned off."

Her hands froze as she gave him a sidelong glance.

"I'll give you the space you want," he went on, gripping the door handle. "But you better get ready because I won't be far and I won't wait long."

With that vow, Graham stormed out. *Game on.* Graham wasn't concerned about how their families would react to the baby. He refused to allow anything other than complete and utter love and acceptance. No, what Graham needed to concentrate on was the fact he wasn't done with Eve, in the personal sense that had nothing to do with their child.

And if she thought he was going to walk away from her or their child, well, she was about to find out that a Newport always got what he wanted.

Seven

"What the hell is wrong with you?" Carson threw his cards down onto the green felt and leaned back in his seat. "You're moping like a woman."

Graham wasn't in the mood for company, let alone playing poker and chatting with his brothers. But when Carson had stopped by earlier, he'd apparently picked up on Graham's doldrums right away and called for reinforcements, texting Brooks to come, as well. Now here they all were.

Graham proudly laid down his royal flush and raked in the chips. Maybe he wasn't in the mood, but he'd been on a winning streak. After sorting the chips by color and putting them away, Graham got to his feet and took his empty tumbler back to the built-in bar.

"I'm done here." Graham refilled his glass with his favorite bourbon. "I'll go put on *The Maltese Falcon*."

They had an ongoing tradition that stretched back

to a time when they lived with their mother and Gerty. Gerty introduced them to the Hollywood classics and insisted they watch them together. To this day, they continued to honor her tradition.

Graham missed her. She was a strong woman, a woman who refused to let life knock her down, and she'd do anything to help others. His mother had been just as strong. A lump formed in his throat as he slid his fingers over the remote to start the movie. Each day seemed to be better than the last, but he knew he'd always feel the void from the loss of Gerty and his mother.

Graham had so many questions now that his mother was gone. She'd been single, pregnant and scared when she'd come to Chicago. Had she even told Graham and Brooks's father that they existed? Had he knowingly turned his back on her or did he have no clue he'd fathered twin boys?

These were questions Graham may never have an answer to. Cynthia took her secrets to her grave. The truth would be something he and Brooks would have to uncover all on their own. At least they had ruled out Sutton as their father, which was a blessing in itself. But the bastard knew the truth and was dodging them. His time was limited, which meant that Graham had to take drastic action if he wanted answers.

The idea of using Eve to obtain the information had his stomach in knots, but she was carrying his child and if Graham had to let that news slip to Sutton in order to get information…well…

Graham heard his brothers behind him as they came into the home theater. But his mind wasn't on the movie or even the idea of his father out in the world somewhere. His mind was on Eve. The parallel between her and his mother's experiences wasn't lost on him, but there was a huge difference. Graham planned on being part of this child's life. Eve wouldn't be alone, she wouldn't have to worry about facing this without support.

"He's still got that look," Brooks muttered. "He won every damn hand and still looks like he's ready to punch the wall."

"Your face would do," Graham replied without glancing over. "I like my walls intact."

"If you're going to fight, at least pause the movie," Carson interjected. "I know we just watched this one a few weeks ago, but it's still my favorite."

Graham shook the ice cubes around in his glass. "I'm not going to hit anything, but if you two keep discussing my mood, I'm likely to change my mind."

Graham turned the volume up until the surround-sound speakers hidden around the room were blaring. He'd had enough of the chitchat and getting in touch with his feelings.

There was no mention of Sutton tonight, which was a relief. Brooks had his PI on the hunt for their father, and apparently there was still no news. Maybe they could just have a regular night like they used to. Something bland and boring. Graham never thought he'd wish for such a thing, but lately his life seemed to be heading in about twelve different directions.

His cell vibrated in his pocket. Setting his glass on the table next to his theater recliner, Graham slid the phone out and held it down to his side so his brothers couldn't see. The screen lit up with Eve's name. He wasn't going to reach out to her just yet. He wanted to leave her wondering when he'd be back, when he'd make a move. There was an ache in him that drove him insane and he wanted her to be just as achy, just as needy.

He quickly read her message.

Dr. McNamera November 17 9:00

That was all. Nothing more, nothing personal. The dynamics of their relationship had changed. Because he was apparently a masochist, he scrolled through their previous messages. Flirting, hookup times, codes for what they would do to each other once they were alone. He shifted in his seat as he recalled doing exactly those things.

It was late, but that didn't mean she wasn't at her office. She worked even on weekends, not that he could fault her because he knew that drive to stay on top of the career you'd worked so hard for. But he wanted to see her, needed to see her.

For the first time in…ever, Graham willed this movie to end. He loved spending time with his brothers, valued their special bond, but right now he had other plans.

Plans that involved Eve, a dark room and no interruptions from the outside world. He didn't want her to get swept away into the fear of being pregnant. He wanted her relaxed and he knew exactly how to make that happen.

Intending to make it through the next couple hours, Graham opted not to refill his bourbon. Two glasses were enough because he wanted his head on straight.

"You all up for more poker?" Brooks asked as the credits rolled.

"I need to get home," Carson replied, coming to his feet. "I don't have to spend my nights looking at you two anymore."

Carson had found love. Good for him. Graham wasn't jealous, he just didn't believe in such things. Still, whatever Carson and Georgia had together was genuine. The way they looked at each other, the way they were always looking out for the other was a testament to their deep bond.

"Can't say I blame you," Brooks countered. "You're a lucky man."

Brooks wanted that home life. He wanted the wife, the kids, all of that. Graham wanted to nail this case he was working on and get Eve to come around to seeing they didn't need to cool it in the sheets simply because they'd created a child. "I actually need to run an errand," Graham chimed in.

Both brothers turned to look his way. Brooks smirked. "Really? What's her name?"

Graham busied himself putting the remote away and taking his glass back to the bar, which was just off the theater room. His brothers followed him. No way were they going to leave him alone.

Empty glass in hand, he whirled around. "It's just work. Relax. I'm in the middle of a big case. That's all I can say."

They both stared at him, clearly not believing the lie. With a shrug, he turned to the bar and started stacking the glasses and returning the bottles to the shelves on the wall.

"I'm out," Carson said on a sigh. "I'd rather be home with Georgia than try to figure out what Graham is being so cryptic about."

Fine by him. One down. One to go.

From the corner of his eye, Graham saw Brooks eyeing him, arms crossed over his chest. The sound of Carson headed down the hall, the sound of his footsteps growing softer before eventually disappearing. Now that Carson was gone, Graham waited for the accusations from his twin.

"Whatever you're smirking about, get it off your chest," Graham finally said, turning to face Brooks.

With a shrug, he replied, "Nothing in particular. Just curious as to why you're rushing off. I'm sure you could do anything work related from here. I know you have your laptop at the ready at all times. And I'm sure you know whatever case you're working on like the back of your hand without having to look at any files."

Graham hadn't gotten to the top at such a young age by depending on anyone else. Every case, every file, every opponent in the courtroom was filed away in his mind. He knew every detail backward and forward. He studied his rivals and found their weaknesses so he could annihilate them when they came face-to-face. So Brooks was right, but no way was Graham going to admit such a thing.

"You don't have to know every detail of my personal life," Graham fired back. Okay, maybe that was harsh, but right now, he wanted to get to Eve. "Are we done here?"

Brooks blew out a sigh. "For now. I'll let you have your little secret, but all secrets come out eventually. Just ask Sutton."

The jab hit too close to home. Yes, Sutton's secret baby, aka Carson, had taken nearly three decades to come to the surface. Graham highly doubted Eve's secret would last three months. Soon both families would know that the Winchesters and the Newports were going to be bound together for life.

That thought had Graham reevaluating everything. Eve had every right not to put his name on the birth certificate. She had every right to fight him for custody. She'd lose, but that wasn't the point. The point was, he refused to let his child come into this world in the midst of a feud.

So now Graham had to show her who he really was. Eve had to see him as a compassionate, loving man who would do anything for his child. She had to see that working together was the best thing for all of them. Because he refused to allow any other man to come in and take away this little family. Love didn't have to be a factor. Graham held the power here, and he would get Eve to marry him, ensuring their child carried the Newport name. A marriage based on sexual chemistry was more than enough for him to rethink saying his "I dos."

And that was why Graham was even more eager to get to her house. Soon Eve would see just how perfect they were together.

Eight

Seven o'clock. Most nights she'd still be at the office, but it was Saturday so Eve had opted to come home. She really needed to cut out the weekends for a while. She was exhausted, and her doctor had told her to listen to her body. Well, she was listening and her body was telling her she needed to get rid of these heels and kill the suit. Yoga pants and a tee sounded pretty good right now. Oh, and a ponytail.

She rarely was off her game. Even at home she was always professional because she often did video meetings and had to look the part. Sure, the other day she had on yoga pants and bunny slippers beneath her desk, but she'd put on makeup, earrings and a suit jacket. Boom. She so owned this corporate world.

She'd nearly cried with relief after she washed her face and pulled her hair back. Now that she was comfortable, she had a little boost of energy...and an extremely empty stomach. She'd had an early lunch to work around meetings, but she seriously needed to keep some snacks in her office at work. Her assistant would've gladly gone and gotten her anything, but Eve had her assistant doing so much lately with the acquisition of the Australian company, Eve hated to even ask for a pack of crackers.

Maybe she'd lie in bed, gorge on food and watch a movie on Netflix. A date with herself? Sounded heavenly and completely relaxing. Just what the doctor ordered.

When someone knocked at the back door, Eve nearly cried. Only one person came and went via the French doors overlooking the outdoor living area. The door was conveniently located by the garage Graham used.

She peered down at her attire and shrugged. He'd seen her in her suits, in a ball gown and in her birthday suit, but he'd never seen her in sloppy, I-want-to-be-left-alone mode.

Circling the kitchen island and bypassing the breakfast nook, she reached the French doors. Only the soft glow from the motion lights illuminated Graham's broad frame, slashing a streak of light across one side of his face. His eyes pierced her straight through the glass. There was an intensity to this man that her body couldn't deny. She hated how, even now, especially now, she didn't want to deny him anything. But if she didn't watch out, she would end up hurt. Right now, she had to focus on her baby.

Flicking the lock, she opened one of the doors. Because she knew he wasn't just here for a quick visit, she stepped aside and let him in.

The second Graham was inside, she clicked the lock back into place. When she turned, his eyes raked her, as they always did. She shivered, but was too tired to even appreciate her instant arousal. There had to be some sort of stop button where this physical relationship was concerned. Shouldn't they focus on how to make this parenting thing work? The time for selfish desires and needs had come to an end.

"If you're here for—"

He held up a hand. "I'm not."

When he took a step forward, closing the gap between them, Eve waited for his familiar touch. But he simply held her gaze and offered a gentle smile. "I'm here for strictly innocent reasons."

Eve laughed, waiting for him to deliver the rest of the punch line. When he only quirked a brow, she sobered. "Innocent? Honey, you don't have an innocent bone in your body."

Honey? Had she seriously just used that term? Exhaustion had obviously stolen her common sense.

"I don't mean to be rude, but really. Why are you here?"

Graham took her elbow and guided her through the house. Her house. As if he owned the place. And she was allowing this to happen. Then he led her up the stairs, toward her bedroom, and pulled back the pristine white duvet on her king-size four-poster bed. Eve darted her eyes between the inviting bed and the confusing man.

"Okay, what's going on?"

Graham took her hand and ushered her into bed. "I had no plans until I got here. But now that I see you're practically swaying on your feet, we're going to relax."

"We?" Eve slid into bed because the temptation was far too great for her to fight.

"That's right." Graham picked up the remote, hit a few buttons. The flat screen slid up from the entertainment island that separated the bed from the sitting area. "I'm going to watch a classic with you."

Okay. So if she had all of this straight in her head, Graham had just appeared at her back door not looking for sex, but to watch a movie and...snuggle?

Eve continued to stare as Graham as climbed into bed beside her and began studying her remote. After several minutes of muttering under his breath—something about his law degree being useless—he finally figured it out. Instantly the room filled with music as the movie popped up, and Eve had to brace herself. He was legitimately here to watch a movie. They were in her bed...completely clothed.

"You're still staring and you're going to miss this opening," Graham said without looking her way.

Her gaze went to the large screen and she instantly recognized *An Affair to Remember*. It was one of her favorite movies. But how did he know? They'd certainly never discussed such personal things.

"Why are you doing this?"

Graham sighed, paused the movie and glanced her way. Those striking blue eyes pierced her heart. But she couldn't have her heart involved, not with him, not now. Her emotions were simply all over the place. She couldn't act on any temporary feelings.

"I love old movies. I want to do absolutely nothing right now but watch one with you. We both work too hard, and now we're having a baby. Maybe it's time we get to know each other."

Without another word, he took the movie off pause, turned the volume up and reached for her hand. The detail-oriented nerd in her wanted to know what was going on. Was this a date? Albeit a warped version of one. Was this some ploy to get her to fall for him? If so, he was doing a damn good job. Did he truly want to get to know her?

Eve attempted to concentrate on the movie, but between exhaustion and the way Graham's thumb drew lazy patterns over the back of her hand, she was having a difficult time.

What was Graham up to? The man was ruthless in a courtroom, if his reputation around Chicago was any indicator. He could've easily had her undressed and beneath him had he tried, because denying him was nearly impossible. Yet he seemed all too happy to lie here, hold her hand and do absolutely nothing.

Graham Newport was playing some sort of game and if she didn't figure out the rules soon, she was going to find herself on the losing side. And that was not an option because she'd end up hurt. Eve had been dealt enough by the hand of grief to last a lifetime and she wasn't looking for more.

Graham knew she'd fallen asleep within the first ten minutes of the movie. Her hand had gone lax beneath his and she even began to snore quietly. He found himself watching her and smiling. Okay, this little plan of his had backfired in a major way.

He'd come here for one reason—to start his plan of seduction. Getting her to trust him, to maybe even develop stronger feelings for him, was a must for making sure they came to a mutual understanding where their child was concerned. And when he asked her to be his wife, he was determined that she'd say yes.

Graham refused to get into a tug-of-war with her over the baby. He refused to allow his child to be a pawn in any family feud, let alone between him and Eve.

But the second she'd opened the door and let him in,

he'd seen just how tired she was. She was struggling to keep her eyes open. Was she not sleeping well at night? Was she not feeling well because of morning sickness? Was she working too hard?

Knowing Eve, she'd put 110 percent into her day as usual and then dragged herself home to rest in private. He knew she was trying to figure out what he was doing here, why he'd shown up and hadn't stripped her and made love to her right away. Every part of him wanted nothing more than to peel her out of her T-shirt and leggings. She'd looked damn good dressed down.

And that was a problem. Seeing Eve in an evening gown was heart-stopping. The way a killer suit hugged her hips nearly had him begging. But when she was just herself, makeup-free and wearing casual clothes, she was the most dangerous. He wanted to think this side of Eve was only for him, that she didn't expose this part of herself to anyone.

He shouldn't want to get more deeply involved with her, but he was a selfish bastard. He wanted all of her. She was the mother of his child and she was his. He didn't give up on anything he wanted, and he'd never wanted anything more than to be a father.

This realization hit him hard. Never before had he thought about having a child, yet now he could think of little else. He may not have had a father figure growing up, but he knew the love of a parent. He knew how to put his own needs aside to care for a child and make sure they had a secure life.

The movie had ended, and the room got dark. Graham turned off the TV, sliding the screen back into the island. Silence filled the room, save for Eve's soft snores. Pale light from the hall lamp gave enough of a glow for him to see. Graham reached across the bed and smoothed the silken strands of hair from her face. Instantly Eve startled awake. Her heavy-lidded eyes locked onto his.

"Sorry," he murmured. "I didn't mean to wake you."

Eve blinked and sat straight up against her mound of pillows. "I never make it through a movie on a good day, let alone when I'm already tired."

"Are you not sleeping well?" Concern had him scooting a bit closer. There was too much space between them, literally and figuratively.

"I'm sleeping fine. That's the problem. I want to sleep all the time. The doctor said that was normal in the first trimester."

A wave of relief washed over him. He knew absolutely nothing about pregnancies, so hearing any morsel of doctor's advice was comforting. He needed to start reading anything and everything he could get his hands on about this. He wanted to be able to connect with her, to comfort her, and somehow show her that he was there and she wouldn't be doing this alone.

"Maybe you should cut back a bit each day at work until this trimester passes." Her bored glare was all the answer he needed. Not that he thought she'd readily agree, but still. "You've only got a few more weeks. Then, when you're feeling better, you can add those hours back on."

"Can I?" she asked, her tone mocking. "I'm so glad to have your permission."

Raking a hand through his hair, Graham came to his feet and rounded the bed. "That's not what I meant and you know it. I'm worried about you."

"About the baby," she corrected.

"Fine. I'm worried for both of you." And he was.

Only a total jerk would ignore the mother's needs. "I want what's best for both of you."

Eve stared up at him. A red crease mark from her pillow marred the right side of her cheek, but her eyes were actually refreshed. Her ponytail had slid to one side of her head, random strands had escaped and hung down one side. Yeah, he knew nobody got this view of her, and part of him puffed up with conceit that he was the one here with her.

"I can't do this with you."

Confused, Graham lost focus on her sexy, disheveled look. "Excuse me?"

She waved a hand in the air. "This…whatever this is. Your attempt to get to know me or vie for some affection. I don't know what you're doing, but I'm not playing games now, Graham. We're having a baby—that doesn't mean we have to be a couple."

Why did those words feel like a slice to his…what? Heart? His heart wasn't supposed to be involved. But he sure as hell didn't like that she was so quick to put him on the back burner. That wouldn't work with his plan, not one bit. But he wasn't about to give up. He'd barely gotten started.

"Maybe I want to make sure we stay on the same track," he retorted. "Perhaps I want to stay friends with the mother of my baby so we can make this child's life as amazing as possible without turmoil."

"Are we friends?" she asked. "Seriously. We have amazing sex and we're both workaholics. That's about all we have in common. Can a friendship be built on that?"

Graham shrugged. "I've had friendships built on less."

Eve seemed to study him for a moment before her

eyes darted down to her lap where she toyed with the hem of her oversize tee. "It's getting late," she whispered.

If she thought he'd take that as a cue to leave, she didn't know him. Obviously that was the entire point of his being here. Why did this seem so forced? Why had everything seemed so easy up until very recently?

Because sex was easy. It was all the emotions that made the struggle real.

"Do you want me to go?" he asked, needing to hear her say it, but refusing to beg for anything. He eased a hip onto the bed next to her. "Do you want me to leave you alone and simply wait for texts about our child? Because you have to know that's not my style. I'm not a man who waits for anything. When I want something, I take it."

Her mesmerizing eyes slowly came up to his. "And what is it you want? The baby, I know. But we're a package, Graham. Don't you see that? I don't even know how we're going to make this work. You and I aren't together, our families hate each other and your brother is so angry and hurt, he's ready to destroy my father given any opportunity."

Tears welled up in her eyes and the sight was something Graham wished he never had to see. "Right now, all that matters is this child. Not your father, not my brother and not this fight. I don't want you worrying about this, Eve. It's not good for the baby."

She burst into tears. Full-on, hands-over-her-face sobbing. What had he said? Obviously the wrong thing when he was only trying to help. No wonder men and women never seemed to be on the same page. They weren't even in the same book.

Clearly words were getting him nowhere and he wasn't about to leave when she was so upset. Wrapping an arm around her, he pulled her against his chest as she continued to cry. Stroking her back, he attempted some comforting words, but he doubted she could hear them.

Moments passed and Graham had to wonder if there was something else that was upsetting her. Surely this wasn't just him. But with all the weight of everything coming down on her, she was bound to break. He didn't want her broken, but if she had to lean on someone, he wanted it to be him. No other man would be coming in here, not when she was carrying his child.

Eve wasn't weak, she wasn't vulnerable, yet right now she was having a moment. He wouldn't embarrass her by asking what he could do. She wouldn't want anyone coming to her rescue. He may not know much about her, but he recognized pride. Actions always trumped words anyway, so he'd show her how he cared instead of just talking about it.

Finally, Eve eased away, wiping at her damp cheeks with the back of her hands.

"Don't say you're sorry," he interjected when she opened her mouth.

"I'm not." She offered a soft smile. "You should've left me to have my meltdown. I can't believe you stayed."

"What kind of jerk do you think I am? I'm not just going to leave."

Closing her eyes, she blew out a breath. "I don't know what to think right now or what your angle is, but I don't think you're a jerk."

His angle? Simple. He wanted his child to be raised with the Newport name. He wanted her to willingly give him rights, and if he had to marry her to get them, then he would. Being around Eve was no hardship and his ache for her hadn't diminished in the slightest.

Before he could comment, her stomach growled. Graham laughed. "Hungry?"

She wrapped her arms around her waist as if to ward off any other sounds. "Actually, I was going to get something when you knocked. Then you guided me up here and the bed was so inviting. I haven't eaten since early lunch."

Graham came to his feet. "Stay here. I'll get something."

Eve rolled her eyes. "I'm not bedridden. I can make myself something to eat."

"I'm sure you can, but I'm here." Graham stepped back when Eve swung her legs over the side of the bed. "Stubborn, aren't you?"

Even with her red-rimmed eyes and pink-tipped nose, her smile was like a kick to his chest.

"A trait we both possess. Sounds like we'll have a strong-willed child."

Graham smiled. The idea of his child being strong, independent and a go-getter was absolutely perfect. A healthy combination of mother and father…he'd never given it much thought, but their child would be a perfect Newport.

Eve got to her feet and attempted to readjust her hair. Finally, she jerked the ponytail holder out and gathered up the fallen strands. In a flash, she had the mass of hair piled back atop her head.

"You don't have to stay," she told him. "I'm just going to make a quick sandwich and go to bed."

"You're trying so hard to get me out of here." He tipped her chin up and stepped in closer, so close the heat from her body warmed him. "I'm going to make sure you eat and then I'm going to make sure you're all settled in. We'll make small talk—we may even share a laugh. We can talk about the weather or we can talk about the baby. Up to you. But I'm not leaving, Eve. I'm going to be here, so you better get used to it."

"Is that a threat?" she asked with a soft smile.

He kissed her, hard, fast, then released her. "It's a promise."

Nine

Eve rolled over in bed, glanced at the clock and closed her eyes again.

Wait. She jerked up in bed and stared at the glaring numbers. How did it get to be so late? Sleeping in had never been an issue for her. She always showed up before anyone else and got a jump start on her day. At this rate, she was never going to make it into the office on time.

The sudden jolt of movement had her morning sickness hitting her fast. She rushed to the en suite bathroom and fell to her knees.

She'd had worse mornings, but still, she didn't like this feeling one bit. How could she remain professional if she was showing up late and looking like death?

Once she was done, she wiped her face with a cool, damp cloth and realized two things: one, it was Sunday so she wasn't late for anything. And two, there was a glorious smell coming from the kitchen and overtaking her home.

Surprisingly, whatever that scent was, it didn't make her more nauseous. If anything, her stomach was ready to go. This roller coaster of emotions and cravings was extremely difficult to keep up with.

Eve thought back to last night when Graham had made a simple grilled cheese sandwich and cut up an apple for her. Then he'd practically patted her on the head and sent her to bed, saying he'd lock up.

So, either he'd stayed and that was him in the kitchen, or one of her sisters was here. She highly doubted Nora or Grace had come by just to do some cooking, so she had to assume Graham had made himself at home.

Considering that she'd just tossed her cookies, so to speak, she opted to brush her teeth before heading down. By the time she hit the bottom steps, her mouth was watering. The magnificent aroma filled the entire first floor. Suddenly her belly growled and she had no idea how she could go from sick one second to hungry the next. Pregnancy sure wasn't predictable.

Heading down the wide hall toward the back of the house and the kitchen, Eve tried to figure out what to say to Graham. She'd seriously had a meltdown last night. He'd been so concerned about the baby, about her. But she hadn't been able to control those insane emotions.

Years ago when she'd thought herself in love, she'd have given anything for her boyfriend to have cared about her, about their baby. But she'd endured the first trimester and part of the second alone. Then she'd struggled through the miscarriage, the D & C, the grieving. All of it on her own. She'd pushed her sisters away because nobody could fix her broken heart. Nobody could bring back her baby and she wanted to be left alone.

Graham was most likely worried about his place in their child's life. He wasn't the type of man to sit back and let someone else raise his child. Still, the fact he'd stayed last night showed the type of man he was. He could've walked away.

So what did this mean? Did he want more than just shared parenting? Did he want to try at a relationship?

Good morning, shoulders.

Freezing midstride, Eve stared straight ahead to the sexiest cook she'd ever seen. She'd seen Graham countless times with nothing on, but finding him in just his jeans standing at her stove was like some sort of domestic porn. Seriously. This was calendar material. Forget the firefighters, sign Graham up. The way those back muscles flexed and relaxed as he did...whatever it was he was doing.

There was a man cooking in her house. The sexy, hot father of her baby was cooking in her house.

This sight alone was enough to make her want to strip and see if they could make use of that kitchen island, but she'd promised herself no more. She needed to focus on so many other things and her sex life was going to have to take a backseat for a while. What a shame, when she was facing such a delectable sight.

"You're just in time."

He didn't turn around as he spoke, just continued to bustle about getting breakfast ready as if this were the most normal thing in the world. As if he belonged here.

Eve couldn't move from the doorway. Between last night and this morning, she had no clue what Graham had planned next. Not one time did he try to get her undressed. Maybe he didn't find her as appealing as he used to. Perhaps pregnant women were a turnoff. Granted, it wasn't like she felt sexy at the moment.

No matter, she wasn't looking for more. At this point, her only hope was that she could keep the peace in her family when they found out she was carrying a New-port's baby.

"Why did you stay?"

Graham froze, plates in hand. Throwing a glance over his shoulder, he held her with his intense stare. "Because someone needs to make sure you're taking care of yourself."

"So you're my keeper now? I'm old enough to take care of myself."

She didn't mention the fact that he was younger than her. There was no need to state the obvious. But the fact that he'd stayed out of pity didn't sit well with her. Maybe she'd gotten her hopes up too high to think he'd stayed simply because he cared.

"I'm not saying you can't." He dished up some type of casserole and...was that fried apples? "It's the weekend. I wanted to stay and make you breakfast, so I did."

She wanted to argue, but the second she took a seat at the island and he placed that plate in front of her, she had no idea what they'd been on the verge of bickering about.

Eve stared down at her plate of food, which looked like it came from some cooking magazine—not the kind featuring light cuisine, either. Then she glanced at Graham, who was scooping up his own servings.

"You cook?" Okay, that was a stupid question. Clearly elves weren't involved. "I mean, this is more than just oatmeal or cereal for breakfast. Where did you learn this?"

Graham set his plate down and went back for two large glasses of orange juice. After putting everything on the island, he took a seat on a stool next to her.

"My grandma Gerty taught us all about cooking. It may have seemed like punishment at the time, but looking back I can see she did it out of love, and as a way to bond."

The wistfulness layered with the love in his tone told her this grandmother was one special lady. Eve pierced one gooey apple with her fork. The buttery, cinnamon sugar flavors exploded in her mouth. She prayed this food stayed with her. This was definitely too good to waste.

"Tell me about Gerty," Eve said, forking up a bite of some egg, sausage and cheese casserole. "Is she still alive?"

Graham swallowed and shook his head. "No."

That one word, full of sadness, had Eve pausing with her fork midway to her mouth. "Oh. Um…sorry. I didn't think."

Graham barely spared glance look her way. "No reason for you to be sorry. She passed away several years back. But she was like a second mother to us. Mom met Gerty at a coffee shop. Gerty was retiring, but she'd already taken a liking to Mom. The two were close and Mom moved in with Gerty because she needed help."

A single, pregnant woman. Eve's fork clattered to her plate as she thought of the parallel between Graham's mother's situation and hers. Did he see it? Is that why he was so adamant about helping her? Did he want to make up for the sins of some faceless man? Graham was so loyal, so noble where his family was concerned.

"Don't go there."

Eve jerked her gaze to Graham, who had shifted on his stool to face her.

"Don't let your mind betray you," he added. "I'm not pitying you because of my mother's circumstances. I'm sure she was scared being single and pregnant, but that's not why I'm here."

Resting her palms on the edge of the counter, Eve tipped her head. "Why are you here? What do you want, Graham? Just say it."

His aqua eyes sparkled, and his lips pursed just slightly, reminding her of what she'd been missing out on the past few days. "Maybe I want to get to know you more. Maybe I think you need to know me better, as well. We need to be strong together, for the sake of our baby and our families."

Eve couldn't agree more, but the way he looked at her said he wanted more than just pleasantries. Could she deny him? Probably not, but she did wholeheart-edly agree with him that they needed to work together.

"Then you'll have to stop eye-flirting with me," she told him, resuming her amazing breakfast.

"Eye-flirting?"

"Yes." She stabbed another apple with her fork. "You look at me and I can see you undressing me in your mind, but you haven't made any attempt to do so. I can't figure you out, but I can't be on the receiving end of that stare anymore."

Eve froze midchew as Graham's fingertip slid along her jawbone. Quickly, she finished her bite so she didn't choke. Her body responded instantly and he'd barely touched her. Why did she have to still want him? Why couldn't she get him out of her system?

"I'll strip you right now and take you on this counter." He turned her head toward him, his eyes darting to her mouth. "Say the word."

Oh, she wanted to say the word. Any word. Anything that would turn this passion into action. But she had to think straight…didn't she? She'd told herself not to fall back into the pattern of sleeping with him. That would be all too easy…and all too amazingly delicious.

No. She couldn't. They couldn't work as a team to figure out how to deal with the pregnancy and their families if their clothes were always falling off.

"Oh, my word, that wind is…"

Eve and Graham jerked their attention to the back door where Nora stood, her hair blown around her face, her mouth wide, her eyes even wider. There was a toss-up as to who was more shocked.

"You've got to be kidding me," Nora finally stated, shaking her long hair away from her face.

There was no reason to deny anything. Seriously. What could Eve say? Graham was sitting right here, shirtless, and Eve had clearly just crawled out of bed. Denying anything at this point would only make Eve look like a fool and insult her sister's intelligence.

"Plenty of breakfast if you want some," Graham supplied with that darn sexy grin. Clearly he was going the hospitable route instead of the awkward one.

Eve couldn't help the laugh that escaped her.

Nora's eyes narrowed on Graham before she turned to Eve. "You think this is funny? I thought you two were done…whatever it was you were doing."

Eve started to stand, but Graham put a hand on her arm. "We're not done, as a matter of fact."

Eve cringed. If he said anything about the baby, there would be nothing to stop Nora from telling Grace. Eve really needed to be the one to tell her sisters…and not in front of Graham. This was definitely a private matter she needed to handle on her own.

"Eve, come on." Nora stepped into the kitchen, her eyes locked on Eve's. "They're trying to destroy Dad's name, his reputation. You of all people should get how damning that could be, not only to our family, but to the company. They think he's hiding secrets, but he's a dying man. Why would he keep secrets at this point?"

Nora had just wrapped up and delivered the crux of the entire situation in that one question. Why indeed? That the matter was out of her control made this whole pregnancy even scarier. There had to be a way to keep this baby safe from family backlash.

"You're not telling me anything I don't already know," Eve replied, purposely keeping her voice calm, though her heart was pounding hard in her chest. "Graham and I are keeping everything private." For now. "So this doesn't need to go any further." Also, for now. "Did you need something from me?"

Nora blinked, then shook her head. "Seriously? You're going to brush this off?"

"There's nothing to brush off," Eve corrected. Now she did slide out from beneath Graham's touch so she could stand and approach her sister. "What Graham and I are doing, or not doing, is really only our business."

Was she honestly going to put Graham above her sisters' feelings right now? Eve was dangerously close to relationship territory, to an area neither of them ever wanted to be. But he'd stood firm against Brooks regarding the media backlash; that much was obvious from the pullback in the coverage. Perhaps they had already crossed that line and that was something she'd have to think about later.

"Eve wasn't feeling well last night, so I stayed to make sure she was okay," Graham chimed in. "Then I made breakfast and was going to head home after we ate. Now that I know she's feeling better, I'm comfortable leaving."

The weight on her chest vanished as she realized he wasn't about to share their secret.

Nora gave him a suspicious look. "You mean you stayed and took care of her because…why? You care about her? Eve, come on. You have to see he's using you. He's using you to get closer to Dad."

The accusation hurt. She knew for a fact Graham wasn't using her. He wasn't. He wouldn't take what they shared and turn it against her. Just because he hated her father didn't mean he'd be so cruel to her. And she hated that her sister didn't think someone like Graham would want to be with Eve simply because he found her attractive.

"I'm not using her. In fact, I asked Brooks to retract the media statements he made regarding your father."

Nora's eyes narrowed once again. Eve couldn't blame her sister for being so skeptical. Eve would feel the same way if the roles were reversed. Nora wouldn't understand there was much more to Eve and Graham than met the eye. And Nora wouldn't understand because Eve didn't fully understand it herself.

Another wave of nausea swept over her and Eve swayed on her feet. She gripped the stool and closed her eyes. Instantly Graham had his strong hands around her waist.

"Eve? What?"

She squeezed her eyes tighter, willing the unwanted nausea away. She couldn't answer for fear of getting sick right here. She hoped staying still for just a moment would help…

"Eve, talk to me," Graham urged. "Is it the baby?"

"Baby?" Nora exclaimed.

Suddenly Eve's fear of getting sick wasn't the issue. Now her sister knew and there was nothing Eve could do to stop this train wreck.

Ten

Graham didn't give a damn about the slipup. And he could care even less if Nora was shocked. When Eve swayed and caught herself on the barstool, his protective instincts took over.

Scooping her up in his arms, Graham ignored her weak plea to put her down as he carted her over to the living area off the kitchen. Once he laid her on the sofa, he noticed her pallor and the sheen of sweat that dotted her forehead. He eased himself onto the sofa beside her and lifted her legs onto his lap.

"Get her a cold cloth," he ordered Nora without taking his eyes from Eve. What if something was wrong? Why did she look so damn pale?

Eve laid one hand on her stomach and the other over her forehead. "I'm fine. Just give me a minute."

Seconds later, Nora waved a washcloth in Graham's face. He used it to wipe Eve's forehead, her neck. He didn't like this helpless feeling one bit. He'd seen his grandmother and his mother grow weak and pass. Not that Eve was dying, but the thought that there was nothing he could do for her right now really pissed him off.

"Eve." Nora stood over the back of the couch and reached down to smooth a damp strand of hair from her sister's face. "Are you pregnant again?"

Eve groaned, muttering something Graham didn't comprehend because he'd homed in on the key word in Nora's question.

Again?

What the hell did Nora mean by that? When had Eve been pregnant before?

"I'm pregnant," Eve mumbled. "Don't tell Grace. I'll tell her."

"Oh, honey." Now Nora's voice took on a compassionate tone, one that Graham instinctively knew had everything to do with this former pregnancy. He was almost afraid to find out the details, but he would. "How far along are you?"

"Seven weeks now."

Graham listened to the sisters, but his mind was overloaded. A spear of unexpected jealousy hit him square in the chest. He had no right to be jealous of a faceless man who'd created a baby with Eve. Clearly they weren't together anymore. But still, Graham didn't want to think of her experiencing this with anyone else.

"Promise me," Eve was saying, her eyes pleading with Nora. "Don't say anything. Let Graham and me handle this. We want what's best for the baby, and our families have to come to some sort of peace."

Nora glanced at Graham before looking back down at Eve. "I promise. I know what it's like to be pregnant and unsure of what to do next."

Nora had been a single mother before she and Reid

had fallen in love. Graham didn't know much about Nora's circumstances, but it sounded as though she'd been alone and scared. Fortunately, Eve wouldn't be alone. Ever, if he had any say.

Eve started to sit up, waving her hand when Graham tried to ease her back down. "It passed. I'm fine. I'm just going to sit here for a bit." Looking over her shoulder, she asked, "What did you need this morning, Nora?"

"What? Oh, it's not important." Nora smiled, then wrapped her arms around her sister. "I thought we might go shopping for party costumes for Halloween, but we can go another day."

Again, Graham didn't like being left out of this little shopping trip. Didn't like being so easily dismissed as though he was replaceable.

"I'll feel fine in the afternoon if you want to wait."

Nora stood straight up and nodded. "Sounds good. Text me later. Reid doesn't want to go, so I'll just pick something up for him. But I was given a list of things he refuses to wear. Tights being at the top of the list."

"No Robin Hood for him, then." Eve smiled. "Thanks for understanding and keeping this to yourself. I know you have questions, but I'll address them. Just not now."

Graham watched the younger Winchester sister as she adjusted her cardigan and smoothed her hair back. "I promise to keep this all to myself, but if you need any help with doctor's appointments or someone to—"

"She's got someone," Graham stated. "Just be sure to keep that promise."

Nora pulled in a breath as if she wanted to let him have it, but Graham flashed her what he hoped was a charming smile. No way in hell was he letting anyone else care for Eve and his child. They may not be a couple, but she belonged to him now.

Closing her mouth without saying anything, Nora turned on her heel and left out the front door. Silence filled the spacious room. Eve's legs were still in Graham's lap, but she sat up with her arm stretched across the back of the sofa.

"We're going to have to tell your brothers now," she said, rubbing her head. "I'll have to talk to Grace and… this is just going to be a mess."

"This isn't a mess. If our families can't see that a child is more important than our rivalry, then—"

"Tell me more about Gerty." Eve's eyes held his. She reached down and took his hand.

"Excuse me?"

Eve glanced down, traced a pattern over his palm. "You seemed so happy when you were talking about her. You seemed nostalgic and that's a side of you I don't know."

Graham swallowed. She didn't know this side because it was the one that was most vulnerable. But he wanted her to fully know him, to gain her affection so that his plan would be flawless. In order for that to happen, he'd have to bare all his emotions where his past was concerned.

"Gerty was amazing." Because he couldn't sit still, he shifted from beneath her and went to the kitchen for her plate. After putting it on her lap, he set her juice on the side table. "She'd swat our hands with a wooden spoon if we cursed, then just as lovingly show us how to bake homemade bread. I've never known anyone like her."

Eve continued to hold on to her plate. Graham picked up the fork and got a small bite for her. When he lifted it to her lips, she kept her gaze on his as he fed her.

"When I fell off the monkey bars in the first grade, she came right to the school because she didn't want to worry my mom or disrupt her shift at the coffee shop. By the time Mom got home, Gerty had bandaged me up, given me ice cream for dinner, and we were watching *Casablanca*."

Eve smiled as he lifted another bite to her mouth. "You get your love of old movies from her."

Graham nodded. "I get many things from her. She would always say how she was just a waitress, but she took pride in her job. She told us to do whatever job we wanted, whether it be a janitor or a doctor. She wanted us to know that every job was important and to make sure we worked hard."

Graham recalled her harping on how important hard work was time and time again. No matter the career, they had to put 110 percent into it. She was a proud woman and Graham knew his mother had found a real-life angel just when she'd needed her. Or perhaps they'd needed each other, considering that Gerty's husband had just passed when she took in Cynthia.

Graham continued to feed Eve. He shared random stories about his childhood. Whatever popped into his mind, he shared. For once, he was completely relaxed. Surprisingly, he wanted Eve to be fully aware of where he came from. He didn't come from money. He'd worked his ass off to get where he was at the law firm.

After her plate was completely clean, he reached for the juice and handed it to her.

"That was amazing," she told him. "Feel free to cook for me anytime."

Graham stilled. He wasn't prepared to play house. He had no road map, no plan here. All he knew was the end result had to be that his child was raised as a Newport.

"I'm sorry," she told him, glancing away. "I didn't mean that the way it sounded."

"Don't be sorry."

Shaking her head, she put her plate and glass on the table before leaning back on the couch. "You may be able to keep those emotions hidden in the courtroom, but I can read you better than you think. I understand you don't want a relationship with me, or any type of commitment. I wasn't implying that."

Graham raked a hand over his face; the stubble on his jawline was itchy and annoying. "Neither of us is at a point in our lives when we can put forth the time and attention a relationship needs."

Eve nodded. "I agree."

"But that doesn't mean everything that happened before I found out you were pregnant is over. I can't just shut off my desire for you, Eve. If you want to cool it in that area, tell me now. I'll respect your wishes and I'll still do everything in my power to keep you and this baby safe and cared for."

He had to say what she wanted to hear. He couldn't scare her off this early. He couldn't even hint at what his true intentions were.

Eve pushed to her feet and started pacing. She stopped in front of the fireplace and turned her back to him. His eyes focused beyond her, on the photos she had arranged across the mantel. Every silver-framed picture showcased her family. The sisters, Eve and her mother, a young Eve on her father's shoulders. He didn't want to get into that aspect of her life. Graham couldn't afford to see Sutton as a loving father. Graham didn't give a damn about Sutton, save for the fact that he knew who Brooks and Graham's birth father was. Or he at least knew a name. The old bastard was keeping this information to himself and Graham would do anything to find it out.

But he wouldn't use Eve or his unborn child to get it.

"I don't know what I want," Eve finally said. "This passion clearly isn't going away anytime soon. But I need some space."

When she turned around, Graham had to force himself to remain seated. She didn't need him cutting her off, she needed him to be strong for her. But he wouldn't stay away long.

"Wanting you has never been a question," she went on. "But—"

"I know." And he did. Graham came to his feet, pleased when her eyes raked over his bare chest. Let her look, let her continue to want and need just as he did. If she needed him, then that would play right into his hand. "I'll give you space, Eve. But you need to understand, I'm not going away. I won't pressure you or point out that you're looking at me like you want to take the rest of my clothes off."

Eve rolled her eyes. "So arrogant."

"Accurate, not arrogant," he corrected as he slowly closed the space between them. "I'm going to check on you every day. I'm going to be involved with this pregnancy. But you're going to come to me on your own."

He now stood so close to her that his bare chest rubbed against her T-shirt.

She tipped her head back. "You're sure of that?"

Graham eased closer, his lips within a breath of hers. "Positive."

He brushed his lips against hers, not quite kissing her, but feeling her warm breath. The slight whimper that escaped her was reassuring, but he stepped back. Fisting his hands at his sides to remain in control, he counted backward from ten.

She wanted space? So be it. She'd see just how difficult ignoring this desire would be.

"I'll call you later."

Graham forced himself to walk away. After getting his clothes and letting himself out, he reevaluated the plan in his head. Carson and Brooks needed to know about the baby, but he couldn't tell them just yet. He needed to formulate a better strategy for dealing with the Winchesters that didn't involve obliterating Sutton, and in turn hurting Eve. He didn't want her hurt, he wanted her to be completely and utterly his. But he also wanted Sutton to divulge the name of his father before he died.

Damn it. There had to be a way to get everything he wanted and not hurt Eve in the process.

If Roman could find their birth father soon, Graham knew Brooks would ease off Sutton. Or if Sutton somehow found it in the deepest part of his dark heart to share the information he knew, that would be even better. But Graham feared the man would go to his grave with the secret.

Just like his mother had. Why hadn't she just told them? All Graham had ever heard was how their father wasn't in the picture and she didn't want to talk about him.

So here they were with no answers, other than that Sutton was Carson's father. But that was it.

Putting thoughts of Sutton out of his mind, Graham pulled away from Eve's house, already planning on how to gain her attention, to make her come to him. Because he wouldn't beg for any women...not even the mother of his child.

Eleven

Graham eased back in his chair and thanked God the case he'd been waiting on to go to trial was finally scheduled. This would be a slam dunk for his client, and another win for Graham and the firm.

Since she'd last seen him, he'd randomly texted Eve. He purposely didn't flirt, didn't get into anything sexual or do the whole pathetic what-are-you-wearing thing. Nope. He wanted to keep her guessing, because if she was guessing, then she was thinking about him and his next move. And if she was thinking about him, then her thoughts would travel to the bedroom all on their own.

But the wait was killing him. It had been too long since he'd touched her properly. The thought of having another woman didn't excite him in the least. Eve was the woman he wanted in his bed, or anywhere else he could get her all to himself.

He knew she was getting ready for her sister's upcoming costume party, but he still wanted to see her. She couldn't come to him fast enough.

"Mr. Newport." His assistant's soft voice came through the speaker. "You have a visitor."

Eve? No, that was ridiculous. She wouldn't come here, not after she'd exploded when he'd shown up at her office during business hours.

"Shall I send Carson in?"

Graham came to his feet and pressed the speaker button. "Yes. Thank you."

Graham's door swung open and Carson stepped inside, closing the door at his back.

"You have a minute?"

Graham gestured to the seat across from his desk. "Of course."

"I'll be brief." Carson remained standing, so Graham did, too. "I'm going to see Sutton this evening. He called me yesterday and wanted to meet. I've been hesitant, but his time is limited, so I'm going."

Graham stilled. "Alone?"

"I know you and Brooks want answers from him, so if you want to go, we can all meet there. That bastard thinks he can always get what he wants, but we're a team, so we're in this together."

Another encounter with Sutton? Why not. The more they pumped him for answers, the greater the odds he'd wear down and just tell them what they wanted to know.

"Is Brooks going?"

Carson nodded. "He's meeting me there."

Graham glanced at the files on his desk, the open emails on his computer screen waiting to be answered. Nothing was more important than another shot with Sutton. Their time was running out.

"What time?" he asked, turning back to his brother.

"Seven."

Graham gave a firm nod of his head. "I'll be there."

Carson pulled in a deep breath and shoved his hands in his pockets. "I have no idea what I'm going to say. It's still awkward for me, especially now that he's dying…"

Graham couldn't imagine the emotions Carson was dealing with right now. "Are you sure you don't want to take Georgia instead?"

"No. She understands the need for the three of us to be there. I want to help you guys get the answers you need, plus I want to see what he has to say."

Graham wondered what Eve would say if she knew he was going to see her father. She was protective of him, wouldn't want anyone going to him on his deathbed and pumping him for information. Still, Graham was going to try one last time. Who knew when the man was going to pass? Sutton may have still been getting the best care at his sprawling estate, but that was only because of his billions. He was too proud to be in some facility like everyone else.

Had Eve told her father about the baby? Doubtful, or Sutton would've called Graham to meet with him, as well. Was Eve planning on exposing their secret or was she hoping to avoid telling her dad?

"You okay?"

Graham blinked and focused back on his brother. "Yeah. Fine. I'll finish up here and meet you all over at Sutton's."

Carson let himself out and Graham hurried to finish up the work that needed his attention right now. Once he was done, he grabbed his cell and thought about firing off a text to Eve but opted not to. She didn't need to know what was going on. If Sutton wanted her to know, he could tell her. Graham wasn't putting himself in the middle any more than he already was.

Sutton's affairs were his business, but Sutton's affair with Graham's mom was clearly out in the open now. Considering that Carson wasn't much younger than Graham and Brooks, Graham knew the affair had started when he and Brooks were mere infants. There was no way in hell Sutton wasn't aware of the first name of their father at least. Why did the old bastard care enough to keep it secret? Any information he provided would go a long way to helping them discover who their father was.

But maybe they wouldn't like the answer. Maybe their father was fully aware of the twins he'd given up. Maybe he didn't want anything to do with them. Still, that was a risk Graham and Brooks were willing to take.

In the end, Graham texted Eve, asking if she'd found a costume for the party. Simple enough, but effective in keeping her on her toes and their lines of communication open.

As soon as he started to shut the lights off in his office, the cell vibrated in his pocket. He pulled it out and nearly sagged against the wall. The image of Eve dressed as some sexy goddess with a white wrap hugging all her tempting curves had him gritting his teeth and cursing himself for telling her he'd give her space. The little vixen was playing games with him. She wanted him begging. He was sure that was her angle.

But two could definitely play at that game and he never played without every intention of winning.

Sutton Winchester's house was a vast estate not too far from the offices where he'd once controlled the real estate world. Graham and Brooks moved in behind Carson as they were led toward the back of the house. The butler was solemn and said nothing as he gestured for them to follow. Not that Graham was expecting a warm welcome, but still.

He tried to take in the surroundings, tried to imagine Eve growing up in this cold mansion. There wasn't a thing out of place and it looked more like a museum than a place where children played.

Graham instantly thought of his penthouse and cringed. Not exactly a playground, but he would make damn sure his child had a fun place to be a kid even if he had to remove his wet bar and put in an indoor jungle gym.

How pathetic was this? He was already one-upping Sutton in his own mind in regards to parenting. Ridiculous.

The servant escorting them motioned toward a set of double doors. Carson thanked the man and threw a glance back at his brothers.

"We've got your back," Brooks stated. "Go in when you're ready."

Carson turned back around, placed his hands on the knobs and eased both doors open. Graham didn't know what he expected, maybe a gray-toned man lying in bed hooked up to machines keeping him alive. But the reality was Sutton sitting up in a plush chair with his feet up by the fire in what Graham assumed was the master suite. A thick, plaid blanket covered his lap.

Sutton was once a kingpin in the corporate world, but right now he looked to be someone's loving grandpa waiting for children to gather around for story time.

Actually, this was his child's grandfather, but Graham would rather forget that little fact and focus on the reason for their visit now.

"I was hoping you'd come alone," Sutton stated. "But I'm not surprised you brought your brothers."

Graham didn't reply. This was Carson's show...for now. Carson had received the invite and it was Carson who had the most to get off his chest. Graham and Brooks were most likely beating the proverbial dead horse. Okay, really poor choice of words, but he couldn't help what popped into his head.

"My brothers and I are a unit. You know all about family loyalty, right?" Carson mocked.

Sutton merely nodded, not answering the rhetorical question.

"I don't even know what to say to you," Carson admitted.

Graham exchanged a knowing look with Brooks. They both knew Carson was on edge, and it definitely cost him to admit it. The poor guy had been on the fence about whether to fully accept Sutton as his father, whether to approach him and listen to what the old man had to say. But they were here now and Graham was more concerned about Carson's feelings than anything else.

"Have a seat." Sutton turned his attention to the twins. "All of you."

Carson remained still, staring at his father. Graham moved first to take a seat on the sofa on the other side of the oriental rug across from Sutton. Brooks sat beside him and finally Carson took the last spot on the end.

Sutton shifted in his seat. Graham wasn't sure if it was nerves or if the old man was simply trying to get comfortable. Sutton wasn't the type to show his emotions, so Graham doubted he was feeling anything but smug. He'd called Carson to come, and he had.

"Why did you want me here?" Carson finally asked, breaking the silent tension.

"You're my son."

Graham snorted, ignoring Sutton's frown and quick, disapproving look.

"So you're expecting us to get to know each other now that I know the truth and you're sick?" Carson asked.

Sutton turned his face to the fire. Orange flames licked against the black stone. The Chicago air was cooling quite a bit, hinting at an early winter. Graham found it easy to focus on the weather, on the fire, on anything other than the fact he didn't want to be here. Oh, he wanted to be here if he was going to get a name, but the chances of that happening were about as good as Sutton recovering from lung cancer.

"What you decide to do is up to you." Sutton coughed, and that's when it was apparent how sick the man was. This coughing fit wasn't short and it wasn't quiet. Finally, when he was done, he turned back to Carson. "I wanted you to know that I truly loved your mother."

Brooks tensed beside Graham. Of course he'd bring their mother into the conversation. He'd pretend that he knew her well, that he was heartbroken to leave her. Sutton had left Cynthia alone and pregnant, just like he'd found her. Only this time she'd been pregnant with *his* kid and he hadn't known it. Still, a lowly waitress and outsider wouldn't have fit into his high-society world of luxury homes, cars and diamonds.

The atmosphere of anger and bitterness in this room enveloped them all. There was so much to be said, but at the same time they were dealing with a dying man... and Eve's father. The grandfather of Graham's baby.

Graham stared at Sutton and tried to imagine the man

from the picture on Eve's mantel. The man who held his daughter on his shoulders at some amusement park. Sutton may be ruthless, he may have had countless affairs, but he loved his children. Considering that he had been shocked by the news of Carson's paternity, Graham wasn't surprised he'd called Carson to his home. Sutton wouldn't sit back and just ignore his child.

But he had no problem ignoring his ex-lover's other children.

"If you loved our mother, then tell us the name of our father," Brooks stated. "You were with her long enough. She would've confided in you."

Sutton shook his head. "It's because I loved Cynthia that I won't betray her confidence. If she'd wanted you to know, she would've told you."

"Tell them." Carson's low demand shocked Graham.

"It's not my place, son."

Carson let out a humorless laugh, eased forward and rested his forearms on his legs. Hands dangling between his knees, he glanced toward Brooks and Graham. Trying to offer silent support, Graham nodded for Carson to go on.

"My brothers deserve to know their father," Carson said, looking back at Sutton. "They keep hitting dead ends. If you can help them—"

"I didn't call them here," Sutton interrupted. "I wanted to see you. I don't have much time, though my doctors keep telling me I'm a fighter. I'm realistic."

"All the more reason for you to tell us," Brooks stated. "You may be the only other person who knows. We don't even know if our birth father is aware of us."

Sutton simply stared back. He gave no hint of what he knew, no sign that he even cared if they were struggling. Graham never liked the man from his dealings with him in the corporate world. He'd been sneaky and underhanded. He kept secrets, even from his staff. Graham had actually seen one of Sutton's previous employees win a case against the old man, but that had been during Graham's internship so he hadn't had a hand in that win.

Graham knew Sutton wasn't about to give up the name, if he even knew a name. For all Graham knew, Sutton was just stringing them along. How had Eve turned out so loyal and honest?

Obviously Eve's mother had a hand in raising her daughter right and was smart enough to finally leave Sutton after years of unfaithful marriage.

"I want to make something clear," Sutton went on. "Cynthia was the love of my life."

Graham didn't want to hear this, didn't want to be subjected to more lies. But one glance at Carson made Graham realize that his younger brother wanted to know. Not that Carson was naive, but Carson was more prone to forgiveness than Graham or Brooks. So Graham remained silent, though he had plenty of thoughts racing through his mind.

Sutton's eyes didn't leave Carson. "I would've given anything to be with Cynthia. But my wife was so well connected in Chicago society, it would've been career suicide to leave her. Plus, she would've made life hell for Cynthia, and I couldn't allow that."

"Would you have made the same decision if you'd known about me?"

The underlying tone of vulnerability was something Graham had never seen from Carson. Graham's younger brother was a rock, he was always in control, but this little meeting was getting to him. Graham prayed Carson would hold it together.

"I would've gone through hell to be with my son."

Sutton's answer sounded honest. Graham fully believed the man would've sacrificed his marriage to Eve's mother. No doubt Sutton would've wanted a son to raise, to mold into his heir. But Eve had filled that role, and she was doing a remarkable job. Maybe too remarkable.

And just like that, his thoughts had once again strayed to Eve during this meeting. He'd be checking on her again when they left here...especially after that little picture she'd sent to torture him.

"I want to hate you," Carson muttered.

Graham glanced over in time to see Brooks give a manly, reassuring pat to Carson's shoulder. They were here for Carson, to support him. If he wanted to embrace Sutton as his father and live out these days happily ever after, then that's what they'd do. But Graham wasn't so willing to forgive the bastard.

"I know you do," Sutton agreed. "And you have every right. But I couldn't die, not without telling you that Cynthia meant the world to me and I regret not having been there for you."

Graham wasn't surprised that their mother had kept the baby from Sutton. She'd probably been scared of the backlash and it was just as easy to live with Gerty and raise her boys in secret as opposed to facing legal proceedings, which she wouldn't have been able to afford.

Silence filled the room. The fire continued to crackle, sending out wayward flickers and orange sparks. Graham glanced around the room. He thought for sure that he'd see pictures of Eve and her sisters here, but there was nothing. Images of Eve staring at pictures of her father on her computer flashed through Graham's mind. She'd been so eager to get those images uploaded and she'd scrolled through them as though they were her lifeline to her ailing father.

Graham didn't want Carson to give his loyalty, his love to Sutton, but this wasn't Graham's choice to make. Who knew what would happen if and when he ever found his birth father? Maybe Graham would find a jerk who knew about his kids and just didn't care. What then? Would Graham still forgive him or want to try to make a relationship with him?

"I don't know what to say, honestly." Carson stared at his hands dangling between his knees. "I'd like to visit you, maybe see you a little more and talk. For whatever time we have—"

"I'll take anything," Sutton said, a soft smile forming on his pale face.

Graham had only seen that smile in Eve's pictures. Apparently he reserved the emotion for his children. Graham was a bit jealous of how Carson's journey had ended; he deserved a dad, even if it was Sutton.

Brooks came to his feet and sighed. "I'm done here. Carson, stay as long as you like. I'll be outside."

Once Brooks was gone, Graham also stood. He approached Sutton, knowing this may be the last time he ever saw the man. He had no intention of ever coming back.

"I'm glad you're not my father," Graham said, leaning down just enough so only Sutton could hear. "But Carson is happy to finally know. If you have to fake affection, do it. He deserves a father who isn't a jerk."

"I love my son," Sutton said simply.

Graham nodded and straightened. It was so tempting to tell him about the baby. So tempting to get just one final jab in. But Graham wasn't that much of an ass and he'd never do that to Eve. He wanted a chance to show her what a good father he could be and harassing *her* father was not the way to go about that.

Graham turned to his brother. "I'll wait outside with Brooks. Seriously, take your time."

Before Graham had gotten outside, he'd fired off a text to Eve indicating what he'd do to her if he were to ever see her in that Halloween costume.

"That man can rot in hell for all I care." Brooks rested his back against one of the thick, white columns of the portico. "I'm happy for Carson, but damn it. That man is infuriating."

Graham stepped forward, shoving his hands into his pockets and hunching his shoulders against the chilly breeze. "Carson has been on the fence for a while now. He wants to forgive Sutton. I hate to come to the guy's defense, but he didn't know Carson existed."

Brooks jerked his gaze around. "Are you serious? You're going to stand there and make excuses for the guy? If Mom was the love of his life, as he claims, then he would've moved heaven and earth to be with her. And he damn well would give a portion of his estate to his biological son."

When Graham didn't reply, Brooks narrowed his eyes. "This has to do with Eve, doesn't it? You're still hung up on her."

He was the father of her child. Which was a few levels above being "hung up on her."

"I'm stating the obvious, that's all." Graham wasn't about to bring Eve into this discussion. She had enough on her plate without being further caught up in this battle. "Sutton and Carson need time to talk alone. You and I will only make things worse."

Brooks started pacing on the stone walk. "I need

Roman to come up with something concrete. I'm putting all my faith in him to find our father."

"I know," Graham said, hating how much this issue was controlling Brooks's life. "But it will happen. We can't run into dead ends forever. Something will turn up. Someone somewhere knows the truth."

Brooks snorted and jerked his thumb toward the house. "Yeah. He's in there."

Graham stared at the double doors. Sutton knew. Absolutely without a doubt he knew. But Graham refused to beg the man. He would find out on his own. He would not give Sutton any satisfaction in getting one up on him. Ever.

Twelve

Seven weeks pregnant and her body was already showing signs of change. Eve attempted to adjust her cleavage in the strips of fabric covering her chest. The white goddess costume had seemed like a good idea at the time, but now she felt very exposed.

Glancing in her floor-length mirror, she shivered as she recalled Graham's text. The man wasn't playing nice. He was trying to get her to give in and…well, she was having a difficult time recalling why she needed to stay away.

Oh, yeah. Someone had to be responsible and think things through right now. Someone had to step back and think straight. When he sent those messages, and there had been many, Eve found it more and more difficult to keep him at a distance.

She hadn't seen him for several days. Too many. The messages hadn't started out as flirty, but then she'd sent that picture and she'd opened up some sort of dam. He'd flooded her phone with messages that would've made her high-society mother blush.

With the cool, windy October weather, Eve would definitely need a coat this evening. Otherwise she'd freeze her butt off.

Eve glanced at the antique clock on her vanity and sighed. She was running late because insecurities over the changes in her body had her doubting her costume. But she had no plan B so goddess she was. Nobody would guess she was pregnant; of course Nora already knew, but she hadn't said anything yet. There was no reason for anyone to believe she was expecting, so worrying over her fuller chest was ridiculous.

Still, she feared that when the rest of her family found out, when her *father* found out she was not only expecting, but carrying a Newport child, there would be trouble. She'd already gotten a glimpse of things to come from Nora. Her family wouldn't be happy. Granted, she was going into this situation with her eyes wide open and not full of stars. Eve had lost a child before when she thought herself in love. Now her family would probably criticize her for making a mistake with another man who was all wrong for her.

Not that her baby was a mistake; the first person to even hint at that would have to deal with her wrath. No, her mistakes came in the form of choosing the wrong men. Clearly she had bad judgment.

By the time Eve pulled onto the Winchester estate, she was confident that she needed to tell her family. The sooner they knew about the baby, the longer they'd have to get used to the idea. After the party tonight, she'd tell Grace and their father when they were all together. It would be the perfect time. Not that there was a perfect time to drop a bomb like this. But there was no changing the fact that she was having a baby.

A baby. The thought thrilled and terrified her at the same time. She was still ten weeks away from the seventeen-week mark. She would feel so much better once she got past the hurdle that had left a hole in her heart during her last pregnancy. Eve honestly didn't know if she could bear another loss so great. She was already facing the inevitable loss of her father, but to add a second baby to the…

No. This baby was just fine. She wasn't going to even think that way… From now on she would have only positive thoughts. Her child was a Newport and a Winchester, which immediately equaled a fighter.

Eve pulled in behind Grace's car and grabbed her clutch and the present she'd brought for her father—a framed photograph. Sliding her phone into her purse, Eve headed toward the grand entrance. Her childhood home was nothing short of spectacular—Sutton Winchester would settle for nothing less than the best.

Instantly memories of growing up here flooded her mind. The house always looked like a museum, but there had been a toy room on the third floor where the kids were given free rein. She and her sisters had spent hours in there playing, dreaming, fighting…all the things close sisters did. They'd run around outside playing tag, chasing each other and fantasizing about being grown-ups. Seriously, growing up was so overrated. They should've enjoyed those carefree days a bit more.

Pulling her wrap tighter around her, Eve made her way to the door. Without knocking, she let herself in. The aroma of something spicy, maybe cinnamon, hit her. Definitely a hint of pumpkin, too. Whatever the cook had prepared—or Nora had had catered—smelled absolutely divine. And thankfully in the evenings, Eve was fine; she didn't have to deal with a queasy belly. So she was ready to have her fill of the party food, but not the wine.

Eve had just pulled her wrap off to hang it on the coat tree in the foyer when Nora came gliding down the hall. Eve put her wrap up and set her clutch and gift on the marble entryway table.

"You look gorgeous," her younger sister declared. "I knew this goddess costume would be so perfect for you."

Eve took in her sister's vibrant green historical ball gown. "Talk about stunning. Nora, you're glowing."

Nora beamed. "I know it's not what I bought when we were out, but then I saw this the other day and had to have it."

"So what is Reid?"

"Lucky." Eve glanced at Reid, who'd just stepped from the formal living space. He wrapped an arm around Nora's waist and kissed her cheek. "I'm damn lucky," he added.

Reid was dressed as a Civil War–era soldier, complete with sword dangling at his side. He and Nora looked as though they'd stepped out of a time machine. Eve was jealous of Nora's itty-bitty waist; no doubt she'd gone for the whole corset and all. Eve's hourglass shape was not long for this world.

"That you are," Eve agreed, giving her sister a wink. "How's Dad feeling today?"

"Good. He's even donned a bit of a costume for the occasion, though he said he'd stay in the study since his oxygen and everything is set up in there. Visitors are welcome, though."

Eve gripped the present beneath her arm and nodded. "I'm going to see him now before everyone else arrives."

"You doing okay?" Nora asked, keeping the question vague.

Eve glanced at Reid, who showed no sign of knowing anything. "I'm great. If you'll excuse me."

Eve made her way to the study. She hated thinking of her father being so sick that he was confined to one room, but she knew that if he truly wanted to move about the house, his caregivers would make it happen. Her father remained in the study more out of pride than anything else. There was a bathroom right off the spacious room and hospice care had set everything up to look like a master suite. Her father's old desk where he'd spent countless hours when he worked from home sat in the corner. Next to the desk was a large built-in shelf housing all of his favorite books.

As she walked down the hall, Eve took stock of all the memories. She hated the thought of his estate being split up when he passed. She wanted her childhood home to remain in the family, but that might not be possible. Who knew what would happen with Carson and how far his brothers would go to make sure he received his share.

Just the thought of Graham stirred mixed emotions within Eve. The ache she had for him kept growing with each day that passed without him, but on the other hand, she hated knowing he was one of the forces waging war against her father.

Pulling the framed picture from beneath her arm, Eve tapped lightly on the double doors and let herself into the study. The cozy fire welcomed her. Her father was actually in his chair beside the flickering flames. The last time she'd visited, he'd been sitting up in bed but hadn't felt like going much farther. To see him in a chair was such a surprise, Eve's eyes instantly filled with tears. The eye patch and pirate hat combined with his navy blue bathrobe made her laugh, though. He'd dressed up for the guests that would come through. If it weren't for the oxygen, she'd swear he was back to normal. But he'd never be himself again. He'd never be the man he once was and she was slowly coming to grips with the harsh reality.

"Look at this beautiful goddess who came to visit." He lifted a hand toward her. "Come on over. You look stunning, Eve. Just like your mother."

Of course she looked like her mother; everyone told her as much growing up. The honey-brown hair, the bright eyes, curvy figure. Eve had seen enough pictures of her mother in her younger years to know she was practically a clone. But Eve didn't want to discuss her mother right now. She wanted this evening to be fun, to be filled with love since the entire family would all be under one roof.

"What have you got?"

Eve flipped the frame around. "I had this made for you. It's from my visit the other day."

Sutton stared at the picture for several moments before finally reaching for it. With both hands, he gripped the sleek pewter frame and settled it on his lap. Eve waited, watching as her father continued to look at the faces staring back at him. Sutton with his daughters, an image that hadn't been captured since they were little.

"This means everything to me," he said, his voice thick with emotion. "You've always had such a good eye for photos."

Eve leaned against the side of the chair and laughed. "It was just a selfie, Dad. But I thought it turned out nice and wanted you to have something in your room."

He glanced up at her, his bushy brows drawn together. "You always know what to do. This is perfect."

"I'm glad you like it."

He looked at the image once more before turning his attention back to her. "Tell me about Elite. How are things going?"

The man was on his deathbed and wanted to know about business. He would probably die with his company—his baby—on his mind.

"We're doing great." Eve was thrilled with the direction they'd taken since she'd been placed at the helm. "We actually just signed on a Sydney office two days ago."

Sutton's smile spread across his face. "I knew you would take a great company and make it even greater. I'm so proud of you, Eve. You've not let anything stand in your way."

"I learned from the best," she declared, wrapping her arm around his shoulders as she settled a hip on the arm of his chair.

"Some women are cut out for husbands, kids, which is fine. But I knew you were the one to follow in my footsteps. You never had—"

"Let's not talk about work." She had to steer him in another direction. Because even though she hadn't wanted the whole family lifestyle once she'd gotten a taste of corporate world, clearly she wasn't going to be able to dodge it for long. "Nora said you were feeling pretty well today. You look good."

He started to laugh, but his robust chuckle quickly turned into a coughing fit. Eve rushed to the wet bar in the corner and refilled his water. She hated seeing him suffer even the slightest bit. For a man who was known to be a ruthless shark in the real estate world, he was now as weak as a baby. The vulnerable side of Sutton Winchester would only be known to his family, though. He'd never let outsiders see him in such shape.

Eve let him hold the cup while she took the framed picture and set it up on the table near the sofa.

"Thank you," he said after taking a few sips. "Damn disease."

Eve went back to his side and took his cup. She placed it on the small table next to him.

"You girls don't have to lie to me," he went on, taking her hand and squeezing it between both of his. "I know what I look like."

Eve kissed the top of his head. "Like my handsome father."

"You're going to find some man and charm him one day," her father teased. "Just make sure when you do that you don't leave my company in a bind."

As if she'd ever settle down and take the time to nurture a relationship. A global company and a new baby were definitely enough to keep her occupied. "I'll never leave Elite," she promised.

"I hate to bring this up—"

"But you will because you're honest," she joked. "Go ahead."

"I know that before all the questions came up about me being the Newport boys' father, you and Graham were—"

"Nothing," Eve interrupted. "We were nothing." And that was the truth. It was *after* the paternity test results came back that they tore each other's clothes off.

This conversation was entering dangerous territory, and that was putting it mildly. Guilt squeezed her chest like a vise. There was no way to avoid it much longer, but she wasn't going to tell anyone about the baby until after the party. No way was she going to ruin Nora and Reid's evening. There would be enough time to discuss it after the guests were gone and only family remained.

"I saw how he looked at you, Eve," her father went on. "Getting involved with a Newport would be the biggest mistake you could make."

Eve bit the inside of her cheek to keep from saying anything. What could she say? She could deny that she was involved, but that would be an obvious lie. She could even pretend they weren't going to be anything more than parents sharing a child, but since they were still flirting and she couldn't get him off her mind, it was only a matter of time before her control crumbled and they ended up intimate again.

Pulling her hand from her father's grasp, she leaned down once more and kissed his head. "I'm going to go see if Nora needs help since the guests should be arriving any minute. I'll be back in a bit."

To tell you I'm expecting a Newport's baby.

"You'd better," her father winked. "But keep in mind what I said, Eve. Graham and Brooks have an agenda. They think I know their father's name and they'll use any means necessary to get it. I wouldn't put it past him to use you to get to me."

Eve stilled. She'd never thought for a second that Graham was using her for anything other than a bedmate…and she'd used him right back. But did her father's words hold any truth? Nora had hinted at the same thing the other day. Was her family just being overly cautious or did they truly believe Graham would use her to get to Sutton?

No. Graham wasn't the type of man to play games. He was a lethal attorney and when he wanted something, he went straight at it. He wasn't the type of man to hide behind a woman and let her do the work.

Eve let herself back out into the hallway and pulled in a deep breath. Voices filtered through the house and it was clear guests had started arriving. Giving her cleavage one last glance in a mirror, she gave a mental shrug and headed toward the formal living room.

Grace, Nora and Reid stood near the mantel, talking and laughing. Grace was dressed as a sexy witch with glittery hose, a sparkly black hat and some killer black stilettos. Their guests were dressed in various fun costumes. Eve glanced around the room and saw an oversize Mrs. Potato Head—presumably the Mr. Potato Head by the wet bar with an appetizer in his hand was the spouse. There was another couple dressed as Vikings and a few others in glamorous gowns and masks. Some reminded her of Mardi Gras with their ribbons and gems.

Eve was stopped by Lucinda Wilde and Josh Calhoun. Lucinda was their father's main caretaker and had pretty much morphed into being one of the family. She and Josh had fallen in love recently and Eve smiled as the couple approached her.

"If there's a contest for best costumes, you two win hands down."

Lucinda smiled as Josh wrapped his arm around her waist. "Josh isn't one for dressing up, so he basically threw on things he already owned."

Eve gave him an approving nod. "The cowboy look works. And your saloon girl is perfect," she told Lucinda. "I could never pull that off, but you guys look so authentic."

"I'm here for the food," Josh joked as he tipped his hat down in a typical cowboy fashion. "And I'd use any excuse to have Lucinda dress up like this."

Lucinda gave him a playful swat. "Eve, you look amazing. This is such a fun party, and I think it's just what Sutton needs. He may come out later."

"Really?" Eve asked. "I hope he does. Everyone here loves him and I know it would do him good."

"I agree," Lucinda said. "I'm going to talk to him in a bit and coerce him to join the party. I even dressed him up."

"I saw," Eve laughed. "I love the pirate."

"It's all he would agree to."

Lucinda glanced around the room, pushing her curls to the side so they slid over one bare shoulder. "If you'll excuse me, I'd like to talk to Nora and Reid. They look great, too."

Eve watched as the two couples met in the middle of the room. They laughed and chatted. Eve stared for a moment too long because she caught Grace's curious look and quirked brow, silently asking if Eve was okay.

Eve pasted on a smile and gave a brief nod. Everything was fine. Seriously. Just because she was expecting a child by a man who was an enemy of her father, just because the two families would go ballistic once the pregnancy was revealed, and just because her father was dying…why shouldn't she be fine?

Thirteen

She needed air desperately. The more guests that filled the house, the more Eve felt as though she was suffocating. She'd spent over an hour smiling, making small talk and wondering if anyone noticed how she kept her water glass full and ignored the wine.

The Winchester mansion was vast, but still, the walls had been closing in on her.

Escaping out the back patio doors, Eve slid off her gold sandals and padded barefoot around the pool. The stones were cool on her feet and for once she welcomed the brisk breeze. She'd started getting so warm inside, but then her body temperature had been off lately. *Thank you, hormones.*

When an arm snaked around her waist, Eve gasped.

"It's me," a familiar voice whispered in her ear.

Her entire body tingled at the warm breath against the side of her face, the taut chest against her back. But as much as she relished the feel of Graham against her, fear gripped her. "What are you doing here?" she whispered.

"My invitation got lost in the mail."

Eve smiled, but quickly composed herself before turning in his arms. "You're—"

Words died on her lips when she realized he was wearing a mask…one of those Mardi Gras masks she'd seen a few of the guests wearing earlier. And a tux. Mercy sakes he had on a tuxedo and looked just as perfectly packaged as he had the night of the charity ball.

Graham slid the mask over his head and took her hand. Without a word he pulled her toward the pool house. A thrill of excitement rushed through her as Graham tried the knob and it turned beneath his palm.

He ushered her inside, closed the door and left the lights off. She waited for him to devour her, to run his hands over her heated body. But nothing. Her eyes hadn't adjusted to the darkness and she couldn't see him.

"Graham?"

"I'm right here."

His voice was close. The heat from his body had her shifting, hoping to brush against him…waiting for him to make contact somehow.

"What are you doing?" she asked.

"I told you, my invitation got lost in the mail."

Eve rolled her eyes, even though he couldn't see her. "No. What are you doing in here?"

Material rustled. Something, his sleeve maybe, brushed against the back of her hand then was instantly gone. Her body was wound so tight in anticipation of his touch. What was he waiting on?

"I wanted to see you," he said in that low tone that had shivers racing through her. "You sent me that picture and I knew I had to find a way to be at this party."

"Did anyone—"

"No. Nobody saw me. I even talked to a few guests, but no one caught on."

Relief washed over her, but was quickly replaced once again by arousal. "Are you…why are we…"

"Are you achy, Eve?"

That sultry voice filled the darkness. Her eyes were finally starting to adjust somewhat, but there were no outside lights coming in because the entrance to the pool house faced the back of the property. Damn it. She wanted to see him better, to touch him. What game was he playing?

"Have you thought of me these past few days?" he continued. "I know you have or you wouldn't be sending me pictures of you in that sexy costume. Did you think I'd come begging for you? I told you, you'd be the one begging."

She was damn near ready to do just that. "Is that why you're here? To get me to beg?" she asked, hoping her voice sounded stronger than she felt.

"I'm here because I told you I wanted to be your date."

Eve eased away from the door, only to stop short when she ran into Graham's hard chest. "So what are we doing in the pool house?" she asked, holding her hands up to steady herself. She couldn't stop herself from gliding her palms up the tux jacket toward his broad shoulders.

"Your call, Eve. I told you I won't be the one to make a move."

Why did life have to be full of so many tempting choices? Why was her greatest need the exact opposite of what she should be doing? But the lengths he went to in order to be with her was rather…oh, fine. It was flat-out arousing and exciting.

"You're quite cocky to come into my family's home," she told him, roaming her hands up toward his neck, her fingertips teasing that smooth jawline.

"Call it what you want, but there was no way in hell I was going to let some damn picture pacify my need for you."

He'd never admitted he needed her before. Granted he was talking in physical terms, but the words still sent a thrill of desire through her.

Eve leaned in until her lips barely brushed against his. "So you're here to give in after all? Dare I say, beg me?" she whispered.

With a groan, Graham snaked his arms around her waist and gripped her backside, pulling her flush against him. "Hell no. I'm not begging. I'm taking what I want, what you've teased me with, and I'm saving your pride so *you* don't have to beg."

Eve laughed. "So this is all for me?"

"I'm a selfish man, Eve. Never forget that."

His lips crushed hers as he backed her up a few steps to the door. She hit with a thud, but she barely noticed. With the way Graham's hands were wrestling the hem of her dress up her thighs, she couldn't concentrate on anything but the endless possibilities of what was about to happen.

"Never tease me again," Graham muttered against her lips. "Did you think I'd avoid you, knowing you looked like this?"

His mouth made a path down her neck, to the deep V of her dress. For the first time tonight, she was all too happy to be this exposed. Better access for Graham was exactly what she needed, what she ached for.

Eve arched her back, cupping the side of his face as he jerked the thick straps down her shoulders. The second her dress fell to her waist, Graham filled his hands with her bare breasts.

"If I'd known you weren't wearing anything beneath this, I would've intercepted you at your house before the party and we never would've left."

Eve gasped as his lips found her sensitive tip. "The dress…it has…um…"

"Yes?" he asked, a smile in his tone. "How close are you to begging?"

About a second.

"The dress has a built-in liner. No bra necessary."

"It's my new favorite."

When his hands trailed up the back of her thighs, Eve had to bite her lips to keep from crying out. He knew every single place to touch her and have her squirming. He knew she was on the brink of begging and he was practically gloating over it.

Time to turn the tables, so to speak.

Eve reached between them. The second she stroked her hand up his length, Graham let out a hiss.

"I'm not playing games, Eve."

She couldn't help but smile against his mouth. "You wouldn't have come here if you weren't playing."

She. Was. Killing. Him.

And his slow descent had started the second she'd sent that picture of her wearing the dress. But, seeing her in person, touching those curves, was absolutely everything he'd ever dreamed and fantasized about. Yes, he'd had her multiple times, but knowing she was carrying his child bumped up the sexual appeal. There was something so primal, so…damn it, *his*. She was his. That child was his. There would never be another man coming into her life, into their child's life. Not so long as Graham was around.

Maybe he'd come here to seduce her, most likely. But he'd intentionally decided to crash the party simply because he knew he could. He'd taken matters into his own hands.

Speaking of matters in hand...

"Take off your dress."

Eve stilled. "Here?"

"We can go back inside to the party to do this, but I'm sure your family wouldn't approve."

Graham backed away and waited until the rustling and soft swoosh of fabric indicated she was indeed bare for him. Closing the space between them, Graham wasted no time in grabbing hold of her and lifting her until her legs wrapped around him.

He eased over slightly so her back wasn't against the grooves in the door. But once he had her against the wall, he reached between them, unfastened his pants and kissed her. Hard. This wasn't a sweet encounter; he didn't have time for gentle touches and nurturing words. He was in this dark pool house with his own goddess for one reason only.

"Hurry," she panted against his mouth.

Clearly Eve was in here for one reason, as well. This was why they got along so well. Their needs, their wants were identical in nearly every single way. Convincing her to be his wife would be the easiest case he'd ever made.

The soft pants, the occasional groan from Eve were begging enough. Graham slid into her, smiling when her fingers curled around his shoulders and gripped tighter. The way she whispered his name as she threw her head back and closed her eyes only fueled Graham to move faster.

"It's been too long," he growled as he kept a firm hold on her hips. "Never again."

"No," she murmured, her eyes locking with his.

Graham couldn't go another day without touching her, let alone several. His stupid pride and the ridiculous game he'd played…it had backfired in his face. Now he was the one needing her, but damn if he'd admit it.

"I'm the only one, Eve." He didn't know why he needed to express this, but damn if another man would be keeping her bed warm. For now, she was his. "Say it."

Nodding, she gasped when he pushed harder. "The only one. Only you."

Feeling too vulnerable, way too close to the edge of exposing feelings he wasn't ready to come face-to-face with, Graham angled his mouth across hers once more. His hips quickened, and her knees tightened around his waist.

When her hands came up to frame his face, Graham ignored the tingle of awareness. He wanted it fast, hard, intense. Little sweet gestures weren't for him. They weren't for *them*.

Eve tore her mouth from his and squeezed her eyes tight.

"No. Look at me," he demanded. His eyes had adjusted to the darkness and he wanted to see as much of her as possible.

When her body convulsed, Graham could no longer hold back. He buried his face in the side of her neck, inhaling that familiar, jasmine scent. Holding tight, he waited until their bodies ceased trembling before he lifted his face. Her heart beat so fast against his chest, matching his own frantic pace.

"My family is going to wonder where I went," Eve murmured, breaking the silence.

Graham nipped at her lips. "Tell them you needed some fresh air."

"I don't even want to look in a mirror. They're going to wonder why I'm so messed up."

"Then leave with me."

Why had he said that? They weren't inseparable. But there was something about knowing they shared this baby…the bond was already too strong. Graham needed to rein things back in or he was going to find himself in a position he wasn't ready for.

Eve slid her legs from his waist. "We'll both pretend you didn't say that."

Once she was standing and had her balance, Graham stepped back and adjusted his clothes. He'd barely taken the edge off and if he stayed at this party, he was going to have to find a spare bathroom or walk-in closet to drag her into.

He pulled out his phone to use as a light, shining it on Eve. The instant the glow hit her face, she froze and blinked at him. But it was the tousled hair, the swollen lips and pinkened cheeks that held him captivated. There was no denying what she'd been up to and the thought of her putting that dress back on while looking so rumpled sent a jolt of desire through him.

"I can't see your face with that light in my eyes," she told him, holding up a hand. "But if I don't get back in there, my family is going to worry."

Angling his phone toward her body as she pulled her dress back up, Graham reached a hand out to help her. "I'm going in, too. I'm not going to leave."

"Why would you want to stay?"

Because he wanted to touch her, he wanted to catch a glimpse of her across the room…because apparently he was a masochist. Mostly because she was trying to push him away when she clearly didn't mean it, and he wouldn't let her.

"Because I can," he said simply.

Once she'd adjusted her dress, she pushed her hair back behind her shoulders. "I'm going to tell the rest of my family about the baby after the party."

He tightened his hold on his phone. No. He had to get her to agree to marriage before she told her family. They would instantly tell her what a mistake it was to be involved with him. They'd get inside her head and have her doubting.

"Are you sure that's a smart move? They already think I'm using you."

"Are you?"

He couldn't blame her for asking. Apparently they'd already gotten to her. "If you thought I was, you wouldn't be in here with me," he countered. He hadn't used her, not by any means. But now that she was having his baby, he would marry her to ensure that their child had a Newport name. A detail she didn't need to know.

Yes, he could've used her to get to her father, but he hadn't. Didn't that count for something?

"Regardless of what they think, they need to know," Eve continued. "There's so much worry with my father, fear of the unknown, and now with Carson finding out he's our half brother. My family needs to know exactly what they're dealing with. Besides, maybe this baby will be the bond that brings our families together and resolves this ridiculous feud."

Graham wasn't so sure of that, but if she wanted to

tell them, he'd support her…after that ring was on her finger.

"Let's wait a few days," he said, holding up a hand when she opened her mouth. "I want you to come away with me."

"What?"

Yeah, what did he mean? Where had that come from? He hadn't planned it. But now that he'd offered the trip, he had to admit it was a brilliant plan.

"We'll go away for just a couple days," he hurried on. "Nobody has to know, and when we get back, you and I can tell them."

"I'm telling them tonight, Graham. I've waited long enough."

Her inflexible tone told him this battle would be more difficult than he'd thought.

"I need to get back inside," she told him.

"I'm coming in, too."

Eve hesitated, but finally nodded. "Just keep your mask on until after the party, okay? I'd hate to have a scene with so many people here."

Graham would love nothing more than to cause a scene, but out of respect for Eve, he'd keep the mask on. He searched the floor, then found it. After sliding it back into place, he bowed toward her.

"You go on," he told her. "I'll be in later. You won't even know I'm there."

With her hand on the knob, she threw him a glance over her shoulder. "I'll know you're there. I'll feel you."

With those parting words, she was gone.

She'd *feel* him? Of course she would. And even across the room, he'd undoubtedly feel her, as well. The line he'd been teetering on, swearing he wouldn't cross it, was starting to waver. He was losing his grip and it was only a matter of time before he lost his balance and fell face-first into emotions he'd purposely dodged.

This entire situation was messy and if he wasn't careful, someone was going to end up hurt.

Fourteen

No matter how she mingled with the guests, no matter how many jokes Reid told her and no matter how many times she refilled her glass of sparkling water, Eve felt the presence of Graham just the same as if he'd come up and wrapped his arms around her.

Nora and Reid separated, but kept making eye contact with each other. Eve wondered what that kind of connection would be like. To look across the room and have your soul mate watching you. Silent communication passed between the couple. Whatever they were sharing, Reid gave a nod and Nora moved through the crowd toward the front of the formal living room.

"Those two are up to something," Grace whispered behind Eve's back. "They've been sneaking around all evening."

Eve caught sight of Graham across the room in the familiar mask. His face was turned toward hers, but she couldn't see his eyes. No matter, she knew they were on her. The connection across the room…it was just like Nora and Reid's.

No. She and Graham were nothing like her sister and Reid. Were they?

"That's what lovers do," Eve replied, not taking her gaze from Graham. She had to admit, the thrill of having him in her family home was exciting. For someone who was such a stickler for rules, lately she found herself not caring so long as she saw Graham.

No matter how she tried to shift her focus to the baby, to remain in control of her life, she kept getting pulled back into Graham's web. The encounter in the pool house shouldn't have happened, but she wouldn't change anything. How could she keep denying what they both wanted? They were having a baby together. That didn't mean they had to automatically stop seeing each other…did it?

Nerves fluttered in her stomach. She was anxious to get this night over with, to finally let her family know what was going on. If there was an issue, she'd deal with it, but she couldn't keep living this secret life. Keeping her affair hidden was difficult enough, but there was no way she'd be able to keep a child from her family. Soon, very soon, they'd see the evidence.

"Can I have everybody's attention?" Reid called. When only half the room quieted, he put his fingers to his mouth and whistled. Silence immediately settled over the space. "I'd like your attention."

"What's going on?" Eve asked her younger sister.

"No idea, but Dad was just wheeled in."

Eve turned around. Dr. Wilde was heading their way with their father. Sutton had his eyes on Eve and Grace, a smile on his pale face. The cancer had robbed him of his color, his dignity and his normal life. But here he was, attending the party in costume, giving his terminal illness the middle finger.

Eve glanced at Dr. Wilde, then down at her father when he pulled up beside her in his wheelchair and reached for her hand to give it a quick squeeze.

"Nora and Reid asked if I'd come in," he explained.

Reid cleared his throat, drawing Eve's attention back toward the front of the room. "As many of you know, Nora and I have been seeing each other for some time now. I've fallen in love with her, with her son, and I want to make things official."

Nora's wide smile was infectious. Eve found herself grinning, knowing what was coming. She clasped her hands in front of her mouth, mostly to prevent people from seeing her chin quiver. She was so emotional lately.

"I've asked Nora to marry me." Cheers erupted in the room. "I've also asked to adopt her son," Reid went on. Wrapping an arm around Nora's waist, he pulled her flush against his side. "She said yes and we plan to be married on Thanksgiving right here on the Winchester estate."

A burst of applause, and congratulations filled the room. Grace squealed and headed for the happy couple. Eve looked down at her father, who had actually teared up. Apparently she wasn't the only one with high emotions lately.

"You didn't know?" Eve asked.

"I had an idea. She asked if she could host a family gathering on Thanksgiving and I told her that would be great and just what the family needed."

Eve gestured to Lucinda, who was standing behind the wheelchair. "One of us will take him back in a bit. Go mingle."

With a simple nod, Lucinda made her way toward Josh. Eve gripped the chair and pushed her father toward Reid and Nora. Once Nora spotted their dad, she rushed forward, arms wide.

"I hope this is okay, Dad." She threw her arms around him before leaning back to search his face. "I wanted to surprise everyone, to ease some of the tension this family has been dealing with from the trouble with the Newports and your illness."

At the mention of the Newports, Eve searched for Graham, but couldn't find him. Surely he hadn't left. He wouldn't. Somewhere he was waiting for his chance to get her alone again.

"This is perfect, Nora," their father said. "I'm so happy for you guys and having the wedding here is an excellent idea."

Nora straightened and said to Eve, "I hope you'll stand up by my side."

Eve hugged her sister. "I wouldn't be anywhere else."

When Nora pulled away, she looked toward Eve's flat stomach, then back up into her eyes. "Everything okay?"

Eve simply nodded, not wanting to get into this now.

Dread filled her. No, she couldn't get into this now, or even an hour from now. This night belonged to Nora and Reid. The baby news would definitely have to wait, but for how long? As much as Eve would love to shield her child from the fallout, she knew she'd have to just tell her family and not worry about the timing. But telling them right now was definitely out of the question.

Stealing the night from Nora and Reid wasn't right.

A flash from the corner of her eye had her turning. The man in the striking Mardi Gras mask moved

toward her. There was no way Graham could get this
close to her family. He wouldn't purposely give away
his identity, but still the idea of him getting within talking distance had Eve excusing herself from her sisters
and father.

"You need to go," she whispered as she walked by
him.

Eve kept walking, knowing he was right behind
her. When they reached the foyer, Eve smiled at one of
Nora's friends who was heading down the hall toward
the bathroom.

Once the foyer was empty, Graham lifted his mask
to rest it on the top of his head. With his back to the rest
of the house, he stared down at her. He wasn't too concerned about the risk of being seen, not with the way
he was standing.

"I can't tell them," Eve murmured. "Not tonight."

She hated this. Hated that such an innocent child, a
child she loved with all her heart, was being kept a secret like there was something…dirty. A child should be
celebrated, not hidden.

Graham's hands slid up her bare arms, his fingers
curled over her shoulders. "I know."

He pulled her into his embrace and Eve willingly
went. She hated leaning on anyone, but right now, they
were a team, whether either of them wanted to admit
it or not. And she had to admit, having Graham's arms
around her felt…right. But that couldn't be. Nothing
about having him here, let alone his embracing her as
if he cared, was right. This affair had started as a whirl-
wind and they were caught up, that's all. There could
be nothing more.

"Let's go away," he whispered into her ear. "We'll
go to my cabin in Tennessee for a few days and relax.

Nothing will bother us, you can rest, and we can figure out a plan that will work for our child and our families."

Was that even possible? She'd give anything to be able to escape for a few days, to come to terms with everything and figure out a way to work with Graham. But if she went away with him, she knew what that meant...there would be more of what had transpired in the pool house.

Eve sighed and pulled back. "My mind is all over the place." She glanced over his shoulder to make sure they were still alone. "Let's go out onto the porch."

Once they were outside, she led him down to where the lights weren't shining right on them. The chilly air hit her hard and Graham instantly took off his black jacket and draped it around her shoulders. His familiar woodsy scent hit her, and the warmth from the jacket where it had hugged his body was just like having his arms around her.

"I keep battling myself where you're concerned," she went on, gripping the lapels closer together. "I want to keep my distance physically, but then I see you and—"

"I don't even have to see you to want you."

"Graham, we have to think of what's best here."

"I am." He leaned in closer, crowding her against the side of the house. "Right now, I'm thinking that escaping for a few days is exactly what we need. We would have time to talk without interruptions. I can fly the helicopter and nobody would have to know where you and I went. We'll both just say we're away on business."

Eve closed her eyes, giving the idea more thought than she probably should. "You make this seem so simple."

"Say the word and I'll make sure it's simple," he

whispered against her mouth. "All you'll have to do is pack a bag."

There was a reason Graham was one of the top lawyers in Chicago. The man could persuade anyone with that charm of his. He made his case so perfectly, so convincingly. Eve opened her eyes, meeting his bright blue stare.

"When do we leave?"

"You're leaving when?"

Graham held the phone between his shoulder and his ear. "Tonight."

Brooks laughed on the other end of the line. "Who is she?"

After placing a perfectly folded pair of jeans in his carry-on bag, Graham stood straight up and gripped the phone. "I said it was work related."

"We pretty much have the same mind and I know this urgency in your tone has nothing to do with work."

Hell, yeah, he was urgent to get Eve alone in his cabin. The obvious reason of privacy aside, Eve needed rest, she needed to relax and not worry about telling her family she was expecting. Now that Nora knew, Graham prayed she was too focused on her engagement to discuss Eve's condition. Graham had to trust her to keep her word. Plus, he had an engagement of his own to worry about. He wanted to get that ring on Eve's finger, and he'd use this trip to advance his case.

"I have a pressing matter that needs my attention," Graham said to his twin. "I'll only be gone three days."

"And this has to do with what case?" Brooks asked in a mocking tone.

"You know I can't discuss my client cases with you." Totally true. "Besides, I need to finish packing, so this conversation is over. Unless there's an emergency, don't contact me and I'll let you know when I get home."

"If I find out our father's name I'll sure as hell be calling you and you'll have to put your mystery woman on hold."

"If you find out our father's name, I'll be back," Graham promised.

"Wait…tell me you're not sneaking out of town with Eve. I thought you were done messing with her."

Graham turned toward his walk-in closet to grab some shirts. "I'm not messing around with anyone."

It was only partly a lie. Because he wasn't messing with her. He was the father of her child. That went well beyond messing.

"You're lying, but I'll let you off the hook because I'm on my way to meet Roman. He thinks he has a lead. I'll keep you posted."

"This late?" Graham asked.

"He texted me right before you called, so whatever he wants, it must be something important."

Excitement filled Graham as the possibilities swirled through his head. "Did he say what the lead was?"

"No. And he said it was minor, but at this point we're going to explore any option we have."

Graham would love nothing more than to find their biological father. Then maybe Brooks's vendetta against Sutton would ease up a bit and the tension would ease between their families. But that was doubtful, especially when Sutton discovered Eve was pregnant.

"Keep me posted," Graham told his brother before hanging up.

After tossing in the rest of his belongings, Graham zipped up the bag. He couldn't wait to get Eve to the cabin. She could take long bubble baths in the garden tub in the master suite that overlooked the mountains and just relax. He would make sure of it. He'd already called one of his staff members to have certain foods stocked. Eve wouldn't want for a thing these next few days.

The only look he wanted to see on her face was happiness. She was still so early in her pregnancy, and his goal was to get her to take her mind off her troubles because he knew she was worried.

Which left the question he'd had on his mind for days. What did Nora mean when she'd mentioned Eve's previous pregnancy? Graham didn't want to dredge up bad memories for her, but he also felt he deserved to know.

These three days could bring anything their way. But one thing was for sure: Graham wasn't going to let her get away without convincing her to marry him. This child would be a Newport. Added to that, merging the families in such a bold way would show everyone just how serious they were about ending this feud. But time was running out and Graham needed to act fast.

He grabbed his things and set the security alarm on his penthouse. After he swung by to pick up Eve, they'd be on their way to his cabin. Nothing would stop him from putting that ring on her finger. He may not have been looking for a family, but there was no way in hell another man would raise his child. And he'd yet to find anyone as compatible as Eve. No, they weren't in love, but what did that have to do with marriages these days anyway? Being an attorney, he'd seen the aftermath when people entered into holy matrimony solely on the basis of love. *No thank you.*

Graham was confident that by the end of this trip, he'd have Eve convinced this was the best decision for everyone. He knew what to say, how to get her to see his side. After all, he'd gotten her to agree to this trip in no time.

A little seduction, a little charm and she'd have that ring on her finger.

Fifteen

A cabin? Who referred to a sprawling five-thousand-square-foot log home as a cabin?

Being the real estate guru she was, Eve nearly laughed when she saw Graham's home away from home. The place was stunning and she hadn't even walked in the front door yet. It was after midnight, so she couldn't see the views. But the old lantern-style lights on the porch illuminated a beautiful facade and had her anxious to see the inside.

"I've got your bag."

Eve stood at the bottom of the stone steps leading up to the entrance. She'd forgotten all about her things once Graham had opened her car door and she'd seen the beauty of this place. All she wanted to do was take in each and every detail because she knew she'd never be back. She couldn't wait for sunrise. She'd bet money the views were spectacular.

"Ready to go inside?" he asked.

Eve blinked, glancing over at him. He held both bags and offered her a smile she knew she wouldn't be able to resist later.

Was she ready to go in? Was she ready to spend three days with a man she was falling for? Was she ready to let him fully into her life, into her heart? She'd made the decision last night after the party to come clean about her feelings. Graham needed to know. There could be no secrets between them, not if she wanted a chance at making this work.

"I'm ready," she told him.

The wide porch had sturdy wooden swings at each end that swayed in the gentle breeze. The warmer temperature here seemed so inviting and Eve already made mental plans to take advantage of those swings. She'd come to relax and she intended to do just that.

"I have the refrigerator stocked with your favorite foods," Graham told her as he set the bags at his feet so he could unlock the door. "I did a search on foods you couldn't have while pregnant, so no swordfish for you."

Eve laughed. "And here I was hoping you'd show me what you could do in the kitchen with swordfish."

That got a chuckle out of him. "I have something else planned for our meals."

The way he threw a sultry look over his shoulder told her he had more than dinner planned…not that she didn't know that already. Even after being with him so many times, she still anticipated their three days together. Something about being here, being so isolated from the outside, plus being so far from their families, seemed even more intimate. Yes, they were still sneaking, but for the next three days, they could be themselves.

Eve stopped short before she could enter the house.

After all they'd been through, this would be the first time they actually slept together. They'd both been careful about not sleeping over—that would've been another level they hadn't discussed. But here, she had to assume they were sharing a room.

Maybe not, though. Maybe he'd put her stuff in a guest room. If that were the case, then the feelings she wanted to reveal would be a moot point.

Eve knew one thing. By the end of this trip, they were going to have to have some serious plans laid out because she couldn't handle this emotional upheaval anymore.

The second Graham swung the old oak door open, Eve gasped. The open floor plan gave an immediate view all the way through the house. But that wasn't the extraordinary part. The opposite wall was nothing but a showcase of floor-to-ceiling windows overlooking the mountains and valleys. The lights dotting the landscape were so sporadic, so different from Chicago. There was space to breathe here, nature to explore. This was exactly the escape she needed from the city, from the chaos in her life.

As if pulled toward the beauty, Eve slowly crossed the open space. "Whatever you paid for this place was worth it."

Graham laughed as she passed him. "I had the same reaction when I first opened the door, too. I knew the asking price was high, but the second I saw that view, I knew this place would be mine."

Eve threw a glance over her shoulder. "And is that how things normally work for you? You see something you want and take it?"

He let the bags he was carrying fall to the floor with a thunk. "Always."

The intensity of his stare combined with his instant response had Eve turning back toward the million-dollar view. She already knew Graham was a go-getter; it was one of the qualities she found most attractive in him.

The way he'd been protective of her feelings, of her emotions during the party earlier had sealed the deal, though. She'd gone and fallen for Graham Newport, father of her child. Even if the baby didn't exist, Eve wouldn't have been able to stop herself.

But they *had* created a child.

A flashback to a time during her previous pregnancy when her belly had been slightly rounded hit Eve as she placed a hand over her stomach. She longed to feel a baby move beneath her palm, wanted to know there was a healthy child thriving inside of her.

Hands slid over her shoulders. "What are you thinking?"

Eve leaned back against Graham's firm chest. Did she open up to him? Did she fully let him in? If she wanted a chance at this, then yes. But not right now. She didn't want to start these relaxing days by dumping the darkest memories of her life right in his lap.

"Something to be saved for another time," she told him.

One of his hands came down to slide over hers. "No worrying. Remember?"

"I'm trying."

Graham spun her around, framed her face and kissed her softly. "Why don't you look around and I'll work on getting something to eat? I know you barely ate at the party."

She had picked at the appetizers, but then the encounter in the pool house had happened, then Reid and Nora's announcement and, well…here she was.

"More of your hidden kitchen talents?" she asked with a grin. "I am definitely on board with that."

"Then you're going to love these next few days. I plan on cooking for you every chance I get. I want a healthy baby, so I'm making sure his mama is cared for."

A healthy child. What she wouldn't give for that.

"You're going to spoil me and I won't want to leave."

Graham nipped once more at her lips. "That's the idea."

What? Did he mean…

Graham let go and went back to grab the bags. He headed up the stairs, leaving her staring after him as if he hadn't just dropped some veiled hint in her lap. Did he want to have her here longer than three days? Did he see their relationship as something more than physical? As something more than just sharing custody?

Hope blossomed inside her. Maybe this trip would be a turning point. Maybe letting him know exactly how she felt was just what they needed to move forward into a life together.

Graham froze at the edge of the couch where Eve lay on her side sleeping. He'd watched her from the kitchen as he cooked. She'd been sitting there reading a pregnancy magazine, then she'd stretched her feet out across the cushions. Now she was down for the count and the magazine had fallen to the floor.

Guilt slid through him. The ring he'd bought a week ago was in his room. He wanted to wait for the right moment to bring it out, to tell her he wanted their child to have his name.

They'd started out so hot for each other, and that hadn't changed. But the second Graham knew there was a child, he wasn't about to let anyone else get near what was his. This baby would have his name, no matter how he had to go about it.

But Eve's underlying defenselessness kept working its way further under his skin. When he wasn't with her, he was thinking about her—when he was with her, he didn't want to leave. He had never wanted a woman in his life permanently. Being married to his job was hard enough, but to try to sustain a relationship was damn near impossible.

For the first time in his life, Graham thought he actually wanted to try. Maybe he'd lost his mind. Perhaps he'd never had a chance where she was concerned. But no matter the reasoning or the path that led them here, Graham was tired of fighting this battle with himself.

Having Eve in his cabin, knowing she'd instantly loved this place the way he had only made him realize just how much they had in common.

He'd convinced her to come here immediately after the party. Maybe he should have waited until morning, but he was so afraid she'd start thinking and change her mind. So he'd whisked her off when she was exhausted. Sleep was exactly what she needed, and once she woke, they could start talking, planning.

Graham pulled the crocheted throw off the back of the sofa and placed it over Eve. Gerty had made this throw, and several other little items around the cabin. He'd wanted a piece of his past to be here. He'd wanted to hold on to the woman who had helped raise him and shape him into the man he was today.

Looking down on Eve's relaxed face, Graham couldn't help but wonder what Gerty would think of her. What would his mother think? No doubt both women would adore Eve. She was so easy to talk to. She may be president of one of the top real estate companies in

Chicago, but it was her charm, her charisma and her determination that would keep her on top.

Sutton didn't deserve a daughter so perfect. He didn't deserve her loyalty. Sutton had used Graham's mother, not bothering to care what happened to her because he had his wife to go back to when he was done.

Graham hated Sutton more and more each time he thought of how easy it had been for the mogul to end things with Cynthia. She'd been pregnant, not that Sutton had stuck around to find out. She'd already had twins at home and was expecting another child. With the income from waitressing, there was no way she could have survived on her own…or been able to pay for an attorney if she were threatened with a custody battle. And she hadn't taken a dime from him for fear he'd sue for custody. She wouldn't have been able to battle Sutton in court.

Graham didn't blame his mother one bit for not telling the tycoon.

Gerty had seriously been the biggest blessing in all of their lives.

Eve reminded Graham so much of his grandma. Both women were strong. They both clung to their determination to get them through rough times. And they were both stubborn to a fault.

Graham took a seat in the leather chair, propped his feet on the ottoman and laced his hands over his abs. He was perfectly content to watch Eve rest. This is exactly what he wanted her to do.

Now he just had to figure out what he really wanted. Asking her to marry him may give her false hope. But on the other hand, he wasn't so sure his goals in marrying her were quite the same as they once were.

There was no denying that when she woke up, and

once they started talking, the dynamics between them would change.

Graham just had to keep the upper hand and decide how much their lives were about to be altered.

Sixteen

Eve woke to blackness. There wasn't a single light on in the room. Where was she? She blinked a few times, sat up and quickly remembered. She'd fallen asleep on the couch in Graham's cabin.

The slightest glow from the porch lights filtered in through the windows. Eve sat up, turning her stiff neck from side to side. She didn't even recall lying down. She'd started reading a magazine, had gotten swept up by some article on how to make your own baby food, and that was the last thing she remembered.

Turning, Eve went still when she spotted Graham asleep in the chair across from her. His feet were propped on the oversize ottoman, his head tipped to one side. She wished there was more light so she could make out his facial features. Was he fully relaxed? When he'd fallen asleep in her bed, he always had those worry lines between his brows. Now that he was away, did he allow himself to completely let go?

Eve pulled at the throw caught around her legs. She hadn't put that there. An image of Graham covering her had a warmth spreading through her. The little ways he showed he cared couldn't be ignored. The way he cooked for her, opened up about his mother and Gerty, swept her away when life became too much…he was putting her needs first and she couldn't deny the tug on her heart.

Part of Eve wished they could just stay here forever. Ignore their families, ignore the entire mess with Sutton, Carson and the investigator Brooks had hired. Ignore the reality that her father was dying, that her sister was marrying the love of her life and everything was perfect for her. The entire family was thrilled for Nora, and Eve was, too. But there was still that fear that once everyone knew of Eve's pregnancy, she'd never be shown support. That she wouldn't experience such happiness. Her family wouldn't accept the fact that Graham was the father, and worse yet, that Eve had fallen for him.

Eve got to her feet, shaking out the throw. Moving around the ottoman, she started to lay the blanket over Graham. Instantly he gripped her wrist and pulled her down into his lap.

With a yelp, she fell right into the crook of his arm, her head to his shoulder.

"I thought you were asleep."

Graham adjusted her legs to settle them between his. "You thought wrong."

That low rumble vibrated from his chest. His fingertips trailed up her bare forearm. "How do you feel now?"

"Like I slept for days."

"Good. I want you to feel rejuvenated."

Eve relaxed fully against him. "I'm sorry I fell asleep when you were cooking. Did I ruin everything?"

"We can heat it back up whenever. It was late. You needed rest."

His fingertips continued to trail up and down her arm. When she shivered, Graham took the twisted blanket and gave it a flick to send it soaring out over their legs. He wrapped her tighter, in the blanket and his arms. Eve wasn't sure if this was some euphoric state from sleep or if this was really happening. Were they... snuggling? He wasn't trying to get her undressed, she wasn't straddling him and ripping his shirt off. They were just...doing nothing and it felt rather amazing.

"As much as I want you to relax and take it easy, I want to know something."

Eve stilled. "What?"

"About your first pregnancy."

Eve closed her eyes. She'd known the questions would be coming, and he deserved to know. He'd given her time to prepare and hadn't immediately asked when Nora spilled the secret the other day.

Eve was ready to tell him now—*needed* to tell him. There was still a part of her that had to heal before she could move on. Not that she could fully recover from the loss of a child, but talking about the pain with the man she'd fallen in love with would go a long way to preparing her for the next chapter of her life.

"I was in love once," she started, then realized that wasn't the right thing to say. "Actually, I thought I was in love, but I had just been blindsided by lust and charm."

Graham remained silent, but kept his firm hold on her. She appreciated the darkened room, the fact she didn't have to look him in the eye when she was telling him about this portion of her life. There was a deeper intimacy about letting him in this way.

"I met Rick in college," she went on. "The attraction was instant. We dated for six months. I thought he was the one."

The words sounded so cold, so lifeless when she said them, but there was no other way to tell this story. That period of her life was gone and she was only left with the emotional scars.

"I found out I was pregnant." She'd never forget how happy she was to tell Rick. "I thought we'd marry, raise our family and live happily ever after." Eve pulled in a breath, toyed with the edging on the crocheted blanket. "When I told him I was pregnant, he was done with me. Apparently he was interested in being married to Sutton's daughter, but not so much in having a child. No, wait. He was more interested in being married to money. I was nothing."

"I want to kill him."

Eve smiled. "I appreciate the offer, but he married into money, then his wife cheated on him with the pool boy. Clichéd, but I did a small victory dance."

Graham chuckled, squeezing her tighter. "I had no idea you had such a ruthless side. Remind me never to cheat on you with the pool boy."

Smacking his arm, Eve continued. "Anyway, I was about six weeks pregnant then. I was scared, but my family was so supportive. I knew I'd be okay. Losing the baby never even entered my mind. Not once."

Graham slid his hand over hers, their fingers lacing over her stomach. That silent supportive gesture had tears burning her eyes.

"Nora, Grace and I had already picked out names," Eve whispered, her throat full of emotions. "I knew I wanted the nursery decorated in gray and yellow no matter what the sex of the baby was. When I was seventeen weeks, I went in for an ultrasound. The doctor's office had a new machine, one that had top-of-the-line imaging. I was so excited to see that little face, to find out what I was having."

When her voice broke, Eve bit her lip. She wanted to hold it together. She wanted to show Graham that she was strong, but all those past emotions threatened to strangle her and end this conversation. Tremors racked her body as her eyes filled. There was no stopping the wave of memories and feelings as she relived the horrid day.

"Eve, don't—"

"No. I've come this far and you need to know." On a shaky breath, she continued, "The tech kept searching the screen and moving the device over my stomach almost frantically, and I knew something was wrong. Her face wasn't bright like when I'd first come in. At one point she excused herself and stepped out into the hall to ask someone to find the doctor. I knew. In my heart I knew something was wrong with my baby."

"What happened?"

"In simple terms, the cord came away from the amniotic sac. I don't know how far along I was when that happened. The doctor said my body still thought I was pregnant, so my uterus was still stretching." Eve sniffed, wiped at the tears on her cheeks. "I could've lost the baby a month earlier or I could've lost her that day. I honestly don't know. But I know I never want to live through that again. I can't."

"Oh, baby." Graham kissed the top of her head. "I don't even know what to say."

"Nothing can be said," she said. "People told me how sorry they were. They tried to say the right thing, but there isn't a right thing. I lost a piece of myself that day and the following days are a blur. I will never know that face. That's all I kept thinking. What did she look like?"

"She?"

Eve shrugged. "I don't know. I didn't ask. They had to perform a D&C the next day to remove all the tissue. I was getting prepped for surgery, wondering how things had gone from the highest mountain to the deepest pit I'd ever known, when the nurse had me sign a paper. It was a paper stating I gave them permission to dispose of any remains. *Dispose of.*"

"Eve, stop, please."

Tears slid down her face. "How could I sign a paper saying that was okay?" she asked, ignoring his plea. "This was my baby. I know I wasn't far enough along to have a funeral, but the wording was just so cold, so heartless. I'll never forget it."

Graham reached a hand up to wipe her wet cheeks, then smoothed her hair away from her face. "No more. Don't do this to yourself. I'm such a jerk for asking, but I thought I deserved to know. I should've thought of your feelings."

"No." Eve shifted in his arms to face him. "You did deserve to know. I wanted to tell you, but I didn't want to kill our mood here. I want you to know everything about me."

"I don't want you hurt," he murmured against her lips. "I can't stand it, Eve. Never again will you hurt like that."

Reaching up to cup his face, Eve tipped her head back. "I hope I don't. I hope this baby is delivered full-term and healthy. I'm so afraid of how my family will react, how your brothers will take the news. I can handle quite a bit, but I won't let our child be in the cross fire."

Graham slid his thumb along her bottom lip. "Nobody will harm you or our child so long as I'm in the picture."

"And how long will that be?" she dared to ask.

In lieu of an answer, Graham kissed her gently. Eve instantly opened to him. He never had to ask, never had to persuade her. She was always ready for more contact, more of anything that had to do with Graham. He'd listened to her, he'd hurt for her and he was trying to make her forget if only for a short time.

When his hand trailed down to the hem of her shirt, she shifted. Without words, without the usual rush and frenzy, they were undressed and somehow ended up settled right back in the chair.

Eve rested a knee on either side of Graham's hips. "I love you."

She didn't mean to let loose with the words, but there was no holding them back.

"Eve—"

"No." She held a finger to his lips. "I don't need anything said in return. I've been completely open with you tonight and I wanted to get it all out. I needed to. Now show me how you were going to make me forget the rest of the world."

Graham couldn't get those words out of his mind. She loved him. Loved. Him.

No other woman, save for his mother and Gerty, had ever uttered those words to him before. He wasn't sure what to do, what to say. Had she not cut him off, what would've come out of his mouth in reply?

As he put breakfast together the following morning, Graham tried to pull himself together. This was what he'd been waiting for. She'd fallen in love with him and now all he had to do was make this relationship more official.

But after all she'd shared before her declaration of

love, he didn't feel right about using her state of vulnerability to complete his plan. He needed to see what happened today, when they could talk more, explore the area together and just be themselves. Maybe...

What? Nothing had changed. He still wanted this child to have his name.

His cell vibrated on the counter. Brooks's name lit up the screen. Graham slid the casserole into the oven and answered his phone.

"Hello."

"Roman has a major lead. He thinks he has a name, but he's going to make a quick trip before he tells us to be sure."

Could this be it? After all this time could they have found their father?

Since Eve was still in bed where he'd left her, Graham put his phone on speaker so he could start cutting up the fruit.

"How soon will we know?" Graham asked, pulling out various bags of produce from the refrigerator.

"He's heading there today. Hopefully soon."

Graham slid a knife from the block on the counter. "I'm going to be nervous all day."

"Me, too," his brother said. "You ready to tell me where you are?"

"I'm at the cabin."

Brooks made a humming sound, one that mocked Graham and made him sorry he'd even admitted that much.

"With?" Brooks asked.

"None of your concern."

"It's my concern if you're sleeping with our enemy's daughter."

Graham glanced over his shoulder, thankful to see

the living area still empty, which meant she was still in bed. "I'm with Eve, yes. But—"

"What the hell, man? What are you thinking?"

Graham didn't get a chance to reply before his brother went on. "Are you using her to try to get to Sutton?"

Graham slid the knife through the mango. "No. I wouldn't do that to her."

"Then what are you doing?"

Graham swallowed, deciding now was as good a time as any to come clean. "We're having a baby."

The explosion of cussing had Graham dropping the knife to the counter and taking the phone off speaker. "Calm the hell down," he barked.

"How long have you known and how could you keep something like this from me?" Brooks demanded.

"We kept our personal lives from everyone," Graham explained, leaning against the counter. "Between you, Carson and her family, we just wanted—"

"What? To mess around and not get caught?"

Basically.

"How'd that work out for you?"

Graham raked a hand through his bed head. "Listen, we're figuring things out and we needed to get away from the city."

"Sutton is not going to like this."

"No, he's not, but there's nothing that can change the fact." Graham stared at the stairs to the second floor, wondering how long she would sleep in. "I'm going to ask her to marry me."

"Are you a complete moron?" Brooks yelled. "Can you just slow down and think this through?"

"I have." Graham turned around and checked the casserole in the oven. "This baby is a Newport and will be raised as such. I'll do anything to make sure my child has my last name."

"So you love her?"

Graham shut the oven door again. "Love has nothing to do with it. The baby is what I'm concerned with."

When he turned back around, he froze. Eve stood on the other side of the kitchen island. All color had drained from her face as she clutched her silk robe together. The hurt in her eyes gutted him. He'd promised her no more pain, but he'd delivered a hell of a punch.

"I'll call you later," he told Brooks, ending the call without waiting for his brother's reply.

"Don't make excuses for what I wasn't supposed to hear," she told him, tipping her chin. "I'm flattered you want to marry me, but I think I'll decline. You see, I already made a fool of myself for one man I conceived a child with. I don't intend to do so again."

Graham started to step forward, but when she held up a hand and squared her shoulders, he stopped. The sheen in her eyes, the fact that she was fighting back tears, told him he'd completely ruined everything.

But he wasn't going down without a fight.

"Marriage isn't a terrible idea, Eve."

"For us? It's a terrible idea."

"Why?"

Crossing her arms over her chest, she pursed her lips as if choosing her next words carefully. Damn, she looked beautiful this morning. With her tousled hair, bright eyes, face devoid of any makeup, Eve was stunning. And she was pulling away. He couldn't let her end what he'd worked so hard to complete.

"I told you I loved you," she started, blinking away the tears. "I meant it. I didn't expect the words in return if you weren't feeling the same way. I understand.

But to know you only want to marry me because of our baby, it's just so archaic. Did you think I'd keep your child from you?"

Graham didn't care what she wanted. He took a step toward her. "I didn't know what would happen, Eve. All I know is I'm going to be a father and I can't miss that. I can't."

Emotions he hadn't fully grasped came rushing at him. "I grew up without a father," he went on, still slowly closing the gap between them. "I've wondered for the past thirty-two years who my dad is, if he wanted me, if he even knows I exist. It's an empty void that I may never fill."

He stood so close now, Eve tipped her head back to look up into his eyes. The need for her understanding was so great, he had to find the right words. Any charm or wit he normally used to get his way wasn't possible here. All he could do was hope for the best when he opened up with complete and total honesty.

"Do you understand what I'm saying?" he asked. "I can't let my child grow up without me. I don't want another man raising what's mine."

Eve's jaw clenched as she closed her eyes and pulled in a breath. "Do I look like I have men lined up outside my door?" she finally asked, glaring back at him. "Apparently you don't know me at all. And all I hear is how you want to give this child a name and treat him or her like your property. That's not how this works and that sure as hell isn't how a marriage should work."

"Eve—"

"No."

She backed away and held out both hands. Just as she did, she started to sway. Graham reached for her, but she pushed him away. She held her stomach with one hand and covered her mouth with the other. Alarmed, he waited to make sure she wasn't going to get sick or pass out. He was a complete ass for…well, everything. He remained close, though, in case she needed him. Not that she'd take his help now.

Moments later she pulled herself together and smoothed her hair from her face. "I'm going back to Chicago as soon as I call my pilot to come get me. Elite has a private helicopter at our disposal."

"I'll take you."

She was going. There was no stopping her. She'd erected walls he couldn't penetrate, not when she was so angry, so hurt. But he'd continue to chip away because he wasn't lying. There was no way he'd let his child grow up without a father.

"I'd rather call my pilot," she told him.

Eve turned on her heel and headed toward the stairs. Graham couldn't take his eyes off her. He silently pleaded for her to understand where he was coming from, why he was so adamant about marriage.

With her hand on the post, she turned to look over her shoulder. "You know what's sad? I thought you brought me here because you cared about me. I was naive enough to think you might have stronger feelings for me, that you wanted to get closer to me. Not because I was pregnant, but because of me."

Graham couldn't breathe, couldn't move.

Eve dropped her head between her shoulders, her grip tightening on the post. "You were using me all this time. I should've listened to my family when they first told me to stay away from you. But I defended you."

Now she turned to face him, her cheeks pink from tears, from anger. Graham hated himself at that moment. He hated the way he'd portrayed himself, the way he'd let her down when he'd promised that no one would hurt her again. He'd destroyed her. Destroyed the light in her eyes, the smile she so freely gave.

"I won't keep you from your child." Her voice shook, her chin quivered. "But I won't marry you, and from here on out, we're nothing to each other."

Without another word, she went up the stairs. Graham listened as the bedroom door clicked shut. The gentle sound seemed to echo through the spacious house. It symbolized everything that had just happened. She'd put a barrier between them, and as he stood on the outside, he couldn't help but wonder how the hell he could ever fix this.

Seventeen

When he left her alone to pack, and then leave the cabin, Eve was even more hurt. She shouldn't have been surprised, but she was. He'd given up. Clearly he only wanted the child and she was an absolute fool to have believed otherwise.

But what hurt the most was that she still loved him. Well, she loved the man she thought he was. He'd been so caring, so amazing these past couple of weeks, but one overheard phone call had revealed the truth.

Eve had been home only a day, but she'd called her sisters and her father for a family meeting. Dr. Wilde had told Eve that Sutton was resting, but he was having a good day and to come on by. Grace and Nora were meeting Eve at the Winchester estate.

As Eve stood outside the front door, she fought back her nerves. Had it only been two nights since she was here for a party? A party announcing her sister's engagement. A party Graham had crashed, and then he'd taken her...

No. There would be no more thinking along those lines. Whatever they'd shared in the past was best left there. Their affair had started out so fast, so intense, there was no way it could've lasted or even morphed into something with deeper meaning. Eve cursed herself for getting so caught up in romanticizing the secret of it all.

Gathering up her courage, she let herself in and headed straight to her father's study. Grace and Nora were already there. Grace adjusted the throw on her father's legs and Nora glanced up, catching Eve's eye. A soft smile from her sister was all Eve needed to get through this. Having Nora here was a huge help since she already knew.

Grace glanced up when Eve shut the door. "Is everything okay?" she asked. "You sounded strange on the phone."

Eve met her father's questioning eyes. "I'm fine, but I have something I need to tell you all."

Grace straightened, taking hold of their father's hand. "You're scaring me. Are you sick, too?"

"What? No." She hadn't meant to scare them. "I'm pregnant."

Silence. Not a word was said as her sisters and father just stared back at her.

"I'm at seven weeks," she went on, in a rush to fill the dead air. "The doctor has assured me that everything looks great, but I'm scared." There, she'd said it. "I need your help and support, no judgment, please. I can't deal with it right now."

"Because Graham is the father?" Grace asked.

Eve bit her lip in an attempt to battle back the emotions. Afraid to speak, she merely nodded.

"He didn't say a word when he was here the other day," her father chimed in. "Does he know?"

Eve moved farther into the room. "What? He was here?"

"With Brooks and Carson."

Eve's mind spun. He'd been to see her father and hadn't said a word. The betrayals kept on coming. He'd been sleeping with her, telling her everything she wanted to know, but sneaking to see her father behind her back.

"Was he pressuring you?" Eve demanded as she eased a hip onto the side of the bed.

"I actually invited Carson here," he stated. "I wanted a chance to tell him I'm sorry, to see if there was a possibility of connecting now that I know for sure he's my son. I didn't want to die without him knowing that I loved his mother, that I would've fought had I known he existed."

Eve listened as her father exposed his emotions. She'd never heard him this passionate about anything other than business. Sutton Winchester was one of the most prominent, powerful men in Chicago and he'd been deprived of raising his own child.

Was that truly what Graham had thought she'd do? Had she ever indicated she'd be so heartless? He'd been determined to marry her, so much so he'd swept her away on a trip away from everything she knew. She'd been easily swayed because she honestly thought he cared about her, when in reality he was softening her, getting her to fall for him, all so he could convince her to marry him.

"Wait, has he pushed you away?" Grace asked.

"No." Eve took her father's other hand. "He...it's complicated. I don't want to go into the details, but—"

"Complicated? You two were on the same page when I saw you the other morning."

Eve glanced at Nora, who had pulled up a chair by their father's bed. Grace and Sutton both turned to Nora.

"She knew?" Grace asked.

Nora shrugged, sending Eve an apologetic glance. "I happened to stop by her house when Graham was there making breakfast for her."

"Things have changed since then," Eve explained. "All I need right now is for you guys to know I won't let Elite down. I'm 100 percent committed to the company and—"

"This baby comes before any company."

Eve stilled at her father's words. He'd never said anything like that. He was loyal to his family, yes, but he always put business first. Always.

"I can handle both," she assured him.

"I'm sure you can." He turned his hand over and held on to hers. "But I want a healthy grandbaby. I want you to take care of yourself. We have enough staff that can assist you, so put some of the burden on them. That's my greatest regret—not having been there more for my kids."

Eve glanced to her sisters, who had both started tearing up.

"When you're faced with the end, you start thinking about the beginning," he went on. "And if I could go back, I'd definitely put some work off onto my assistants so I could be with you all more. Learn from my mistakes, Eve. Take care of yourself."

"That's what I've been telling her."

Eve jerked at the familiar voice behind her. Graham stood in the doorway with the butler right behind him.

"I tried to stop him, Mr. Winchester," the poor man explained.

"It's fine," Sutton replied. "Close the door and leave us."

Eve continued to stare at Graham, who hadn't taken his eyes off her. "What are you doing here?" she demanded, coming to her feet. "You can't just barge in here—"

"I can. And I did."

Eve didn't risk looking behind her to her sisters or father. The tension in the room had multiplied, threatening to take over.

"I don't want you here," she told him, pulling her cardigan tighter around her. As if such a simple gesture could keep any more pain from seeping in.

"I realize that." His tone softened as he inched closer. "I know I hurt you, but the moment you left I knew I wasn't finished."

Eve didn't have much energy for a battle. The past forty-eight hours had been hellacious at best.

"Then say what you want to say and get out."

He'd reached her now, but didn't touch her. "I meant I wasn't finished with us."

Eve stared into those striking eyes that had first drawn her in. "There is no us. If that's all, then leave."

"Do you two want to go outside for privacy?" Grace asked from behind Eve.

"No," both Eve and Graham said at the same time.

"I don't care who hears me," he went on, keeping his eyes locked on hers. "When you left yesterday I knew I had to take drastic measures to get you back. So, if I have to make a fool of myself in front of your family, then so be it."

Eve didn't want to hear it, though she wouldn't mind

him looking like a fool considering she'd been played for one.

"I'm not discussing the baby's last name. I know that's all you care about." Eve stepped back because being this close, knowing she still loved him but couldn't touch him was agonizing. "If you'll excuse me, I'm visiting my father."

Eve had just turned away when Graham's soft, "I love you," hit her hard.

Frozen in her steps, she looked to her sisters, her father, to see if she'd heard correctly. And saw three pairs of eyes wide with shock staring back at her. Yeah, he'd said that.

Eve looked back over her shoulder, her heart aching more than she'd ever known possible. "That was cruel," she whispered as tears clogged her throat. "Throwing those words around won't make me marry you."

Graham reached for her, turning her to face him fully. "I'm not proposing. I love you, Eve. I want to be with you. Not for the baby, for you."

If he'd said those words two days ago she'd have believed him. "Revelation has certainly come at a convenient time."

His hands curled around her shoulders as he stepped in closer. Her entire body brushed against his, as if she needed the physical reminder of how much she'd missed his touch.

"Nothing about us has been convenient," he told her. "I didn't want a child, a relationship, but now I can't live without either. I don't want to try. I know I hurt you, I know I destroyed everything we'd started building, but I'm asking for another chance."

Eve couldn't say anything. What was there to say at

this point? He was a shark in the courtroom because he knew the exact thing to say at precisely the right time.

If she even thought he was serious, she'd wrap her arms around him and start fresh. But she knew better. Graham was only looking out for his best interests where the baby was concerned.

"You need to go," she whispered.

The muscle in his jaw clenched as he nodded, dropping his hands from her shoulders. "I'm not giving up, Eve. I love you. I've only had two women in my life who heard those words from me."

His mother and Gerty.

Eve turned away from him and went back to her father's bedside. She listened to Graham's footsteps as he left the room. Once the door was closed behind him, Eve couldn't stop the emotions from washing over her.

"I hate him," she sniffed. "I'm sorry you had to see that."

Her father reached for her, tipping her chin up so she could look him in the eyes. "I'm not sorry at all. I saw a man who loves a woman. I saw a man who stood in the same room as his sworn enemy and didn't give a damn what anyone else thought."

"He's only saying those things because he wants to marry me so the baby will have his name."

"The baby can have his name without marriage," Grace pointed out. "He could fight you for custody in court and probably win, if that's the way he wanted to go about it."

Eve knew all of this. She wasn't stupid, wasn't ignorant when it came to laws. But she had been blindsided and refused to let Graham have another swipe at her.

"I'll agree he didn't go about things the right way,"

her father said, swiping a tear from her face. "But men are fools when they're in love. Most of the time they don't even know it until they've lost someone."

Eve knew her father was referring to Cynthia. There were no secrets about the fact that Eve's parents didn't love each other. Eve fully believed that her father was in love with Graham's mother at one time. But he'd let her go.

"I can't let him back in," she whispered.

"You can't let him out," Nora countered. "He loves you, Eve."

Eve met the eyes of her family. "Are you all defending him?"

Sutton smiled. "I'm just as shocked as you are, but I want my daughter and grandchild to be happy. When I saw the way he looked at you, the way he didn't care how he laid his feelings on the line, I knew he loved you. Any man who is that strong and passionate is exactly what I want for you."

Eve couldn't believe what she was hearing. "You want me to forgive him? Just like that? It's that easy?"

When her fathered smiled, wrinkles formed around his sad eyes. "I want you to follow your heart. I don't believe Graham will give up and that has everything to do with his feelings for you. Grace was right. He could fight you in court, where things would get ugly if he only wanted the child to have his name. I don't think he realized how much he cared for you until you left."

Eve shook her head. "I can't just take him back. Right now, I only want to be here with you guys. I want to visit and laugh and… I don't know. Pick out nursery themes."

"I'm thrilled that's your attitude," Nora said, reaching over to squeeze Eve's shoulder. "This baby will be perfectly healthy and come home to a beautiful room and a family who loves her."

"Her?" their father asked, raising his brows.

"I think Eve is having a girl, too," Grace laughed. "Another Winchester girl? That has a nice ring to it."

Eve didn't care about the sex, she just wanted a healthy baby. Now more than ever, she wanted that happiness in her life. She prayed her father would live long enough to see her child, but the odds were against them.

For now, though, she wouldn't dwell on the sorrow. She'd live in the moment.

Later she'd deal with the ache...and she'd deal with Graham.

Three days had passed since she'd seen Graham... since he'd exposed himself before her family. But he'd texted her. He'd checked on her, asked if she was eating, joked that he'd send over some of the fried apples she loved. He didn't tell her he loved her again, didn't pressure her to meet him or to make a decision regarding this relationship they'd thrown up in the air and left hanging.

He'd genuinely been...well, caring. And she was positive this wasn't some game to him. He wasn't using her. Eve realized that if he'd wanted to use her all along, then he would've tried to use her to get closer to her father. If he was that sure her father held secrets about Graham's past, then he could have easily used his charms and sneaky maneuvers to find out what she knew. Or have her find out what her father knew.

He'd done neither. When they were together, he'd avoided the topic. It had taken Eve two restless, sleepless nights to replay their last seven weeks. There were no red flags, nothing other than an intense affair and unexpected emotions.

Now she stood in the lobby of his building, clutching a photo, more scared than she'd ever been in her life. This was the biggest risk she'd ever taken, but this could also be the greatest thing to ever happen to her.

By the time Eve reached the top floor and stood outside the only door in the hall, she was a little more under control…until the door swung open and Graham stood there in a pair of running shorts, beads of sweat running down his chest.

"Doorman told me you were on your way up," he explained. "I was on the treadmill."

Eve still didn't say anything. Now that she was here, all the speeches she'd rehearsed vanished from her mind. The picture in her hand crinkled, drawing her attention to the reason she needed to gather up that Winchester courage.

"I, um…can I come in?"

Graham stepped back, opening the door wider. The second she passed by him, she was assaulted with that sexy, sweaty, masculine scent. She wanted this to be easy, didn't want a messy reunion…if he'd take her. They'd been through so much already, Eve wasn't even sure a relationship was possible.

Eve crossed the spacious entryway and stepped down into the living area. Her eyes were fixed on the skyline.

"I never got to appreciate the view in Tennessee," she muttered. "I was numb when I left."

When he said nothing, Eve turned, only to find he'd moved in closer behind her.

"I was still numb when I saw you at my dad's house," she went on. "But then I realized you didn't have to be there. You could've let me go, could've waited and fought me."

His intense stare hit her as fiercely as his words. "I'd never fight you, Eve."

"I'm tired," she whispered. "Tired of worrying, tired of questioning and tired of wondering what we're doing."

Graham reached for her, pulling her into his arms. She didn't care that his chest was damp with sweat. All she cared about was that he didn't seem to have changed his mind.

"Put it all on me," he murmured against her ear. "Every fear, every worry, give it to me. I want to be everything for you, Eve."

She eased back, hope spreading through her. "Can our lives be that easy? Can we make this work?"

"I'll do anything to have you in my life, Eve. Anything. Not just the baby, but you." He framed her face with his strong hands. "I've never loved a woman the way I love you. I've never wanted to. But we fit, Eve. We get each other and I can't imagine life without you."

Sliding the black-and-white image between them, she held up the picture for him to see. "This is for you."

Graham took a step back and stared at it. It was a sonogram of their baby. His eyes instantly misted as he slowly reached for the glossy image.

"I didn't think you'd had the appointment yet."

"I called the doctor for a favor." Eve smiled, unable to stop herself as she saw how in love Graham was with this child already. "I wanted to give you this. I wanted you to know that we are both yours if you'll have us. If you can forgive me for doubting you, for doubting us."

His eyes instantly sought hers. "There's nothing to forgive. I'm the one who nearly ruined the greatest thing that's ever happened to me. I won't ask you to marry me. But know that the second you want to, I'm ready."

Eve started to say something, but he held up his hand.

"Because I love you both. I want to build a life with you, raise all the babies you want."

"My father defended you," she told him.

Graham looked shocked. "He did?"

"I know you think he has a secret about your father, but this disease, it's changed him. I—I'll go with you if you want to ask him. He won't lie to me."

Graham pulled her in once more. "I have everything I need right here. I won't put you between your father and me. Besides, Brooks has a lead with the investigator."

Eve pulled back. "That's great."

Graham smiled. "Roman is out now searching and he's pretty sure he has the name we've been searching for."

"Oh, Graham. Are you excited?"

"I am." He kissed the top of her head. "But not nearly as excited as I was the second I knew you were here to see me. Don't leave. Stay with me."

Eve leaned up on her tiptoes to kiss him. "Maybe we should start with a shower and then talk."

Graham set the picture down on the accent table and scooped her up into his arms. "That's the best idea I've ever heard."

* * * * *

MILLS & BOON®

Desire™

PASSIONATE AND DRAMATIC LOVE STORIES

A sneak peek at next month's titles...

In stores from 20th October 2016:

- **Hold Me, Cowboy** – Maisey Yates *and*
One Heir...or Two? – Yvonne Lindsay

- **His Secretary's Little Secret** – Catherine Mann *and*
Back in the Enemy's Bed – Michelle Celmer

- **Holiday Baby Scandal** – Jules Bennett *and*
His Pregnant Christmas Bride – Olivia Gates

Just can't wait?
Buy our books online a month before they hit the shops!
www.millsandboon.co.uk

Also available as eBooks.

MILLS & BOON®

Why shop at millsandboon.co.uk?

Each year, thousands of romance readers find their perfect read at millsandboon.co.uk. That's because we're passionate about bringing you the very best romantic fiction. Here are some of the advantages of shopping at www.millsandboon.co.uk:

* **Get new books first**—you'll be able to buy your favourite books one month before they hit the shops

* **Get exclusive discounts**—you'll also be able to buy our specially created monthly collections, with up to 50% off the RRP

* **Find your favourite authors**—latest news, interviews and new releases for all your favourite authors and series on our website, plus ideas for what to try next

* **Join in**—once you've bought your favourite books, don't forget to register with us to rate, review and join in the discussions

Visit **www.millsandboon.co.uk**
for all this and more today!